UNBOUND

JIM C. HINES

Magic ex Libris: Book Three

DAW BOOKS, INC.
DONALD A. WOLLHEIM, FOUNDER
375 Hudson Street, New York, NY 10014

ELIZABETH R. WOLLHEIM
SHEILA E. GILBERT
PUBLISHERS
www.dawbooks.com

For Amy, Skylar, and Jamie.

Acknowledgments

This is my tenth novel with DAW.

Shadowstar's twinkling bells, this is my tenth novel with DAW!

Wow. I don't even know how to process that. It feels like a lifetime since *Goblin Quest* first came out back in 2006, and at the same time it couldn't possibly be that long. (I have much the same reaction when I realize how old my children are getting . . .)

That's roughly a million words of published fiction about goblins and princesses and flaming spiders and dryads and magic librarians. And it wouldn't have happened without the help and support of some incredible people.

Sheila Gilbert has been my editor since day one, offering suggestions and input that have strengthened every one of those ten books.

I've been with JABberwocky literary agency for even longer, and I don't want to imagine what my career might look like today without the help of Joshua Bilmes and everyone else at JABberwocky: Eddie, Brady, Sam (aka the Right Hand of Darkness), Lisa, Krystyna, and Eeyore.

I've been very fortunate when it comes to cover artists, but with the cover for *Unbound*, Gene Mollica has gone above and beyond. He actually built the armillary sphere and the ray gun you see on the front cover of the U.S. edition. (I'm pretty sure he didn't build his own Mackinac Bridge, but you never know.)

Thanks also to author Kelly McCullough for beta reading this one, and to author Scott Lynch, for his knowledge and insight into the events of chapter 14.

Much love and gratitude to my family. I was working to write two novels in the past year, while at the same time juggling the day job. Thank you to my wife and children for putting up with me.

And finally, thank you, my readers. Because all the rest of this would mean very little without you.

My name is Bi Wei. I was born in the Ming Dynasty, shortly before the alleged death of Johannes Gensfleish Gutenberg, the man most people today know as the father of the printing press.

We knew this man not as a creator, but as a force of death and destruction. Johannes Gutenberg was a thief, a fraud, and a murderer.

Gutenberg did not die in 1468 as history claims. His body was not laid to rest at a Franciscan church in Mainz, a church later destroyed, conveniently erasing any evidence of his deception.

Johannes Gutenberg, like myself, survives to this day. And he is not alone.

At the end of the fifteenth century, Gutenberg founded an organization known as Die Zwelf Portenære. The Porters, as they are more commonly known, devote themselves to the elimination of all those Gutenberg views as a potential threat, and to the secrecy of magic.

I learned the art of magic from my great grandaunt. I touched the power of printed words my ancestors had passed down for generations. I added what strength I possessed to their work. I served my family and my people. I harmed no one.

Most of my friends and family were killed the day Gutenberg attacked our temple. My teachers fought to give the rest of us time to escape. My brother died to protect me. To this day he walks with me in my dreams. He knew death approached, and he couldn't hide his fear from me, but he was determined to complete his duty.

Gutenberg has hidden many things from you. He has rewritten history and buried fact beneath myth and legend. He has worked to control magic, to keep it from the larger world, and he has committed atrocities for the sole purpose of "protecting" you from the truth.

He has failed.

Gutenberg and the Porters have brought this world to the edge of destruction. They have awakened the sǐ guǐ jūn duì, the Ghost Army. They are the restless dead, bound as slaves to one who would devour this world. They grow in number and in power, and they are coming. They wait like a tiger in the shadows, unseen as they creep ever closer. Their claws are bared to strike.

No doubt you will laugh and dismiss my story as the fanciful imaginings of a child. For you *know* that such things are not possible in the real world.

We are descended from a man called Bi Sheng, who explored the magic of books centuries before Gutenberg's birth. The Bì Shēng de dú zhě survived Gutenberg's assault on our home. We have returned. We ask only to be left in peace. In exchange for that boon, we offer you the gift of truth.

From Gutenberg's computers, we have pulled the location of all Porter archives: secret libraries hidden from public view. They house magical artifacts and books deemed too dangerous for magical use. Those locations are listed below.

Use caution when investigating these archives. The Porters will defend themselves from perceived threats. They will deceive you, twist your perceptions, and alter your memories. We have watched them do all this and worse.

They would kill us for telling you this, but they cannot hide the truth forever. A friend from your time recently said to me, "You can't stop the signal." We will learn soon enough whether he was correct.

To Gutenberg and the Porters, the Ghost Army is coming. Give up your efforts to find and destroy us, and abandon your centuries-old lies. Turn your attention to the true enemy.

Like Shen Yuanzhi, whom stories say slumbered for

a hundred years at Lanchang Palace to cheat death, we escaped our fate. We slept for five centuries, trapped alone with our nightmares, and awoke to find the world changed.

It is time for the rest of the world to do the same. It is time for you to awaken.

—From a letter that appeared in George R. R. Martin's A Dance with Dragons

Chapter 1

TED BOYER—hunter, fisherman, vampire, and general pain in my ass—was gone.

Dirt and gravel crunched beneath my sneakers as I crossed the empty lot where his yellow doublewide trailer once stood. A rectangle of flattened earth, striped by old, cracked cement, marked the site of Boyer's former home.

There was no sign of the secret basement he had dug to hide his coffin and store his blood supply. Wherever Boyer had fled to, he wasn't planning to come back.

"There are weeds starting to poke through the dirt." Short, heavyset, and stronger than five humans combined, Lena Greenwood looked as tired as I felt. She crouched on the cement and touched one of the tiny green shoots. "He left at least a week ago."

There had been a time, back when I was a field agent for the Porters, when I would have been thrilled to see Ted gone from Marquette, and preferably gone from Michigan's Upper Peninsula. Let someone else take on the responsibility of checking in on him and blowing the bomb in his skull if his blood tests ever showed he had gone back to feeding on Boy Scouts.

But Ted was a lifelong Yooper, stubborn as hell and determined to live out his afterlife here in Marquette. I had resigned myself to sharing the peninsula with him until one of us was dead and buried for good.

"Do you think he left willingly?" Lena asked.

I shrugged. Ted didn't exactly have a lot of friends, and he had collected a decent list of enemies over his lifetimes. If one of them had used the chaos last month as cover to come after Ted, he could be dead by now. Deader. But why would they bother to haul away his trailer and his truck? More likely, he simply wanted to get away before all hell broke loose.

Some would say hell had broken a month earlier, when my home town of Copper River ended up in the crossfire of a three-way magical battle between the Porters, the Bì Shēng de dú zhě—a group thought to have been wiped out more than five hundred years ago by the aforementioned Porters—and an army of mindless ghosts fighting to return to this world to kill . . . well, pretty much everything.

At least thirty-four of my friends and neighbors had died in that battle. Then there were the Porters and werewolves who had fallen trying to protect Copper River in a conflict that promised to be merely the precursor of things to come.

"Keep looking." Fossilized beagle shit, half-hidden by weeds, turned much of the grass into a minefield. I crouched by one pile and stared as though I could use the droppings to divine where Ted had gone, but all they told me was that we were too late.

I continued to search. Cigarette butts littered the ground by the woods beyond the driveway, where Ted used to work during the night, skinning and butchering whatever game he brought back. I found a couple of old beer cans by the trees.

"Isaac ..." Lena studied my face, then shook her head. "Never mind."

Anger tightened my jaw. I knew what she was going to say, and I didn't want to hear it.

The manager of the trailer park said Ted had simply vanished. He had left an envelope full of cash to pay off his bills, which was more than I would have expected from Ted. More likely, he had simply messed with the manager's mind to make him believe everything was squared away. That would better fit Ted's style and budget. "I need to find him."

"How? By staring at dog crap all day? This must be a new school of magic I hadn't heard about. My lover, the fecomancer."

On another day, I would have smiled. That was before I had lost a fourteen-year-old girl to the Ghost Army. A girl who was potentially more powerful than any libriomancer in history, with the possible exception of Johannes Gutenberg.

A girl who had been under my care and protection.

Jeneta Aboderin had the ability to perform libriomancy using electronic media. The rest of us needed printed books to shape our magic. We could reach into the pages to create anything from futuristic laser pistols to fizzy lifting drinks from *Charlie and the Chocolate Factory*, as long as we had a physical copy of the book.

Jeneta could pull the mockingjay pin from *The Hunger Games* out of her smartphone, and carried an entire library around on her e-reader. Nobody fully understood how she did it, nor did we know the limits of her power.

I searched the dirt driveway next. This was my third time studying the dark patches of oil that had leaked from Ted's old Ford Bronco. I knew a Porter who could have used that stain not only to track Ted's truck, but to bring it to a screeching halt wherever he might be. Or there were books whose magic could help me to find him myself . . . if I had still been a member of the Porters.

If Johannes Gutenberg hadn't locked my mind to prevent me from ever using magic again.

I closed my eyes and fought off a now-familiar surge of despair.

"There's nothing here," Lena said softly.

"I know." I took a long, slow breath, trying to ease the walnut-sized lump in my throat. "We'll have to find someone else to help me. Ted isn't the only one who can touch people's minds."

"Would you really want that man messing around in your nightmares?"

"I *saw* her, Lena." Two nights before, I had jerked awake, my body dripping with sweat, my hands reaching helplessly for power I no longer possessed. For two days that memory had stalked me, taunting me from every corner.

"Jeneta?"

"The woman who took her." The name darted into view like a dragonfly and vanished again before I could grasp it. "I know who she is, but something's blocking the memory. I need help. Someone who can help me remember."

Wisps of black hair hung over Lena's red-veined eyes. Her lips pressed together with worry and helplessness, along with a dash of skepticism. It was an expression I had come to know well over the past month.

She wore a snug green T-shirt with the sleeves and collar cut off. The words "Tree Hugger" were written in yellow block letters across her chest. She was armed with a pair of curved wooden swords—Japanese bokken— thrust through the belt of her cutoff jeans.

Heat flared at my hip. From inside the rectangular metal cage clipped to my belt, Smudge watched the road like he was expecting a horde of zombies to claw up through the pavement and devour us. Faint red flames rippled across the fire-spider's back. A layer of fire-resistant black fiberglass on the side of the cage prevented him from burning holes through my pants.

Lena moved to the opposite side of the lot while I returned to the relative safety of my car. The protective enchantments on the black TR-6 convertible were stronger than anything I could have prepared myself, even when I could still manipulate magic. I waited by the passenger door and searched for whatever had set Smudge off this time.

There were no zombies, only a lone man carrying an aluminum baseball bat. He had a good five inches and fifty pounds on me, and a scowl like I'd just pissed in his Budweiser. "What are you folks snooping around for?"

Normally I would have tried to talk my way around this guy, making up a story that explained our presence without raising suspicions. But I no longer had any reason to care about keeping a low profile, and in the words of a coworker, my give-a-shit gauge was stuck on Empty these days. "Ted Boyer. Have you seen him?"

He rested the bat on his shoulder, wrapping both hands around the black-taped handle. "Ted said there might be people nosing around in his business, looking to give him a hard time."

"Do you know where we could find him?" Lena hadn't touched her weapons. Against a man armed with a bat, she wouldn't need them.

"What I know is that you'd better get the hell out of here by the time I count to five."

I reached into the car, popped the glove box, and pulled out a gun. The man's eyes went huge. "Do you know where Ted Boyer went?" I repeated.

He shook his head. "He wouldn't say."

"And did Ted ask you to threaten anyone who came along, or was that your idea?" I pulled the trigger without waiting for an answer. Lightning spat from the barrel, spinning a cocoon of electricity around his body. He collapsed face-first in the grass, the bat dropping to the ground beside him.

"Isaac, what the *hell?*" Lena ran toward him.

"The gun was on setting one." I blinked away the afterimage of jagged light. Ozone bit my nostrils. "He'll be fine."

I had created my sidearm from a novel called *Time Kings*, back before Gutenberg locked my magic. Disguised to look like an ordinary revolver, the shock-gun had a two-stage firing mechanism. First, it shot a tiny ionized pellet toward the target. A split second later, it brought the lightning, which could deliver anything from a light stunning burst to a full-on, Earth-shattering ka-boom.

"You're sure about that?" Lena was checking the man's pulse and respiration. "You made sure he didn't have a pacemaker before you electrocuted him? You reviewed his medical records for any preexisting conditions?"

I felt like she had reached into my gut and tied my intestines in a knot. "He looked healthy . . ." That was a stupid excuse, and I knew it. "Is he all right?"

"He seems to be, considering you just *shot him with a lightning bolt.*" She brushed her fingers over the singed spot on his shirt. "What were you thinking?"

"That he didn't know anything, and we didn't have time for this."

"Oh, do you have plans tonight? Another exciting evening of hiding in your office with your books and shutting away the rest of the world?"

I wanted to apologize and I wanted her to keep arguing with me and I wanted her to leave me the hell alone. I didn't know *what* I wanted anymore, except to find Jeneta and fix the things that had gone so damned wrong.

I circled around to the driver's seat. "There's nothing here. Let's go."

Like a paroled felon, Ted was supposed to let the Porters know if he moved, but I no longer had access to the Porter database. He might not have bothered, trusting them to be too preoccupied with the Ghost Army to worry about a lone vampire. If so, he'd better pray he found a black-market magic-user to deactivate the bomb in his skull before anyone else noticed he was missing.

I unclipped Smudge's cage and let him climb onto the dashboard. A stone trivet protected the dash from his heat. He watched me closely, his body low against the trivet. For a big black-and-red spider with a penchant for setting things on fire, Smudge could be surprisingly expressive. He wasn't worried about random strangers with baseball bats anymore. *I* was the one making him anxious.

Tension drained from my body, guilt and exhaustion replacing anger. I let my head thump against the steering wheel. I should apologize. For scaring Smudge. For snapping at Lena.

For a lot of things.

"We'll find someone else." Lena sat down beside me. "You've got other vampires who owe you favors, not to mention the Porters—"

"None of the Porters are allowed to talk to me," I reminded her. "I'm not exactly on the best of terms with the undead, either. The last time I asked them for help, I got several of their people dusted, including a rather powerful ghost-talker."

"The Porters are searching for Jeneta, too." She didn't say anything more, but those seven words carried the weight of hours of previous arguments.

What could one librarian with no magic of his own do that Gutenberg's people couldn't? The Porters had magic and a worldwide network of hundreds of libriomancers and other magic-users to help them track Jeneta down.

To which I always replied, *"Then why haven't they found her yet?"*

I gunned the engine and got the hell out of there.

Driving into Copper River meant passing one reminder after another of the damage the Ghost Army had done to my home. The Porters had repaired much of the destruction, hoping to bury evidence of werewolves and wendigos and magic. They couldn't bring back the dead, but they had rebuilt homes and rewritten memories.

Sometimes I wished they had rewritten mine. To the right was the drugstore, where Becky Luhtala's body had been found behind the counter. A block away was the intersection where Phil Gutzman had died when his truck collided with a metal dragon made of magically animated mining equipment.

Every road conjured memories of metal insects, their serrated pincers tearing my skin, or white-furred monsters smashing through doors and windows. I remembered every detail save the identity of the one responsible.

By the time I reached my street, my neck and shoulders were tense as steel. I felt like I was driving through a war zone. This was where the trees had turned against my neighbors, crushing roofs and ripping through homes. A dryad named Deifilia, another servant of the Ghost Army, would have tortured and murdered everyone on my block if Lena hadn't killed her.

Despite everything the Porters had done to erase the damage, "For Sale" signs had appeared in five different yards.

My own home was untouched. From the outside, the

dirty aluminum siding and metal roof showed no sign of anything unusual.

It was another story entirely once you stepped inside. Books, maps, and haphazardly organized printouts covered the kitchen table. My laptop sat in the center, a single orange LED blinking wearily. It looked like the laptop had gotten drunk and vomited up a copious amount of paperwork and sticky notes.

I returned Smudge to his tank, a large terrarium sitting on the edge of the kitchen counter. I dropped a pair of crickets in with him, replaced the lid, and turned on the heat lamp. He raced over to dig a little nest in the obsidian gravel in the center of the light.

Lena grabbed a package of Twinkies from the freezer. She took the majority of her sustenance through her tree, and as far as anyone could tell, her human diet had absolutely no effect on her health or physique. She took shameless advantage of that fact. Though why she preferred her Twinkies frozen was a mystery. She tore open the package and held one out to me.

"I'm not hungry." At the edge of my vision, a red light blinked at me from my phone's base unit, signaling a waiting message.

Lena followed my attention, and her forced cheer vanished. "You don't have to listen right now."

"Yes, I do." We both knew who the message was from. I considered deleting it, but I owed them at least this much. And the longer I waited, the longer that blinking light would taunt me. I jabbed the button.

The machine beeped, and then a woman began to speak in a British accent. It was a voice I had come to know as well as my own. "Mister Vainio, this is Paige Aboderin again. I know you said you'd call if you learned anything more about Jeneta, but it's been weeks since we last heard from you."

Buried somewhere on the kitchen table was a copy of the paperwork Paige and Mmadukaaku Aboderin had signed earlier this year, giving their daughter permission to spend the summer at Camp Aazhawigiizhigokwe. Another form allowed Jeneta to work with me as part of a "summer internship" at the Copper River Library, an internship that had mostly involved sitting around in my backyard practicing magic while I tried to understand her power.

"We've hired a private investigator to look for Jeneta. He has copies of everything you've shared with us, but he might be calling you to follow up."

Jeneta should have been safe. Camp Aazhawigiizhigokwe was far enough from Copper River to keep her out of the fighting, and the Porters had assigned a field agent named Myron Worster to keep an eye on her, just in case.

They had found Worster a day later, wandering aimlessly through the Detroit Metro Airport with no memory of who Jeneta was or where she might have gone. He recalled picking *someone* up from the camp, but the details were wiped so thoroughly from his mind that not even the strongest Porters had been able to retrieve them.

"I'm hoping to come back to Michigan by the end of the month," continued Paige Aboderin. "We think . . . we hope the police might do more to find her if we meet with them in person again."

They had flown out immediately following Jeneta's disappearance. Paige stayed in Detroit, while Mmadukaaku rented a hotel room here in Copper River so he could talk to everyone who had seen or interacted with Jeneta in the days before her disappearance.

Every time I spoke to them, it got harder to lie, to pretend I knew nothing about what had happened to their daughter, or to try to reassure them that Jeneta would be all right.

They never blamed me. Even though I was the reason Jeneta had come to Copper River. I was the Porter assigned to work with her, to try to understand her magic and teach her to control it.

I was the reason the Ghost Army had found her. Whatever she became, whatever they did with her power . . .

"The investigator thinks Jeneta is still in Michigan. We know she didn't get on any departing flights."

No, we didn't. We knew only that the airport had no record of Jeneta boarding a flight. Given her magic, and the power our enemies commanded, that meant nothing. She could be anywhere in the world.

I forced myself to listen to Paige's slow, precise words. I could easily imagine her standing at the front of a classroom, lecturing her college seniors about poetry.

"Mmadukaaku believes—" Her voice broke. "He said there could have been a mistake when the coroner was identifying the bodies in Copper River last month. He thinks our daughter might have been buried. I'm planning to look through all of their reports and photographs. I hoped you might be willing to help. You're familiar with . . . with what happened, and Mmadukaaku said you read faster than anyone he's met."

She sounded as determined as ever to find her daughter, but the strength in her words had grown brittle. I couldn't imagine how hard it must be to go to bed each night without knowing. To pour every resource you had into trying to find your child, knowing it might not be enough to bring her home. To admit it might be too late to save her.

This was the first time I had heard either of them acknowledge the possibility that Jeneta could be dead. They might be right. But if so, it hadn't happened during the attack on Copper River.

"Please call if you learn anything at all." She left her number. I had memorized it weeks before.

The message ended. The machine saved it automatically, along with the rest.

"It's not your fault," said Lena.

I sat down at the table, started up the laptop, and dug out a wrinkled list of all departing flights from Detroit Metro Airport on the day Jeneta vanished. Tiny check marks covered the list, along with notes about my conversations with flight attendants, pilots, and a handful of passengers I had managed to track down.

There were too many possibilities, particularly when you looked at connecting flights. I had no way of knowing the Ghost Army's plans, and without more information, no destination was any more or less likely than the rest. All I really had was an eight-second clip from a security camera, showing Jeneta swiping an enormous cinnamon roll from the Starbucks shop in the airport.

I studied one of the printouts, a grainy photo showing Jeneta reaching for the roll. She wore the same clothes she had at camp, and I didn't see that she had brought any luggage, though it could have been outside of the camera's field of vision.

Jeneta had her phone in her other hand. The people around her appeared dazed, staring in random directions at nothing in particular, suggesting she had used magic. Or that whatever had taken her was able to use her magic, which was far more frightening.

"How long since you've eaten?" asked Lena.

I looked at an airline map, trying to match the location of the Starbucks to terminals with flights that departed after these images were taken. "I grabbed a sandwich at lunch."

"You mean this sandwich?" She picked up an abandoned plate from beside the sink and poked at a sad, barely touched stack of bologna, cheese, and lettuce on wheat bread. "I'm ordering pizza. You're going to eat some. End of discussion."

With a sigh, I set the map aside and pulled a book on self-hypnosis from another stack. I had picked it up yesterday morning from the library. Torn scraps of paper—makeshift bookmarks—protruded from the top like tiny white feathers, each one marking a technique I thought might help me to retrieve the elusive memory from my dreams. None had worked yet.

I needed to hack my own brain. I *knew* I had seen the face of our enemy, the person or thing behind the Ghost Army, but that image had been cut out of my thoughts, leaving only a ragged-edged pit filled with frustration.

Had our enemy hidden themselves from me, or was this a side effect of the invisible padlock Gutenberg had snapped through my mind to stop me from using my magic? I was only aware of one person who had successfully bypassed one of Gutenberg's locks, and I wasn't quite ready to try that technique. Not yet. I preferred to save do-it-yourself trepanning for a last resort.

"Did you want bread sticks?" Lena asked.

"Whatever." I stood and fetched Smudge from his tank. "I'll be out back."

If I stayed inside, I'd end up taking my frustrations out on her. Better for both of us if I spent this time alone. I would have left Smudge behind too, if not for the fact that his presence repelled the mosquitoes.

A ring of oak trees transformed the ground into a wrinkled tangle of roots and dirt. If they grew much more, the roots would start to undermine the foundation of the house. Lena's oak stood at the center of the circle, a queen protected by her guardsmen.

Her tree bore the scars of last month's battle in the form of broken branches, gouges in the bark, and blackened streaks of dead, cracked wood.

It was here Lena had killed the dryad she called her sister. She had stabbed Deifilia with her sword, pinning her to the central oak. She stayed with Deifilia as she died, as the tree slowly enveloped her body, a reclamation that was simultaneously touching and horrifying.

And it was here that rabid minds of things long gone from our world had clawed at my thoughts. Where I had lost the ability to distinguish fiction from reality. Where I had seen . . . something. *Someone.*

I stepped between the outer trees. The air within was warm and still. The grove muffled the sounds of the outside world, though I had never figured out exactly how or why that worked. The leaves turned the sky a deep green.

What had the Porters been doing for the past month? They had all but vanished after completing their repairs to the town. I wasn't exactly getting their newsletter anymore, and the few friends I had tried to contact said Gutenberg was threatening to personally turn anyone who spoke to me into a garden gnome. I suspected they had somebody keeping an eye on Lena and me, possibly from one of the now-vacant homes on my street, but beyond that, I knew nothing.

Given the letter Bi Wei had written to the world, revealing the existence of magic and the Porters, they were probably busy increasing security on their archives or transferring the books to other locations. How many Porters were busy working damage control when they could have been out looking for Jeneta, or coming up with ways to stop the rest of the Ghost Army from entering our world?

I understood Bi Wei's reasoning. The Porters weren't just hunting Jeneta and the ghosts. They were looking for her as well, and for every surviving student of Bi Sheng. The more Bi Wei did to divert the Porters' energies, the safer they would be.

I touched a pale scar running down the side of Lena's oak. The bark peeled back, revealing a red cloth-bound book. I gently slid the book free, then sat with my back against the trunk of her tree. Smudge scurried from my shoulder to stalk a purple-tinged moth.

With a sigh, I opened the book and began to read. The first section of the book was in Mandarin, and had been block-printed onto the rice paper pages centuries ago. Lena had penned the rest by hand.

Bi Wei and her fellow students had used books like this to preserve themselves after Gutenberg's attack five hundred years earlier. Bi Wei had given this one to Lena in the hope that it might preserve her as well.

Lena Greenwood was literally magic brought to life, having been "born" from the pages of a lousy fantasy novel called *Nymphs of Neptune*. The nymphs in that book were little more than sexual wish fulfillment for overly hormonal teenaged boys. The nymphs were written to mold their personalities to the desires of their lovers.

Years after her creation, Lena had found and fallen in love with Doctor Nidhi Shah. They were together for years before they learned the truth about Lena's origins. By then, Lena had become exactly what Nidhi fantasized about: a magical superheroine, strong and clever and powerful.

Enter Isaac Vainio, magic-using librarian. Lena's relationship with me had introduced an element of conflict into her existence. For the first time, she wasn't defined solely by one lover, but was shaped by us both. Pulled between our overlapping desires, she discovered choice. It was the closest thing she had known to true freedom.

Nidhi and I both struggled with the ethical implications of our relationship. Nidhi might not have known Lena's origins in the beginning, but she *had* been Lena's therapist. She had chosen to begin a romantic relationship with a former patient. Had Lena been human, that choice could have cost Nidhi her license. As it was, she had been severely reprimanded by the Porters, something she hadn't admitted to me until recently.

Lena was what she was. Not even Gutenberg could change that. If not Nidhi and myself, she would have no choice but to find someone else, perhaps someone who would use her as cruelly as her first lover had.

Lena said she had pursued me deliberately, knowing me well enough to guess at my desires, and choosing to let those desires shape her. But the fact remained, she was bound to the two of us, and when we died, the person she had become would die with us, subsumed by whoever she became next.

This book from Bi Wei might change that. If it worked, the things Lena had written in these pages would one day define her, allowing her to choose for herself who she would be.

But the basic tenets of libriomancy still applied. A book had no power without a reader. I had read this book almost every night for the past month, trading it back and forth with Nidhi. We had no way of knowing if our efforts made a difference, or if the book could truly change Lena's nature, but it was the best hope she had found.

I rubbed my eyes and tried to focus. Every time I opened a book, part of me expected to touch the power humming within the text, waiting to be used. Instead, the book was dead, a stiff corpse of paper with dried ink for blood.

"That image is too damn depressing, even for me." I thumped the back of my head against the tree, as if the impact might reset my mood or jar loose my missing memories. When that failed, I turned the page and started reading.

I had gotten through about fifty pages when I heard footsteps beside me. I dropped the book and yanked my shock-gun from its holster, even as my brain pointed out that Smudge would have alerted me to any true threat.

"A librarian should be more careful with rare and

valuable texts." Nidhi Shah stopped a short distance before the grove and nodded pointedly at the fallen book. She wore a black blazer over a blue shirt, with a necklace made up of interlinked copper disks the size of silver dollars. The cuffs of her black trousers brushed blue sneakers. She must have come straight from the office. I hadn't realized she was working weekends now.

While I picked up the book, she entered the grove and sat down across from me, crossing her feet at the ankles. I could feel her studying my posture, the tension in my neck and jaw, the way I had jumped when I heard her approach. Nidhi had been my psychiatrist for years, and even though that relationship had changed, old patterns continued.

"Lena told me about Ted," she said. "I'm sorry."

"I can't blame him for running. A lot of people—and non-people—have gone into hiding to wait for things to blow over. Trouble is, I don't think it's going to. Not this time."

"Gutenberg likes to say most people have no concept of change. Our 'short-lived perspective and poor intergenerational memory' create the illusion of stability." She twisted a braided silver ring on her right hand, a gift from Lena. "How long do you think you can continue—"

"Don't." I stared at the dirt, fighting to keep my temper under control. "I'm not a Porter, and you're not my therapist."

"I know that." A hint of pain and reproach edged her next words. "I don't *have* any Porter clients anymore, remember?"

More than half of Nidhi's client base had been magical, from a werewolf with crippling anxiety disorder to libriomancers who played God so often they started to believe in their own divinity. But in the eyes of the Porters, Nidhi was part of my family. The lover of my lover is my . . . I don't know exactly how they classified her, but they had kicked her out the same day they did me.

"If I was your therapist," she continued, "I'd probably talk about how you're grieving for your lost magic. Or point out that your insistence on blaming yourself for what happened to Jeneta suggests an unrealistic sense of power, as well as an overly developed ego. I'd also start you on at least fifty milligrams of Zoloft."

This wasn't our first time through that particular script. "I'm not suicidal, and if I'm a little depressed, I'd say I've got good reason. Right now, the last thing I need is drugs messing up my brain."

"You think depression hasn't already done that?" she asked gently.

"If anything screwed up my head, it was Gutenberg."

"Oh, good. Then we agree your head is screwed up." Her delivery was perfectly deadpan. She waited a beat, then sighed. "How long has it been since you laughed?"

I shrugged.

"Lena says you've been having trouble sleeping, and I can see that you've lost weight. How are things going at work?"

"I've read the *DSM-V*. I know the diagnostic criteria for depression, too," I snapped. "This is different."

"I've read *Gray's Anatomy*. That doesn't make me a surgeon." She stood to go. "Oh, I almost forgot what I came out to tell you. I've found someone who might be able to help you uncover those dream memories."

I set Lena's book aside—carefully this time—and jumped to my feet.

"I haven't worked with her in a while, but I've been keeping up on her research. Best of all, she's only a few hours away."

"Who is it?" When she didn't answer, I folded my arms. "Come on, Nidhi."

"First, put that book away and come eat. Then I'll tell you." She headed toward the deck.

"Since when do therapists use blackmail?" I called out.

She turned around and cocked her head. "Like you said, I'm not your therapist anymore. See you at dinner."

BEIJING—Additional details are finally being released about what appears to be a burglary three weeks ago at the National Library of China. Authorities have confirmed that six people were killed, and another thirteen hospitalized.

Initial accounts described the perpetrators as "inhuman." One was said to have hair like living snakes, similar to the legendary Medusa. Her companion was allegedly twelve feet tall, strong enough to smash brick with his bare hands. Some eyewitnesses claimed the pair was accompanied by a teenaged girl.

Social media site Xīnlàng Wēibó, a Chinese microblogging Web site similar to Twitter, has been abuzz with speculation. Theories range from terrorist activity to an American CIA mission gone wrong. However, the library is now announcing that the attackers' primary target seems to have been the Rare Books Restoration Center. Most of the books and scrolls stored there are centuries old.

The library's Web site provides a partial list of missing items, including works of religious, historical, and mythological significance. A fire that began in the rare books section damaged hundreds, perhaps thousands of other works. It's not known whether the attackers deliberately set the fire.

Some are speculating that this break-in and the supernatural appearance of the perpetrators are somehow related to a message that appeared in a popular fantasy novel last week purporting to reveal the existence of a magical secret society headed by Johannes Gutenberg.

The library is closed indefinitely for repairs. The U.S. Library of Congress has offered to send a team of rare book librarians to Beijing to assist with restoration efforts.

Chapter 2

"HER NAME IS EUPHEMIA SMITH," said Nidhi. "She's a siren."

I set my pizza crust down on the top of the box. Given the state of my kitchen table, we had elected to eat on the deck instead. Nidhi and I sat on old plastic chairs, while Lena perched on the railing, her bare feet pressed to the wooden post.

Nidhi had refused to share any information about her mysterious lead until I finished at least three pieces. She looked pointedly at the crust, and I crammed it into my mouth.

"A siren?" I chewed fast. "As in, Odysseus binding himself to the mast so he could listen to their song, sailors throwing themselves overboard to drown, ships run aground on the rocks, and all that jazz? How is that supposed to help me?"

Most magical creatures these days were book-born, like Lena. Libriomancy had brought hundreds of new species into our world from the pages of books. Intelligent beings generally couldn't make the transition from fiction to the real world—in part because they simply didn't fit through the pages—but there were other paths. Lena had been created as an acorn that grew into her first oak. Vampires—so many different flavors of vampires—spread to our world when overimaginative readers reached into the stories and got themselves bitten.

Other species had evolved naturally. Or supernaturally. There were ongoing debates among the Porters whether sirens and their cousins the merfolk were a result of natural selection or deliberate magical manipulation from millennia ago.

Nidhi sipped her iced tea. "Euphemia and her husband Carl run a hypnotherapy clinic in Marinette, Wisconsin. Neither mental discipline nor magical barriers are proof against a siren's song. She lulls clients into a trance and helps them face the roots of their problems. She and Carl generally help people to quit smoking, lose weight, things like that. I was one of three Porter therapists assigned to supervise the first five hundred hours of her work while they were getting licensed. Nicola wanted to be sure there was Porter oversight."

Nicola Pallas was the Midwest Regional Master of the Porters, responsible for keeping tabs on all things magical for much of the United States and a chunk of Canada. "Marinette isn't that far," I said. "Why haven't I heard of this siren?"

"Because Euphemia works very hard to keep quiet and out of sight. The Porters have a long file on her, of course, but as long as she doesn't hurt anyone or openly use her power, they consider her harmless. She has a speech impediment that limits the more dangerous aspects of her power. She's not strong enough to lure ships to their death anymore. But she and her husband have an impressive success rate. I believe she could help you recover your fragmented memories."

I downed the last of my Pepsi. "I'll grab my keys."

"You'll want to grab your checkbook, too." Nidhi

didn't move from her chair. "The Smiths aren't cheap, and I doubt your insurance covers this. I made you an appointment for tomorrow afternoon."

I was already in the doorway. "Tomorrow? But—"

"If we left now, it would be close to eleven when we arrived," Nidhi said. "I'm sure you'd happily pay extra for a late-night session, but they have concert tickets tonight. Carl is taking Euphemia to see Big Daddy Kane in Green Bay. They'll be exhausted, and Carl tells me his wife's song gets rather *intense* after two hours of live rap."

I wondered briefly if Euphemia and Nicola had ever done a duet. Nicola was a bard with a preference for jazz-based magic. I had once seen her knock a man unconscious with a single bar of music sung over a cell phone.

"Is it dangerous?" Lena asked.

Nidhi hesitated. "It shouldn't be. Usually, Carl does the intake. He meets with Euphemia afterward, and she tailors a recording for him to use in follow-up sessions. But given the nature of Isaac's mind, the magical and psychological barriers he's dealing with, we both agreed this needed to be a 'live' session with Euphemia present."

I slid the door closed and turned around, resting my back against the glass. "You're saying you don't know what will happen?"

"Lena and I will be there to keep an eye on things."

My boss wouldn't be happy about me calling in sick again. I'd used up most of my leave time over the past month. Jennifer had pulled me aside on Friday to discuss my less than stellar job performance. I should check the schedule to see if anyone was available to cover. Alex might be willing to pick up the extra hours. He was trying to save up for a new electric guitar. "I'll see you both tomorrow. What time do we leave?"

Lena and Nidhi looked at one another, and I saw pages of unspoken discussion pass silently between them. "I thought I'd stay here tonight," said Lena.

"But you normally stay with Nidhi on Sundays." I hesitated, double-checking my mental calendar. This wouldn't be the first time I had lost track of the date.

"Not tonight." Lena gestured at the pizza box. "I'm not going to let half a deep-dish sausage and pepperoni go to waste."

I should have been happy. Instead, I found myself resenting that they believed I needed a babysitter. Guilt immediately followed resentment. They were only trying to help.

It might be better for all of us if they left me alone. Given Lena's nature, what was my recent mood doing to her? How much had I dragged her down with me? It was one more reason she should go with Nidhi tonight, to get away from my negativity. It wasn't like I was going to drive to Marinette to track Euphemia down myself, showing up on her doorstep at midnight to demand she dig the answers out of my brain.

Probably.

I rubbed my eyes. Maybe Nidhi was right about the Zoloft.

The laptop baked my thighs as I sat on the couch, searching the Internet while *Star Trek* reruns played in the background. Online, librarian circles were buzzing with speculation about the attack on the National Library of China. I found plenty of theories, but not a single photograph of the attackers.

A gorgon, a giant, and a teenage girl. No mention was made of the girl's appearance, but who else could it have been?

On another day, I would have been fascinated by the prospect of a living gorgon, a creature thought to exist only in myth. I would have loved to see an MRI scan of her head. I had always been curious about how the serpentine hair might work. Each snake presumably had a brain of its own. Did they have independent thought, or was it more of a hive mind? And did the snakes eat? If so, what happened to their meals? Either their intestinal system needed to link into the gorgon's, or else the gorgon would need some truly potent shampoo.

I switched Internet windows and pulled up a list of my preprogrammed search spiders. I had customized more than a hundred automatic searches, monitoring the Web for any information about the Porters, the students of Bi Sheng, or Jeneta Aboderin.

I found two more reports of people digging up the sites of old Porter archives, working from the information in Bi Wei's letter, but in both cases the excavations turned up nothing. The Porters must have either cleared out the contents or found a way to trick the searchers into forgetting what they found.

Lena settled onto the couch beside me and studied the screen. "What are you looking for?"

"Anything I can find." Almost as bad as losing my magic was being shut out of that community, cut off from every reliable source of information and gossip. I might have been sent to the sidelines, but I still wanted to know what was happening in the game, dammit.

I switched to a report from South Africa. "A lightning storm two weeks ago fried every electronic device in a five-mile radius near the edge of Polokwane. That sounds like a magical EMP, one of the tricks the Porters use to avoid being recorded. But I have no idea what they might have been doing there."

I was more certain about the next thing I showed her, an e-mail from one of six publishing-related lists I was on. I opened the attached press release and read, "'Rose Hoffman takes over as CEO at one of the top UK publishing houses.' I don't know the name, but the photo is familiar. I'm pretty sure I met her three years ago. She's a Porter researcher. She was trying to prove the existence of magical resonance between different translations of the same books. Her findings suggested there could be some minimal resonance, but it wasn't conclusive, and she wasn't able to point to the mechanism that would explain it."

Lena's smile made me realize I was beginning to ramble.

"Sorry. The point is, she's almost certainly a plant." The Porters had always had people in New York and other publishing hubs, but it sounded like they were working to take more control of what books—and what potential magic—got into readers' hands. How many books made the bestseller lists not because they were particularly original or well written, but because they included something the Porters wanted to use?

Another open folder contained copies of scholarly articles I had downloaded for review, primarily about the development of printing technology in Asia. Gutenberg's press and the invention of libriomancy had launched a new era in magic, at least in Europe, but China had been working with book magic for centuries before Gutenberg came along. If I could uncover more of that history, I might find clues as to where Bi Wei and her fellow students had disappeared to. If the Porters wouldn't help me, maybe they would.

"Time for emergency measures." Lena bounced to her feet and grabbed the remotes. A minute later, the opening notes of Christopher Franke's *Babylon 5* soundtrack blasted from the television speakers, making me jump.

Lena yanked the laptop away from me, set it on the

coffee table, and plopped down beside me. She turned sideways, leaning her body against mine and crossing her legs on the arm of the couch.

Annoyance and amusement fought it out and decided to call it a draw. That alone should have been enough to make me realize how far gone I was. When a bright, fun, beautiful woman resting against me was a source of frustration, I had a problem.

I wrapped my arm around her and tried to relax, to ignore the part of my brain that refused to stop obsessing. We were five minutes into the episode when I realized how tightly Lena was holding my arm. With my other hand, I combed the thick, black hair from her face.

She caught my hand and kissed my palm, never taking her eyes from the show.

I ended up drifting off about halfway through the episode. But I jolted awake when Lena switched off the TV and set the remote on the table.

"Damn," she whispered. "I was trying not to wake you."

I smothered a yawn. The sky outside was black. "How long did I sleep?"

"Two and a half episodes."

I slid my hand around her waist, feeling the warm skin of her back. She tilted her head to kiss my chin. A second kiss, this one to the base of my neck, carried an unspoken question. I kissed the top of her head in response, but nothing more. After that, neither of us moved for a long time.

I mentally checked off another box on the list of diagnostic criteria for depression: anhedonia, a decrease in enjoyment of most day-to-day activities, including a loss of interest in sex.

Eventually, she stirred enough to ask, "Walk me out to my tree?" Her breath tickled my neck.

"Sure."

The air outside had cooled, and the night was quiet save for the whisper of leaves. We walked hand-in-hand to her grove. I tensed as we approached. Memories of sharp-featured metal constructs and white-furred monsters flashed through my thoughts.

"We're alone here," Lena said.

She would have known had anyone violated her grove. I knew that, but it didn't help my heightened sense of wariness. We were safe tonight. How long would that last?

Jeneta knew about Lena's grove, as did the Ghost Army. Even if Lena transferred herself into another oak tree, a process that was a hell of a lot harder than moving into a new apartment, they had found her tree once before.

I had watched one dryad devastate an entire block. If they took Lena away, turned her into another Deifilia . . .

"I'm sorry about Deifilia," I said suddenly. I couldn't recall if I had ever spoken the words.

"Thank you." She pulled away, her movements tight. One hand touched her tree where Deifilia had died. "I can still hear her sometimes. Only whispers and shadows, impressions of who she was, preserved in the wood like insects in amber."

I wasn't sure how to react to the revelation that Lena's oak contained the echoes of a woman who had been prepared to kill us both.

She must have seen my concern. "They're little more than memories, Isaac."

"I'm glad you have them."

It was the right thing to say. She smiled and kissed me. "Do me a favor," she said as she pulled away. "Don't stay up until three in the morning again searching for answers that might not exist."

"There are always answers," I said automatically.

"That doesn't mean you'll be able to find them," she

shot back. "Or that the cost of those answers is worth paying." She pulled me in for another kiss, ending the argument quite effectively, and in a way that left me with no complaints.

"Promise me?" she asked when we broke away. "If you can't sleep, fine, but no reading anything related to ghosts, Jeneta, Gutenberg, Bi Sheng, or the imminent end of the world."

"I promise." I waited while she entered her tree, her flesh merging into the wood like the bark was clay molding itself around her. I put a hand on the tree once she had disappeared, but felt nothing of Lena or the power in her oak. "Good night, love."

After a brief debate the following morning, we ended up taking my pickup truck to Wisconsin. Neither my convertible nor Lena's motorcycle could comfortably carry three, and the last time we used Nidhi's car to do something magic-related, wendigos had pretty well totaled it. Nidhi was still fighting the insurance company over that one.

Lena drove, giving me time to read. I had kept my word the night before, trying to lose myself in an old Terry Pratchett novel and finally falling asleep around two in the morning. But I hadn't made any such promise about today. I leaned against the passenger door, books and papers around my feet, trying to track down any references to the Ghost Army from the past five hundred years.

Nidhi sat in the back, working on what I guessed to be case notes, though I couldn't be certain since I didn't read Gujarati. Smudge rode on the dashboard, contentedly watching the passing scenery.

I doubt any of us said more than a dozen words until we reached Marinette. Nidhi guided us to a large house less than two miles from the Michigan/Wisconsin border and even closer to the waters of Green Bay. Twin spruce trees stood in the middle of a circular driveway. The American flag flew from a pole in the front yard.

"Euphemia and Carl work out of their home," Nidhi said.

There were no signs to distinguish it from the other extravagant houses along the road. Most people who worked a magical day job tended to do business through word of mouth, since it wasn't the kind of thing you could advertise.

They seemed to be doing quite well for themselves. A brick walk led past beautifully precise landscaping, full of purple coneflowers and black-eyed Susans. To either side of the house, decorative spruce trees grew along the front of a brown privacy fence, blocking the backyard from view.

I could see Lena studying the flowers and taking mental notes. Her garden had been destroyed by the oak grove in our backyard, but she had hinted about plans to turn my front lawn into a floral jungle.

Tall, etched windows framed the storm door, which was a single rectangle of stained glass showing a sailing ship on the waves. A disproportionate amount of the glass was devoted to the water, showing plants and fish of every color imaginable. The ship appeared cramped in its relatively small rectangle of sky at the top.

Nidhi rang the doorbell. A silhouetted head peeked through the blue glass, and then the door swung open to reveal a middle-aged man in plastic flip-flops and a green Speedo. His wet hair was slicked back, and water dripped down his well-rounded stomach, creating random swirls in his graying chest hair. He grinned at Nidhi. "Doctor Shah! How long has it been?"

"A little over a year." Nidhi stepped to the side. "Carl, this is Lena Greenwood and Isaac Vainio."

I shook his hand, then dried my palm on my jeans.

He beckoned us to enter. "Euphemia's been in the pool all morning. How was the drive? Can I get you anything to drink?"

"Cherry Coke?" Lena was staring unabashedly at our host. He was hardly swimsuit model material, but then, neither was I. Lena had much broader standards of beauty than most.

"You got it. Isaac, if you need privacy, you can change in the sauna."

I blinked. "Change into what?"

"Your swimsuit." He paused. "Didn't Doctor Shah tell you?"

I folded my arms and turned toward Nidhi. "No, Doctor Shah forgot to mention anything about needing a suit."

Nidhi looked like she couldn't decide whether to apologize or laugh. "Euphemia didn't say anything . . ."

"No sweat," said Carl. "I used to be closer to Isaac's size. I'm sure I can find him something that will fit."

He ducked through an arched doorway. As soon as his back was turned, Nidhi mouthed the words, *I'm sorry.*

I debated making a run for it. "If he comes back with another Speedo—"

"I like him," Lena announced, grinning merrily at my discomfort. "If he can't find anything that meets your standards, I get the feeling he'd be okay with letting you go skinny dipping instead."

Anything I said to that would only dig me in deeper. Instead, I studied the three long aquariums that lined the hallway, their filters and pumps humming quietly. The closest looked like someone had carved a chunk out of the Great Barrier Reef. Another brimmed with goldfish. The third held guppy-sized fish in neon colors.

"Go on out back," Carl shouted. "Through the hall, then take a right. I'll be right there."

A door to the left opened into what appeared to be Carl's office, judging by the license and diplomas framed on the far wall. To the right, a glass door led onto a small patio.

Lena took one step outside, pointed to the pool, and said, "I want one."

"Where would we put it?" Larger trees and the privacy fence surrounded what was more a lagoon than a pool. Enormous orange carp swam lazily along the algae-green bottom, and a turtle sunned itself on a log near the edge. Flowers and plants, mostly tropical in appearance, bordered the pool. I spotted hibiscus and some kind of stunted palm, along with large red and yellow blooms I couldn't identify.

"Isaac Vainio?" The question came from a woman on the far end of the pool, her face partially shaded by an overhanging palm. I wondered briefly how they maintained these plants in the distinctly nontropical climate of the Midwest.

"Doctor Euphemia Smith?" I guessed.

The way she glided through the water reminded me of a swimming serpent. She swam not with her arms or legs, but with her body. One look, and I understood the speech impediment Nidhi had mentioned. An inch-wide strip of scar tissue slashed the left side of her neck, vivid pink against the deep tan of her skin. The scar thinned in the middle, and the raggedness made me suspect some kind of bite. Given the angle, I was amazed the wound hadn't killed her.

The gray in her hair and the lines on her face made her look a good ten years older than her husband, though for all I knew she could have been Gutenberg's age. Her hair was thick and matted, like seaweed. Or feathers. Sirens were sometimes said to have had bird-like characteristics.

"I'm not a doctor." Her words rasped, reminding me

of my grandmother in her last days after a lifetime of smoking. "I dropped out midway through my first semester."

"Here you go, son." Carl emerged from the house, and I was relieved to see him holding a thigh-length pair of red-and-white Hawaiian-print trunks. He pointed me toward the wood-walled sauna a short distance away.

"Let me know if you need help," Lena offered.

The sauna was spacious, clean, and utterly lacking in personality. It looked like a kit built from a box. The slats of the walls and benches were too perfect, too identical. The electric heater with its uniform gray stones caged atop the heating elements could have come out of a Sears catalog. There was even a small flat-screen TV built into the wall behind a layer of glass or plastic to protect it from the steam. My father, proud Finn that he was, would have refused to dignify it with the name "sauna."

I turned the heater on low and set Smudge's cage atop the grate, then stripped down and folded my clothes on the wooden bench. I should have been excited. Anxious. I was about to experience a form of magic I'd never seen or heard before. Instead, there was only impatience.

I yanked on the old swimsuit. It hung a bit loosely, even after I tightened the drawstring, but that shouldn't matter. When I emerged, Carl had joined his wife in the water, dragging an inflated yellow raft behind him.

Lena grinned when she saw me. "I like the look, but we have *got* to get you outside more often. You're so pale there's a very real danger you'll get yourself staked as a vampire."

Carp shot away as I eased into the warm water. Algae turned the bottom slick. I grabbed the edge to keep my footing. Carl took my other arm and helped me climb onto the raft.

"You just lay back and relax," he said. "Euphemia's

going to sing you a little lullaby, that's all. You should be thankful. Few people get to hear her sing in person these days."

"Why not?" I asked.

"My voice isn't what it once was." The water barely rippled as Euphemia ducked and swam beneath the raft, emerging to my left. "But the unfiltered song of a siren, even a crippled one, can be disturbing."

"What do you mean, 'disturbing'?" Lena asked sharply.

"She's talking about the yearning," Carl said. "Her song cuts deep into your heart and dreams, digging up the things you most desire. It's how her kind lured men and women back in the old days. Euphemia sings promises. The first time I heard her, I wept for a week."

"Is it dangerous?" I asked.

"Eighteen years, and we've never lost a patient."

Nidhi frowned. "That's not an answer."

"It's the best I can give you," Carl replied, uncharacteristically serious. "I'm not gonna lie. There will be aftereffects, and they won't be pleasant. But if you really want to find those answers buried in his thoughts, Euphemia can guide him there."

"Do it." I rested my head on the gently bobbing raft and closed my eyes.

"Nidhi told me about the rumble in Copper River. What's the last thing you remember about your fight with that other dryad?" Carl's words were calm but strong. It was much easier to take him as a professional with my eyes shut.

"Lena tried to . . . to connect with her." *Seduce* would have been a more accurate word, but I didn't want to get into that. "Deifilia resisted."

"This isn't going to be fun, but I need you to relive that day," said Carl. "Play it back in your thoughts and tell me what happens next."

Metal creatures swarm down the trunk of the oak—magically created rats and insects with clicking legs and gleaming teeth. Some jump onto Lena, biting her skin. Wooden weapons slam together as Lena and Deifilia duel. The impacts crack like gunshots.

The students of Bi Sheng look on helplessly, bound in the tangled roots of the new-grown grove. All save two who have been corrupted by Deifilia's ghosts, the spirits Jeneta had named devourers. Their magic stretches toward Lena, ripping her apart from within.

Lena collapses, dying as I watch. The possessed students remind me of vampires, draining Lena of the magic that defines her. Soon there will be nothing left but a desiccated corpse.

"I took control of the oak. Lena's oak, I mean." Deifilia had seized it for her own, but she was distracted by the battle, allowing me to act.

"No shit? How'd you manage—" I heard a splash and a sputter from Carl, and a murmured chastisement from Euphemia. His voice turned smooth once more. "Right. Nidhi said you were injured."

"My knee. I dislocated it."

My leg throbs, pumping agony through my body with every heartbeat. I shift my body, trying to ease the pressure. Roots pin my leg in place, holding me trapped.

"Focus on the sensations of that battle. The pain. The noise. The sweat dripping down your face and back. The way your perception of time stretches out when you're frightened."

As I recalled the details, Euphemia began to sing.

I recognized the language as Greek, though I couldn't understand the words. *Haunting* was the first word that came to mind. It was what whale song might have sounded like, if the whale was suicidal and her song was being performed by Stevie Nicks.

Tension drained from my muscles. My body grew

warm, as if the shade had been burned aside and the sunlight was baking my muscles from within. The raft cradled my body. Small movements in the water made me feel like I was flying.

"You grabbed hold of Lena's oak," Carl prompted.

Lena is dying. So is Bi Wei, the first of the students of Bi Sheng to be restored to the world. The Ghost Army is fighting to claim her. They're too strong. I don't know how to fight them.

But Deifilia's power, like Lena's, comes from books. I know the book that gave birth to them. I look beyond the tree to the magic flowing through it, layer upon layer of familiar text. I reach for that story.

My hand sinks into the roots. I use Lena's roots to trap Deifilia in place, just as she had done to me.

"I pushed too far." My throat was dry. Pain throbbed through my leg as I remembered my senses stretching through the roots, the branches, even the individual leaves. I had manipulated the magic of *Nymphs of Neptune*, and when I did, that magic sank its roots into my thoughts. "The air was cold."

"You heard voices?"

"Characters from the book, yah."

"I am yours now, John Rule of Earth." A nymph kneels on the ice, blonde hair flowing like a golden river over the voluptuous curves of her body. Arousal pounds through my veins, and I forget about the pain.

"I was hallucinating. It happens sometimes, when libriomancy goes wrong." I shivered, remembering the chill of the Neptunian caves, the ice beneath my body. "They told me there was no returning from this place."

"They were wrong." Carl sounded like a father soothing a child after a nightmare. "You're safe here, Isaac. But this is where the ride gets a little bumpy. So far, Euphemia's just been helping you relax, settling you into a nice trance. You're in control, and everything that happens next is up to you. The answers are in your mind, but you have to want them."

"I do." Euphemia's song couldn't completely suppress my annoyance.

"What happened next, Isaac? You saw someone else. Not a character from a book. Someone real."

My muscles tightened. My breath caught. It was as if I had fallen from the raft and plunged not into the warmth of the pool, but a frozen lake. Swirling currents seized my body, tugging me down.

Euphemia's song grew louder. The rhythm was uncomfortably sexual, an erotic melody sinking its hooks into my bones. My months with Lena had taught me a great deal about desire, but this was different, more primal. I had felt sensations like this only once before, when Lena demonstrated what her unfiltered power could do. It was like a shot of adrenaline directly to the libido.

Euphemia sang of mystery and promise and dreams fulfilled. I could no more turn away than I could stop my own heart from beating. I imagined her swimming through my memories. I followed, desperate to reach her, but she kept just out of reach.

"What do you hear, Isaac?" Carl pressed.

I swallowed. "Gutenberg was there." *He stands over me, his anger palpable even in my delusional state. He and Lena are arguing.*

"He's lost," Gutenberg insists.

"None shall harm him while I live." Lena's words blur with those of the book.

"Even if I wanted to help the man who betrayed the Porters, he's too far gone."

I knew what came next. The tip of a golden fountain pen pressing against my brow like a scalpel, cutting away my magic. Tears slipped down my face, rolling past my ears to the sides of my neck. "Please don't."

My words sounded distant. I reached for happier

memories. Using magic to transport myself to the surface of the moon. Making love to Lena for the first time. Watching Smudge play in the glowing coals of a barbeque grill, jumping about and flinging ash into the air with his forelegs.

Euphemia slowed her song, calling me back to that moment of loss. Her words promised me everything I dreamed of, all of the joy of those memories and more, if only I swam deeper.

"There was another voice," said Carl. "The book wasn't the only thing trying to get inside your head."

The Ghost Army. In fighting Deifilia, I had opened myself to their assault. The ghosts rode the currents of magic, and I was channeling a hell of a lot of it. "I can't see her."

"Her?" he repeated. "It's a woman?"

Memories rushed past, swirling too quickly and violently to grasp. If I tried, they would tear me apart. This was a place of death, a place where something had burned my thoughts to ash and salted the ground to make sure I would never remember her attempt to drown me.

"Listen to Euphemia. She can't read your thoughts, but her song can lead you to what you most desire."

Her voice whispered to me from beneath the ash, offering knowledge, magic, love. I could have it all. I could reverse the spell Gutenberg had carved into me and restore my magic. I could move beyond the limits of libriomancy, figure out exactly how magic made the universe work, manipulate the gears of creation.

Lena was there as well. Beyond her waited treasured memories and moments from my past. Christmas morning. My mother baking brownies. Seeing *Star Wars* for the first time. Helping take my eighth grade Knowledge Bowl team to nationals, where we placed third. Anything I had ever loved or desired.

"Focus, Isaac." Carl sounded far away.

That wasn't right. We had won second place at nationals. Silver medals, not bronze. Yet it was bronze that edged my vision, framing my thoughts. My focus narrowed with each word of Euphemia's song. Stone walls shut me out of my own memories, but her music pulled me irresistibly through the cracks.

I heard myself whispering, *"Who are you?"*

"Would you like me to show you, Isaac?"

Pinpricks grip my chin, turn my head to one side then the other, as if I'm a prize poodle at a dog show.

"She wore a metal mask. Bronze, I think."

The stones crushed together, sealing memories and cauterizing thought. Euphemia's song grew stronger in response, dragging me downward. Euphemia hammered the shell of my prison, every word ringing through my thoughts. New fissures appeared, and through the gaps I saw a woman clad in bronze armor. She was short and inhumanly beautiful, though I wasn't sure how I could know that, since the armor hid every inch of her skin. Even her eyes were shielded by thin shells of bronze.

The bronze woman stretches out a hand. Through her eyes I see an empire of the dead. I watch her slaughter half of humanity to build her army. Jeneta is the key to her victory. Libriomancy transforms every book into a potential weapon, and Jeneta's e-reader holds all those weapons in a single device.

I couldn't breathe. Cold fingers tightened around mine, pulling me closer. My heart felt like a balloon about to burst. Panic clawed within my chest like a trapped animal. I was no longer flying, but falling—

I landed hard on stone tile, coughing and gagging. Strong hands rolled me onto my side. I vomited water from my mouth and nose.

"Don't struggle." Lena held me in place while I fought to breathe. "You rolled off the raft. Carl said it was the final step in the process, that when you came back up, you'd have the memory you needed." Her face was pale. "You didn't come back up."

I blinked at her. Memory and reality blurred. I saw a ghost trapped in bronze, the living cut down by the dead. Most of humanity knew nothing of magic. We were unprepared to fight such a one-sided war. She would rip her ranks from our corpses.

"Isaac!" Lena's cry pulled me back. Water streamed from her hair onto my chest. Goose bumps tightened my skin. She pulled me up and wrapped her arms around me. I could barely force my arms to return the embrace. I felt like I had finished a marathon on a planet with twice Earth's gravity.

Euphemia lay unconscious on the edge of the pool, a short distance away. Carl sat beside her, his eyes wide.

"What happened?" I asked hoarsely.

"I told her to stop singing." Lena's body was tense. "She didn't."

"She was *helping* him." Carl started to rise, looked at Lena, and apparently thought better of it.

"You said you've never lost a patient." Nidhi stood beside me. Unlike Lena, she neither raised her voice, nor was her body language in any way threatening, but the clipped intensity of her words made Carl flinch. "If Lena hadn't stopped your wife and brought Isaac up, he would have died."

"You don't know that for certain." Carl swallowed. "Look, that was no simple repressed memory. It's like you asked us to heal a cut, then brought us a patient with terminal cancer. The only way to treat that sort of thing is to burn it out."

"Even if you kill the patient?" Nidhi turned to me. "Isaac, I didn't know. I swear to you. I've consulted on their cases. Carl promised you would be safe."

"It's all right." I closed my eyes and rested my head

on Lena's shoulder. A part of me didn't care about drowning. I wanted Euphemia's song back, yearned to return to that place of memory and hope and desire, and to escape the vision of a world where the living were enslaved to the dead. "It worked. I remember her name."

"There you go." Carl stretched his hands toward me, like a magician's flourish after a grand trick. "Exactly what you asked for. No harm, no foul."

Nidhi silenced him with a look. "This man was your patient, and you almost killed him." She crouched beside me and touched my wrist, checking my pulse. More quietly, she added, "He's also family."

It was the first time she had used that word to describe me. I turned to look at her, to respond, but the words wouldn't come. Nor did she give me the chance to speak. Her attention and anger were utterly focused on Carl.

"When Isaac fell into the water, you told us this was normal. You've done this before."

"Sometimes recordings aren't enough," he said defensively. "Some patients need a more immersive treatment."

"Why wasn't that included in your reports?" She slashed a hand through the air, cutting off his reply. "When I get home, I will pull up every patient record you ever signed. I will follow up with each and every one of those people. If I find a single person who suffered thanks to your negligence, you're through."

Carl glanced down at his wife, then scowled. "Who the hell do you think you are? You think the state will yank my license because you tell them fairy tales about magic songs?"

"Why would I waste my time reporting you to the *state*?" Nidhi countered quietly.

"You don't work for the Porters anymore," Carl said. "You can't—"

Nidhi continued as if he hadn't spoken. "I've worked with many powerful, dangerous people over the years. I helped them through traumas nobody should have to endure. I taught them to rebuild relationships torn by magic and secrets. I fought for them, helped them find hope, helped them to retain their humanity." Her voice dropped even lower. "And I have most of those people on speed dial."

I had never seen Nidhi like this. Carl looked like he was the one who had almost drowned. His eyes were round, and the color had faded from his cheeks.

"Thank you for your assistance." Nidhi joined Lena in helping me to my feet. We started toward the house, pausing only long enough for Lena to fetch Smudge and my clothes from the sauna.

I made it to the driveway before the tears began. Carl had warned me about the yearning, but words couldn't convey the sense of loss. I was hollow, as though everyone I loved had been ripped away from me, killed without warning. Every dream crushed, every possession stolen, every hope turned to dust. It was ridiculous and irrational and I couldn't control it any more than I could hold back the sunset.

But one memory remained. Through the tears and the grief, I saw the woman who had taunted me that day in Lena's grove. I saw the one who commanded the Ghost Army, who had taken Jeneta. I saw her, and I remembered.

Meridiana.

WEREWOLVES VS. BIGFOOT

Summary: Viral video claims to show shotgun-wielding werewolves hunting Bigfoot from the back of a pickup truck.

Status: Inconclusive.

Sample E-mail:

Hey, check out this cell phone video, captured by a 17-year-old girl in Copper River, Michigan.

You can't see the driver, but look at the two shotgun-toting hicks in the back. And before you say it's just a couple of hairy guys in masks, wait for the 0:42 mark, when a white-furred giant streaks across the road.

A good makeup artist can create a convincing werewolf, but that dude in the back jumps at least ten meters FROM A MOVING TRUCK to tackle what looks like an albino sasquatch. Both of them bounce back from the impact like it was nothing.

Copies of this video have already been pulled from YouTube and other sites for "copyright violation." Screen caps are below, in case they yank this link, too.

Background: Many rumors have been spread about the recent tragedy in Copper River. At least 34 people are known to have died, but initial reports of property damage appear to have been wildly exaggerated. The official cause of most deaths was listed as accidental, according to police reports. [Sources: Associated Press, Copper River Journal, CBS News]

The video in question first appeared on the Internet on August 5 of this year. On August 8, Reddit user BlackCapsFan12 posted a detailed analysis of the background motion to demonstrate that the "impossible" jump was a result of camera trickery. Other users argued the video was genuine, and submitted evidence suggesting BlackCapsFan12 was a sockpuppet account.

Another theory is that the video is part of a viral marketing campaign for an upcoming movie or television show. (See also "*Vampire Photobombs Live News Report.*") Hollywood is certainly capable of producing a video of this quality. However, no studio has claimed responsibility, nor has anyone been able to connect the video to a specific forthcoming release.

Conclusion: While most people scoff at the idea of magic and monsters, there is no conclusive proof that the video was faked. In addition, materials such as the *George R. R. Martin Letter* suggest that we must at least consider the possibility of such things being genuine. Therefore, ChainBusters.com has given this story a verdict of INCONCLUSIVE.

Related Stories:

• Iron Dragon Escapes from Copper River Mine, Attacks Local Library

• Secret Government Drug Testing Goes Horribly Wrong in Michigan's Upper Peninsula?

Chapter 3

I CALLED NICOLA PALLAS from the truck. Whatever the Porters might think of me, we were all working toward the same goal, and they needed to know what we'd learned. Nicola's phone went straight to voice mail.

"I got a name. Meridiana. That's who's trying to raise the Ghost Army. That's who took Jeneta. And this whole process would be a lot easier if we could share resources." I glared at the screen, willing her to pick up. When nothing happened, I added a bitter, "You're welcome," and hung up.

Nicola Pallas was one of the most powerful people in the country. More importantly, she had argued for letting me keep my magic. Granted, she hadn't argued as loudly or strenuously as I might have liked, but it was more than most had done, and made her a potential ally.

"You know the Porters are keeping an eye on you," Lena said. "Just stick a note to the front door and they'll get it."

"I know. You think they're living in the Mileskis' old place?" The Mileskis had moved out a week ago, and while I'd miss the family, I didn't mind being rid of their dog, an elderly mutt who had barked nonstop for three days following the assault on our block. I felt bad for the trauma the poor thing had suffered, but she had apparently taken it as an excuse to start sneaking out to use Lena's new grove as a bathroom. My sympathy dried up the third time I stepped in one of her "presents" in the backyard.

"Probably. If I was going to take over an abandoned house, I'd want one with a hot tub."

There was one other person I could ask for help. I checked my contacts list, but Ponce de Leon's information had disappeared. No surprise there. His number only showed up when he wanted something from me, which had been rare even when I had been a Porter. Fortunately, I had memorized his number years ago.

Juan Ponce de Leon, former conquistador and ex-Porter, was perhaps the strongest sorcerer alive. While the rest of us needed books or song to control our magic, he could manipulate that power through his will alone. To say he and Gutenberg had a complicated history was putting it mildly, but if the Porters wouldn't help me, maybe he could.

Assuming he wasn't still pissed at me for stealing his car.

Ponce de Leon didn't answer, either. He had been sticking to the shadows for months, but knowing him, he'd be keeping tabs on events in the magical world. I left a message giving him just enough information to whet his curiosity.

I could feel Nidhi watching me as I hung up. "Thank you," I said quietly. "For what you said and did back there."

"How much do you remember from Euphemia's spell?" she asked.

"Too much." I swallowed and looked out the window,

watching the grass and trees pass by in a blur of green. My legs bounced with restless energy. The aftermath of the siren's song was like reliving every missed opportunity, every wrong choice I had made in my life.

I leaned forward to grab the GPS. If I stopped moving, stopped *doing something*, I would shatter. I programmed a new destination, then returned the unit to its mount. "We need to stop at Brown County Central Library in Green Bay."

There was magic, and there was magic. Thanks to Gutenberg, I could no longer pull wands, potions, and light sabers out of books, but when it came to research, give me a well-stocked library and I was a goddamned Merlin.

I climbed out of the truck and hurried toward the library, leaving Lena and Nidhi to search for a parking spot. The moment I stepped inside, a little of the hollow pain from Euphemia's magic began to ease. I had never set foot in this particular library, but this place *felt* right. From the familiar conversations behind the circulation desk to the tapping of keyboards. The slightly sweet, papery smell of cellulose. The sight of row upon row of books, the colorful chaos of their spines unified by the white tags affixed to each. I was home.

An arched skylight made the whole place feel warmer and more welcoming. I smiled at a woman behind the desk and headed for the public computers.

By the time Lena and Nidhi found me, I had scribbled half a page of notes on the back of a flyer, and was well into my fourth search. "I knew I'd heard the name Meridiana before."

Lena looked over my shoulder. "Pope Sylvester II?"

"Born Gerbert d'Aurillac, in France. They called him

the scientist pope. According to legend, he ascended to the papacy in 999 AD with the help of a demon named Meridiana. Other stories say the name referred to a bronze head, an oracle of some kind that provided him with supernatural advice."

Lena pulled out a chair and sat down beside me. "How does a pope's thousand-year-old oracular head end up kidnapping Jeneta Aboderin from northern Michigan? Assuming there's any truth to the stories."

"We know d'Aurillac practiced magic," I said. "He believed a deeper knowledge of the universe was the key to seeing the mind of God. He studied mathematics, astronomy, rhetoric, music, and more. Including magic. He did his apprenticeship at al-Karaouine in Morocco."

"That's all in the article you're reading?" asked Nidhi.

"All but the magic part. That's up here." I tapped my temple. "Gutenberg took my libriomancy, but he didn't take the years I spent studying Porter records and histories."

Unfortunately, whereas the life of Pope Sylvester II had been well-documented, Meridiana was little more than rumor and superstition. One author linked her to a secret cult of Mary Magdalene, while another described her as a succubus sent by Lucifer to corrupt and destroy the pope.

I tried and failed to pin down the origin of the name. Meridiana could be Italian or Latin, possibly Spanish. It could also be a corruption of the word "Meridian." As far as I could tell, it had never seen popular use as a proper name.

A librarian named Louanne was kind enough to set me up with an account to use the printer. The library had little information about Sylvester II or Meridiana, but she jotted down the address and phone number of the Archdiocese of Green Bay and suggested we try there.

"What I really need are his firsthand writings," I muttered as Louanne returned to the front desk. "D'Aurillac's collected letters, his work on the nature of man and God." Though if he had written anything directly about magic, the Porters would have snatched those documents and hidden them away in one of their archives. Probably in Rome or France.

I printed out a timeline of d'Aurillac's life and career and studied the dates. "Bi Sheng would have been a child at the time of Sylvester II's reign."

"Five thousand miles away," Lena pointed out.

"Right, but there *was* contact between continents back then. Commercial as well as magical." Meridiana had survived for a thousand years. Centuries later, Bi Sheng's students had preserved themselves by using specially prepared books to anchor their thoughts and memories.

"You think Bi Sheng got the idea from Meridiana?" asked Lena.

"I don't know. They could have both learned from an older source, or maybe they developed similar magic independently, a parallel evolution of ideas." I pulled up an academic article on the history of brazen heads and sent it to the printer. "When I saw Meridiana, she was encased in bronze."

"If it exists, the head might be a kind of prison," said Nidhi.

"Or it's the equivalent of the book Bi Wei and the others used to preserve themselves. Either way, it explains how she endured all these centuries. If we could find it first . . ." Assuming Jeneta hadn't already done so.

"From the obnoxious grin, I take it you have a plan for how to find it first?" asked Lena.

"Yep." And neither Lena nor Nidhi was going to like it. I sat back and brushed my hands together. "I figure the quickest way to get the answers we need is to ask Gerbert d'Aurillac directly."

Only a handful of vampire species had the ability to speak with the dead. A ghost-talker named Nicholas had helped us talk to a deceased Porter earlier this year. Unfortunately, Nicholas hadn't survived the attack that followed, making it unlikely that the vampires would be willing to help me out a second time. Especially now that I lacked the ability to make it worth their while.

I called Deb DeGeorge, who had been a friend back in the days when she had a pulse and didn't snack on bugs. When I told her what I needed, she spent the next thirty seconds laughing at me.

"Isaac, the first time you got involved with us, a madman bombed the shit out of our Detroit nest," she said when she recovered. "Then you got a very expensive ghost-talker killed. If I so much as mention your name, they're likely to feed me to the ferals. Unless you're interested in converting—"

"No, thank you," I said quickly.

"Then I'm sorry, hon. You're on your own." Deb sighed. "Be careful, okay? Try not to get yourself killed."

The phone went dead before I could answer. I leaned my head against the window and sorted through my remaining options. There were books with the power to show limited glimpses of the past, but nothing that would let me contact a man who died a thousand years ago. Even if they could, the Porters were forbidden from working with me.

The students of Bi Sheng could probably help. Assuming I could find them. Given that they seemed to be successfully hiding from Gutenberg and his automatons, the odds of me tracking them down were slim.

Our next stop was the archdiocese. I pretended to be a graduate student in theology, and came away with several photocopied references about Pope Sylvester II, but nothing new about Meridiana.

By now, frustration and the aftereffects of Euphemia's magic had thoroughly darkened my mood. It had been all I could do to keep from snapping at the priest, let alone Lena and Nidhi. So when Lena asked where else we could look for answers, I said only, "Tamarack."

Nidhi wasn't the only one with friends who owed her favors.

Evening found us driving through Tamarack, home of the majority of the Upper Peninsula's werewolf population. Those who weren't living in the wild, at least. Tamarack was a broken-down, half-empty, ex-mining town, and made Copper River look like the big city. We pulled to a stop at the home of Jeff and Helen DeYoung.

Jeff was an arthritic werewolf with a take-no-shit attitude and a penchant for flamboyant dress. More importantly, after the events of a month before, he considered me a member of his pack.

We found Jeff and Helen sitting together on an antique wooden porch swing. Jeff took a swallow from a half-empty beer bottle as he watched us climb out of the truck. Both he and Helen visibly relaxed when they saw who we were.

Jeff removed his right hand from the revolver holstered to his hip. Helen slipped a knife back into a sheath beneath the bottom of her sweater. With magic's veil of secrecy beginning to unravel, every sentient nonhuman was on edge. At least a quarter of Tamarack's werewolves had retreated to the woods over the past month.

Jeff greeted me with a back-cracking hug and a quick sniff of my neck. "You smell like algae."

"Long story." I turned to hug Helen, who finished the spinal rearrangement her husband had begun on me. "We need a favor."

"Beer first. You look like you could use one." Jeff finished hugging Lena, then scooped up Nidhi. "Favors after, eh?"

He disappeared into the century-old house, returning with three beers and a plate of what appeared to be bacon-chip cookies. Given the choice, I grabbed one of the bottles and leaned against the railing, waiting impatiently as Jeff and Helen filled us in on the latest werewolf gossip, most of which centered around who was sneaking into bed—or into the woods, or the backseat, or in one case the middle of the gas station parking lot—with whom. Werewolves treated sex like a professional sporting event, occasionally with spectators and cheerleaders.

I held my silence for as long as I could, which turned out to be approximately half a bottle. "Jeff, I need you to hook me up with some black-market magic."

The wrinkles in his forehead furrowed like fresh-plowed farmland. Helen turned dagger eyes toward her husband.

"Don't start," he said to Helen. "You know I haven't run in those circles for decades. Isaac, this is a bad idea. Even for you."

"What's that supposed to mean?" I shook my head. "Never mind. This is important. I have to talk to a ghost. A man who died a thousand years ago."

Helen set her beer on the porch. "Why?"

I was ready for this. "To find whoever took Jeneta. She was my student. My responsibility. My pack."

Jeff rolled his eyes. "You throw that damn pack thing at me every time you want something."

"Only because it works."

He flipped me off, but he was chuckling, too. "Do you have any idea what you're getting into? If these people suspect for one second that you're still with the Porters, they'll kill you. Not to mention what the Porters will do if they catch you going after underground magic."

"I did my time as a field agent," I reminded him. "I know what's out there."

"Didn't the Porters have to pull you out of the field?" Helen asked. "The Mackinac Island incident, wasn't it?"

"First of all, I stopped those zombie horses, didn't I? Second, that's beside the point. Jeff, what did it cost you to get your moonstone?" I was referring to the magical crystal he used to control his transformations into wolf form. It had come from one of Kristen Britain's *Green Rider* novels, meaning he must have gotten it from a libriomancer.

"They asked me for a favor." He stared at the porch. "I don't want to talk about it."

"That should tell you everything you need to know," said Helen. "I've been married to this mutt for forty years, and I can count on one hand the number of times he *didn't* want to talk."

"Look, I hate to ask, but isn't this something the Porters should be doing instead of you?" Jeff continued to avoid eye contact.

I took a drink before answering, using the beer to force back the anger his words triggered. The despair was stronger than before, no doubt a side effect of Euphemia's song. "Yah, it is. But they've had a month to search, and haven't found her. They haven't stopped the Ghost Army. Far as I can tell, they haven't accomplished shit. I've learned who we're hunting, and I've seen what she means to do. I can track her down, but I need more information."

"What happens when you find her?" asked Helen. "You make a citizen's arrest? Blow your bad guy whistle?"

Jeff leaned close. "How far are you willing to go, Isaac Vainio?"

"You saw what they did to Copper River. Not to mention that Meridiana has done her best to strip away my sanity on two separate occasions."

"Did a pretty good job from the look of it," Jeff muttered.

I let that pass. "Jeneta called the Ghost Army 'devourers,' and the name fits. They're not true ghosts, just shadows of hunger and rage and charred magic. Lena and I fought one in Detroit. The two of us together could barely stop the damned thing. We had to drop an entire building on its head, and even that only stunned it. Meridiana's planning to use Jeneta's magic to create a true army."

"You're telling me this Meridiana and her ghosts whupped your ass twice when you *had* magic. What do you think's gonna happen this time around?"

I shrugged. "That depends on whether or not the dead pope can help us."

"Idiot," Jeff muttered.

"No more than you were at his age," Helen said.

"Which is why he should listen to me." Jeff walked to the corner of the porch and stared out at the empty street. "My libriomancer contact died eight years ago, but I know a black-market troll living in Niagara who deals in architectural magic. I might be able to bargain a name out of her. But if you mess up, these people will eat you alive. Some of them literally. Do you understand what I'm saying?"

I nodded.

"Go home. I'll make some calls."

"Thanks, Jeff."

He snorted. "Thank me by coming back with your body and soul in one piece."

For the next two days, I read everything I could find about Pope Sylvester II, taking shameless advantage of our interlibrary loan system and the library's access to various online collections.

I heard nothing from Nicola or the Porters, nothing from Ponce de Leon, and nothing from Jeff DeYoung. The news outlets were all but useless for updates on anything magical. Beijing had clamped down on information about the library, and so far, it looked like the Porters were continuing to stay ahead of efforts by the public to uncover their archives. The only interesting thing I found was a rumor about a biology teacher who captured and dissected a bunyip in Australia, but after spending half an afternoon tracking the story down, it turned out to be a hoax.

The hardest thing was finding the energy to care about my day-to-day responsibilities at the library. Today, Jennifer had me working on one of my least favorite duties: culling our collection. Books that hadn't been checked out for at least three years had to go, and Jennifer had preemptively forbidden me from checking them out myself to save them.

I had pulled more than a hundred so far. Those in reasonable condition would be sold at our fall library fair next month, while the rest were supposed to be recycled.

Personally, I thought "brought back to Isaac's house to be repaired and donated to kids at the local high school" qualified as recycling. I wasn't all that good at bookbinding and restoration, but you could add years to a book's life with a plastic jacket cover, book repair tape, and the right adhesives.

Jennifer leaned out from her office. "Isaac, did you take care of those subscription renewals I left in your box last week?"

"Shit." A father sitting with his preteen son at the computers gave me a death stare. "I mean, shoot. Sorry."

I rubbed my eyes, abandoned the half-sorted piles of books, and headed for the break room. Employee mailboxes lined the wall opposite the old fridge. My cell phone went off before I could retrieve the papers stuffed into mine. When I saw who was calling, I spun around and called out, "Alex, could you watch the desk for a few minutes?"

"Sure," he said. "I did your job all day Monday. Why stop now?"

I ignored him and ducked back into the break room. "What have you found, Jeff?"

"Hello to you, too. Rocky—that's the troll I mentioned—didn't know anyone who could talk to the dead directly. But she put me in touch with someone who might be able to help. You're not gonna like it."

"What else is new?"

"I called in a lot of favors for this, Isaac."

"Understood. What exactly am I getting into?"

"A little late to ask that question, don't you think?" His chuckle sounded forced. "Do *not* trust this guy. He's the next best thing to a vampire ghost-talker, but he's slimy as six-month-old meat. He won't do anything that puts him on the Porters' radar if he can avoid it, but he will screw you over six ways from Sunday, and I don't mean in a good way."

"What is he, and what's the price?"

"His name is Mahefa. He's a Ramanga."

"No kidding?" Ramanga had originally been servants whose duties to the nobles of Madagascar included consuming nail clippings and spilled blood to prevent such things from being used for evil magic. Considering I knew at least one Porter who could knock you unconscious with a single hair from your head, it seemed a wise precaution. Ironically, the Ramanga had spent generations learning to do exactly what their masters feared, developing and refining a type of magic that drew power from the blood of others. From all I had read, they were few in number, and their magic was limited in both strength and duration. "Last I checked, Ramanga weren't known for chatting up the dead."

"He's also a drug dealer, not to mention a smuggler, a thief, and a vindictive little snake. Rocky says he has something that should fit the bill."

"And the cost?"

A male voice with an unfamiliar accent answered from behind me. "The cost is simple. You're going to do me a favor."

Jeff growled. "He's there, isn't he?"

"Yep." I had left my shock-gun at the house. I casually checked the room for potential weapons as I turned around, just in case. The dirty bread knife in the sink was probably my best bet.

"Isaac, be careful. Rumor has it Mahefa once cut a customer's heroin with basilisk blood after a fight over a woman. It took three days for the poor bastard to die as his veins and organs petrified."

"Good to know. And thank you." I hung up the phone and examined the new arrival. He was stout but strong, one of those men whose mass was more breadth than height. He had a close-trimmed beard, walnut skin, and sunken, bloodshot eyes. His lips were ashen, as were the tips of his fingers. His fingernails were ragged, bitten to the quick. He wore a black suit over a pink shirt with no tie.

I extended my hand. "Isaac Vainio."

"Mahefa Issoufaly." His hands were soft-skinned, but thick with muscle. His temperature felt normal enough for a human.

"Bienvenu à Copper River." French was one of Madagascar's two official languages, and I didn't speak Malagasy.

"Merci." He smiled. "Your friend tells me you need to speak to a dead man."

I checked to make sure nobody would overhear. "That's right."

Mahefa opened the fridge and helped himself to a bottle of water. "I believe I can get what you need, yes."

"And the favor?"

His smile grew. His teeth were perfect, bleached bone white. "There are three. To begin with, I want a sample of your blood—250 milliliters should suffice."

I wasn't thrilled, but neither was I particularly surprised. "Why?"

"Why does an oenophile seek new varieties of wine?" His words dripped condescension. He shut the fridge with a sniff of displeasure. "I am the world's finest connoisseur of blood, Isaac. Just as the lover of grapes can discern the subtlest flavors, I can taste the life contained within your blood, your memories and experiences, even your magic. For more than a hundred years, I've sampled kings and paupers, sea serpents and sorcerers. All blood has power. With mundane blood, I can heal my body, extend my life, and more. But the blood of a libriomancer is potent indeed."

I almost told him Gutenberg had locked my magic, so my blood was likely to be disappointing. But why undercut my own bargaining position? "What else?"

"An equal amount of your dryad's blood."

"No deal." I tried and failed to keep the anger from my tone, but that only seemed to amuse him. "I can't pay you what's not mine to give. I'll give you 400 milliliters of mine instead."

"I've tasted libriomancers before, but the dryad would be a new flavor. I'm told she's book-born?" He nibbled a hangnail on his thumb. "Very well. What can you offer me in her place?"

Without magic, it was a painfully short list. I assumed money wouldn't interest him, and I didn't have all that much anyway. I wondered if he'd ever tried siren blood. But I couldn't in good conscience barter Euphemia's blood any more than I could Lena's.

There was Smudge, resting in his cage behind the front desk. Though he probably wasn't resting anymore.

Hopefully Mahefa's presence hadn't upset Smudge enough to set him alight. The lack of shouting was a good sign.

Smudge had been hurt last month, and the fluid from his wound looked and behaved much like kerosene. But I wasn't about to jab a needle into him and let Mahefa have a taste.

Mahefa's eyes narrowed as the silence grew. A bead of blood swelled from his hangnail. His tongue flicked out to capture it. "How badly do you need this, Isaac?"

"Lena isn't a possession to be bargained."

Amusement lightened his reply. "That's not what I've heard."

All things considered, it was probably a good thing I wasn't armed. He watched me, obviously enjoying my struggle.

"Shouldn't this be Lena's decision, not yours?" he pressed. "If you truly consider her a person, why are you making the choice for her?"

I definitely wanted to shoot this guy. Yet there was truth to his barb. Was it my place to refuse on her behalf? Reluctantly, I said, "I could ask her."

"Excellent." He wiped his thumb on his suit jacket. "Shall we?"

"Right now?"

He looked surprised. "I thought this was important."

"What about the third favor?"

"All things in time." He gestured toward the doorway.

Dammit, Jennifer was going to kill me. I headed for her office, where she was sorting through budget paperwork. "I have an emergency I need to take care of."

"Another one?" she asked without looking up.

"This is Mahefa. He's my insurance adjuster. He's finally getting around to assessing the damage to my house from last month."

"Your house looked fine the last time I drove past,"

she said. "That would be two weeks ago, by the way. When you hadn't called or come in for two days, I decided to swing by and make sure you weren't dead."

Mahefa cleared his throat. "Isaac, would you like me to—"

"No!" I didn't know what powers he might have to manipulate minds, but I didn't want any of them in my library. "Jennifer, I'll make up the hours."

"No, you won't." Her shoulders slumped. With a sigh, she pushed her paperwork aside and focused her attention on me. "You've been with this library longer than I have, and you're *good* at your job. One of the best people I have. When you're *here*. I've tried to be flexible, and I've cut you as much slack as I could.

"I was happy to fight to get you a full-time position, but this isn't working. Even when you show up, your mind is elsewhere. I'm not the only one who's noticed. I don't want to be the bad guy, but I have to think of what's best for the library, and for the staff as a whole."

"Are you *firing* me?" Before, I had always had a salary from the Porters to fall back on. A grant through one of their dummy companies had funded my position here, guaranteeing my job security. Now that grant was gone, along with the bulk of my income. If I lost this job, I was well and truly screwed.

She hesitated only a few seconds, but they stretched out like hours. "I'm willing to keep you on, but I'm cutting you back to part time. Twenty hours a week." She held up a hand before I could speak. "Show me you want this job, and we'll revisit things in three months."

Part time meant reduced income and no benefits. Health insurance hadn't been a concern when I could pull Lucy's healing cordial out of *The Lion, The Witch, and The Wardrobe* to fix anything from a cold to a severed limb, but without magic or insurance, a simple broken bone could bankrupt me.

"Or I can let you go altogether," Jennifer added.

"No." I hated myself for how quickly I answered. For the desperation, and for *needing* this job. I should be out in the world reading and discovering the true power of books, not reshelving and recycling them. Music echoed in my thoughts, the siren's song weighing me down with yearning and despair. I had to grip the doorframe to keep from falling.

"Go home," Jennifer said wearily. "Take care of your house. I'll talk to you about scheduling tomorrow."

"Thanks." I grabbed Smudge's cage on the way out. He scooted into a corner, crouched in the gravel that lined the bottom, and watched Mahefa closely.

Alex called after me to ask where I was going, but I couldn't bring myself to explain. Let Jennifer fill him in.

Once we were outside, Mahefa reached into his inside jacket and produced a circuit board encased in clear plastic, about the size of a business card. A tangle of ribbon cables emerged from one end. "I got this from a libriomancer in Mozambique," he said. "It should be able to hack just about any electronic lock."

I didn't like where this was going. "It sounds like you have a particular lock in mind."

"I do." He squinted up at the clouds. "And it should be passing over the Midwest later today."

BOOKSTORE OWNER HOSPITALIZED
AFTER ATTACK

ANN ARBOR, MICHIGAN—Clarissa Andress, owner of Drumming Goddess New Age Bookstore, was hospitalized yesterday following the alleged firebombing of her store.

Flames broke out near the front of the bookstore at approximately 6:15 PM. Andress was quick to usher customers out of the building, but went back inside to attempt to find the store cat. Andress apparently collapsed from smoke inhalation. Firefighters pulled her from the building and administered oxygen. She regained consciousness at the hospital, and is expected to make a full recovery.

"Never go back into a burning building," said Edward Hubbard of the Ann Arbor Fire Department. "Get outside and leave the window or door open behind you so your pets have an escape route. They'll find their own way out. Call to them, and let the firefighters know your pets are still inside, but *don't* go in after them. People don't realize how quickly smoke can overcome you, or the flames can spread and trap you."

Witnesses claim to have seen two youths fleeing the scene immediately after the fire began. The police have no suspects in custody, but say they are following up on several leads, including a number of threatening letters delivered to the store in recent days.

"There have always been people who see 'New Age' and immediately think of witches and incense and weed, but it's getting worse," said Annette Botke, a University of Michigan sophomore and employee at Drumming Goddess. "Our sidewalk sign was vandalized twice last week. One commenter on our Web site said people like us should be burned at the stake."

The fire department was unable to save the twenty-year-old store. The area is cordoned off for safety, and the site will be bulldozed later this week. The stores to either side, an antiques shop and an Indian restaurant, sustained minor damage, but should reopen soon.

Padfoot, the store cat, was found huddling beneath a car in a nearby parking lot. He was checked out and found to be in perfect health. Padfoot is staying with a friend until he can be reunited with his owner.

Chapter 4

I FOUND LENA IN the backyard, pulling up the poison ivy vines that had begun to encroach from the edge of the woods. She yanked them from the dirt bare-handed, unaffected by the oils that would have transformed me into a miserable mass of red, itchy bumps and blisters.

Most days during the week, she would have been out doing odd landscaping jobs or volunteering around town, but lately she had been spending more time near her grove. She brightened when she saw me, and then her gaze moved to Mahefa. She grabbed a wood-handled rake and walked toward us.

I wondered if Mahefa had any idea how quickly Lena could grow that handle into a spear, or how many bones she could break with it. A part of me hoped he'd get the chance to find out.

"You're home early." Lena kissed me, careful to keep her oil-covered hands away from my skin. "What's wrong?"

"This is Mahefa Issoufaly. Jeff said he could help us to speak with Gerbert d'Aurillac."

She frowned and looked at my arm. I didn't try to hide the Band-Aid near the elbow. There was almost no bruising. He had hit the vein on the first try. The remaining warmth evaporated from Lena's expression.

"He's not a vampire," I said. "He's . . . you could probably call him a hematophile."

"You make it sound like a medical condition," Mahefa complained. "Blood magic is just as real and valid an art as your libriomancy."

"You let him drink your blood?" Lena's fingertips pressed into the rake's handle like it was clay. "And then you brought him here."

"His price for helping was a sample of my blood." I rubbed my arm. I should have said no. Should have told him to go to hell the second he said Lena's name. Let Jeff find someone else who could help us. "And yours."

She took a step back. "I see."

"You don't have to say yes."

"What's wrong, Isaac?" Mahefa asked. "You'll share your dryad with your friend Doctor Shah, but not with me?"

"She's not—"

"Not what?" He circled Lena, studying her up and down. "She's certainly not human. Isn't this why she was created? For men like you and me?"

Forget saving the world; right now I wanted my magic back so I could turn this loathsome man into a cockroach and drop him in a cage with Smudge. But since I couldn't do magic, I settled for punching him in the nose.

He staggered back, eyes watering. Blood dripped from his nostrils. He snarled and started forward, only to find the sharpened tip of the rake handle barring his way.

"I told you I would ask her," I said. "I didn't say anything about letting you come to my home and insult the woman I love. You have until the count of five to get off my property."

"If you want to speak to your dead man, you'll let me sample your woman's blood."

"If you want to join my dead man, you'll keep standing there." I folded my arms. "One."

"Wait," said Lena. "Isaac, tell me why you need to do this."

"Jeneta—"

"The Porters know about Meridiana and Jeneta," she interrupted. "You're not the only person in the world clever enough to make the connection to a dead pope. Why do *you* need to be the one to go chasing answers?"

It was arrogant as hell to believe I could succeed where the Porters had failed. But then, being one of the few who could use magic to rewrite the universe tended to reinforce both ego and arrogance.

The problem was that I wasn't just risking my life. If I died, who and what Lena was could be lost as well. We hoped the book Bi Wei had given her would help to stabilize her identity, to end her dependence on her lovers, but we had no way of knowing it would work.

There were hundreds of Porters, all better prepared to protect themselves against magic. Was I truly the best person to find Jeneta, or was that the twin brain weasels of guilt and depression pulling my strings?

Why not simply stop? Let the Porters worry about Meridiana. Focus on my job at the library. Visit the cemetery and finally pay my respects to those who had died the month before.

I couldn't do it. I had been suspended from the field for two years after Mackinac Island, forbidden from using magic except in emergencies, but I had still been a part of that world. I had touched the magic of books every day. I had clung to the hope of returning to the Porters as a field agent or researcher. From the moment I discovered magic, I had been unable to imagine a life without it. "Because this is who ... this is what I am."

Lena turned to Mahefa. "Fine. How do we know you'll keep your word?"

"I've never cheated a customer," Mahefa said indignantly. He held a handkerchief to his nose to slow the bleeding. "It's bad for business. I will procure what Isaac needs. When he goes to his friend's final resting place, he'll be able to have his little chat."

Lena nodded. "You can have my blood, but not until Jeneta is safe."

Air hissed through Mahefa's teeth. "Given that Isaac is very likely to end up dead, I'm afraid—"

Lena stabbed the end of the rake through the edge of Mahefa's leather shoe, pinning him to the earth. He reached for her, and she casually thumped him in the face with the other end.

"And you drink it in front of me," Lena continued as if nothing had happened. "I'm not risking you magically cloning yourself a dryad, or whatever else you might want to do with my blood."

He chuckled. "A counteroffer, then. I take your blood when Jeneta is safe, *or* when Isaac gets himself killed, whichever comes first. I promise I'll do nothing to facilitate the latter possibility."

"Good. Because if you do, I'll take an acorn from my tree, ram it down your throat, and start it growing. Do we understand one another?"

He lowered the bloody handkerchief. His tongue cleaned the remaining blood from his upper lip. "We do."

Lena yanked the handle free and gripped his hand, sealing the deal. From the look on his face, she squeezed quite a bit harder than necessary.

"I'll meet you out front, Isaac. Don't take too long." Mahefa whistled as he strolled away.

"I'm sorry," I said as soon as he was gone. "He wouldn't accept anything else."

Lena didn't look at me. "Promise me you'll give me an hour's notice before he comes to take my blood."

"I will."

"Good. I'll wait until then to finish pulling up the poison ivy. The work is relaxing, and my skin soaks up the oils like aloe." She glanced over her shoulder, giving me a crooked smile that didn't touch her eyes. "I can even absorb it into my bloodstream."

Mahefa insisted we take his car, a freshly waxed black BMW that smelled like antiseptic and Chinese food. He also strongly advised against taking Smudge. On the other hand, he hadn't objected at all to my bringing my shock-gun along. If anything, he seemed amused, which made me nervous.

I studied him more closely as we drove. I couldn't be certain, but I thought the blackening of his lips and fingers was a form of magical charring. With my magic locked, I shouldn't have been able to see it. How much power had burned through his blood to leave visible damage?

His veins were swollen. One mapped a dark, jagged line down the side of his forehead. Others bulged along his arms and the backs of his hands.

He swerved around curves at speeds I wouldn't have attempted without magic, finally pulling off near the old railroad bridge about five miles south of town. He parked in the grass and popped the trunk. "Time for favor number three. You're going to help me break into a satellite."

We climbed out, and Mahefa pulled a pair of metallic silver suits from the trunk. My mouth went dry.

"Relax, it's not a CIA spy satellite or anything like that. Nothing to tie you up in any ethical conundrums. Just your everyday illegal vampire-built space junk."

"When you said this thing would be passing over the Midwest, I assumed we'd be meeting it at an airport somewhere."

He chuckled. "The only way to override one of these things from the ground is to fight our way into the Chernobyl vampire nest and take over their system. I don't think either one of us are up for that." He tossed me one of the suits. "Put this on."

I held the ridiculously flimsy fabric. A deflated transparent bubble topped the one-piece jumpsuit. "What the hell is it?"

"Some old sci-fi writer's idea of what a futuristic space suit would look like. I bought them off a libriomancer in the early eighties. They hold twelve hours of compressed air, and there's a radio unit in the collar."

I couldn't process the idea of going into space in a thirty-year-old magic spacesuit, so I tried to focus my thoughts elsewhere. "Are you saying the vampires have their own satellite?"

"More than one. This is blood bank number six, out of ten that I know about. I've been wanting to get into this one for years."

Ten blood banks in orbit, and the Porters had no idea. What else had we—had *they* missed? And why satellites? The cold of space would provide cheap, effective refrigeration, but as far as food storage went, it was ridiculously impractical. You couldn't just fly into orbit every time you wanted a snack. What a satellite did provide was secrecy and security. "They're storing samples."

"Very good. They've built up a library of blood from every known species and hybrid of vampire. It's all treated with glycerol to preserve the cells, which does nasty things to the flavor, but it's worth it."

And we were going to steal from them. To break into a blood bank. In orbit. Wearing tinfoil jumpsuits. "All right, next question."

"Why do I need you?" Mahefa guessed.

"I was going to ask how the hell we're supposed to reach this satellite, since I didn't see a rocket ship in your back seat. But sure, let's start with that."

"The damn vampires put a bomb in my head last year. I get within a hundred meters of one of their vaults, and *boom*." He pantomimed the explosion.

"Sounds unpleasant." It also sounded similar to what I had done to Ted Boyer a few years back. I wondered if they had used the same hardware. "So you need someone who can get inside and loot the satellite without getting atomized in the process."

He shoved a pair of fire extinguishers into a beat-up canvas backpack. A coil of nylon rope followed, along with an oversized metal thermos. He zipped the whole thing up, then grabbed a laminated index card from his rear pocket. He handed me the card and an empty cooler. "I got my hands on a copy of their cataloguing system. This card lists the samples you'll need. One of these will let you talk to your dead pope. Bring them all back, and I'll tell you which one."

"Wait, let *me* talk to him?"

Mahefa paused. "Is that a problem?"

"I'm not a Ramanga. I can't use blood magic."

"Which is why I'll be prepping your drink, cutting it with a bit of my own. Your body is used to channeling magic, so it shouldn't burn your guts out or anything like that."

"This is vampire blood we're talking about. What if I drink it and then burst into flames the first time the sun hits me?"

"This particular strain shouldn't turn you," he assured me. "You might have a nasty migraine for a few hours, but that's all. If you're scared, trick someone else into taking it. I'm sure Lena would drink it if you told her to, yes?"

Gutenberg's spell had locked my magic, but that shouldn't interfere with the effects of the blood. Euphemia had demonstrated quite well that magic could still affect me.

"It goes without saying that if you tell anyone about this, I'll rip out your throat." Mahefa clapped me on the back. "Go ahead and put on your suit. Don't seal it yet, though. Sealing the helmet starts the airflow, and there's no need to waste oxygen."

Flying—heights in general, really—ranked right up with do-it-yourself root canals on my list of things I'd rather avoid. Maybe Lena had been right. Let the Porters find a way to speak with the dead. Once they dug up the pope's secrets, they could hunt Meridiana.

Assuming they took my vision seriously enough to pursue it. And what would they do to Jeneta if they found her? Gutenberg had done his best to destroy the students of Bi Sheng, and Meridiana was a far greater threat. They would kill Jeneta without a second thought.

It might come to that, if I couldn't save her. If I couldn't pry Meridiana out of her mind. But I intended to make damn sure that was a last resort.

I sat down on the hillside and pulled the suit over my legs. Following Mahefa's lead, I didn't worry about removing my shoes. The material felt like heavy satin. It clung to my jeans, outlining every fold and wrinkle. A pair of thin silver canisters on the back presumably held my air. There were no gauges to verify whether they were full.

Mahefa was already sealing the front of his suit, using a zipper-like tab that left no visible seam. The plastic bubble hung down behind him like a sweatshirt hood. These suits were far simpler and more maneuverable than anything NASA had. I imagined most astronauts would kill for something like this...assuming they worked.

Mahefa opened a second cooler in the back of the car and pulled out a plastic packet of blood, the kind of thing you might find hanging from an IV stand in a hospital. He jabbed a metal straw into the top and sucked it down like a child's juice box.

I started to seal my suit, then changed my mind. This thing had no built-in plumbing, and I had no idea how long our flight would be. I hiked to the base of the bridge to relieve myself. When I finished, I glanced back to make sure Mahefa wasn't paying attention, then tucked my shock-gun into the bag, along with the laminated list.

He tossed the empty pouch onto the ground, strapped on an oversized harness, and slammed the BMW's trunk shut. "You ready?"

I thought about Jeneta, about the hate and hunger I had sensed from Meridiana and her minions, and about my friends and neighbors who had died without understanding why. With a sigh, I stepped into the harness.

Mahefa might be an ass, but he was all business as he cinched the straps around my chest, shoulders, and thighs. Heavy steel rings locked us together like tandem skydivers, my back to his front. I resisted the urge to seal my helmet to block the foulness of his breath. "How long does the blood last?"

"Depends. The stuff I downed should be enough to get us there and back. The kind you'll be stealing will give you several hours of talking to the dead." He wrapped his arms around my chest. "Relax. Flying is as easy as falling, only backward."

Before I could stammer a response, he jumped hard enough to make me bite my tongue. I spat blood and gripped his arms, trying to stop the pressure of the harness from cutting off the circulation to my legs. I had no clue how fast we were accelerating. The average human being passed out around five gees, and I could feel the blood in my body draining downward. I clenched my muscles and tried to hold on.

"It will take a few minutes to escape the atmosphere," he shouted. "I'll let you know when to seal your helmet."

For as long as I could remember, I'd had nightmares about tumbling out of airplanes, off cliff sides, or over the edge of the Mackinac Bridge. This was worse. I was falling *away* from the Earth, significantly faster than terminal velocity. The wind dried my eyes and tore the breath from my mouth.

Already the air was getting colder. When I looked down, I could make out the outlines of the Great Lakes, the mitten and rabbit shapes of Michigan's lower and upper peninsulas. My neck cramped, and my jaw was clenched so tightly I expected my teeth to shatter.

"If you need to puke, do it *before* you close your helmet," Mahefa yelled.

The Earth's curve was clearly visible, which would have been awe-inspiring if I had been looking at a photograph from the safety of my desk. Shadows stained my vision, congealing from the edges. Passing out might be a blessing, but I had no faith that Mahefa would bother to seal my helmet.

We were through the upper clouds now. The sun was brighter, and when I wrenched my head up, I could just begin to make out the stars overhead.

Mahefa let go.

I shouted and clawed at his arms as the harness took my full weight. My fingers were numb, little more than useless stubs.

"Helmet," he yelled, his voice tinny.

I fumbled to pull the clear bubble over my head. After three attempts, Mahefa snatched it from between us and yanked it into place. He grabbed a tab at the collar and pulled it around my neck. I heard hissing, and the bubble expanded, filling with cold, stale air.

The plastic wasn't as clear as I had thought, or perhaps it was designed to polarize in direct sunlight. The world below took on a smoky tint.

"Radio check." Mahefa's words crackled through a speaker by my neck. "You done screaming yet?"

My suit bulged outward. Rings of stiffer fabric kept it from bubbling too much. I looked like a shiny Michelin Man. I forced myself to breathe slowly. "Yah. Starting to hate you a lot, though."

I tried to distract myself by figuring out the physics of our magical flight. There was no visible propulsion—at least, I was 99 percent certain Mahefa wasn't somehow shooting rocket exhaust out of his ass. The state of my stomach meant his vampiric blood-magic hadn't completely excused us from the normal rules of acceleration and momentum.

How much energy did it take to fly the two of us at this rate? Call it 350 pounds total, guesstimate our speed at several hundred miles per hour and climbing ... by my off-the-cuff calculations, we should have caught fire five minutes ago.

One way or another, movement obeyed Newton's Third Law. Mahefa could fly upward by basically jumping off the Earth, but how could he change directions, especially once we reached the vacuum of space? What was he pushing against? Everything in the solar system was chained to the sun's gravitational pull, but gravity was a relatively weak force for the speed and power of this flight. On the other hand, once you escaped Earth's atmosphere and gravity, you should need far less energy to maneuver.

With adequate blood supplies, could we send a vampire out to explore Jupiter?

That thought summoned a new fear. *What if somebody already had?*

"Hold on," Mahefa said over the radio. "Let me get my bearings."

We coasted higher, rotating at a slow speed that was perfect for inducing vomiting. I tried to focus on the sun, using it as a fixed—if moderately blinding—point on the horizon. My inner ear kept trying to tell me I was falling in every direction at once.

The cold was unpleasant, but no worse than a typical November morning in the U.P. I gripped the harness straps and waited.

"We're early," he said. "You're lighter than I expected. Looks like we made better time."

We sped higher, angling away from the sun. The stars were so much sharper than I was used to, without the Earth's atmosphere to distort their light and color. I tried to engrave the sight in my memory for later, when I might be able to appreciate it.

"There we are." Mahefa changed course again, moving slower this time.

We headed for a rectangular shadow that blotted the stars from view. "All this needs is *Also sprach Zarathustra* playing in the background," I muttered.

"What's that?"

"Nothing." Save the *2001: A Space Odyssey* reference for someone who might appreciate it.

The orbiting blood bank made me think of a stealth bomber. The skin was matte black, and the closer we got, the more I could make out the irregular angles of its surface. It seemed to hang motionless in the darkness, hiding in the edge of the Earth's shadow.

Before I realized what was happening, Mahefa unbuckled the harness holding us together. I tried to twist around, but he slipped free before I could grab him.

My efforts had started me rotating. I spread out my arms and forced myself not to panic. Slowly, my body

and brain realized I wasn't plummeting to my death.
Though given our current vector, the Earth's gravity
would pull me back down eventually, which meant I *was*
plummeting. I was just plummeting very, very slowly.

I brought my arms in, and my body spun faster. I extended my legs, testing how each change affected my
movement. I slowly stretched out both arms and pin-
wheeled them backward, trying to visualize the different
angles and their effects in a frictionless environment.

"Your maneuvering jets." Mahefa caught my shoulder
and handed me the two fire extinguishers from his backpack. "Don't overdo it. Your instincts will make you
overreact. A little thrust goes a long way up here."

I took one extinguisher in each hand. Mahefa pulled
the pins and tossed them aside. They tumbled end over
end until they vanished from sight.

"Once you reach the satellite, plug the card into the
console by the door. There's no air inside, so do *not* remove your helmet. The computer system should come
up automatically." He seized my harness. "You have the
list?"

"Yes."

"Gather everything on that list, then get the hell out
of there and jump toward me. You get your long-distance
phone call to your dead pope. I get my new vintages.
Everybody wins."

I raised the extinguisher in my right hand, lining it up
on a path that should take me to the satellite.

"Save your fuel until you need it." Mahefa spun me
around and gripped the back of my harness. Before I
could react, he hefted me overhead like a javelin and
hurled me at the distant satellite.

My muscles went utterly rigid, as if the cold of space
had turned my body to ice. My mind was little better,
stuck on an infinitely repeating loop of *oh shit oh shit oh
shit*. Then my radio crackled, breaking the spell.

"Veer up and to the right, or you're going to miss it."

I positioned the extinguisher in my left hand and gently squeezed the handle. Mahefa was right about the thrust. A split-second burst corrected my course and started me rotating backward like a slow-motion boomerang.

"A little higher. There you go."

I did my best to stay on target and minimize my body's excess motion. Half of my corrections made things worse, but I managed to keep the satellite in sight.

I was glad I had left Smudge behind. He might have enjoyed zero gravity, but he had a severe phobia when it came to fire extinguishers.

I guessed that our flight into space had covered at least a thousand miles, but these last hundred meters seemed to stretch out the longest. My hands cramped from holding the extinguishers. Sweat burned my eyes, and I had no way of wiping them. My jaw and neck were locked like rusted steel.

One moment I was flying through space. The next, my brain rebooted my perspective, and I was falling head-first toward a satellite the size of a semi-truck trailer. At this speed, I'd bounce like a basketball, breaking who knew how many bones in the process. I brought both fire extinguishers around and tried to slow my approach.

It wasn't enough. My left arm struck the satellite first, hard enough to bruise the elbow. The satellite's black skin felt like brick. One of the fire extinguishers bounced from my grip and tumbled free.

Mahefa's voice blasted my ears. "Watch it! You screw up and get stuck out there, I can't come save you."

I used my remaining extinguisher to shoot myself back toward the satellite at a more oblique angle. I skipped along the wall twice more before reaching the end my mind insisted on calling the bottom, as it was facing the Earth. I made my way around the corner and looked up at a black computer screen alongside the out-line of a small rectangular door.

There were no handholds. Flying vampires wouldn't need them. I floated in front of the door and pulled the bag off of my shoulder to retrieve the electronic lock-pick. The interface looked like an ATM machine, with oversized plastic buttons, a curved glass screen, and a single data port.

The first time I attempted to plug the cable into the port, all I managed to do was shove myself away from the satellite. I tried not to look at the Earth stretched out beneath me. "How did they get this thing into orbit with-out anyone noticing the launch, anyway?"

"They carried it," Mahefa said.

Vampires. Right.

I made my way to the console and tried again. This time, I managed to align and insert the cable without knocking myself away. The circuit board lit up, and a blinking cursor appeared on the screen. "Now what?"

"Don't touch anything. Just cross your fingers and hope they haven't upgraded their security."

Seconds later, oversized text scrolled across the screen, welcoming me to Satellite Theta. The doorway—little more than an oversized doggie door, really—cracked open, and lights flickered on inside.

"Here goes." I left the lockpick in place and squeezed inside.

Glass-fronted storage cabinets ran the length of the satellite. Orange text scrolled down the computer screen on the far side. I grabbed my list and pulled myself toward the screen. The cabinets took up most of the space, and the remaining crawlspace was perfectly sized for inducing claustrophobia.

"Hurry up." Mahefa sounded antsy, like a getaway driver waiting for his partner to finish robbing a bank safe.

Each sample on his shopping list was coded by wall,

cabinet, tray, and position. I left the list floating in front of me and searched for the first one: *2-8-3-E4, 2007.03.18— Burtley6.*

The satellite was clearly labeled and organized, at least. I turned to wall number two, slid open the glass door to cabinet eight, and pulled out the third tray. Each aluminum tray was segmented like a checkerboard, and each square held the gleaming steel hybrid of a thermos and test tube, roughly three inches in diameter. I pulled out E4. A black plastic label from an old-fashioned label maker confirmed this was the Burtley6 sample from March of 2007.

One by one I raided trays and began to fill my bag with frozen vampire blood. There was little room to maneuver, and I banged my knees and elbows repeatedly. When I was about a third of the way through the list, I noticed black smoke leaking from beneath the monitor.

My first thought was a computer failure of some sort. My second was that it would be too much of a coincidence for the computer to break down just when I was robbing the place. Though it was possible Mahefa's hack had somehow damaged the system.

My third thought was that gas in a zero-gravity vacuum should diffuse into an ever-expanding cloud, not twist and branch out, condensing into what appeared to be a man. "Mahefa, I may have a problem here."

I moved toward the exit, but a hand clamped around my ankle. A pale, emaciated man, little more than a skeleton, slammed me against the nearest cabinet.

"You're human."

I heard his words inside my head. "Mahefa, you didn't say anything about an undead rent-a-cop!"

"What exactly do you expect me to do from out here, Isaac? Scold it?"

Blue-black lips peeled back from the vampire's fangs. Cloudy, frozen eyes seemed to peer through my body.

His tongue was a pale, desiccated lump of flesh. He moved stiffly, as if his joints were continually freezing and had to be broken loose. *"It's been four years since I've fed. Shall I drain you now, or wait for your blood to freeze, then chew you up like a popsicle?"*

I had used up a month's worth of fear on the way here, and I had nothing but anger and impatience left. I reached into my bag for the shock-gun. The lightning bolt normally required a path of ionized air, which wouldn't work here, but direct contact with the barrel should conduct the charge into his body. The gun's insulation would hopefully prevent it from frying me as well.

The vampire yanked me closer, seized the bag with his other hand, and tossed it behind him. Canisters of frozen blood tumbled loose, bouncing soundlessly off the walls. So much for that plan. His reaction suggested he could probably read minds as well as project, and I had no defense against telepathy anymore, dammit.

What else did I know about him? He could dissolve into mist and didn't need a spacesuit. Or clothes of any kind. That narrowed down the list of possible species, but not enough to figure out how to fight him. The oversaturated market in vampire fiction had led to countless new book-born species of vampire, each with their own customized—and far too short—list of vulnerabilities.

I kicked him in the face, but he didn't release my leg. His claws pressed harder. Hunger hadn't robbed him of his strength, which made sense. If you were going to leave a guard in space for years at a time, you'd want someone who could take out an intruder after four years of hibernation.

I grabbed for the fire extinguisher and slammed it against the side of his head.

He smiled. The tip of his tongue poked between his teeth like a swollen blue slug emerging from a cave of yellow bone.

I tried the fire extinguisher again, this time bringing it down on the back of his hand. I bruised my own leg, but his fingers loosened enough for me to pull free.

Four years since he last fed. Four years of starvation, surrounded by blood. What had he done to earn such a punishment, and how did they stop him from gorging himself on bloodsicles? I could feel his hunger pressing into my mind. There was no way he had voluntarily refrained from sampling the merchandise.

I threw the extinguisher at his face and snatched one of the blood canisters. I tried to unscrew the lid, but the gloves of my suit made it difficult, and then he was on me. We flew against a wall hard enough to crack the glass. I hoped it was the glass. It might have been my shoulder.

"Too late, Porter." He wrenched his jaw open and brought his fangs toward my neck. I could see his thoughts, his eagerness to bite through my suit and into my neck, to rip me open and gorge himself.

I wedged the metal canister into his mouth. It barely fit, popping into place behind his fangs with what I'm sure would have been a gruesome scraping sound. He jerked back. For a moment he reminded me of a dog with a metal bone. He let go of me and reached for the canister.

I grabbed the top of his head with both hands and slammed my knee into his jaw. Fear and desperation gave me strength, and I felt his fangs punch through the side of the tube.

His mental agony was like a blowtorch to my senses, searing my eyes and forcing acid into my throat. The flesh of his cheeks and jaw eroded like a crumbling sand sculpture. The pattern of dissolution would have probably given me another clue to his species, had I cared enough to watch.

I dragged myself away. Whatever they had added to

the blood to turn it toxic, it worked quickly. It would need to be something that could be easily filtered out later. Silver, maybe? You could probably rig up a way to separate out the silver using electrolysis.

The broken tube tumbled past me. Blood sprayed from the holes like morbid little geysers, boiling away in the vacuum.

When I looked back, nothing remained but a slightly pitted skeleton drifting in a slowly expanding cloud of gray dust.

I brought the skeleton out with me. The idea of leaving his bones trapped in a floating vault in space was too horrific, no matter what he had tried to do to me. Bracing myself in the open doorway, I shoved his remains toward the Earth. He shot away like a torpedo from a submarine. Between the sunlight and the heat of reentry, he should be gone soon enough.

I double-checked my bag and fire extinguisher, pulled myself through the doorway, and yanked the electronic lockpick loose. The door slid shut. I tucked the lockpick into the bag and made sure my gun was at the top where I could reach it.

Mahefa shone a light in my direction to orient me. I crawled to the side of the satellite, braced myself, and jumped. I was a little off course, but Mahefa had no trouble intercepting me. He caught my harness with one hand and reached for the bag.

"Not yet." I yanked it out of his reach. "Tell me which sample will let me talk to the dead."

He looked genuinely saddened by my mistrust, like a disappointed parent. "Søndergaard18."

The name sounded familiar. I prayed it wasn't the one I had sacrificed fighting the vampire. I dug through the bag, checking one tube at a time. I found it near the bottom. According to the label, this sample was twenty-seven years old.

"Go ahead and hold on to that if you'd like," said Mahefa. "I'll carry the rest—"

"Not until we're on the ground." I kept my hand in the bag, gripping my shock-gun.

He laughed. It was an ugly sound, heavy with mockery. "You think I plan to double-cross you? Perhaps to 'accidentally' drop you on the way down?"

"Most criminals don't like letting witnesses go free," I said warily.

"You're not a witness, Isaac."

He was too damned confident. "How do you figure?"

He pointed to the satellite. "If this was simply a matter of bypassing a lock and fighting a single guard, I'd have gotten myself a magical signal dampener and helped myself to their stock years ago."

It was like the vacuum of space had seeped into my chest. "What are you saying?"

"I needed someone with no connection to me," Mahefa continued. "Someone who could have plausibly discovered the vampires' secrets." He smiled. "Someone who would appear to be acting alone when the controllers in Chernobyl reviewed the video feed."

Oh, shit. "And it never occurred to you to wear a damn mask?"

"A mask wouldn't block the scanner you passed through on the way in. They peeked right through your suit to record every wrinkle and birthmark on your body." He pulled me closer, until our helmets touched. "You're not a witness, Isaac. You're a scapegoat."

I can't decide whether to kill him or commit him.

I don't pretend to know what Isaac is going through. The entire town mourned the loss of so many innocent people, but Isaac hasn't allowed himself to grieve. He blames himself. I don't know if he's searching for punishment or redemption. And then Gutenberg took away the thing that most defined him. I watch him fight to hold on to that world and that purpose, clinging like his life depends on it. He's lost and angry and terrified.

Isaac isn't the only one in pain. I lost most of my career. I lost clients and colleagues I worked with for years. Lena was forced to kill Deifilia, the only blood-family she's ever known. Lena has been spending far more time in her tree than she used to, and grief blunts her joy. Whether that grief is her own or Isaac's, or even mine, I couldn't say.

I worry about them both, but if Isaac continues on like this, with the depression eating away at him, his pain could smother Lena as well.

In some ways, his reaction tracks closely to the grief and anger that follow an unexpected amputation. So far, he's turned most of that pain inward or tried to focus it through action. His tunnel vision keeps him pursuing a vanished child and a thread of hope.

It was a mistake to bring him to Euphemia. The aftereffects of her song have driven his loss deeper, like shrapnel seeking his heart. I want to help Jeneta, too, but not at the cost of Isaac's life.

I can't force him to get help. I can't stand by and watch him self-destruct. And I can't leave, not without tearing Lena apart. I love her, but that love chains the three of us together, and if Isaac's downward spiral goes on . . .

He bargained his blood and Lena's for a chance. What was he thinking? And what else will he sacrifice?

If things don't improve soon, I may call Jeff and Helen and have them lock Isaac in a damn kennel until he gets his head together.

—From the personal journal of Doctor Nidhi Shah

Chapter 5

I HAD MADE ENEMIES of an entire species in exchange for a single vial of blood.

How long before they discovered the theft? Whatever alert had triggered the release of the guard within the satellite had likely signaled the vampires on Earth as well. They had an impressive security database, which presumably included records of known Porters and ex-Porters. All they had to do was match the video and scan from the satellite to their information on Isaac Vainio.

Trying to explain Mahefa's part in it wouldn't change the evidence. Whatever my reasons, I had broken into their secret satellite. Simply knowing the thing existed was probably enough to earn me a death sentence.

It was almost enough to distract me from our head-first dive back to Earth.

"Where are we going?" My helmet muffled the wind rushing past.

"Copper River." Mahefa sounded as happy as a kid going to Disney World. A drink of dryad blood would be the cherry on top of his bloody sundae.

"Not yet. First you're taking me to Rome." The bastard had made me a target for every vampire in the world. The least he could do was give me a lift.

"Do I look like a fucking taxi cab?" he snarled.

"How do I know the blood will work?" I shot back. "Once I've tested it, then we can go home."

I half-expected him to drop me. It would be a simpler death than waiting around for the vampires. At this speed, I'd probably fall another hour, but I wouldn't have time to feel the pain of impact.

"Sure, why not?" he said cheerfully, his annoyance seemingly forgotten. We veered to the right. "I haven't been to Italy in years. It's a beautiful country, full of beautiful, delicious women."

Lower and lower we flew over the blackness of the Atlantic. My stomach lurched as Mahefa flattened out his path, skimming the waves so closely the spray hit my helmet. We had slowed a bit, but the air still battered my suit and helmet, and the harness felt like it was about to sever my legs.

We sped across the water for another hour, with nothing but the waves below and the stars overhead. Monotony dulled my thoughts. I was half asleep when Mahefa struck my shoulder and pointed to lights illuminating the coastline ahead. "Wake up, and welcome to Ostia Beach!"

He unclipped my harness from his, and I went from flying to falling. It was like being on a swing set and feeling the chains snap. I braced my head with my hands and doubled over. The first time I struck the water, I bounced like a stone skipping across a lake. The second time, my arm and shoulder sank beneath the surface. I flipped heels-over-head and ended up underwater.

Mahefa hauled me to the surface. "Better to be seen swimming than flying. You *can* swim, yes?"

You didn't grow up in the northern part of the U.P. without learning to swim. I pulled free of his grip.

"Shouldn't you have asked before you dropped me in the ocean?"

Hotels, nightclubs, and bars illuminated the beach ahead. Folded umbrellas lined the sand like soldiers at attention, guarding the nightlife against marine invasion.

By the time I was close enough to shore for my feet to touch bottom, I could hardly feel my legs, and my arms and chest felt like they were on fire. I staggered toward dry sand, one hand fumbling uselessly with the helmet seal.

"Be careful with that," Mahefa snapped. "It's practically an antique."

I considered shooting him, but firing a waterlogged lightning gun while soaking wet probably wasn't the wisest idea. It wouldn't be the dumbest one I had ever had, either. But that said more about me than it did about the idea in question.

I finally got the helmet off. The beach smelled of salt and sunscreen. I peeled the suit from my body and grabbed my phone.

"Damn." The screen was cracked. I doubted the warranty covered getting tossed around a satellite by a starving vampire.

An older couple waved as they strolled past, probably thinking we were out for some late-night scuba diving.

"Where do you need to go to talk to your corpse?" Mahefa asked.

"The Basilica of St. John Lateran." But not like this. My clothes were wrinkled and reeked of sweat. Now that I was back on solid ground, exhaustion was battering me from all sides. I needed a bed, a good meal, and a hot shower.

Most of all, I *desperately* needed to pee.

Mahefa accompanied me only long enough to deposit his blood in the hotel fridge. He examined each vial closely, opened one, and used a Swiss Army Knife to cut a frozen chip from the end.

"What's that for?"

After licking the blood from the blade, he sealed the vial and returned it to the fridge. "Blood magic is all about absorbing the strength of the donor. In this case, the vampire's strength and endurance. As long as I'm here, I'm going to party like the undead." As he left, he called over his shoulder, "You understand what will happen to you if you touch a single drop of my stock, yes?"

"Whatever. Just be back by morning." I collapsed on the bed, kicked off my shoes, and reached for my cell phone before remembering it was dead. Groaning, I rolled out of bed and stumbled over to grab the phone on the desk. Lena would be asleep in her oak, so I called Nidhi. She answered after the second ring. She sounded alert and awake, despite it being past midnight in Copper River.

"It's Isaac. Are you and Lena all right?"

"We're fine. What the hell have you done, Isaac? Lena said you sold her *blood?*"

A dozen excuses and justifications clambered through my thoughts. I stomped them down. "I did," I said flatly. After a long silence, I added, "I may have also pissed off some vampires."

"How many vampires?"

"I can't give you an exact number, but I'd estimate roughly . . . all of them. You should probably stay with Lena until I get back. If they can't find me, they might come after one of you. I'm sorry, Nidhi. If I'd known this would put the two of you in danger—"

"Isaac, stop."

"I got the blood. I'm about twenty miles from the

tomb of the man who can answer our questions about Meridiana." I rubbed my eyes. "No, wait. Don't stay with Lena. The vampires know where I live. The two of you should get a hotel room somewhere. I promise I'll find a way to—"

"Isaac, Elne Cathedral in France was destroyed tonight. Two Porters were killed, along with six civilians. Eleven others were hospitalized."

My fingers tightened around the handset. "Was Jeneta involved?"

"All I have are the public news reports and secondhand rumors. From the photos, it looks like a sinkhole swallowed the entire cathedral, and then a bomb leveled anything that remained. They're calling it terrorism, but if the Porters were there . . ."

"Elne Cathedral." Fatigue blurred my memory, but I remembered the name from one of the books I'd skimmed at the archdiocese in Green Bay. "Miro Bonfill."

"Who?"

"He was a friend of Gerbert d'Aurillac. Probably a mentor as well. There's a stone at Elne—was a stone—with their names carved into it." Nobody knew what purpose it served. It couldn't have been a magical artifact, or else the Porters would have confiscated it years ago.

"You think I should come home and let the Porters take it from here," I said. If Meridiana was going after sites connected to d'Aurillac, there was a good chance she'd be watching his tomb as well.

Nidhi said nothing.

"Answer me one question. Given everything we know about the Porters, everything we've learned about Gutenberg and his history, do you trust them to take care of Meridiana? Are you *certain* there's nothing I could accomplish here that they can't?" I rested my head against the back of the chair. "Tell me that there's no chance of me digging up some fact the Porters missed or making a connection that might help us save Jeneta. Tell me there's nothing I can do here, and I'll come home."

Nidhi hesitated. "I ought to lie to you."

"Probably."

She sighed. "I also know that with your magic gone, a part of you feels as though you have nothing left to lose. I worry that you'll continue to take more dangerous risks."

"That's not why—"

"Shut up," she said calmly. "Your life has changed tremendously over the past year. Magic or no, you have a great deal to lose. And so do we. Remember that."

She hung up before I could answer.

I left the hotel hours later, clothed in knee-length shorts and a bright blue T-shirt from the gift shop in the lobby. A shoulder bag with the hotel logo held my clothes, shock-gun, and stolen blood. I bought an enormous croissant and a caffè latte on the way out.

I found Mahefa sleeping on a bench outside, nursing what looked like a grande-sized magical hangover. When he opened his eyes, blackened lines spread like lightning from the irises: charred blood vessels, inflamed by whatever power he had burned last night. He snatched the caffè latte from my hand without a word and downed the whole thing before we were halfway to the metro station.

The subway got us to Rome, and from there we hiked to the Basilica of St. John Lateran, the resting place of Pope Sylvester II. What was left of him, at any rate. When his tomb was opened during the seventeenth century, Gerbert d'Aurillac's body had crumbled to dust like a staked vampire. I just hoped enough of that dust remained for us to communicate.

When we reached the basilica, I had to stop to absorb the sheer grandeur of the place. Reading about the cathedral hadn't prepared me to stand on the stone steps looking up at pillars eight times my height. A statue of Christ stood atop the highest point of the façade. To either side, statues of various saints looked out at the tourists.

"While we're young?" Mahefa muttered.

"Right." I scanned the crowd for anything or anyone out of the ordinary, wishing I had Smudge along to warn of danger. I saw nothing unusual, nor did anyone appear to be paying undue attention to us.

Mahefa was already heading inside. I followed, then stopped again once I passed through the entrance. "I have *got* to start traveling more."

I gawked openly, trying to absorb 1700 years' worth of history. Every inch of the cathedral was a work of art, from the intricate patterns of the stone tile floor to the fluted pillars and statues on either side of the nave. Gold leaf covered sculptures on the ceiling, which had to be a hundred feet high. Framed paintings hung on the walls above giant statues of the apostles.

Reluctantly, I quickened my pace and made my way past tourists posing for photographs or reading travel guides on their phones. A small crowd had already gathered around the cenotaph of Pope Sylvester II.

Marble framed a stone inscription and a sculpture depicting Sylvester II. I watched an older man press forward to touch the stone. According to legend, the monument wept to foretell the death of a pope. If the stone was merely damp, it predicted the death of a bishop or cardinal.

I pulled the blood from my bag and carefully unscrewed the lid. Chilled air rose from the opening.

"Dumbass. You didn't let it thaw overnight?" Mahefa snatched the canister away from me. He took a test tube from his shirt pocket and popped the rubber stopper loose.

"What are you doing?" I whispered. We were attracting some very odd looks.

Mahefa spread his arms in mockery of a crucifix. "This is my blood, which I give up for you." He poured the contents of the tube over the frozen blood like a dessert topping. "Blood and saliva both, actually. They help release the magic. Relax, this isn't the first time I've whipped up a mixed drink for a mundane."

People had begun to move away from us. I hoped none of them called security.

"Don't drink it all at once. You don't want to overdose. I'd hate to have to put a stake in your heart after all this."

I brought the canister to my lips, at which point I discovered another problem. The interior was cold as dry ice. Mahefa's blood had frozen to the rest, and none of it was budging. I cupped the mouth and exhaled onto the blood, trying to warm it. When that failed, I whacked the bottom with one hand until a dark red cylinder began to slowly slide free.

An older couple stared in horror and disgust. I don't know if they were more upset about the noise I was making in church or the contents of my thermos. I offered them a weak smile. "Cherry smoothie. I must have left it in the freezer too long."

The woman said something in Italian, and they both turned back to the papal cenotaph. Mindful of Mahefa's warning about overdosing, I brought the frozen bloodsicle to my mouth and bit down.

I don't know what was worse: the metallic syrup that coated my mouth and tongue like paint as it melted, or the icy pain that started in my teeth and raced like electricity up my nerves, giving me the worst case of brain freeze I could remember. I hadn't thought to bring anything to wash down the blood. I wondered if they had a font for holy water, and whether anyone would object to me using it as a drinking fountain. Though given that I was trying to absorb vampire magic, using holy water as a chaser probably wasn't a great idea.

"How is it?" Mahefa whispered.

"Foul." I forced myself to take another bite and did my best to keep from vomiting. "How much do I have to eat before it starts working?"

"Depends on body mass and sensitivity. You'll need more than those two swallows, though."

I had just finished my fourth bite of blood slushee when magic jolted my bones. My gasp drew more annoyed glares. I made my way to a wooden bench, sat down, and closed my eyes, concentrating on the whispers in my mind. They were too faint to understand, but they were *real*.

I chomped more blood, swallowing so quickly I started to gag. I covered my mouth with both hands until the coughing fit passed, then licked the melting droplets from my palm. The taste was no less repulsive, but the return of magic after a month of being unable to reach into a single book overwhelmed all other sensations.

"I think he likes it," Mahefa said dryly.

With libriomancy, I needed to concentrate, to deliberately forge a connection between my will and the belief anchored within the books. But aside from an ashen aftertaste and what felt like the start of heartburn, the blood's magic was *effortless*. It was like the blood had reawakened something dormant within me.

My coughs turned to giddy laughter. Through tear-blurred eyes, I saw a man approach, heard him ask if I was all right. Mahefa waved him off. By now, half the people here probably thought I was stoned out of my mind.

Reluctantly, I sealed the canister and tucked the rest

of the blood away. I felt more awake and alert than I had for weeks.

"Good stuff, no?"

I nodded. Despicable he might be, but Mahefa had delivered exactly what he promised. He took my elbow and guided me back to the marker of Pope Sylvester II.

"Keep your eyes open," I said. The whispers grew clearer as the blood continued to pump magic through my body. I heard multiple voices now, a veritable choir of dead popes and other ghosts. And not one of them spoke English.

"Dammit." I didn't realize I had spoken out loud until a new wave of glares turned my way. "Sorry. *Mi dispiace.*"

What language would d'Aurillac speak? Latin? French? I knew several Romance languages well enough to get by, but the French of today was very different than that spoken a thousand years ago. "Gerbert d'Aurillac?"

The response was incomprehensible. I felt their disorientation, but the words were foreign. After so long, was anything of Gerbert d'Aurillac even left for me to contact?

My mouth had gone dry as cotton. I ran my tongue over my teeth, tasting the faint traces of blood in the crevasses where tooth and gum met. My fingers tightened around the stolen blood. If I consumed it all, would I better understand the voices of the dead? Would I be able to distinguish d'Aurillac from the rest?

"Je suis Isaac Vainio," I whispered. Modern French might be too different for d'Aurillac to understand, but maybe he would at least recognize the language. *"Où est Gerbert d'Aurillac?"*

Nothing but confusion and fear. Latin might be a better choice, assuming these were true ghosts. I couldn't even be certain I was communing with the afterlife. This could just as easily be a hallucination brought on by bad blood.

I thought back to Nicholas, the ghost-talker who had communicated with a murdered Porter earlier this year. Nicholas hadn't spoken in English. But when he first made contact, he had described not the Porter's words, but his emotions.

Ever since my "session" with Euphemia, I had been trying to wall away my fear. But perhaps fear would work where words failed. I opened those walls to all who might be listening, remembering the terror of a woman in bronze dragging me down into a world ruled by the dead. *"Meridiana is here."*

One voice grew louder, honed by despair and grief. I concentrated, separating him from the noise. *"Gerbert d'Aurillac?"*

Wariness supplanted fear. He neither recognized nor trusted me, but at least he heard me. From him, I felt the pain of betrayal. His emotions carried flashes of thought and memory. Hopelessness showed me a teacher and scientist who found himself thrust instead into a world of politics. He had watched so many allies die or turn against him. His fears stemmed from those memories of betrayal: was I a man, or the Devil sent to tempt him?

For a moment, I saw his dreams. I saw a world in which science and magic and religion were one and the same, tools to better understand the mind of God. I saw him happily sketching out a clever poetic puzzle, or working with a friend to find the formula for calculating the area of a circle.

"Pi times radius squared," I said automatically, visualizing the equation in my head.

Fear vanished, replaced by joy and disbelief. Gerbert d'Aurillac, the man who had helped bring Arabic numerals to Europe, who had designed an abacus capable of near-infinite calculations, had never uncovered the concept of pi.

"Volume equals four-thirds pi times radius cubed," I said, sensing his next question.

Silent laughter followed. I felt his delight that humanity had mastered such knowledge and understanding of God's most perfect shape. He pulled the value for pi from my thoughts and marveled at its mysteries.

This was who Gerbert d'Aurillac had been. Not a politician, nor a master of dark magic as legend once painted him, but a man of learning and dreams. A man who had lived to see those dreams broken.

Gerbert had hoped to bring about the renaissance of the Holy Roman Empire, an empire built upon knowledge and wisdom and faith. Like him, Meridiana dreamed of an empire, but her ambitions were grander than anything Gerbert could have imagined.

I showed him what I could of my encounters with Meridiana. How she had first become aware of Jeneta Aboderin when I asked for Jeneta's help in fighting off an infestation within Lena's tree. I remembered Jeneta screaming in fear as darkness and death reached through her e-reader, devouring her magic and seeking to do the same to her.

I was the one who had brought Jeneta and her power to Meridiana's attention. *"What is she?"* I asked. *"Where is the mask, the bronze head?"*

Confusion. He knew of no mask.

"Who was Meridiana?"

The name conjured the image of a child, a little girl named Anna, twin sister to the Holy Roman Emperor Otto III. Gerbert's memories carried fear and regret, even love.

"I don't understand." I had read only a single reference to Otto III's twin, a girl who had died before her first birthday.

Gerbert's memories gave lie to the history. When Anna was born, the navel cord had encircled her throat like a noose. Her tiny body lay blue and dying, despite Gerbert's prayers. When God's mercy failed to save the child, he turned to magic.

Millennium-old guilt and regret made me stagger. Gerbert *knew* God had chosen to let Anna die, but in his arrogance, he had ignored God's will. He conjured spirits from the air—*jinn*—and sent them into Anna's lungs, forcing her to breathe. His power warmed her blood and restored life to her body.

Her spirit was another matter, one Gerbert wouldn't discover for years to come.

Anna grew to be a plain child, smaller than her brother, with slurred speech that fooled many into thinking her dimwitted. But she was oh so clever. She often spoke to the shadows, preferring her imagined companions to family and playmates. I could feel Gerbert's fondness for the girl he had saved, his joy at her childlike questions and unexpected insights.

Anna was raised in the background of her brother, all but invisible. By the time Otto III was crowned king of Germany at the age of three, Anna had begun to recite lines of age-old poetry or repeat seemingly random phrases in Latin or Greek. Gerbert dismissed these things as signs of Anna's eager mind and brilliant memory. He assumed she was merely mimicking what she had heard.

As the twins grew, Anna remained close to their mother Theophanu, who served as regent. Anna watched and whispered, sharing advice both keen and ruthless. In time, her quiet intensity and unnatural knowledge came to disturb even her mother. Anna's demeanor was more that of an aged empress and scholar than a young girl. Knowing Gerbert's skill in things magical, Theophanu begged him to help her daughter.

He began by preparing a detailed horoscope. Initially, he assumed he had made a mistake. He had misread a chart, or perhaps his algebra contained an error. Gerbert repeated his calculations. When they returned the same results, he consulted with a former instructor in Spain, who confirmed his reading several months later.

Anna had been born a medium, able to commune with the dead. With her strength, she could have heard their voices alongside her mother's while still in the womb.

Gerbert had brought Anna back from the dead on the day of her birth, but she hadn't returned alone. She had clung instinctively to those that comforted her: not her living parents, but the spirits of her ancestors. Her horoscope revealed fragmented lives and histories, all of which Anna had incorporated into her own being. Her mind was a monstrous patchwork of life and death and power.

Gerbert tried to save her, to heal her scarred soul and pacify the dead. For a time, he thought he was succeeding.

Anna had absorbed the lessons of politics and empire. Watching her brother struggle to expand his kingdom, she came to believe herself better suited to rule. She had the power of her magic and the experience of the dead.

At the age of twelve, Otto led a campaign to retake the city of Brandenburg. Gerbert couldn't be certain, but he thought it was this defeat that pushed Anna to begin laying the groundwork for the murder of her brother and her own ascension to power.

She began with Gerbert. In all of Rome, his magic was second only to Anna's own. But to truly take advantage of Gerbert's potential, he needed to be moved into a new role.

She began by stirring instability in the papacy, encouraging the tensions that resulted in the torture and removal of Pope John XVI, who later came to be known as antipope. His successor was Anna's cousin Bruno of

Carinthia, who sat as pope for only a year before disease—or poison—took him. With his death, young Anna cleared the way for her mentor to ascend to the papal throne.

But Gerbert had taken notice of her machinations. When confronted, she confided her plans to Gerbert, whom she had come to love as a father. She planned to make him the spiritual leader of her empire. With Gerbert's help, she would succeed where her brother and her ancestors had failed. Not only would she restore the Holy Roman Empire, she would unite Heaven and Earth, the living and the dead, and rule over both worlds as Empress Meridiana I.

I caught Gerbert's bitter appreciation for the word-play. "Meridiana," from the Latin for midday, that moment when morning was left behind and the world began its journey toward nightfall. The beginning of the end.

"How did you stop her?" I whispered.

When I saw what Gerbert had built, I could have wept. I had seen armillary spheres before, series of metal rings and bands designed to show the orbits of the planets and the positions of the stars, but this was a masterpiece.

A bronze model of the Earth sat at the center, affixed to a slender rod through the poles. A series of vertical and horizontal rings and bands gave the impression of a spherical cage. Curved rods held polished metal marbles representing the moon and five other planets.

Through his memories, I saw the working of the sphere, though I didn't understand it all. I recognized the horizontal rings that represented circles of latitude. The flat band intersecting the equatorial ring was broken into the twelve signs of the zodiac. The armillary sphere could be adjusted to show the motion of the Earth and moon, the movement of the stars, or both.

He must have used magic to achieve that level of detail: etchings of the constellations so precise they appeared alive, fittings with less than a hair's width between them. The whole thing was perhaps eighteen inches in diameter, and rested within a plain wooden cradle. A brass sighting tube jutted from the sphere like a drinking straw.

Gerbert lured Anna with news of an armillary sphere so perfect it could be enchanted to reveal the mind of God. They ventured outside, where he had aligned the sighting tube and brought his metal stars into symmetry with the Heavens.

He had constructed a model of the known universe, lacking only one thing: a true model of Gerbert d'Aurillac's universe required the presence of God.

Anna was that final piece. Gerbert invited her to look through the sighting tube, not from the bottom, as a mere mortal gazing up at the sky, but from the top, like God peering down at his creation. When she placed her eye to the end of the tube, her soul was drawn into that bronze universe, bringing completion to Gerbert's masterpiece. The entire model began to move on its own. Planets rotated through their orbits. Stars began their inexorable seasonal journeys.

Meridiana wanted the universe. Gerbert had given it to her.

"JACKSONVILLE COACH SUSPENDED FOR ALLEGED USE OF MAGIC,"
BY LAURA MCKINSEY

The Jacksonville Journal *is not responsible for the views expressed in the comments section of our articles. We reserve the right to delete any comments that violate our terms of service.*

"This whole story is bullshit! Magic? What is this, the 18th century? Even if you believed the accusations, they can't fire Coach Lutz without proof. That's the very definition of a witch hunt! So much for innocent until proven guilty."
J. Davies | August 8, 2:15 p.m.

"J. Davies—Did you even read the article? Nobody's been fired. Lutz was placed on administrative leave *with pay* while they investigate the accusations. The police have three different witnesses. What if three people had witnessed him molesting kids? Would you still want him around your son or daughter? Shut up and let the system work."
WildcatsFan31 | August 8, 2:44 p.m.

"Gandalf would make an awesome football coach, especially on defense. NONE SHALL PASS! ☺"
FrodoLives | August 8, 3:51 p.m.

"I've read some shoddy stories in the Jacksonville Urinal before, but this is the worst. McKinsey should be fired, along with whatever editor approved this garbage. It's yellow journalism at its worst, nothing but sensationalism at the cost of a man's career and reputation. There are no facts, no proof, nothing but rumors. Shame on you all!"
Carla Clark | August 8, 4:01 p.m.

"The mainstream media is a dinosaur."
   DFG | August 8, 4:22 p.m.

This comment has been flagged for review. Click Here to Show Flagged Comments.

"@Carla Clark—Did you see the video of the last game? It's on YouTube. Look at the 5:02 mark and watch the pass Johnson makes to Hayes. They say the wind made that ball shift direction, but I was at the game. THERE WAS NO WIND."
   T.L., Former Referee | August 8, 4:50 p.m.

"Coach Lutz should sue the district, the parents, the school board, the newspaper, and everyone else spreading these lies."
   Diane Rodgers | August 8, 6:24 p.m.

"Check out the YouTube video I made: <u>Hitler weighs in on accusations of football witchcraft.</u>"
   Steven P | August 8, 6:41 p.m.

This comment has been flagged for review. Click Here to Show Flagged Comments.

"I don't know about Coach Lutz, but I'm pretty sure Mrs. Black who teaches seventh grade math is a zombie."
   Jason | August 8, 8:40 p.m.

Chapter 6

GERBERT D'AURILLAC WAS TOO late to undo the damage Meridiana had begun. She had manipulated kings and queens, bishops and popes, planting the seeds for what would come to be known as the Dark Ages. And though d'Aurillac could never prove it, he believed her final act had been to curse him for his betrayal. Or perhaps it was God punishing him for his mistakes and his arrogance.

His life began to crumble. King Robert of France burned two of Gerbert's students as heretics. A rebellion drove Gerbert and Otto III from Rome. Rumors spread that Gerbert d'Aurillac was a sorcerer in league with the devil.

"Meridiana is searching for the sphere," I said. She hadn't been able to free herself from her metal prison, but nothing was eternal. Over time, Gerbert's magic would have weakened enough for her to begin building her army of the dead, and eventually, to reach out and take Jeneta.

Through Gerbert's memories, I watched him prepare a poem in careful Latin. It was a work that took three months to finish, a puzzle with layer upon layer of meaning. He laid the letters out in the shape of a triangle. Within the triangle was a wheel of text. A second, smaller circle sat within the first. A cross divided both circles, and three additional lines connected the inner circle to the outer one.

When at last the poem was complete, he removed the bronze sphere from its wooden frame and set it atop the poem. He spoke to the sphere as if Meridiana—as if *Anna*—might yet hear him. He prayed over her for a full day and night, then recited an incantation I couldn't understand.

The sphere melted into the text.

I had dissolved magical items into books using libriomancy, transforming them back into potential magical energy, but this was different. Both the prison and Meridiana had survived the transition. Gerbert had simply transferred the sphere to somewhere else, or perhaps transformed it into the text itself. A prison within a prison.

It was an amazing work of magic, and I would have loved to understand how he had done it. I pushed the yearning aside, and tried to focus on Gerbert d'Aurillac. *"What did you do with the poem that held the sphere?"*

"He sent it away," came a familiar voice.

Oh, shit. I tore myself away from the cenotaph. I blinked, trying to focus on the real world. People were whispering and backing away. To my left, Mahefa rummaged through his bag of blood.

Jeneta Aboderin stood in the center of the aisle about twenty feet away, flanked by two large bodyguards. One was clad head to toe in an emerald green burqa. A matching veil hid the eyes from view. The other was clearly inhuman, eight feet tall and covered in orange fur. Some kind of sasquatch?

"He's a *yeren*, not a sasquatch." The unspoken *"Duh"*

beneath her words was so familiar, I felt an instant of hope that she had somehow thrown off Meridiana on her own. Hope that died when I saw the arrogance and disdain in her expression.

Jeneta looked much as she had the last time I saw her. Her hair hung in tightly braided cornrows. Blue polish on her nails matched the plastic frames of her sunglasses. She had lost weight. Her cheekbones were more defined beneath her brown skin. She wore loose cargo pants with oversized pockets, and clutched a black e-reader with both hands.

I glared at Mahefa. "I told you to keep an eye out."

"I did," said Mahefa. "But I spotted this hot little bambolina, and then your friend showed up with her pet gorilla, and—"

"Stop talking." Jeneta tapped her screen, and Mahefa's left hand turned to stone. The canister he had been holding slipped from his fingers and spilled blood across the floor.

The only person I'd ever seen perform magic like that was Johannes Gutenberg, and even Gutenberg needed the physical book.

"What the hell did you do?" Mahefa's fingers were perfectly sculpted obsidian. His arm muscles tightened from the weight.

"Get everyone out of here." I kept my voice calm and tried not to do anything remotely threatening.

"Fuck this." Mahefa gripped his bag in his good hand and bolted for the closest exit. Neither Jeneta nor I tried to stop him.

I studied Jeneta's shrouded companion. Beneath the veil, her scalp bulged and shifted like boiling molasses. If this wasn't the gorgon who had helped Jeneta break into the library in Beijing, I was betting it was another of her kin. All she had to do was pull back her veil, and this church would have a lot more statues.

"Where'd you get the muscle?" I nodded toward the yeren and the gorgon.

"I made them."

Whispers and questions surrounded us. The tourists hadn't switched over to full-on panic yet. Few of them had seen or understood the transformation of Mahefa's hand, and the yeren was alien enough that they weren't yet certain how to react. For now, they kept a safe distance and snapped pictures.

"Jeneta ..." I had spent the past month searching for her, and here she was, ready to kill me with a flick of her fingers. "I'm sorry."

She looked around. "I expected to find more of your Porters here."

"The Porters lost you at the airport. Your parents haven't stopped searching for you." I hoped Jeneta could hear me, that she understood we hadn't given up. "I'll find a way to fix this."

She drummed her fingers on the e-reader's screen. "Do I need to turn your limbs to stone to get your attention? I could transform you to gold or a pillar of salt. I've an entire library of possibilities at my fingertips."

I fell back on the oldest defense I knew: smart-assery. "When I get home, I'm firing my travel agent. I specifically asked for a *monster-free* vacation. All I wanted was a few days to relax and enjoy my retirement. You do know I'm retired, right?"

Jeneta and her monsters moved closer, stepping in eerie synchronicity that reminded me of the children of Camazotz from *A Wrinkle in Time*, bouncing balls and jumping rope in perfect unison.

"What have you learned, Isaac?"

"Well, the basilica's façade was built by Alessandro Galilei in the eighteenth century, and—"

The yeren growled, a sound so low I could feel it. More and more people were scurrying from the church.

Those who remained gawked like this was some new form of street theater. How long before the police showed up, or had Meridiana taken steps to make sure no one stopped her from interrogating me?

"Where did he send the poem?" she continued. "Not to his colleague in Beijing. Nor to Miro Bonfill. He certainly didn't hide it here."

"Why don't you ask him yourself?"

She made a brushing-off motion with one hand, a gesture both regal and utterly foreign to Jeneta. "He won't speak to me, or to anyone under my control. Dead for a thousand years, and still he thwarts me. But he shared his poem with you. I can see the design in your thoughts."

Other voices tugged at my awareness: fragmented whispers that seemed to come from Meridiana's monsters. The yeren's lips were pulled into a taut snarl. Even if that muzzle was capable of producing human speech, there was no way it was speaking Mandarin without moving its jaw or—

The realization was like ash in the back of my throat. The blood I had consumed let me hear the dead, and whoever these two people used to be, Meridiana had killed them to create her inhuman guardians. She had likely picked up the yeren during her attack on the Beijing library. I wondered if he had been one of the students of Bi Sheng.

The gorgon—rather, the woman whose body Meridiana had transformed into a gorgon—called to me in English. Her name was Deanna Fuentes-McDowell, and she had been a Porter. She told me how Meridiana had tracked her like an animal, following the scent of her magic and exhausting her until she fell, then turning her body into a vessel for one of her ghosts.

I started to reach for my shock-gun. The gorgon touched a slender hand to the corner of her veil. I spread my hands and did my best to look harmless.

"Now that we're all acquainted, it's time for you to choose," said Meridiana. "Help me, and I'll restore you in return. I'll remove the spell Gutenberg carved into you."

"Sure, why not? That kind of bargain always ends well."

She rolled her eyes, and once again, I saw flashes of the teenager who had gotten so exasperated while trying to talk to me about poetry.

The yeren leaped into the air, coming to land atop the head and shoulders of a statue. His next jump took him past me, cutting off any escape. The impact cracked the tile floor.

"An angel waits for you outside," whispered the dead Porter, Deanna.

I could tell she was trying to help, but I had no idea what she meant. I was standing in front of a would-be destroyer of worlds, and the ghost decided it was time to play it cryptic?

One of Deanna's memories floated like smoke across my vision. I saw Jeneta standing in a Porter archive. I didn't recognize the facility, but the layout and contents were unmistakably ours. Deanna lay powerless and exhausted on the ground. Meridiana used her e-reader to pull up a book on Greek mythology. I saw her reach into the screen and fling *something* toward Deanna, like an inky cobweb made of words.

That was how Jeneta had transformed her servants. Instead of reaching into the text and pulling out a fully formed object, she had seized the pattern of belief, using it as a template to reshape living bodies. It was as if she had inverted libriomancy.

Meridiana reached out, fingers curved like claws. I doubled over. My stomach convulsed, and I coughed up blood. The same blood I had swallowed to speak with Gerbert d'Aurillac. "You think to hide your conversations with the dead from *me?* Your thoughts are as simple to read as a children's book, Isaac Vainio."

The whispers in my head fell away. Gerbert d'Aurillac shared one last memory, and then he was gone.

I continued to heave. My mouth tasted of blood and ash.

The sight of me puking blood pretty well emptied the church. By the time I managed to stand, we were alone. My skin was clammy, and my stomach spasmed. "I finally get some magic back, and you had to steal it away."

If Meridiana could read my thoughts, I'd just have to act without thinking. Lena would say that was one of my strengths. I concentrated on d'Aurillac's final message, letting that memory fill my mind.

Meridiana gave an anguished cry as she saw Gerbert d'Aurillac holding his poem to the flames. "Damn him. He didn't send the poem away. He destroyed it."

I was already moving. I lunged at the gorgon and seized her veil. With my eyes squeezed shut, I pulled hard. Cloth tore in my grip. Angry hissing and the snapping of tiny, fanged jaws told me I had successfully unveiled one of the most dangerous creatures in Greek mythology. Way to go, Isaac.

I turned my back on the gorgon to face the yeren. The yeren who had maneuvered around behind me, putting himself directly in the path of the gorgon's gaze. He had one enormous paw over his eyes, like an oversized "See no evil" monkey. I yanked out my shock-gun and pulled the trigger. Lightning crackled over his body, and he fell to the ground with a whimper.

I sent my next shot into the ceiling. The gold leaf conducted the charge, and the light momentarily blinded everyone who remained. Droplets of molten gold rained down, searing my skin like acid. I hoped Jeneta would forgive me for any scars, but hopefully the pain would distract her for a few seconds.

I heard shouts behind me, but didn't dare turn to see what had happened. I sprinted toward the closest exit, emerging into a crowded stone courtyard where the church walls joined the Lateran Palace.

The crowd's panic and confusion would give me a little cover. It looked like the commotion had caused at least one accident in the street beyond. Traffic had come to a halt. So much for catching a taxi.

I slowed when I realized most of the people weren't looking at the church itself, but at the roof. A large figure wielding a double-edged broadsword stood atop the church between the statues. Broad wings stretched from his shoulders. He jumped from the edge, and his wings turned the fall into a glide. Long, ragged red hair framed a face twisted with righteous fury. He swooped past me, cutting me off from the street.

An angel waits outside. This was what Deanna had tried to warn me about. I shot at the angel, but the lightning died before it touched him. I feinted left, then sprinted to the right, keeping close to the wall of the palace. On foot, his wings slowed him down as he fought through the crowd to try to intercept me. My feet hit the blacktop. I wove between parked cars. Two seconds later, I heard the slap of his sandals behind me.

When I reached the other side of the road, I turned the shock-gun up to level six and blasted the blacktop directly in front of him.

The angel was moving too fast to stop. His sandals sank into half-melted tar, and he fell hard. His sword slipped away and clanged against the sidewalk.

I cringed at the sight of so many cameras and cell phones. Hopefully I wouldn't end up on the news or online. I turned a corner and searched for a place to hide. I didn't have much time before—

I didn't see who cast the spell, but I felt it encase my body like quickly hardening mud. The road swelled toward me as if I was falling, though I had stopped moving. I reached out to catch my balance. My arms were little more than swollen stubs of slick flesh. My shouts of alarm emerged as gurgling cries.

I fell to all fours. My clothing tightened around my shrinking body, turning a bright orange. My skin was the same shade. Weirdest of all was the sensation of a tail growing out of my backside.

A gloved hand scooped me from the pavement and dropped me unceremoniously into a jacket pocket that smelled like spearmint gum. "Don't struggle."

Like I had a choice. I tried to climb out, but the swift, uneven strides of my captor bounced his jacket against his body with every step. I squirmed and twisted until my tail was curled comfortably around my body, then settled down to wait. I wasn't dead, and the way today was going, that was probably more than I had a right to expect.

A crack of light appeared overhead, and oversized fingers dropped a wriggling worm in with me. I pounced without thinking, devouring half of it in one gulp. The worst part of my instinctive response was that the thing tasted so *good*. I could feel the worm twitching in my throat, trying to escape. I wanted to vomit, but I also wanted to chomp down the rest, to feel its juices sliding down my gullet.

We were moving again. I crouched as low as I could, waiting for the danger to pass. There were noises nearby. Loud and sharp and dangerous. I tried to burrow, but wherever I was, I couldn't dig.

The worm twitched in my mouth. I gobbled it down in a single movement. Had anything seen me? My eyes flitted to and fro, searching the darkness. My skin was too dry, and this hole constricted my body. Fear held me motionless.

I don't know how much time passed before my own thoughts started to return. My captor was no longer

walking. From the steady growl of an engine and the vi-
brations passing through my body, we were in a vehicle.

My body was covered in some sort of slime or mucus,
and the taste of worm lingered in my mouth. I hoped
whoever had done this would restore my clothes and gun
when he changed me back, because I was going to shoot
him in the face.

"We're almost there, Isaac. Be patient."

On second thought, maybe I would accept my indig-
nities in silence. Gerbert d'Aurillac would be proud.
Rather than seek retribution, I chose to turn the other
cheek. Because while the sound was muffled and distorted—newts lacked external ears—I recognized that
voice.

Even I knew better than to try to shoot Juan Ponce de
Leon in the face.

I felt the lopsided gait of my rescuer—or kidnapper, depending on the role he had decided to play today—when
he climbed out of the car. As I understood the story,
Ponce de Leon had been struck in the leg by a magically
poisoned arrow during his conquistador days, and the
wound had never fully healed.

My hearing was distinctly subpar, but my sense of
smell had been turned up to eleven. While pipe smoke
suffused his clothes, I could have still picked the nutmeg-
and-rosewood scent of his cologne out of a lineup. His
hard-soled shoes echoed against cement. The smell of oil
and exhaust lingered in the air. I guessed we were in a
parking garage.

A door opened, and we hurried across carpeted floor,
passing voices too muffled for me to make out. We
stopped briefly, until an electronic ding announced the
arrival of an elevator.

I figured this was either an office building or a hotel, but it was impossible to be certain while trapped in Ponce de Leon's pocket. I waited impatiently as we left the elevator and limped a short way. I smelled wine and cleaning solutions. Another door opened, and we hurried inside.

"Welcome to the Westin Excelsior." His hand dipped gently into his pocket, closing around my body and carrying me to the bathtub. My feet found little purchase on the wet ceramic, and then I was doubling over as my body returned to its normal size. I remained fully clothed, thank Heaven for small favors.

I looked up at the man who had snatched me from Meridiana's grasp. This was the first time I had seen Juan Ponce de Leon in the flesh. He had a long nose and a narrow face, and was more disheveled than I expected. His wrinkled, ivory-colored suit looked like it cost more than I earned in a year. Stubble blurred the edges of his black goatee. He rested heavily on a cane of flawless black wood with an opera-style hooked chrome handle. Veins of gold were spread through the cane's handle and collar.

It was his eyes that made me nervous. They were constantly searching, examining every corner of the room, even checking the mirrors to make sure nothing could take him by surprise. If Juan Ponce de Leon was jumpy, we were in serious trouble.

I ran my hands through my hair and rested against the tile wall above the tub. "You turned me into a *newt!*"

He tilted his head and said, deadpan, "You got better."

"Oh, no. Quoting Monty Python isn't going to make this go away. Why would you—wait, don't tell me. Meridiana could hear my thoughts, right? Forcing me into that form, making me *eat a worm*, was your way of overriding my human thoughts long enough for us to escape without her finding us."

He brought his hands together in a silent golf clap.

"Am I confined to your bathtub, or am I allowed to get up?"

He stepped back and offered a mocking half-bow, gesturing with both arms. "Watch your step. Remember, you're walking on two legs again."

I pressed the wall for balance. The ground did seem awfully far away, and my butt felt oddly light without a tail. I stepped slowly, determined to make it out of the bathroom without asking for help or falling and breaking my nose.

I emerged into a room that could have swallowed my first apartment. Thick white carpeting covered the floor. Heavy gold curtains hid tall windows. A flat-screen television, fifty-two inches at least, hung flush on the wall opposite a queen-sized bed with a red velvet canopy. The ivory-and-gold wallpaper looked like something out of a mansion, as did the crystal chandelier over the small dining area.

I settled into a leather sofa, the cushions stuffed with softness and extravagance.

"Make yourself at home," Ponce de Leon said dryly. "Would you care for a drink?"

"Anything that will wash the taste of worm out of my mouth."

He retrieved two tulip-shaped glasses and a bottle. "Scotch, I think."

It was fortunate I was sitting down, because the first swallow would have knocked me on my ass. I blinked hard as the vapors seemed to rise through my head, leaving a layered, smoky taste. "How old is that bottle, and where can I find one?"

"Older than you. Not as old as me. And you couldn't afford it."

I took another sip. "Thank you, by the way. For getting me away from Meridiana."

He raised his glass in acknowledgment. "Meridiana, is it? I thought the girl was named Jeneta. She's your student, if I'm not mistaken?"

"She's going through an identity crisis." I set my drink on a marble end table. "So there I was. Isaac Vainio exits stage right, pursued by an angel. When suddenly one of the world's most powerful sorcerers just happens to wander by. The same sorcerer who refused to answer my calls. What a coincidence, eh?"

Amusement peeked through the fog of his fatigue. "I truly had no idea you were in Rome. I was more interested in why both the Porters and your friend Meridiana had set magical wards to watch over an old church."

I rubbed my arms. I knew it was all in my head, but I still *felt* like I was covered in newt slime. "She's a thousand-year-old princess who consumes and commands ghosts, and plans on killing off half the population and setting herself up as empress of the living and the dead. Gerbert d'Aurillac trapped her in a miniature bronze universe. She's spent the past millennium searching for a way out and working to capture the minds and souls of other magic-users. She's trying to escape into the world, and has been using Porters and the students of Bi Sheng as vessels for her deranged ghosts. Oh, and Gutenberg fired me last month."

"I see." He stepped closer and rubbed his thumb gently over my forehead, in exactly the spot where Gutenberg had inscribed his spell. "I'm sorry."

He sounded like he meant it. Only another magic-user would understand what it was like to have that part of yourself ripped away. "Thanks."

"What prompted Johannes to do this?" he asked.

"Meridiana was trying to get into my head, to possess me the way she had the others. Locking my magic locked her out, though it obviously wasn't enough to stop her from reading my mind." I took another swallow of

Scotch. "Also, Gutenberg was pretty pissed at me. I kind of allowed the students of Bi Sheng to escape."

"Johannes' conflict with Bi Sheng's followers was before my time with the Porters," he said. "He never spoke of it."

"Five hundred years ago, Gutenberg sent his automatons to destroy them," I said flatly. "Only a handful survived, trapped in limbo until earlier this year." I stared through my glass at his elongated form. "Do you know how to counter Gutenberg's spell and restore my magic?"

I didn't want to ask the question, but I couldn't *not* ask. Ponce de Leon was the one person who might have both the knowledge and the power to undo Gutenberg's magic.

But the question was like Schrödinger's box. Just as Schrödinger's cat was potentially both alive and dead until you opened the box, so was my hope for restoration. One way or another, his answer would collapse the possibilities into unforgiving reality.

Though hope didn't really fit, thematically speaking. Hope had been Pandora's thing. All right, fine. It was like Schrödinger opening Pandora's box.

The weariness and sadness in his eyes told me his answer. "I'm sorry, Isaac."

With those three words, the damn box imploded, splinters piercing whatever hope I had clung to for the past month.

"I always believed removing the memory of magic was a kindness," he continued. "Better not to know what you had lost."

"Better for whom?" I asked.

He didn't answer. "I assume Bi Wei is one of the survivors you permitted to escape? Her letter to the world was impetuous and poorly timed. I see why the two of you would have gotten along. I can only imagine Johannes' dismay. Not to mention poor George R. R. Martin. Many of his fans believe the letter is a publicity stunt foreshadowing a new series by Mister Martin. Their reaction has been . . . *passionate*, to say the least."

"I understand why she did it," I said. "The students of Bi Sheng are as terrified of the Porters as they are of the Ghost Army. But in the process, Bi Wei gave Meridiana the address of every Porter archive."

He sat down on the other end of the couch. "From what I've observed, Meridiana would have found them without Bi Wei's help. Though most of Meridiana's energies have been focused elsewhere."

He pointed a finger at the television, which turned on. Apparently his index finger was a magical remote. Nice.

A map of the world filled the screen. Red dots appeared like chicken pox. Not just a television, but a computer monitor as well.

"The National Library of China," he said. "A museum in Cairo. Three Porter archives, including the Library of Congress. Even the Bibliothèque nationale de France, though the French police have kept that out of the media."

"She's searching for a way back into this world," I said. "And creating pet monsters along the way."

"Yes, I wondered how she had recruited an angel into her ranks. They generally prefer not to intervene in mortal affairs so openly."

That comment raised a thousand questions, temporarily derailing my train of thought. Reluctantly, I pushed them aside. "Libriomancers—even Gutenberg—can only access one book at a time. Jeneta could potentially draw on millions of books through her e-reader. She was just learning to use her magic, but Meridiana was trained by Gerbert d'Aurillac, not to mention what she's learned from the dead." I thought about how easily she had petrified Mahefa's hand, then took another drink of scotch.

Ponce de Leon's finger twitched, and the screen filled with photos and video feeds showing the chaos at the basilica. Someone had gotten a jumpy three-second clip of the angel leaping to the ground, sword drawn. Another photo showed the yeren stumbling around, one paw covering its eyes.

"Meridiana knew d'Aurillac wouldn't tell her how to free herself," I said. "She waited for someone else to come along. Someone d'Aurillac would trust with the key to her prison. Someone whose thoughts she could peel open."

"Someone who would charge headlong into the situation, seeking answers without weighing the risks," he added dryly.

"I wasn't—" I stopped myself. "I haven't been at my best lately."

"I can imagine. Do you know where to find this key?"

"I'm not sure." D'Aurillac had destroyed the poem that contained his armillary sphere, but Meridiana was still imprisoned. I closed my eyes, remembering the shape of the poem, the carefully inked letters stretching together to create interwoven shapes on the parchment. Far more than any other memory d'Aurillac had shared, that poem was burned into my thoughts.

"Good. Then Meridiana should be equally lost." He turned back to the map. "The students of Bi Sheng have done an admirable job of concealing themselves, though I believe them to be hiding somewhere in eastern Asia. I've felt currents of their activities. Instead of openly trying to battle Meridiana or the Porters, they seem to have focused their efforts inward in some way. As for Meridiana, her targets have no obvious geographic pattern. Her base of operations could be anywhere in the world, assuming she has one at all."

Another flick of his hand cleared the screen. "You've met her gorgon, angel, and sasquatch." He snapped his fingers as he spoke, each time pulling up an image of the monster in question.

"Yeren, not sasquatch," I said.

"Really? I believe that would make this the first verified yeren sighting in history, though I'd need to dig into Johannes' records to be sure." Additional pictures and sketches continued to fill the screen. "Meridiana also has what appears to be an ogre of some kind, as well as a naga, a kitsune, a manticore, and a pair of mermen."

"Nine monsters and one out-of-control libriomancer."

"That we know of. We should assume she hasn't revealed her full hand yet." He slashed his fingers through the air, and the screen switched to a men's tennis match. "How many ghosts do you think she's gathered over the centuries?"

"Hundreds," I said. "Maybe thousands."

"Now that you've communed with Pope Sylvester II, she'll be hunting for you."

"I know." And if she couldn't find me, she'd go after whatever leverage she could get, starting with Lena. Everything I did lately put them in greater danger. "Could I borrow your phone?"

"I texted Miss Greenwood and Doctor Shah from the car to warn them. They're none too happy with you, by the way."

"Yah, I got that feeling." And rightfully so. First vampires, now Meridiana. Lena could protect them from most threats, but not this. "I need to get home."

"I've already made arrangements, but the flight doesn't depart for another four hours." Trust Ponce de Leon to be two steps ahead of me. He watched the tennis game for several minutes. "There's no suppressing this, Isaac. You can't cram an oak tree back into an acorn. What Meridiana and Bi Wei have begun will change this world."

"I know."

He chuckled. "I doubt that. No slight intended, but you lack perspective. You've never watched empires rise and fall, nor the chaos that erupts in their death throes. You've not seen intellectual, philosophical, economic, or technological revolutions sweep the globe like ocean waves, each one greater than the last. Do you know what led to my split with Johannes?"

I tried to keep up with his train of thought as it lurched off the rails. "No clue."

"Nothing is eternal. Magic could be kept secret for a time, centuries perhaps, but not forever. Johannes and I both knew people would discover the truth, and when that day came, we knew the world would change. We had both seen what such changes could lead to. Fear. War. Genocide.

"Johannes believed such change could be controlled. That we could minimize the damage and guide the world through its turmoil. His personal texts are full of plans for the revelation. Several such plans involve rather extreme actions."

"What kind of actions?"

He waved a hand, dismissing my question. "What are the three oaths each Porter takes?"

"To preserve the secrecy of magic, to protect the world from supernatural threats, and to expand our knowledge and understanding of magic." I tried to ignore the hollow feeling the words triggered in me.

"And what gives them the right?"

"I didn't know we needed permission to save people's lives." I thought back to an assignment from three years ago. "Who exactly should I have asked about that smog elemental I fought in Grand Rapids?"

"I've tried to change the world before. The Moors. The Indians. I believed—I *knew*—I was on the side of right. I intended to save them, to spread knowledge and civilization, even if I had to slaughter half the population to enlighten the rest." He downed the rest of his Scotch and poured a second glass. "Countless cultures paid for my arrogance. I vowed never to put myself in a position to make such mistakes again."

"The Porters aren't conquering anyone." I wasn't used to being the one to defend Gutenberg and the Porters.

"Not this week, perhaps. But conquest and control come in many forms, Isaac. Time after time Johannes and I fought over this point. God's plan may be infallible, but ours are not, no matter how well-intentioned. It's not our place to shape the world."

"Is that why you refused to answer my calls? Why you've disappeared and done nothing while Meridiana works to turn this world into a planet ruled by ghosts?"

His eyebrows rose. "I wouldn't call saving your life nothing. But you're correct, the time for hiding is over. Whatever Johannes' plans, Meridiana's are far worse. You can't fight this war alone, Isaac. Nor can he. I will return to America with you, and we will decipher the clues Gerbert d'Aurillac shared."

I nodded gratefully. The Porters could ignore my calls, but they couldn't ignore Ponce de Leon. I finished my drink and asked the other question I had been scared to ask. "I heard the ghosts of the people Meridiana transformed into monsters, but I didn't hear Jeneta. If she was dead, I should have heard her voice, too. Do you think there's a way to free her from Meridiana?"

"Perhaps. The best chance might be the same spell Johannes used to protect you from Meridiana and her ghosts."

Lock Jeneta's magic. She would never forgive me. "What would that do with Meridiana already rooted in her body?"

"I don't know, Isaac. But our first priority is to stop Meridiana. Even if it costs an innocent child her life."

The dude was messed up, mumbling to himself and talking to people who weren't there. I thought about finding a cop, but he wasn't really hurting anything, you know? I'd only been in Rome for two days, so what did I know? Maybe this sort of thing happens all the time there. Plus he had this accent, like he was Canadian or something, so I figured he was probably harmless. Just a tourist who partied too hard and was trying to walk it off. And then he started puking right there in the middle of the church, and there were monsters and s—, and we got out of there.

I looked back through the doors, and that mother—— started waving a gun and flinging *lightning bolts* out of his hands. Everyone was running and screaming and s—. Next thing you know, some clown in an angel costume with a sword is chasing the guy into the street.

Don't ask me what set it all off. The guy didn't look like a terrorist or anything. He was all skinny and pale, like someone who spends too much time in his mom's basement playing World of Warcraft and downloading porn, know what I mean? But I know what I saw. That nerd was doing magic.

You've seen the pictures, right? Blackened walls. Melted gold. They're trying to say lightning hit the church. Really? Lightning hit *inside* the church? In the middle of the day, with the sun shining? I've got two words for that. Bull and s—.

There is some *seriously* weird s— going on. Bad enough we've got to make sure terrorists don't sneak onto another plane and blow our country to hell. Now we've got to worry about magic Canadians, too? That's just not right.

—Excerpt from a CNBC News Interview

Chapter 7

IF YOU HAVE TO FLY, I strongly recommend taking a sorcerer as a traveling companion.

No papers? No problem. Ponce de Leon purchased a postcard at one of the shops outside the airport and transformed it into a passport, complete with stamps showing I'd also been to France, Spain, and Austria. The shock-gun became a large digital camera, and the half-empty vial of vampire blood a telephoto lens.

"The spells will wear off after twenty-four hours," he warned. "Under *no circumstances* should you try to take anyone's photograph."

An hour later we were waiting on the tarmac while what seemed like the entire Italian commercial air fleet taxied down the runway ahead of us. I leaned over the armrest to whisper, "I don't suppose you could jump us to the head of the line?"

"Even my magic has limits, Isaac."

I returned my attention to the brown paper bag spread flat on my seat tray. I had sketched the general shape of Gerbert d'Aurillac's poem from my memory. A large triangle contained two circles, and a series of intersecting lines. The next step was to work Latin characters into each shape.

I drew the letter A in the seven places where the spokes intersected the outer circle. The inner circle was the same, but with Ns instead of As. I moved on to the words within the triangle.

"Interesting." Ponce de Leon studied my work through the thin rectangular lenses of his reading glasses. "A carmen figuratum, yes?"

"Not just a visual poem, but a puzzle." Recreating the poem was only the first step. Once I finished, I then had to decipher it.

He touched the letters. "Anna. Meridiana's true name."

That name had to be part of the key to understanding d'Aurillac's poem, but the rest of the text seemed to be the Latin equivalent of word salad, as if the author had cut apart every word from the original and flung them into the air with no care for where they landed. I continued to write them out as best I could from memory, taking a brief break for takeoff.

Ponce de Leon touched one such fragment. "This says, 'Temperate bull expires Caesar urine.' I'm a fair poet, but the metaphor eludes me. Unless we're to assume Meridiana is imprisoned by the power of dead bulls and the piss of emperors."

I rubbed my eyes. I had filled in only a fraction of the text, and already my head was beginning to throb. Fortunately, we had a long flight ahead of us.

I finished the outer triangle and part of the vertical spoke before my eyes gave out and I surrendered to sleep, but the poem stalked my dreams. Geometric shapes unraveled in my hands, brown-inked letters slipping through my fingers before I could grasp their meaning. I made a little more progress during our layover in New Jersey.

Ponce de Leon woke me shortly before our descent into Detroit. I rubbed grit from my eyes. "Do you ever sleep?"

He shrugged. "When I have time."

He had made additional notes on a separate piece of paper, playing with words as if they were anagrams. He had also penciled the first letter of each word in a single column, but if those letters held any hidden meaning, it was beyond me. I folded the sketch and tucked it into my back pocket.

Lena and Nidhi waited for us by the baggage claim. My shoulders sagged with relief to see them standing there, unharmed by Meridiana or pissed-off vampires or Mahefa or anyone else I might have crossed in the past week.

Lena rested her weight on a thick oak cane that would have gotten her thrown out of the airport or arrested if security had realized what she could do with it. I slowed, uncertain how to greet them.

She handed her cane to Nidhi and strode toward me, her expression unreadable. She stopped with her face inches from mine and looked me over, as if searching for injuries. Her nose wrinkled. "We need to get you a shower."

"Hey, I've been stuck on planes for—"

Before I could finish, she twisted her hands into my shirt, yanked me close, and kissed me.

I wrapped one arm around her shoulders and slid my other hand up her neck, my fingers combing through her hair. As her arms encircled my waist and her lips pressed against mine, she shared her desire, her anger, her relief, and her pain more effectively than words.

She kept hold of my shirt when we finally broke away.

"I'm sorry," I said.

"We saw the reports about the lightning storm inside that church." Her nose touched mine. "Get into a brawl

like that without me again, and I will drop Smudge down
your pants."

"That seems like an awfully cruel thing to do to an
innocent fire-spider."

She flexed her arms ever so slightly, and my ankles
lifted from the floor.

"Right," I said hastily. "No weenie roast necessary."

That earned a crooked smile. She hugged me one
more time, then stepped away so I could greet Nidhi. I
hugged her, too, which I think surprised us both. "Are
you and Lena okay?"

"Yes, thank you. We had one undead visitor, but Lena
took care of her."

"What about Mahefa?" I forced myself to look at
Lena. "Did he show up to claim the rest of his price?"

She took her cane back from Nidhi and wrapped her
fingers tightly around the wood. "No sign of him yet."

Maybe the petrification of his hand had been enough
to scare him away from anyone associated with me, but
I doubted it. That wasn't the way my luck had been
working lately.

"What about you, Isaac?" asked Nidhi. "Are you all
right?"

I started to give her a flippant response about uncom-
fortable airline seats and leftover newt slime, then
caught myself. At the very least, I owed them honesty.
"No. Not really."

Oddly enough, that drew a smile from Nidhi. She gave
me a small, understanding nod. After glancing around to
make sure nobody was watching, she reached into a canvas shopping bag and pulled out Smudge in his traveling
cage.

He skittered around in quick, tight laps when he spotted me. I took his cage and grinned. "I feel the same way,
buddy." I searched my pockets for something to feed
him, but came up empty.

Lena handed me a half-empty package of M&Ms. Smudge reached a bristly leg through the bars to nudge my hand, like a child searching for a prize. I slipped him a yellow one. "What's the media been saying about Rome?"

"It made CNN's roundup of 'Magic Watch,'" she said. "There were reports of a magical commotion inside, but the only decent photographs were after the fact. They did have footage of what looked like an angel standing on top of the church." Her voice trailed off as she spotted Ponce de Leon, who had stopped a respectful distance behind me. Her stance shifted slightly, and she adjusted her grip on her cane.

"Who is this?" Nidhi asked.

"He's the reason I survived the attack on that church." I stepped to the side. "Juan Ponce de Leon, this is Doctor Nidhi Shah. You've met Lena once before."

"Not in person." He shook their hands, his attention lingering on Lena. "You are quite the interesting snarl of conflicting magic, aren't you?"

"I'm sure you say that to all the dryads."

"Have the news reports come up with anything else?" I asked.

"They've connected Bi Wei's list of Porter archives to the fact that both the Michigan State University library and Fort Michilimackinac suffered 'unexplained incidents' this year," said Nidhi. "It's slow, but they're piecing the truth together."

Ponce de Leon was already walking toward the exit. "Revelation is a foregone conclusion. Johannes will be working to control the message and minimize the damage to his organization, but Meridiana's actions force him to respond quickly. Men under pressure make mistakes, and he is no exception."

Lena jerked a thumb at Ponce de Leon's back, her cocked head voicing her silent question. *What is he doing here?*

"He's here to help," I said quietly. "I think."

"Did you find the answers you were looking for?" Nidhi asked.

"Not exactly." I slowed as we reached the parking lot, but Ponce de Leon seemed to know exactly where he was going. "I have a better idea what we're up against, and what Jeneta—Meridiana—is searching for. And I know who Meridiana really is."

Nidhi's car waited for us on the far side of the Mc-Namara Parking Garage. I recognized the car first, then the man standing in the shadows beside it. "Oh, crap. Hi, John."

John Wenger was a Porter field agent, tall and slender and dangerous. He held a hardcover book in one hand and a small silver-and-black pistol in the other. "Lightning in the middle of a church, Isaac? How could you? The artwork you destroyed was irreplaceable."

"In my defense, they started it." I saw Lena readying her cane. I put a hand on her arm. John wasn't a bad guy. And even if she took him down, he wouldn't be alone. They wouldn't send a lone field agent after an ex-Porter, especially an ex-Porter whose lover had fought everything from vampires to one of Gutenberg's automatons. "How goes the effort to protect the archives?"

"Not good." John grimaced, but the gun never wavered. "We've kept anyone from getting inside our facilities, but the mundanes have used satellite and radar imaging to confirm the existence of at least two archives we know of. They've halted the reconstruction of the MSU library in East Lansing, and there's a fight brewing over whether or not to reexcavate the site."

I folded my arms. "If you're not too busy worrying about hiding your archives and hunting down a rogue ex-Porter, maybe Gutenberg could spare some people to help me stop a reincarnated empress who wants to make herself a god?"

"Rogue ex-Porters, plural." John was one of the most polite, easygoing people I knew, but there was violence in his words. "We've lost seven that I know of, not including yourself. For some it's national or religious loyalties. They're worried about all-out war, and want to make sure their 'side' wins. Others see the secret getting out and figure this is their chance to cash in. There's also a libriomancer who may have gotten herself imprisoned or killed in Pakistan, we're not sure. And the EARM has a team looking for another one who's gone missing in North Korea."

I couldn't recall the name of the East Asian Regional Master, but I didn't envy him that job.

John pointed his gun toward my bag. "Where's the blood, Isaac?"

Moving as slowly as I could, I pulled out the telephoto lens. "You know about that, too, eh?"

"What were you thinking?" John asked. "We've already lost one Porter to the vamps this year."

"I'm as human as you are," I said.

"So was Deb DeGeorge, in the beginning."

My hand shook slightly as I remembered the rush of magic surging through my veins and the voices of the dead whispering their secrets. It wasn't magic I could shape and control, but it was magic nonetheless.

My mouth went dry. I tensed my arm, trying to hide another tremor. I had no real need to hold on to the rest of my stolen blood, but I couldn't force myself to hand it over.

Lena tugged the lens from my grip and gave it to John.

"Thanks," I muttered. "Where are you planning to take me? Porter jail?"

"You're to be debriefed and kept under guard until this mess is brought under control. Pallas' orders."

"Good." Hopefully this meant I'd actually get the chance to talk to her.

John hefted the lens. "How did you disguise the blood?"

To one side, Ponce de Leon cleared his throat. "When you say we're to be taken in, did you mean *all* of us?"

I had almost forgotten he was here. His cane was hooked over his folded arms, and he rested one ankle atop the other. He blended into the background so well I suspected magic. A useful trick for someone who had spent so long trying to stay out of sight.

"Are you with them?" John asked. "What's your name?"

Ponce de Leon said nothing. He didn't have to. John's face paled when he realized who he was pointing his gun at. He stepped back and raised his wrist to his mouth, speaking into what looked like an old-style spy communicator watch. "Uh, we may have a problem here."

Ponce de Leon merely smiled.

I would have dearly loved to see what happened next. Unfortunately, that was when someone shot me in the back with some kind of stun beam. Energy seared my nervous system, and everything went black.

I awoke on a ridiculously comfortable bed. I rolled onto my stomach, and my right arm brushed warm flesh.

"Good morning." Lena's voice came from somewhere past my feet. I frowned and opened my eyes.

Nidhi Shah was sprawled on the bed next to me, snoring quietly. I planted my face in the pillow. My head was pounding like a flat tire going down a dirt road. "Where are we?"

Lena understood my muffled question. "Chicago, I think."

"Ponce de Leon?"

"I only woke up a half hour ago. I haven't seen him."

I sat up and looked around. Nidhi and I were in a

queen-sized bed in the center of a small but well-furnished bedroom. Oak bookshelves lined one wall. To the right, blue curtains covered the windows. A wooden ceiling fan hummed quietly overhead.

Nicola Pallas lived in the Chicago area, but I didn't think this was her place. The air lacked the musty blood-and-fur smell of her beloved chupacabra hybrids.

I climbed out of bed, trying not to disturb Nidhi. Smudge was in his cage on an antique bedside table. My shoes sat neatly beside a wooden door, alongside Nidhi's and Lena's. I checked my back pocket and swore. The poem I had been working on was gone.

I tried the door, which was locked, then slid open a small closet with folding doors. An assortment of robes, shirts, and pants hung on wooden hangers. Wherever we were, there was plenty of wood Lena could use for weapons, if it came to that. I started toward the window.

"Brace yourself," Lena warned.

I peered out and swallowed. We were at least thirty stories up, and perhaps a block from the waterfront. You'd think a trip into orbit and back would have made it easier for me to handle heights, but if anything, the vertigo was worse. I forced myself to inspect the windows, but they weren't designed to open. Even if they did, there was no fire escape. We weren't getting out this way. Lena *might* survive a jump from this height, but it would hurt, and I doubted she'd be getting up and walking away.

I turned to let Smudge out of his cage. He scampered up my arm and perched on my shoulder. He was no warmer than usual, suggesting we were in no immediate danger. "What happened after they shot me?"

"They shot the rest of us." Lena shrugged. "I'm pretty sure Ponce de Leon just laughed it off, but Nidhi and I . . ."

"There's always a silver lining," Nidhi said, not opening her eyes. "Isaac desperately needed the sleep."

"They probably did their initial interrogation while we were out," I guessed. Neither Lena nor I had any defenses against mind reading. A tattoo on Nidhi's temple, the Gujarati characters for *balance*, was supposed to grant her some protection against mental assaults, but since the Porters were the ones who had given her that tattoo, I wasn't counting on it.

I returned to the door and listened, but heard nothing from the other side. I knocked hard. "I'd like to order room service, please!"

There was no answer. I turned around, surveying the room more closely. Lena could fashion those coat hangers into something strong enough to smash the window. A couple of knotted sheets would let us go down one floor and break in through another window. If we were fast enough—and assuming nobody lost their grip and plummeted to their death—we might be able to pull it off. Especially if Lena sealed the door to slow pursuit.

The door opened before I could share my plan, which was probably for the best. Nicola Pallas stepped inside. She was alone and appeared unarmed, though in her case, appearances were deceptive as hell. Nicola could probably hum a tune and make me run headfirst into the window until it broke or I knocked myself unconscious, whichever came first.

She looked . . . twitchy was the best word I could find. Her hands were in constant motion, the fingers dancing to and fro. She shut the door and immediately began pacing the room, like she would collapse if she stopped moving. I couldn't tell whether her manic energy was from overstimulation and stress or simple overuse of magic, if not both.

She wore an unbuttoned denim shirt over a red turtleneck, with black corduroys. Her black hair was pulled into a short, fat ponytail. The lines by her eyes appeared deeper than the last time I had seen her.

"Are we prisoners?" Nidhi asked bluntly.

"Yes," said Nicola.

"For how long?" I pointed to Lena. "She's a dryad, remember? Keeping her away from her tree for too long could kill her. Or are you planning to transplant her oak to the apartment, too?"

"We considered it."

"Who is 'we'?" asked Lena.

She ignored the question. "Doctor Karim warned us that you wouldn't be able to let go. Not that I expected you to. But none of us knew how far you would go. Mahefa Issoufaly? That man is a known murderer."

Doctor Karim had been my therapist for that too-brief stretch when I worked as a Porter researcher. The last I had heard from her was when she stopped by my house to conduct a half-hour "exit interview" after Gutenberg stole my magic and kicked me out. "Then why haven't the Porters done something about him?"

"He's one of many individuals on our watch list, but we have other priorities as of late. Like bringing you in so we could protect you."

"And because you need to know what Gerbert d'Aurillac told me," I said.

"That's correct." Nicola sang as she spoke, a weird, wordless undertone that made me wonder if she had given herself a second set of vocal cords. "Do you know how to use the poem d'Aurillac shared with you?"

"You know I don't."

"Not consciously, no." She continued to sing. "I'm trying to help you, Isaac. To sharpen your thoughts and insights."

After being shot and dragged to Chicago, I wasn't in the mood to cooperate, but Nicola's song didn't give me much choice. The words flowed like water through a cracked dam. "From what I saw, he used it like some kind of portal. He put the armillary sphere—Meridiana's prison—inside, then burned the poem. Like sealing off a tunnel behind you. I'm hoping that if you rewrite the poem, you can use it to retrieve the sphere. I can't consciously remember all the details. The words just come to me when I write. I think he wanted me to recreate it." I studied my hands, remembering the rough brown paper with my careful lines and letters of blue ink. I spoke without thinking. "But his poem is wrong."

"Wrong how?" asked Nicola.

Where had that come from? I examined the memory of my effort, comparing it to the poem d'Aurillac had shared. Every letter matched as perfectly as was possible, given that I had used a ballpoint pen and a paper bag instead of a goose quill and parchment. But the tools shouldn't have mattered. This wasn't libriomancy, where perfect physical resonance would enhance the magic. "I'm not sure."

Her song changed to a minor key. "How much does Meridiana know?"

"That depends on what she plucked out of my brain before Ponce de Leon dropped me in his pocket." I caught Lena's expression and added, "I'll explain later."

"We've had little success pulling the memory of that poem from your mind," Nicola said. "Either it somehow defends itself against prying, or else d'Aurillac provided you with a form of mental armor to guard his secret."

"That's a neat trick, coming from someone who died a thousand years ago." I walked to the bookshelves to take a closer look at the titles. Most were hardcovers, ranging from brand-new releases to leather- and cloth-bound works that appeared at least a century old. "I take it Gutenberg is waiting outside?"

Nicola didn't answer.

"Half these books are in English, but the rest . . ." I dragged my finger along the lacquered edge of the shelf. "German, Spanish, Middle English, Japanese, Arabic,

Hebrew, and more. Even among the Porters, most of us can't read this many languages without magic."

"We have fourteen polyglots among the Porters," Nicola said.

"But how many of them would have a disproportionate interest in books from the late fifteenth and early sixteenth centuries?" I tapped the spines one by one. Whatever Nicola was doing to sharpen my mind, I was starting to enjoy it. "My parents were always listening to seventies music, because it's what they enjoyed as kids. These are the equivalent of Gutenberg's oldies station."

Nicola stopped singing. "He thought you'd be more likely to trust me rather than him, given the circumstances."

"You mean the fact that the last time he saw me, he gave me a magical lobotomy?"

"Yes." She opened the door and stepped into the hallway. "Come with me."

Nicola led us past a small kitchen to a hardwood-floored room where Johannes Gutenberg and Juan Ponce de Leon sat arguing over deep-dish pizza and imported German beer. My incomplete poem sat on the glass table in front of them, along with a stack of old books, all safely out of range of their meal. Both fell silent as we entered.

An old upright piano stood in the corner by two walls of floor-to-ceiling windows that looked out on the water. Gutenberg had sprung for a corner apartment. Nice.

More bookshelves filled the third wall. A wood-topped bar separated the kitchen from the living room. They'd converted the bar and part of the kitchen into something reminiscent of the Batcave, with oversized computer monitors hooked up to a series of keyboards and laptops. I could hear the computer fans humming from across the room.

"We need the rest of the poem," Gutenberg said without preamble. Ponce de Leon rolled his eyes.

"That's nice," I said. "I need my magic back."

"Told you so," Ponce de Leon murmured.

Gutenberg shot him an annoyed look. "Given your role in releasing Meridiana in the first place, Isaac, I would have thought you'd be eager to help."

"I've been *trying* to help. I'm the one who figured out who we're fighting, remember? I'm the one who went to chat with the dead pope."

Gutenberg started to respond, and then Ponce de Leon touched him gently on the forearm. Gutenberg sighed and sat back. "That's true enough," he conceded.

He looked and sounded . . . older, which I didn't think was possible. Gutenberg wasn't truly immortal, but he came as close as anyone. One of his first printed works had been an edition of the Latin Vulgate Bible, which he used to create a Holy Grail.

The Bible didn't explicitly reference the grail as providing eternal life, but by that point in time, belief in the grail legend had grown powerful. When Gutenberg reached into the pages and pulled out the chalice from the Last Supper, the faith and belief of those readers came with it. It was quite the trick, but Gutenberg had been bending the rules of libriomancy from day one.

The grail's magic was supposed to keep him young and healthy, but he had lost weight, and his eyes were shadowed. Thick, unkempt hair and a beard framed a narrow face with tired eyes that made me think of a cranky, burned-out schoolteacher.

"This is your place?" I asked.

"It's where I stay when I'm in the Midwest."

I walked to the low table and picked up what appeared to be a bound manuscript of an unpublished novel. "John Porter. Isn't that one of your aliases? You're ghost-writing fantasy novels now?" The answer clicked into place as soon as the words left my mouth. "You're putting weapons into production."

"We've had a number of stories prepared for quite some time," Gutenberg said. "They're updated as needed to keep the language and references fresh. We even have a trunk novel from H. G. Wells that we revised to meet our needs. The problem, as always, is one of timing. Publishing is anything but quick, and until we learn how Jeneta mastered e-books, self-publishing our texts electronically remains unfeasible."

I realized my mouth was hanging open. "Do you, um, happen to have a copy of that Wells novel here?"

"Priorities," Lena whispered.

Right. The end of the world took precedence over an unpublished H. G. Wells. Barely. "Nicola said we were prisoners."

"For your own safety," said Gutenberg.

Ponce de Leon's sigh conveyed volumes, as did Gutenberg's answering glare. They seemed capable of carrying on entire conversations without words.

"We need the sphere," Gutenberg continued. "As we've been unable to draw the details from your mind, you will remain here to complete Gerbert d'Aurillac's poem. Once you've done so, Juan and I will activate its magic and retrieve Meridiana's prison."

"What then?" asked Lena. "What's to stop Meridiana from breaking down your door and taking it away?"

Gutenberg leaned forward and pulled out three thick books. "The armillary sphere acts as a miniature world. Many religions have powerful stories about the end of the world. It's simply a matter of finding and unlocking the appropriate texts and applying them to Meridiana's prison. We will end her world, and her along with it." He gestured to the shelves. "I've brought reference books on Latin and medieval poetry, as well as works about d'Aurillac himself to help Isaac in his work."

"Restoring my magic would help more," I said.

Ponce de Leon's lips twitched in what might have been a smile.

"It's not that simple, Isaac. Even if I trusted you with your magic, it's far easier to remove someone's abilities than it is to restore them. Not to mention that my lock gives you an additional layer of protection against Meridiana."

"So it *is* possible to undo your lock," I pressed.

"You know perfectly well that it is," he snapped. I thought I saw him scowl in Nicola's direction, but it happened too quickly to be certain. "Given our current situation, are you suggesting I neglect the various magical crises breaking out across the world and devote my energies to returning the magic of a single overly reckless libriomancer?"

I said nothing.

"I know you, Isaac. Hate me if you wish, but you won't hold the fate of the world hostage for your own personal needs. You *will* work to complete Gerbert d'Aurillac's poem."

Rarely had I been so pissed about someone else being right.

RIO DE JANEIRO, BRAZIL—Authorities are reporting the discovery of a secret subbasement in the Royal Portuguese Reading Room, believed to be one of the Porter archives described in the "Bi Wei Revelation," a message that appeared as if by magic in a fantasy novel by American author George R. R. Martin.

The governor of Rio de Janeiro praised the efforts of Colonel Raimundo Azevedo, who organized the raid. Shaped explosives were used to open a passageway to the hidden basement. While the contents of the archive are still being catalogued, one source claims that it held more than a thousand books, mostly Portuguese titles. There are conflicting reports that at least one prisoner was escorted from the building following the raid.

The damage to the approximately 130-year-old library has created anger among the people of Brazil and throughout the world. Within minutes of the operation, images of shattered windows and smoke pouring from the Gothic-style building began circulating online.

The Royal Portuguese Reading Room holds more than 350,000 books, and has been described as one of the most breathtaking libraries in the world. Only authorized military personnel are currently being allowed in and out of the building, making it impossible to estimate the damage.

This is the first conclusive verification of the information provided in Bi Wei's letter to the world. Authorities have been quick to stress that this archive does *not* prove the existence of magic or any secret society . . .

Chapter 8

GUTENBERG'S CHICAGO APARTMENT was roughly the same size as Ponce de Leon's luxury hotel suite, but even if it had been twice as large, that wouldn't have been enough space to contain the stress and tension—not to mention the egos—stuck inside.

Nicola spent most of her time monitoring the computers and video chatting with various Regional Masters around the world. Her head and hands were usually moving in time to music playing through the wireless earbuds she wore at all times. As far as I could tell, she never switched them off; she simply lowered the volume a bit when she had to converse with others.

Gutenberg and Ponce de Leon acted like they couldn't decide whether they wanted to kiss or kill one another. One moment they were arguing over the future of the world, the next they were laughing about some obscure magical misadventure from three hundred years ago.

I had been given a large wooden drawing desk, which was set up uncomfortably close to the windows. So far, I'd sketched out more than half of the poem, though the words made no more sense than before. I jotted the translation onto a separate piece of paper as I went.

Nidhi pulled a folding chair over and sat down beside me. She skimmed over my notes. "This looks like the writing of an unmedicated schizophrenic."

"D'Aurillac wasn't crazy." I stared at the poem. "He might be making me crazy, though. Him and Gutenberg. I can't even use the phone to call Copper River." I hadn't spoken to Jennifer at the library since I left with Mahefa. I was so fired.

"Nicola says the Porters have assigned a second field agent to guard your house and Lena's oak. All of Gutenberg's automatons are awake and alert. If anything happens in Copper River . . ."

I twirled my pencil through my fingers. "Will that be enough? How many Porters has Meridiana killed? We know she's taken at least one of Bi Sheng's followers, too."

I spun the pencil again, then slid it behind my ear. I massaged my eyes and temples with my fingertips. "Meridiana doesn't even need to attack. Just drop a spy into the neighborhood and wait for us to return. She knows Lena has to go back to her oak."

"Not for a while," Lena said, strolling across the room. In one hand, she carried what looked like an ice cream float made of Neapolitan ice cream and Mountain Dew. "When Nidhi told me you had started a war with all vampkind, I figured we might be taking a vacation soon, so I took a few precautions."

Lena's grin was almost smug. I glanced at Nidhi, who shrugged.

"Another graft?" I hadn't seen her carrying a branch from her oak, but I had been knocked unconscious before getting into Nidhi's car, so who knew what they had packed in the trunk.

"Not exactly." Lena sipped her float, licked foam from her upper lip, then extended her left hand toward us.

A blister bulged along the length of her palm like a swollen tendon. A long sliver darkened the skin. It stretched, tenting almost a centimeter before a slender spike of wood punched through.

There was no blood. Clear fluid coated the bark, giving it a dark shine. The twig grew faster now, stretching upward and thickening until it was roughly the size of a chopstick. Delicate green buds uncurled into tiny oak leaves.

I reached for her arm, then hesitated. She nodded permission, and I gently probed the skin of her forearm, feeling the hard bulge of the wood. I traced it back to the elbow, where it seemed to merge into the bone and joint. I imagined roots stretching through her arm, twining with her veins, digging into the muscle fibers. "You're carrying a graft inside of you?"

"Grafts, plural." She turned her hand to admire the leaves. "My tree is my flesh. It contains me. Why can't I do the same for it? Do you remember when I smuggled a wooden knife in my arm?"

"Yah." I touched the skin where the branch emerged from her hand. It gave slightly, sliding around the wood.

She smiled and touched the leaves. "This is easier. More natural."

"How much do you have?" asked Nidhi. "How long can it survive inside of you?"

"The wood doesn't do as well without sunlight, but it's thrived for two days so far. It helps when I'm able to get outside and spread my leaves, so to speak." She flexed her hand, and the leaves turned brown. The wood slowly shrank back into her skin. "The thickest segment is near my spine, with thinner, softer branches stretching along my limbs."

"I would love to see an X-ray of that," I whispered.

Nidhi touched Lena's palm. "Does this mean you no longer need your oak?"

"No. I'll need to go back eventually. This body isn't big enough to fully contain that part of me. But I'll have more freedom to wander. The idea seemed insane at first, but I've grown to appreciate a little insanity from time to time." She winked at me.

The tip of the branch disappeared, leaving only a trio of dried leaves that had broken from the branch. A tiny pearl of blood welled from the cut in her skin.

"Please don't do that again." Gutenberg clutched an electronic cigarette between two fingers. The light in the end glowed a soft, steady blue. "This place is as secure as I can make it, but we're keeping magic use to a minimum."

"Save it for the necessities," I said. "Like prying into our memories?"

"Yes."

Lena broke in before I could pursue that argument. "If we're stuck here, could someone bring in a grow light? I'm not used to spending so much time inside with incandescents and fluorescents. It's like trying to live on a diet of plain toast and tepid water."

"Nicola should be able to arrange—" He scowled and spun away, tapping a Bluetooth earpiece. "I don't care what the Brazilian authorities are saying, you need to get her out of there." He paused. "Absolutely not. Humans only. Babs can send reinforcements if you need, but I'm not risking a single photo getting out that could be used to suggest Porters are in league with monsters."

"Monsters?" Lena said softly.

Gutenberg didn't notice. He finished his conversation, jabbed the earpiece, and turned back to us. "I'll talk to Nicola about your lights, but in the meantime, no magic. For similar reasons, the phone won't work unless Nicola or I key in an access code. Your cell phones have been disabled and the batteries removed. The Internet is likewise off limits. Meals and supplies will be delivered to the apartment as needed. The windows are reflective from outside, so you can sightsee to your heart's content so long as you stay within this apartment. Until we have Meridiana, none of you are leaving."

I started to ask if we'd be issued orange prison jumpsuits, but the gentle pressure of Lena's hand on the center of my back calmed me enough to hold my tongue.

"We know," said Lena. "Nicola already explained the rules."

"My phone was a cracked brick anyway," I added.

"Yes, I repaired that for you. You'll need it if we're forced to evacuate." Gutenberg turned toward the window and took a long drag from his cigarette. When he spoke next, he was *almost* apologetic. "Meridiana has declared war on my people. I'm trying to protect you."

I sat back. "I thought I stopped being your people when you kicked me out of the Porters."

"I can understand why you would think that." He still hadn't turned to face me. "This isn't exactly falling out the way I had hoped."

"How bad is it?" I asked.

"That depends on what the followers of Bi Sheng do next." He glanced over his shoulder, but said nothing about my choice to allow Bi Wei and the others to escape. "Their letter to the world was probably the most helpful gift they could have given Meridiana, forcing the Porters to split our attention, to react instead of act. If they continue to aid her—"

"They're not trying to help Meridiana," I protested.

Gutenberg turned his full attention on me, making it feel like the gravity had just doubled. "You know this for a fact? I know you consider Bi Wei an ally, but even if you're right about her, can you be certain about her compatriots?"

"Bi Wei and her friends were terrified of the Porters," Nidhi said. "They're refugees from a battle they fought and lost five hundred years ago. You're their bogeyman. That letter forced you to prioritize, to devote your people to other crises instead of searching for them. For now, as long as they don't feel threatened by you, I doubt they'll do anything that might draw your attention."

"Maybe." Gutenberg brought the cigarette to his mouth, inhaled, then scowled at the glowing blue tip. "But the sooner Isaac can figure out that poem, the better off we'll all be. Doctor Shah, I'd appreciate it if you could work with Nicola. Look over her shoulder at the reports from the field. Anyone showing the slightest hint of instability needs to be pulled out immediately. Lena, would you please join Juan and me in the other room?"

"What for?" she asked warily.

"As we manage the various revelations taking place throughout the world, the existence of magical beings will become known. There's no avoiding that now. Your perspective would be helpful."

Lena didn't answer right away. Given Gutenberg's long prohibition against nonhumans joining the Porters, I suspected "Juan" had been the one pushing for Lena's participation.

She raised her glass. "All right. But I'm going to need a refill."

I was up past midnight, but I had filled in everything save the central circle and inner cross of the poem. When I collapsed on the sofa, visions of Latin swirled through my dreams.

Sunlight woke me at what my body instinctively recognized as a ridiculously early hour. Gutenberg was standing in front of the windows, arguing with someone on his phone in what sounded like Swahili. I groaned and pulled the throw pillow over my face while he finished his call. His footsteps approached, stopping at the end of the couch.

"Isaac, good, I had something I wanted you to see."

"Isaac's not here right now," I said through the pillow. "He's home in Copper River having a nightmare, probably brought on by bad Cudighi. Leave a message, and he'll get back to you as soon as he wakes up."

I waited on the off chance that reality might respond to my wishful thinking, then sat up and tossed the pillow aside. Fatigue vanished when I spotted the book Gutenberg had set on the coffee table. Large, bound in brown leather, with vellum pages. "What's that?"

"*Selected Writings on the Mind of God*. By Gerbert d'Aurillac." He sat down and opened the front cover. "Mostly mathematics and magic, with a smattering of astronomy and music."

I hardly dared to breathe. "How old is this?"

Gutenberg smiled, one of the first times I had seen such an unshielded expression on his face. It made him appear almost human. "It's an original manuscript, penned mostly by d'Aurillac himself. From my private library."

I stared at the pages, imagining Gerbert at his writing desk, dipping a sharpened quill into his inkpot to trace each letter. He would have left blank spaces for the lines of red text that denoted the word of God, and for the larger, decorated drop caps. Sketched constellations filled the margins, along with bisected circles that could have been exercises in geometry or an attempt to map the orbit of the moon. "You just happened to have this sitting around?"

"It was back home in Mainz. I had it delivered last night." He sat back, clearly enjoying my appreciation. In that moment, he wasn't the master of the Porters, nor was he the man who had stolen my magic. He was simply a book collector showing off one of his prizes. "I've had a long time to accumulate old tomes. I've got an early draft of *Frankenstein* you should read someday. Shelley's original ending changes the entire message of the story."

"Why are you sharing this with me?"

"Because I knew what it would mean to you to see it. And because I hoped it might provide additional insight into d'Aurillac's mind. He says nothing of Meridiana or her prison, but he does discuss the structure of magical spells, along with certain principles he learned from an Arabic master." He grabbed a spiral-bound document and set it alongside the book. "I also printed out one of d'Aurillac's known puzzle poems and its solution. He prepared this one as a gift to Anna's father, Otto II. The structure is simpler, and I don't believe there's anything magical about it, but it should help."

"Thank you." Whatever his intentions, the presence of the thousand-year-old book had burned through my fatigue, leaving eagerness and excitement in its wake. I brought the book and printout to my writing desk and sat down to study Gerbert d'Aurillac's poem to Otto II, comparing it to my own notes. This was simpler, yes, but both poems shared some of the same basic structure.

The first page of the solution looked like a word search, only instead of straight lines, the words were hidden in the shapes of Arabic numerals and Greek letters. "'From Gerbert to Otto,'" I read, tracing the loops of a Celtic knot. The puzzle used the letters of Otto's name just as the poem in my mind used Anna's. Each of those letters marked the beginning of a line of text to be stacked one atop the next, creating the grid for the word search.

"Breakfast should be here in an hour," Gutenberg said. "If you and your companions have any preferences . . ."

I shooed him away and turned the page, then snatched up my pencil and began to write.

According to the notes Gutenberg had provided, Gerbert d'Aurillac's original poem to Otto II would have come with thirty-two pages of instructions.

The poem d'Aurillac had planted in my head came with a total of zero.

Once the raw poem was complete, I copied out each line of text to create the word search grid, starting each line with the larger letters from Anna's name. But how to arrange them? Did I work from the inside out or vice versa? Clockwise or counterclockwise? The various As and Ns broke the poem into a total of twenty-six segments, most of which had two or three lines of text. With sixty-four lines in total, there were too many possibilities to simply guess.

I tried following the pattern used to translate Otto II's poem, but after three hours of rearranging and staring, I had yet to find a single hidden word or phrase.

I cut each line onto its own strip of graph paper, which kept the letters evenly spaced and allowed me to move them about. In order to search for word shapes, I borrowed one of Nicola's computers to scan, enlarge, and print the "answer key" to d'Aurillac's older poem. Squares of clear plastic cut from a large freezer bag, plus a black permanent marker, let me trace templates of the shapes from that poem. But no matter how I slid them around, I found nothing in his poem for Anna.

Either the shapes were wrong, or else I hadn't found the proper sequence for putting the text together. I considered asking Gutenberg if he could yank a magic codebreaker out of a book, but if it was that simple, I'm sure he would have done it by now.

Gutenberg and Ponce de Leon crossed the room, heading for Nicola and the computers. Gutenberg was talking sharply into his phone. "Tell Mohamed an automaton will be there in two minutes. He needs to— No, that's what Meridiana wants. Karim is already dead. If he tries to rescue the body, she'll take him, too." He peered over Nicola's shoulder at one of the screens and muttered to himself what sounded like a Middle High German curse. "If Mohamed so much as cracks a book before the automaton arrives, you take him down yourself, understand?"

"Won't work," said Ponce de Leon. "Mohamed and Karim were siblings, and he's too skilled a fighter. Tell her to throw up a sandstorm if she can. It will hold him back and buy them time."

"A sandstorm against a kishi?" Gutenberg snapped. "The damned thing has two faces. Blind the human face, and the hyena will track them by scent."

"Mohamed . . . isn't he the one who likes to use the *Guinness Book of Records*?"

Gutenberg nodded.

Ponce de Leon grinned. "Trinidad Scorpion Pepper."

"Ha!" Gutenberg spun away. "Tell Mohamed to rip open his *Guinness* and hit that thing with the essence of the Trinidad Scorpion Pepper. Whatever you do, make sure the wind is blowing *away* from you both."

I found myself holding my breath along with them and counting the seconds. How long had it been since Gutenberg sent the automaton?

"Good." Gutenberg stepped back and ran a finger through his hair. "Now get the hell out of there."

Ponce de Leon clapped Gutenberg's back. Gutenberg waited a moment longer, then ended the call.

"Meridiana?" asked Nicola.

"She's hunting us like animals." Gutenberg fumbled his electronic cigarette out of his pocket. "She captured Karim, allowed her ghosts to seize control of the body, and used it as bait. I'm sending Barbara Palmer down there to clean up the mess. Mohamed needs a firm hand to keep him from doing anything stupid, and it will get Babs off my back."

Babs was a Regional Master from down south. Other Porters called her the "Tex-Mex Libriomancer," but never to her face. I didn't know her background, but if she was giving Gutenberg a hard time, I liked her.

"If Meridiana is chasing random Porters, it means she hasn't found our location yet," Ponce de Leon pointed out.

"So instead she's taunting us," Gutenberg snapped. "Showing the Porters I can't protect them. Pushing them until they burn themselves out trying to fight her with magic, and once that happens, she crawls into their thoughts and seizes control."

"You can't fight every battle yourself," Ponce de Leon said.

Gutenberg shrugged him off. "Meridiana's ghosts unravel our magic faster than we can create it. Unless we find a better means to fight her, she'll continue to eliminate us one by one."

"You saved two lives today."

"And I lost a third." Gutenberg flung his electronic cigarette at the window so hard I was amazed it didn't break.

"How long has it been since you slept?" Nidhi yawned as she entered the living room. Lena followed behind her.

"Years," snapped Gutenberg. "Not since Nancy Kress released *Beggars in Spain*. I don't have time to sleep. You'd think immortality would give you more time to accomplish things. Instead, every year lengthens the list of what must be done, and time slips past ever faster." He strode over to retrieve his cigarette. "My apologies. Did we wake you?"

"Yes." Nidhi walked up to Gutenberg and poked him in the chest. "You're still human. More or less. Maybe your body doesn't need to sleep, but your mind needs a break. Go watch a movie. Read a book. Play Monopoly. Nicola will let you know if there's another emergency."

He played with his beard, twisting it into a point. "I complain of having too little time, and your advice is to play Monopoly?"

"When was the last time you checked in with your therapist?" Nidhi asked.

Gutenberg frowned. "The network connection isn't secure enough, and the bandwidth—"

"I didn't ask for excuses, I asked how long?"

He blinked, and his lips quirked upward. "Two months," he admitted. "Maybe three."

Porter gossip suggested Gutenberg's therapist was a 130-year-old woman whose mind had been transferred to a computer system in the late seventies. Gutenberg's comments about connectivity suggested there might be truth to the story. I would have loved to learn how that had all come about.

"That's the reason I'm here, right?" Nidhi circled around the bar and dug through the fridge. She surfaced with a small bottle of orange juice. "To protect me and prevent me from being used against Lena and Isaac, sure. But also because you know you need someone keeping an eye on your mental health. You've always known."

Ponce de Leon looked back and forth between them, as if he were appreciating a particularly exciting game of ping pong.

"It is my *professional* opinion that you are physically, mentally, and emotionally exhausted," Nidhi continued. "If you don't take a break, you're going to get your people killed."

Gutenberg retrieved his cigarette from the floor and sighed. "Damned therapists," he muttered. "One hour. That's all I can give you."

"One hour?" Ponce de Leon pulled a deck of cards from his suit pocket. "That should give me plenty of time to trounce you in Noddy."

"I'm not playing with any deck you've had your hands on," Gutenberg said sharply.

"You didn't seem to object when I— Oh, I'm sorry. Did you say *deck?*" He limped into the hallway, cutting the cards one-handed as he walked. Gutenberg shook his head, but followed.

I coughed to hide my laughter. On a whim, I turned back to my work and tried searching for patterns of letters that would correspond to the pips on various playing cards. I did find the word "muria," which meant *to pickle*, but I was pretty sure that was just coincidence.

Lena had brought Smudge out with her. She grabbed a banana and offered him a chunk, but he refused. With a shrug, she popped the piece into her mouth and came over to study my work. She stopped several feet from the table. Smudge was calm for the moment, but neither of us were about to risk him getting close to a thousand-year-old book.

"It's still wrong," I said.

"Everyone makes mistakes."

"That's not it. I wrote the poem exactly as he did, and it was right when he used it. But it's not anymore."

"Maybe *you* need to take an hour to play a little naughty," she said.

"Noddy, not naughty. It was an early version of cribbage from the sixteenth cent—oh."

She chuckled sadly. "What are we going to do with you?" Before I could respond, her eyes fell upon an antique-looking floor lamp that hadn't been there the day before. A post-it note with Lena's name on it was stuck to the stained glass hood.

She dragged a chair over, turned on the lamp, and stretched like a cat in a sunbeam. "Mm. We are definitely getting one of these at your house. And another for Nidhi's apartment."

I pulled my attention back to my crumbled and discarded notes. What was I missing?

"Do you think the poem is somehow keyed to the user?" asked Lena.

"I thought about that. I searched for permutations of Gerbert d'Aurillac and Sylvester, thinking maybe the letters of his name were the answer, and I'd have to rewrite the poem with my own name. I couldn't find anything."

"It's a shame you don't want a lover who's smarter than you."

"What?" I stared at her. Her expression was unreadable.

"I'm what my lovers make me, remember? If you fantasized about being with a super-genius, I might be able to see something you'd missed." She smiled, but it didn't reach her eyes. "It's all right. Being with you and with Nidhi, this is the smartest I've ever been, and I'm grateful for that."

I rubbed my eyes. "I'm sorry. You deserve more."

"I know." This time her smile was genuine. "We all have limitations, and you can't help your insecurities."

"I'm not—"

She laughed. "I'm satisfied with who I am and what I have. At least for the moment."

"What about the future?"

"You mean after you and Nidhi get old and gray and wrinkly and die peacefully in your sleep at the age of a hundred and eleven? I plan to find a kind, brilliant, passionate Michelle Rodriguez lookalike and live a life of shameless, hedonistic luxury."

"Good to know you've thought this through."

She shifted Smudge to her other shoulder and leaned back in her chair. "Just thinking about Rodriguez in that *Resident Evil* film . . ." She shivered. "If you're not careful, I might have to physically drag you away from those books."

"If you could find the answers in this thing, I'd take you right here."

"On the table?" she asked playfully. "Gutenberg wouldn't be happy if anything happened to his antique book."

"Fine, we could move to the couch."

She walked over and studied the poem. For a moment I thought she had been setting me up, that she was about to point out some pattern I had missed. Instead, she pursed her lips and shook her head. "Sorry. I guess I'll have to somehow make it through the day without your manly touch. Alas and woe."

"Laying it on a little thick, eh?"

She grinned. "Just trying to cope with my disappointment. The pain may force me to seek solace in the arms of another woman."

I didn't respond right away.

"I'm sorry," said Lena. "That wasn't—"

"It's all right." I wasn't sure I would ever be one hundred percent comfortable with my girlfriend having a girlfriend of her own, but they say with time you can adjust to anything. Nidhi had described us as family, and in a way, she was right. I certainly spent more time with the two of them than I did my brother or my parents, and the things we had seen and survived created a powerful sense of connection. This might not be the family I had imagined building when I was younger, but when had the universe ever listened to my plans?

Nidhi and I would never be in love with one another. On the other hand, she was a friend and a good person, and I had gotten used to her being a part of my life.

"Tell you what." Lena circled around behind me and kissed my ear. "You solve this thing, and then we'll celebrate together."

The erotic tingles racing down my neck were squashed a second later when Smudge decided Lena had bent down for his convenience, allowing him to jump from her shoulder to the top of my head. Spider feet tickling my scalp turned out to be a powerful mood-killer. I yelped and tried not to make any sudden moves that might cost me my hair.

Lena laughed and lured him away with an M&M. "Gerbert d'Aurillac designed this so people could retrieve the sphere if they needed to. He *wanted* you to figure it out." She kissed me again, then pulled away before Smudge could return. "Let me know when you do."

This is a photo of my nine-year-old daughter Klara.

Three days ago, she was in the ICU waiting for the tumors that had colonized her body to finish killing her.

Today we brought her home.

The doctors can't or won't explain how a terminal patient, a little girl who spent the majority of her young life fighting a losing battle with cancer, could overnight become the model of health. I'm terrified this is a dream, that I'll wake up tomorrow morning and be back in that hell, listening to my princess struggle to breathe.

Klara says the night she got better, she woke up to see a teacher standing over her. Her mother and I asked why she thought it was a teacher. She told us, "Because she had lots of books, and she smelled like coffee."

Whoever it was, she gave Klara a drink of something sweet. Something that "tasted like magic honey."

The next morning, Klara was literally bouncing in her hospital bed.

Go ahead. Tell me it wasn't a miracle. Tell me how else but magic the tumors that riddled her body could literally vanish overnight.

A week ago, I lived in a world where I had to watch my dying child fade one day at a time. Today, I live in a world where Klara won't stop pestering us to go to Disney World in the United States so she can get Peter Pan's autograph.

Klara's magic teacher healed two other children that night. The best medical care in the country had failed our angels. Magic saved them.

There are no words for the relief, or for the terror that it will somehow be yanked away. I prayed for so long, bargained with God and screamed at him, offered my life for hers. I've broken down crying ten times a day since Klara got better.

Most of the time, they're tears of joy. Other times . . .

When your child is seriously ill, you get to know other families struggling through the same thing. You share their triumphs, and you mourn with them when their child finally escapes the pain. When they earn their wings, as one mother described it.

Where was the magic for those children? How many of them could have been saved? Why were we blessed when so many other parents had to bury their little ones?

I don't have the answers, and the questions haunt me every night. But tonight we watched Klara devour an ice cream sundae the size of her head, watched her run through the house like a miniature tornado in Reksio pajamas, and finally tucked her in to her own bed.

I don't understand. I don't know who Klara's magical teacher was, or whether she'll ever see this note. But whoever you were, thank you from the bottom of our hearts.

Chapter 9

G UTENBERG SET A STACK of books on the coffee table and settled down on the sofa with the topmost book. Grateful for the excuse, I abandoned my ever-growing hill of notes to see what he was reading. Though "reading" wasn't precisely correct, given that Gutenberg didn't bother to open the books, let alone look at the text inside. He simply held each one, stared at it for several seconds to absorb the contents, and set it aside.

Learning how he did that was high on my To Do List if I ever got my magic back.

I picked up the book he had just discarded and turned it over, skimming the summary on the back cover. "You never struck me as a Nora Roberts fan."

"I prefer Jude Deveraux for romance," he said. "In this case, however, Miss Roberts had the better preorder numbers, meaning a stronger pool of reader belief."

There was no particular theme to the books, save that all were brand-new, and all were by popular authors. I spotted two thrillers, three more romance novels, a fantasy, a tell-all, and a political memoir. I snatched up the fantasy. "I didn't think Simon Green's new one was coming out until next month."

"We manipulated the release schedule." Gutenberg scowled and tossed another book onto the table. "The official publication date isn't for another week and a half. We arranged to delay printing of the 'corrected' versions as long as possible in order to minimize the chances of anyone noticing our changes and pulling them from production."

"What was corrected?" I asked.

He pointed to the Green. "Chapter nine now introduces a magic wristwatch that allows line-of-sight teleportation. Patterson's novel includes a thumb drive with a program that hacks into every camera in the world—cell phones, satellites, streetlights, security feeds—to locate and track a particular individual. Roberts' book is set out west. In chapter three, we added an old six-shooter that supposedly belonged to Billy the Kid. According to legend, the gun always hits its target dead center in the heart, no matter how far away." For a moment, he almost looked embarrassed. "As this is supposed to be a romance novel, I tried to write it as a metaphor for love, a kind of Old West version of Cupid's arrow."

I stared. "*You* wrote these books?"

"Only some of them, and only the extra scenes." He opened one and touched the first page of the prologue. "None of which do us a damned bit of good until people read the bloody things."

"Tell him about the Rowling," said Ponce de Leon. He and Lena were darting to and fro by the window, bokken and cane clacking together as they fenced. His bad leg didn't slow him down much. His technique was far more precise than Lena's, but her strength and endless energy was balancing that out.

"You have a new book by J. K. Rowling?" I scanned the pile.

He pulled out an oversized hardcover. "*Harry Potter and the Goblin's Scepter.*"

I stared open-mouthed and fought the urge to snatch the book from his hands and barricade myself in the bedroom for the rest of the day. "No. Fucking. Way."

"I'm afraid not. Several years ago, we enlisted a popular fanfiction author to pen a plausible eighth book in Rowling's universe. We needed something that would guarantee instant, worldwide readership."

A new Harry Potter would certainly do that. "When is it coming out?"

"In two days. There will be an immediate backlash, of course. I expect the lawsuits and the negative publicity may utterly destroy a good publishing house. I have eight people working full-time to keep the book's release a secret, even from the printers and publishing staff. Nobody should know anything until the book arrives simultaneously in bookstores throughout the world. The stores will be confused, naturally. Some will contact the publisher for clarification, but once they realize what they have, most will begin selling, unwilling to delay and risk losing out to their competitors."

A sharp, triumphant cry pulled my attention to Lena, who had driven Ponce de Leon into the corner where the bookshelves met the windows. She jabbed her bokken at his leg.

He slapped her weapon aside with his cane while reaching with his other hand to grab a book from the shelf. He flung the book toward her face.

Lena lowered her head, taking the impact on her brow, but it distracted her long enough for him to tag her thigh with the tip of his cane.

Gutenberg coughed. "If you two idiots want to bash each other's brains out, fine. But I'll thank you to leave my books out of it."

Ponce de Leon backed away and mopped his brow

with his sleeve. "I believe that's one point to me," he said calmly. To Gutenberg, he added, "They deserve the whole truth, Johannes."

The Porters were using other authors' work to create tools and weapons for their war against Meridiana. To forge a Rowling book suggested they needed something stronger, something that required the belief of millions. "What does the Goblin's Scepter do?"

"It's a last resort," Gutenberg said wearily. "In the story, the goblins of Rowling's universe design a doomsday weapon for use against the wizarding world. One with the power to end magic."

Lena shoved her bokken through her belt. Nidhi lowered the e-book reader she had curled up with. Even Nicola turned away from her computers.

"What do you mean 'end magic'?" I asked softly.

Gutenberg pointed to my forehead. "What was done to you would be done to the world. It would be irreversible, and it would put an end to the threat Meridiana and the Ghost Army present."

When I recovered enough to speak, I could only whisper. "You're insane."

He took the book from my hand. "Was Hamlet mad, or merely desperate? I won't use the scepter until all other options fail. I'm not keen on the idea of ending my own immortality. But Meridiana could destroy this world, Isaac. If we eliminate magic, we eliminate her power. The mere threat of this weapon may be enough to persuade her to surrender."

"What happens to Lena if you use that thing?" I asked. "To Smudge?"

"That's a fascinating question." Ponce de Leon leaned more heavily than usual on his cane as he joined us. Sparring with Lena had winded him. "Where's the line between natural and supernatural? My body is healthy flesh and blood, which suggests I could live another sixty years without magic, assuming good diet and exercise. But what of your average vampire? What traits are bound to their flesh and blood, and what relies on magic? The truth is, we don't know."

"I never imagined myself saying this, but I vote we continue on in ignorance." I couldn't conceive of how such a spell would operate, let alone the impact it would have. The power required would likely destroy whoever tried to cast the spell. "You can't know what kind of impact that would have on the world. Twenty-six years ago, a Porter researcher theorized that sentience itself was an evolutionary adaptation to magic. It was a crackpot theory, but if there was any truth to it—if intelligence and consciousness are dependent in any way on magic—"

"None of us can foresee the consequences of such a step." Ponce de Leon ran his fingers through his hair, smoothing it back into place. "Though after centuries of watching mankind, I sometimes suspect intelligence is overrated."

Gutenberg returned the last of the books to the table. "As the truth emerges, bookstores and publishers will pulp their remaining stock of our altered titles. Their power will wane. We have only a limited window during which this option will be open to us."

Ponce de Leon cleared his throat. "I believe that's his not-so-subtle way of telling you to get back to work, Isaac."

"Yah, I got that, thanks." Like I hadn't been under enough pressure already.

I paced the length of the bookshelves, shoving another bite of cinnamon raisin bagel into my mouth without tasting it. Nidhi had insisted I stop and eat something. I was finishing up the last few bites when it hit me.

"Two-dimensional thinking!"

My exclamation was loud enough to make Nicola jump. She turned from her computers, searching the room for whatever had made me cry out.

"Sorry." I held up my hands. "It's a line from *Star Trek II*. Spock points out that Khan's pattern 'indicates two-dimensional thinking.'"

Nicola frowned. "I don't understand."

"I've been thinking like a twenty-first-century librarian. Gerbert d'Aurillac was brilliant, but he was also a product of his age. He lived in a time when Arabic numerals were the hot new thing in Europe, and the zero hadn't caught on."

I swallowed the last of the bagel and returned to my desk. D'Aurillac had been fluent in multiple languages, but he had written his poem in Latin, the language of the church. He would have wanted it to be understood by another educated man. Back then, that meant someone familiar with Latin, along with the trivium—grammar, logic, and rhetoric—and the more advanced quadrivium—arithmetic, geometry, music, and astronomy. He would also have assumed that whoever found his poem would have a grounding in magical theory.

I stared at the poem until my vision blurred. I tried to focus not on words, but shape. Geometry and mathematics. Circles and angles and spokes. Seven spokes. That was a deliberate choice. Every stroke of the pen had been drawn for a reason. Seven . . . seven days of creation in the Old Testament. Seven musical notes in a scale. Seven deadly sins.

On a whim, I searched for "septem," the Latin word for seven. In order to help me find potential words, I had jotted down a table showing the frequency with which each letter appeared in the poem. The P was the least-used letter in the word septem, so I scanned for Ps, looking for anywhere they connected to E and T.

I didn't notice Ponce de Leon approaching until he sat down across from me.

"The last time, it was a lost book of the Bible," he said quietly.

Letters crawled across my vision like tiny insects. I blinked and sat back, mentally marking my place in the word puzzle. "Huh?"

"The atomic bomb terrified him." He turned to watch Gutenberg, who had emerged to check one of the computer screens. "The Cold War was before your time. You didn't live through the fear. What could magic do against the power that had devastated Hiroshima and Nagasaki? For years, we watched the sky and waited for the scream of the sirens that would herald the end of everything.

"So Gutenberg prepared his lost book. He knew some would accept it at face value while others denounced it as a forgery, but they would all read the alleged prophecies of Christ. Their belief and imagination would fuel those prophecies. Including one in which 'the sword of the archangel Michael, commander of God's armies, shall lay waste to the wicked and their tools of destruction. The angelic blade shall rip the sky asunder and rain brimstone upon those who would wage war.'"

Most swords fit easily through the pages of a book. "He wanted to create a superweapon."

"A *preemptive* superweapon. In order for his plan to work, Johannes had to strike first. He couldn't watch over the entire Earth, nor could he sit back and wait for the first missiles to launch. We didn't have satellite television or instant social media updates back then. By the time we learned of a nuclear launch, it would be too late to save the world."

"This is what you were talking about in Rome," I said quietly. "The split between you and Gutenberg."

"What gives any of us the right to play God over humanity? To judge and punish?"

I thought about the phrasing of Gutenberg's Biblical prophecy. "What counts as 'those who would wage war'?"

"Exactly." Ponce de Leon nodded slowly. "Had Johannes gone through with his plan, he would have eliminated the world's nuclear stockpile, but slaughtered half the globe in the process. The power of such magic would have certainly killed him as well. We fought for so long over that book. Over his need for control and his lack of faith."

"You stopped him."

"I did." He didn't elaborate. He didn't have to. The haunted emptiness in those two words conveyed how much his actions had cost him. "But this time is different. Even if I wished to do so again, Johannes will have taken steps to prevent me."

"Maybe he's right," I said.

Both black eyebrows rose. "Not a sentiment I expected to hear from you, Isaac. If you're considering the end of magic to be a good thing, perhaps Doctor Shah was right about your depression."

I scowled. "Look at how many people Meridiana has corrupted or killed using magic."

"That has nothing to do with magic and everything to do with the nature of man. Or woman, in this case. Eliminate magic, and perhaps you stop this threat. What of the next?" He reached past me to pick up a crumpled sketch I had done. "What's this?"

I had to stop myself from trying to snatch it away. My cheeks burned. "It started as a picture of the poem's geometry . . . but then I got frustrated and turned it into a plan for a tiny steam-powered airship for Smudge. He'd provide the heat for a tiny, fireproof dirigible, and there would be eight little straps he could use to steer." I had even drawn tiny goggles over his eyes.

An odd smile played over Ponce de Leon's mouth. Slowly and carefully, he smoothed out the picture, as if it

was a lost Van Gogh rather than a silly pencil sketch.
"*This* is where magic is born. No matter what happens,
nobody can take that from you." He returned the drawing to me and stood. "On that note, I should leave you to
your work."

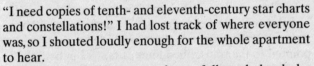

"I need copies of tenth- and eleventh-century star charts
and constellations!" I had lost track of where everyone
was, so I shouted loudly enough for the whole apartment
to hear.

Lena was the first to reach me, followed closely by
Nicola and Gutenberg.

"You have something?" Gutenberg asked.

"Maybe." I jabbed a finger at the poem. "The triangle
is the outermost shape. That's the number three, the trin-
ity. At first I thought it was symbolic, a way of suggesting
that God contains all things, only that's not what d'Aurillac was getting at. It's a matter of perspective. Two-
dimensional thinking. God isn't surrounding the poem.
He's *above it.*"

They simply stared. Nidhi had come up behind Lena,
and I heard Ponce de Leon limping toward me from the
bedroom. None of them understood.

"D'Aurillac created this poem to house his celestial
sphere." I grabbed another piece of paper and drew a
quick set of intersecting ovals. "This is how we'd illus-
trate a sphere today to show it as a three-dimensional
shape, but most artwork from his time didn't use forced
perspective the way we do. This poem *is* the sphere. This
central circle is the Earth. The seven spokes connect us
to the sun, the moon, and the five planets."

I pointed triumphantly. "Look where the top spoke
connects to the outer ring. There's the large A for Anna.
To the left is the word *fortuna*, which means fortune. To

the right, *lucis*, or daylight. Combine the last and first two letters of those two words, and you get *Luna*, the Latin name for Selene, the goddess of the moon."

"But the two pieces of the word are on the wrong side," said Nidhi. "That would make 'nalu,' not Luna."

"Exactly!" I beamed as I drew a faint loop from the end of fortuna to the beginning of lucis. "It's not enough to simply connect the two parts. The letters have to circle around the A. Just as the moon orbits round the Earth."

I slammed the pencil down. "The heavens are all here, just as Gerbert crafted them. All except the stars." I pointed to the transcribed lines of text. "I'm betting the constellations will unlock his message. I need illustrations by Ptolemy and al-Sufi, and for that I need access to either a library or the Internet."

"It's not safe for you to leave," said Nicola. "Meridiana is searching for you. As are several teams of vampires, if our intelligence is correct."

"Great. Internet it is."

Gutenberg left without a word. He returned carrying an old brick of a laptop. "Nicola?"

She ran a network cable from behind the bar to the laptop, then sat down and began typing. "I'm routing him through the same proxy servers and firewalls we're using on the main system."

Ten minutes later, I was downloading excerpts and images of *The Book of Constellations of the Fixed Stars*, by Abd al-Rahman al-Sufi. I had no idea whether Gerbert d'Aurillac had been familiar with his work, but al-Sufi was a tenth-century astronomer, so his illustrations should be similar to what d'Aurillac had used and observed. There was only one problem with the pages filling the screen. "Does anyone here read Persian? I can't—wait, never mind."

I clicked on the thumbnail view option and skimmed through the pages, searching for illustrations.

"Big, smart librarian, and all he wants to do is look at the pictures," Lena murmured.

I enlarged a page with a chart and picture of Ursa Minor. "Printer?"

"Behind the bar," said Nicola.

I printed the first of al-Sufi's constellations and clicked to the next. The scale wouldn't necessarily match my grid of nonsense words, but the stars and lines would show me what patterns to search for. Depending on how obsessive d'Aurillac had been about accuracy—and given what I had seen so far, I wasn't about to underestimate him—finding one constellation should give me a relative idea of the size and positions for the rest.

Ursa Major, Draco, Cepheus, Boötes, Hercules. I sent them all to the printer, then hurried to the bar, unwilling to wait. I grabbed the finished pages and brought them back as the printer continued to spit forth illustrations.

I started with the circumpolar constellations, those that would have been visible year-round from the northern hemisphere. Ursa Major was the most memorable. I traced circles onto clear plastic to use as a template, then attacked the text. Holding the template at varying heights allowed me to expand or shrink the scale.

"How do you know which way is 'up'?" asked Lena.

"It would depend on the season. Logically, the pole star should be in the center of the map, which means Ursa Major would rotate around that fixed point." I scooted my chair back and stood, slowly circling the table to examine the text from different angles. I bumped into someone and muttered an apology without looking up.

"Shall we leave Isaac alone to finish transcribing the universe?" Amusement colored Ponce de Leon's words.

I barely noticed as they moved away. One step at a time, I was decoding a message Gerbert d'Aurillac had left more than a millennium ago. It had all the excitement of being a kid and making up secret codes with

your friends, only this code had been created by one of
the smartest men of his age.

Six hours later, the thrill had pretty much disappeared, replaced by a throbbing headache and dry, ach-
ing eyes. The constellations hadn't turned up a single
usable word. Either I had wasted most of the day racing
down the wrong path, or I was missing a vital piece of the
puzzle.

I knew the dangers of getting too attached to un-
proven theories. If I was wrong about the constellations,
I needed to walk away and find a new angle. But this *felt*
right. The shapes, the numbers, the sphere, everything fit.

I pushed back from the table and stretched. A plate
sat untouched beside the laptop. I picked up the sandwich and called out, "Thanks to whoever made dinner."

"That was Ponce de Leon," said Nicola. "Two hours
ago."

A conquistador and sorcerer had made me turkey,
lettuce, tomato, and cheese on a poppy-seed bagel. Nice.
I crunched down and went in search of something to
drink. The bundled cords and cables Nicola had strung
through the kitchen were as bad as tripwires. "How did
you end up being Gutenberg's personal network guru?"

She didn't look up from her screens. "I have experience with this kind of setup. It's similar to what I used
when I recorded my last album."

I stared at her through the gaps between the monitors. "You made an album?"

"Three. I only made a hundred copies of each. They're
experiments, mostly. Exploring the limits of voice." She
turned to another screen, typed a command, and
frowned. "Also, Gutenberg trusts me more than most of
the other Regional Masters."

"Why is that?"

"Because I can't stand politics. And because I told
him he was wrong to kick you out of the Porters. Most of

the others either don't question his decisions or else they keep their disagreement to themselves. He prefers to know where people stand."

I grabbed a Coke and made my way out of the kitchen. "What's that screen on the left?"

"Our best assessment of Meridiana's powers and limitations. Every attack tells us more about what she can do. All of her magic has been channeled through e-books, suggesting she's limited by Jeneta's own potential."

"That's a lot of potential."

"True, and the fact that we don't understand her power complicates things. In addition to Jeneta's libriomancy, Meridiana maintains her connection to the Ghost Army. She's able to use the dead to possess and control her transformed monsters. The transformation is book-based magic, but the ghosts are something else entirely." Nicola pointed to another monitor. "By the way, someone scoped out your house last night."

I froze, my drink halfway to my mouth. "Lena's tree?"

"They didn't hurt anything this time. They were using magic to shield themselves, but they tripped one of the infrared beams Whitney set up. As far as she can tell, nothing was touched or disturbed, but we can't be certain. They may have just been checking to see if you were home, or they may have wanted a way to track you down."

Depending on the power of the hunter, a single leaf from Lena's oak could be enough to find her. Or a hair from my brush. For the right kind of magic, a sweaty sock was as good as a compass. "How good are the protections on this place?"

"The best we can make." She sang a quick verse in Greek, and two of the monitors changed views. "You should be safe for now. Meridiana wasn't able to steal d'Aurillac's secrets from your mind. That means her best plan is to wait for you to unlock his magic. That's when she'll try to kill us all and take the poem and the sphere."

I snorted. "If she's waiting for me to crack this thing, we could be stuck here for years."

"The constellations haven't worked?" She continued to watch the monitors as she spoke, rarely making eye contact. She was too busy keeping an eye on the rest of the world.

"No, they haven't." I stepped back, turning that image over in my thoughts. Nicola sat on her padded bar chair like a goddess on her throne, looking down at the mortals below. "But that's because I'm an idiot."

She didn't say anything. Which was a little insulting, actually. It would have been nice if she'd argued.

"Tenth-century thinking." I swallowed. "There are *two* perspectives for showing the stars. One is to draw the sky as we see it. That's what I printed out from al-Sufi's text."

I hurried back to the table, snatched up the transparency of Ursa Major, and held it toward the ceiling. "This is what we see when we look up at the stars. But there's a second perspective." I flipped the transparency and held it over the poem. "God sits *above* the stars, looking down! From God's perspective, the stars and constellations would appear backward."

Five minutes later, I had it—the first word of Gerbert d'Aurillac's message. "Octavian," I shouted triumphantly. The seven stars in Ursa Major aligned perfectly. The O and the C were linked together, the C hooked through the circle of the O. I even recognized the reference. "The treasures of Octavian were a legend, a story of hidden caverns full of bones and gold. Historians assumed the stories were about old Etruscan tombs, but according to William of Malmesbury, d'Aurillac knew the secret of entering those hidden caverns. William's account is more myth and superstition than fact, but—"

"But we know d'Aurillac hid the armillary sphere somewhere it would be safe," said Gutenberg. I hadn't even heard him enter. Lena and Ponce de Leon were with him.

"Somewhere inaccessible to mortal man," said Ponce de Leon.

"The elements of the story would seem to fit." Gutenberg stared at the poem as if he could peer right into those shadow realms. "Valuables secreted away, protected from discovery, with dire warnings against disturbing them."

"If Ursa Major is here . . ." I circled the letters on the page and penciled in the lines to complete the constellation. "Someone pass me Virgo."

If Virgo was on the map, it would mean d'Aurillac had used the spring sky as his guide. *That* was why the poem felt wrong. He had prepared it beneath a different sky. If the magic was attuned to the stars, I would need to adjust it to align with the autumn constellations. That meant uncovering the rest of the hidden words, then reverse engineering the overall grid and the original poem.

"What is it?" asked Lena.

I realized I was grinning. "I was thinking about Jeneta. She used to laugh at me when I struggled with poetry. She would love this." My smile faded. "I hope I get the chance to share it with her."

Stormy Knight Publishing would like to apologize to our readers and to author Stuart Pan for the errors in this week's release of *The Foretelling*. While all of our titles are reviewed by multiple editors and proofreaders, it would appear that the file sent to the printer contained portions of another, as-yet-unidentified story, which was somehow inserted into the manuscript.

We are posting the corrected versions of chapters six and seven of *The Foretelling* on our Web site for download, and we have pulped all remaining copies from our warehouse. Bookstores have been instructed to pull the title from their shelves and return it to us. If you have already purchased this book, you can return it for a full refund or a replacement, which should be available within two weeks. If you bought the book electronically, we will be working with e-book vendors to push a corrected file to your device.

After reviewing the inserted text, we have determined that it did not come from any of the books in our catalog, nor does it appear to be from a known published work. We are investigating the possibility that this was deliberate hacking and sabotage.

Here is a paragraph from the affected chapters. If anyone recognizes the excerpt in question, please contact us at editor@skpub.net.

The JG-367 was the pinnacle of military magic, a wand mounted on a handgun's grip, fully programmable through its cutting-edge touch-telepathy interface. The wand was titanium, infused with more than twenty firing modes, including sleep spells, transformation, and temporary or permanent petrification. More importantly, this new model included an exorcism mode, capable of tearing spirits and demons from their human hosts and trapping them in a sphere of magical energy.

For eight years, Stormy Knight Publishing has worked to bring you the best books by some of the most popular authors of our day. We would like to thank our readers for their support and understanding. We look forward to sharing exciting and amazing stories with you for many years to come.

Chapter 10

GERBERT D'AURILLAC HAD USED not the spring constellations, but the winter. Canis Major, Orion, Ursa Minor, Draco . . . each revealed another piece of his message. The name Meridiana was worked into the poem, along with Anna. The next word I found was *paeniteo*, which meant repent. The names made sense. The significance of repentance was less clear. Was d'Aurillac asking for forgiveness, or commanding Meridiana to confess and atone for her sins?

Shadow. Bridge. Spirit. The constellation of Gemini, the twins, revealed the name *Gerbertus* twice, but the second was spelled backward. I stared at that for a time, trying to understand. Was the duplication a play on the image of the twins? And why backward? Twins weren't mirror images of one another, any more than Otto III and Anna had been.

Goose bumps spread up my arms. What if the poem itself was the mirror? Then d'Aurillac's reflection was whoever found and deciphered this poem. I crossed out the letters of the reversed name and inserted my own.

Gutenberg and Lena walked into the room. I took one look and jumped to my feet. "What happened?"

Gutenberg tossed my holstered shock-gun through the air. "Put that on."

He carried a sword, a short, thick-bladed weapon with a flared pommel and a simple S-shaped guard. A Katzbalger, if I remembered my history correctly. The blade was made of a dull gray metal. Tiny lines of black text were etched along the edges. He scanned the room, then sheathed his sword.

Lena's twin bokken had flattened into wooden blades, sharp and strong as the best steel. "Jeneta is in Chicago. They attacked Nicola's home."

The chairs by the computer were empty. "Where's Nicola?"

"Bathroom," Lena said. "Gutenberg won't let her leave. The friend who was taking care of her animals called a few minutes ago. When he showed up today, he found four of them dead and the rest escaped."

"Oh, no." Nicola's chupacabras and the hybrids she crossbred with poodles were as dear to her as family. They were also dangerous as hell. For someone to take down four of them . . .

"How close are you to deciphering the spell?" asked Gutenberg.

"I've got most of it worked out. The next step is to update it with the current constellations." Starting with the keywords, then working those letters into the proper patterns. "I'll need another day to finish the poem. Maybe two. As for infusing it with magic and retrieving the sphere—"

"You complete the poem. I'll perform the magic," he said.

It made sense. Gutenberg knew more about libriomancy than anyone, and given my lack of magic, it wasn't as though I could do it myself. But logic did nothing to stop the crush of disappointment that someone else would finish my work.

"We're out of time." Nidhi hurried out carrying Smudge's cage in one hand. Nicola followed a moment later. Nicola's face was dry, but she was fidgeting more than normal, and she wouldn't look at anyone.

Inside the cage, Smudge was blazing away. I adjusted my shock-gun to level six, which should be enough to make even a sandworm from *Dune* decide to go elsewhere.

Gutenberg gathered the books from the table, shoving them into a brown carpet bag that should have been far too small to hold them all. "Juan?" he shouted. "Sorry to cut your shower short, but we may be receiving guests."

Nicola slid into her customary place in front of the computers and began pulling up what looked like video feeds from the building's perimeter. "One of the cameras is damaged." She turned the monitor off and on again. "Wait, it's not the camera. The screen is partially burnt out."

"Where?" Nidhi looked over Nicola's shoulder. "I don't see it."

"Second monitor from the right. The entire top-left quadrant is blacked out."

I moved to join them, anxiety worming through my gut. I pointed to an irregular blob of dead pixels. "You can't see that?"

Nidhi shook her head.

If this was what I thought it was, I shouldn't have been able to see it either. It looked like black-and-gray smoke had seeped into the screen. Lighter gray circles bulged and popped, as if the plastic was melting. "Is that—"

"Char, yes." Gutenberg touched the corner of the screen with one hand and jumped back as if it had given him an electric shock.

Magical charring was invisible to mundanes. "Are you using magic in your network?"

Nicola shook her head. "Low-level security, nothing more."

"Get away from it." Ponce de Leon raced out of the bathroom. He had thrown on a pair of trousers without bothering to dry himself.

"The manifestation reminds me of a report Isaac filed about his first encounter with one of Meridiana's ghosts," said Gutenberg. "In an abandoned warehouse in Detroit. I believe you called them 'devourers.'"

"We had to drop the whole building on that thing to stop it," Lena said. "I'd prefer to not go through that again. Especially with us inside the building."

Gutenberg stepped around the bar and began yanking power cables from the battery-powered surge protectors. The screens flickered and died, but the ashen stain continued to grow.

"Whatever they are, they're searching." Ponce de Leon gripped his cane in one hand. With his other, he slicked his wet hair back from his face.

"They?" asked Nicola.

"I can hear others throughout the city. If we use magic to fight them, we'll give our position away to Meridiana."

"Excuse me," said Gutenberg. Nicola surrendered her seat, and he sat down to examine the spreading char. He reached into his jacket pocket and pulled out a gold fountain pen.

My mouth went dry. The sight of the pen brought back memories of magical cold, of losing myself to Meridiana and her ghosts. I remembered the sharp pressure of that pen against my skin. The tip had felt like it was cutting my skull, slicing through the bone, though it hadn't left a visible mark. When he pulled it away, he had taken my magic with it.

"Isaac?" Nidhi touched my elbow.

"I'm all right." I unclenched my hands and took a deep, slow breath. "How many are there?"

Ponce de Leon shook his head. "Dozens. This one is exploring a hundred computers and phones in this building alone. They know we're in the area, and I suspect even the residual magic in your network is enough to attract attention."

"We knew this location was temporary." Gutenberg pressed the pen to the monitor and began to write. I couldn't make out the words. "Anything?"

"Whatever it is, it's still coming through. I believe it has abandoned its assault on the other residences, however." Ponce de Leon pointed his cane toward the monitor. "Step aside, *mi corazón*."

I couldn't see what he did, but a web of cracks spread from the center of the screen. He stabbed his cane forward, and the screen bowed inward like a trampoline with a weight in the center. The invisible weight sank deeper, though the cane never appeared to touch the screen. The smoke and ash began to slide inward, pulled into whatever mystical singularity Ponce de Leon was creating.

Gutenberg tucked his pen away and drew his sword. He ran one finger over the flat of the blade. The text in the metal responded to his touch, letters rearranging themselves along the edge. He extended the tip and cut sharply down and to the right, slashing a rift through the air in front of the monitor. Flame flickered from the edges, and the smell of sulfur drifted into the room.

"Ready?" asked Ponce de Leon.

Gutenberg cut a second line across the first, opening an X. Triangles of reality flapped like flags, offering glimpses into a cavern of burning, dripping rock. "Bring it through."

Ponce de Leon spun, yanking his cane with both hands like a fisherman reeling his catch into the boat. The monitor exploded, and a creature of glass and ash and electricity flew out, directly into whatever hellgate Gutenberg had opened.

He sheathed his sword, and the rift vanished, taking the devourer with it. Bits of broken glass and plastic fell to the floor.

Ponce de Leon flashed Gutenberg a lopsided smile. Gutenberg raised two fingers to his brow in salute. Neither one was even breathing hard.

I looked at Lena, remembering what it had taken for the two of us to destroy one of those things.

She folded her arms and asked, "Where can the rest of us get swords like that?"

I shoved the printed constellations and the rest of my notes into an old leather briefcase, along with a Latin dictionary. Gerbert d'Aurillac's poem and my initial efforts to update it were folded and crammed into my rear pocket. I didn't want to keep everything in one place, just in case Meridiana got her hands on the briefcase. Or on me.

Nicola was singing '80s techno to the computers. Each one sparked and smoked in response to what I assumed was a musical self-destruct command.

I clipped Smudge's cage to my belt and looked around. Lena had taken up sentry duty at the door. Nidhi was ready and waiting, watching nervously out one of the windows. Given the nature of our arrival, the three of us didn't have much to pack.

Gutenberg was another matter. This was his home. He had emptied almost a quarter of the shelves, and was tossing more into his bottomless carpet bag. He moved too quickly for me to see which titles he chose to save, though the Gerbert d'Aurillac manuscript was one of the first ones he took.

The telltale *whoosh* of a spider bursting into flames made me jump. The fiberglass lining on the side protected my jeans, but I had to hold my arm away to avoid burning my hand or wrist.

"We need to go, Johannes." Ponce de Leon joined Lena at the door and peered into the hallway.

Gutenberg looked at the remaining books on the shelves and sighed. "Nicola, please let the other Regional Masters know this location has been compromised." His sheathed sword bounced against his hip as he hefted his carpet bag and strode toward the door. "The elevator is to the left, ladies and gentlemen."

We were halfway down the hallway when I noticed Smudge's reaction. "Stop!"

"What is it?" asked Lena.

"The closer we get to the elevators, the hotter Smudge burns."

Ponce de Leon jogged ahead. "He's right. There's a great deal of magic coming up over here." He touched the doors to both elevators. A series of electronic chimes rang out. "I've shut one down. The other is on its way. The ghosts are blocking my efforts to stop them, but I'll do what I can."

Gutenberg pulled his sword. "Lena, would you assist me, please?"

I followed them to the elevator, where Lena wrenched open the doors. Gutenberg leaned out to press his blade against the moving cables.

"Wait," said Nidhi. "What if there are innocent people inside?"

"Nothing in that elevator qualifies as 'people' anymore," Ponce de Leon said quietly.

The text on Gutenberg's blade burned orange, and individual filaments of twisted steel cable began to snap. He pressed harder, slicing through the rest like flame through ice. A deafening screech echoed up the elevator shaft. The emergency mechanisms on the car would prevent it from falling, but it wasn't climbing anymore, either.

Ponce de Leon dug his fingers into the edge of the carpet in front of the elevator and peeled it back. "Lena, I could use your magic here."

They conferred together, and moments later, a thick tangle of black tendrils began to rise from the floor. It reminded me of cotton candy, if cotton candy came in tar flavor.

"Mold," said Ponce de Leon. "Strengthened with Lena's power as well as my own. It won't stop them from climbing up the elevator shaft, but it should give us an additional minute or two."

"If any of Meridiana's thugs have asthma, it might scare them off completely." I heard pounding from within the elevator shaft, along with the ring of an alarm. A particularly loud thump echoed through the building, and the alarm went dead.

"Stairs?" I wasn't looking forward to descending thirty-plus stories on foot.

"They'll have someone on the ground to watch the stairs as well." Gutenberg's sleeve was ripped and bloody. The metal strands must have lashed out like whips. One side of his face was bleeding, and his ear was torn.

His magic started to heal the damage as I watched. The gouge down his face zipped together, leaving a single line of blood. He noticed me staring and grimaced. "It still hurts like hell."

"Take the stairs," said Nicola. "Get out on the second floor, break into one of the apartments, and go out through the window."

Gutenberg nodded and hurried past, leading us toward the end of the hallway.

A door opened behind us. I spun, one hand going to

my shock-gun as an older man peered out and shouted, "What the devil is going on out here?"

"Emergency drill, Mr. Bennett." Gutenberg strode past the door toward the stairs. "Best to stay inside. Things will soon quiet down, one way or another."

Another door opened. Gutenberg sighed. "Juan?"

Ponce de Leon tapped his cane on the floor. Mr. Bennett yelped as the door swung shut in his face. Up and down the hallway, I heard deadbolts click into place.

Gutenberg pushed open the door to the stairs, peered down, and swore. "They're coming up. Back to the apartment."

"We could do that newt thing again," I suggested.

"That's unlikely to work this time," said Ponce de Leon. "Particularly now that Johannes and I have vanquished one of her devourers. She knows we're here. If she can't find us, she might decide to destroy the entire building to prevent us from escaping."

Once we were back inside Gutenberg's apartment, Lena shut the door, locked it, and sank her fingers into the wood. Roots began to grow into the frame and the walls.

Gutenberg and Ponce de Leon were arguing in low tones. Gutenberg glanced at me long enough to say, "I believe the window now offers our best escape. Isaac, if you would?"

I fired the shock-gun, leaving a smoldering hole in the curtains and an empty frame with bits of jagged, semi-molten glass dropping from the edges.

Gutenberg tilted his head to one side. "Dramatic, but effective." He reached into his carpet bag to produce an umbrella with a carved head in the shape of a parrot.

"That's from Mary Poppins," I said. "I *knew* I recognized that bag!"

"The umbrella's magic should carry us safely to the street, so long as everyone holds tight."

"Will it support all of our weight?" asked Lena.

"That won't be an issue. The umbrella's magic creates a field of near-weightlessness." Gutenberg yanked open the curtains. "Poppins wasn't clinging for dear life as she flew about, after all."

"There are people on the street," said Nidhi. "I can't tell whether they're with Meridiana or if they're trying to see why lightning just shot out of somebody's window."

I looked past her. "How close is the nearest automaton? We could try to set up an ambush, or they could teleport us away . . ." I trailed off when I saw the grim expression on Ponce de Leon's face.

"He doesn't feel them," said Gutenberg.

"Doesn't feel what?" I asked.

"The Ghost Army." Ponce de Leon traced a symbol onto the door with his cane. "If Meridiana had simply brought the same handful of warriors she had in Rome, we might have a chance. But the presence of additional ghosts complicates both our defenses and our escape. Teleportation is dangerous at the best of times, but I'd risk it now if not for the ghosts. The slightest interference, and we could end up rematerializing in the sun or scattered across a three-mile stretch. Assuming we reappeared at all."

"And what stops the ghosts from sucking the magic from that umbrella and dropping us in mid-flight?" I did my best to match their calm, though I suspect I failed.

Ponce de Leon twirled his cane. "Me."

Gutenberg opened the umbrella and approached the window. "There's a parking garage across the road, close enough for us to reach."

Something smashed against the door. Books fell from the shelves, and dishes rattled in the kitchen cabinets.

"Television!" Lena shouted.

Ponce de Leon spun toward the flat-screen, which had

begun to bulge outward. He pinned the struggling, partially formed devourer in place with his cane. "Johannes?"

Gutenberg pulled a book from his back pocket, opened it one-handed, sank his thumb into the text, and tossed the book to Ponce de Leon, who caught it and thrust it into the screen. Creature and television both imploded into nothingness.

Ponce de Leon touched the end of his cane and grimaced. "Almost took the tip with it."

"I'm sorry," said Gutenberg. "Next time I'll look for a gentler black hole. Now get over here."

We each grabbed the umbrella's handle, pressing together like we were part of the world's weirdest maypole dance. Lena kicked shards of cooling glass from the window frame. People were shouting and pointing from the ground below.

"Don't look," Nidhi whispered.

I nodded and held tighter.

Wind filled the apartment, rustling fallen books and tugging the umbrella. Then, as if we were standing on an invisible platform, we rose gently out the window.

"Here they come," said Ponce de Leon. "Brace yourselves."

The instant we were out of reach of the building, we dipped like an airplane hitting turbulence. I wrapped both hands around the handle. I didn't know which was worse, the potential fall or the fact that I was helpless to do anything about it.

Not that my magic would have been effective. Meridiana's incorporeal soldiers weren't ghosts in the traditional sense, but beings of magic who had lost their sanity and sense of self long ago. Trying to fight them with spells was like using a squirt gun against a giant squid.

Ponce de Leon simply grinned. The winds around us

grew stronger, pulling trash from the street and books from the apartment into a cyclone. "They feed on magic. Let's see how much they can swallow."

Under other circumstances, I would have loved to watch Ponce de Leon command the wind, but right now, I was more interested in not plummeting to my death.

"Incoming." Lena drew one of her bokken and pointed it toward the roof.

A familiar angel loomed from the edge like a gargoyle, wings spread wide, sword in one hand.

Even if his bones were hollow as a bird's, basic physics meant there should be no way for him to truly fly in this gravity and atmosphere. As was often the case, magic just chuckled and kicked physics in the balls, leaving it groaning and wondering what just happened.

The angel jumped from the roof and swooped toward us. Lena twisted to parry his first strike. The impact spun the umbrella like a merry-go-round.

I pried my right hand from the umbrella and reached for the shock-gun. I needed an angle that didn't risk me shooting through a window and killing innocent people if I missed. "Can you get us below him?"

"Unfortunately, his maneuverability is better than ours," said Gutenberg. We pulled to the left to dodge the next attack. We were halfway to the parking garage.

I heard a siren in the distance. Traffic below had stopped. Horns blared, and people shouted at us and at one another. All I cared about was the glorious rooftop ahead.

The angel curved around to block our way. He hovered in front of us, holding his sword in both hands. He didn't need to take us down. He just needed to keep us here long enough for the rest of Meridiana's brute squad to arrive.

We dipped lower. I adjusted my aim and fired. Lightning stabbed the air, only to dissipate into smoke when it reached the angel. He smiled.

"I see," said Ponce de Leon. His cyclone slowed. "Perhaps if we try a less direct approach."

I couldn't tell what he did, but about five seconds later, a pigeon dive-bombed the angel. Its claws and beak left tiny red scratches on his face.

Gutenberg chuckled as two more pigeons attacked. Others followed, fluttering and pecking as if our attacker was a piñata stuffed with discarded fast food.

The angel fought back against the birds the best he could, but the pigeons were surprisingly difficult targets. For every one he grabbed, another pecked his fingers. His sword slipped away, and Ponce de Leon blasted it into oblivion before it could strike the ground.

"Dumpster?" said Gutenberg.

"Excellent choice." Ponce de Leon twisted to point his cane at the street. A metal dumpster lurched into the air and tumbled end over end. The ghosts might have tried to intercept his magic, but by then, momentum had taken over. Pigeons fled in all directions, giving me a brief glimpse of one royally pissed-off angel wiping away blood, feathers, and pigeon crap. I don't think he even saw the dumpster that slammed him into the building. Angel and dumpster dropped onto the street with a deafening clang.

We landed on the top level of the parking garage and immediately ducked behind a van.

Gutenberg watched the broken window of his apartment. "Nicola, Juan, find us transportation. My own vehicle is parked below my building, regrettably out of reach. Meridiana's ghosts are still here, so be cautious and use as little magic as necessary. Lena, please go with them. I believe your strength might be useful."

Leaving Nidhi and me to hide and wait. Not that I really *wanted* to confront whatever else Meridiana sent after us, but I hated feeling useless.

A resounding crack came from inside the broken window across the street, followed by a puff of dust and smoke. They had broken through the door. It felt like we had stepped out of that window an hour ago, but it couldn't have been more than a minute or two.

In Jeneta's body, Meridiana looked down at us, flanked by the gorgon from Rome—still wearing her burqa, thankfully—and an enormous, misshapen man with yellow skin.

Meridiana clutched her e-reader close to her body. I couldn't make out her facial expression, but from here, she looked like any other kid. Right up until she reached into her e-reader and pulled out a writhing yellow serpent, which she hurled toward us. The snake lengthened and split again and again, until a swarm of indignant and presumably venomous serpents were raining down at us.

Gutenberg was ready with a book of his own. I backed away, wishing my gun had a wide-field setting.

Meridiana's magic must have cushioned the snakes' landing, because they immediately started hissing and slithering when they hit the ground. But they didn't attack. To the last snake, they darted into the shadows, fleeing whatever Gutenberg was doing.

"The legend of Saint Patrick," he said calmly, holding up his book. "If he can drive the serpents from Ireland, I can banish these from a parking garage. We'll send an automaton into the sewers later to gather them up."

Meridiana's next assault created what looked like streams of silver glitter falling from the sky. She directed them not toward us, but to the onlookers below. It wasn't until the screams began that I realized what it was.

"Burn them," I shouted. "Don't let it reach the ground!"

Gutenberg swapped books and launched a jet of flame, but the ghosts must have intercepted his assault. The fire sputtered and died before reaching its target: deadly spores known as Thread, from Anne McCaffrey's

Dragonrider series. Watching it fall from Earth's sky was like reliving the first time I read *Dragonflight*, and the horror I felt at wave after wave of deadly Thread that consumed all organic life it touched.

"Give me d'Aurillac's poem, and I'll end this." Meridiana's words cut through the screams, as if she stood directly in front of us.

The quick beep of a horn announced the arrival of our ride.

"We can't leave," I said. "The Thread will start to burrow." Most of the ground below was blacktop or sidewalk, but there were strips of green, grassy soil where Thread could thrive.

"We both know I'll find you wherever you go," Meridiana continued. "The only question is how many people you'll sacrifice in the meantime."

Gutenberg tucked his book away and pulled out his cell phone.

"I could summon Thread down upon Lena's grove," she said. "This is but one of a thousand plagues I can—"

Gutenberg tapped a button on his phone, and the apartment exploded.

DIET OF THE DAMNED

A popular new diet plan could soon put a stake through Jenny Craig's heart.

Nutritionist Jamie Bergren of Los Angeles, California announced earlier this week that she will be launching her exclusive blood-based weight-loss program online. Doctor Bergren says she has been using this plan with select clients for years, with incredible results.

Her Web site features photographs of slender, attractive men and women drinking blood from wine glasses, but Bergren is quick to point out that human beings can't survive on blood alone.

"Healthy arterial blood is used as a dietary supplement only," she explained in a press release. "Every client's needs are different, depending on weight, gender, physical activity, and other factors."

How did she discover this unusual diet? That's simple. According to Bergren, her father was a vampire.

"He was turned when I was eleven years old," Bergren explains. "Before that, he had always been obese. He couldn't play with me or my brother without getting out of breath. We watched him try one fad diet after another, but nothing worked.

"Within a year of becoming a vampire, he was down to a hundred and seventy pounds. The most significant change to his lifestyle, aside from having to avoid sunlight, was his diet."

The California Department of Public Health is currently investigating Doctor Bergren's practice, and has not yet issued a statement.

"You don't know it, but you've seen several of my success stories in the movies and on television," claimed Bergren. "They look better, and more importantly, they *feel* better. They're healthier, happier, and, if I say so myself, hotter."

Bergren's Web site advises people not to begin the vampire diet on their own. Potential risks include blood-borne illnesses, iron overdose, dehydration, and more. "My clinic takes every precaution to guarantee the safety of donors, the cleanliness of the blood, and the health of the recipients." A one-month trial will cost $250. Everyone who signs up will receive sealed packets of blood-based salad dressing, drink additives, and a flavored syrup said to go great with pancakes.

We want to know what you think. Visit our Facebook page to share your thoughts on this article.

Chapter 11

SMOKE BILLOWED FROM THE shattered windows. People in the streets screamed and fled. Fire alarms buzzed through Gutenberg's building, audible even over the ringing in my ears. Torn and burning books fell like confetti.

By the time I recovered from my shock, Gutenberg had resumed his assault on the Thread. He burned it from the sky, then turned his efforts to the street below.

"You killed her," I whispered.

"Doubtful." Gutenberg flicked his fingers, and a sweet-smelling rain began to fall on the wounded, healing the worst of their injuries. "I can't imagine Meridiana would enter my domain without precautions, and even if her physical host *was* destroyed, her spirit remains bound within the sphere."

"Her *physical host?* Jeneta Aboderin was—is—fourteen years old! She's a kid, a victim."

"You think I want to kill her? She was one of ours, Isaac. One of mine. But if you ask me to choose between the life of one girl and the safety of this world, I *will* make that choice. Be grateful you don't have to."

I understood the logic. I wanted to deck him anyway. It wasn't just the choice he had made, but the coldness with which he made it. There had been no hesitation, no doubt. When I looked at him, I saw not the slightest trace of regret for what he had done.

I looked at the apartment. The interior had caught fire, and smoke continued to pour out the windows. If Jeneta and her monsters had survived, I couldn't see them.

"If you want to save lives," said Gutenberg, "the best thing you can do is finish that poem."

Behind us, Lena stepped out of a red four-door Jeep with oversized mud tires. She looked at the three of us, then to the apartment beyond. Her jaw tightened.

"The ghosts remain, though they appear disorganized," Ponce de Leon said from the driver's seat. "We should be going."

I told myself Gutenberg was right. Meridiana would have taken precautions. Jeneta was still alive.

"Interesting choice," said Gutenberg as he joined us. He took the passenger's seat.

"It looked like a fun car to drive," said Ponce de Leon.

I stared out the window at the column of black smoke.

"Who buys a Jeep this size for Chicago traffic?" Ponce de Leon slid his fingertip along the top of the window, leaving tiny etched characters in the glass. They looked similar to some of the enchantments in my convertible.

"Is everyone all right?" asked Nidhi.

"For the moment." Gutenberg went silent while Ponce de Leon paid the parking attendant. "We'll be safer once we leave the city."

Traffic made that an even slower process than usual, thanks to the damage we had caused. I split my attention between Smudge and the windows, waiting for the next monster to attack. People continued to pour out of the building, but they all appeared human from here. I wouldn't say we had won this battle, but we hadn't lost, and it looked like Gutenberg had disrupted Meridiana's plans enough for us to get away.

"Isaac, can you work while we drive?" Gutenberg asked.

I nodded tightly and pulled my notes from my pocket. Setting the briefcase on my lap, I began to write.

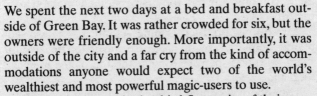

We spent the next two days at a bed and breakfast outside of Green Bay. It was rather crowded for six, but the owners were friendly enough. More importantly, it was outside of the city and a far cry from the kind of accommodations anyone would expect two of the world's wealthiest and most powerful magic-users to use.

The owners put us in the third-floor suite of their converted farmhouse. The old hayloft ceiling curved overhead, the naked timbers an odd contrast to the nineteenth-century wallpaper. The main window looked out on maple trees and fenced-in fields where sheep wandered about, grazing lazily or napping in the shade. Lena spent much of her time outside, sunbathing on the balcony or resting within the trees. At the moment, she and Nidhi were playing chess behind the barn while Smudge hunted grasshoppers.

The sleeping arrangements were, if anything, even more awkward than they had been in Gutenberg's apartment. The owners lent us several extra cots, but there was little privacy. And it turned out that Nicola sang in her sleep.

During the day, Nicola and Gutenberg continued to coordinate with the other Regional Masters while I updated Gerbert d'Aurillac's poem. Nidhi's job, when she wasn't with Lena, was to keep the rest of us from killing one another.

Between being driven from his own apartment and news of additional Porter casualties, Gutenberg was a magical time bomb searching for an excuse to explode. For Ponce de Leon, it was being stuck in the middle of nowhere that was slowly chipping away at his sanity. His latest complaint was the lack of "a single *real* Vietnamese restaurant."

Personally, I preferred the B&B to the cramped, crowded feel of the city. If you had to stack people's homes and workplaces on top of one another to make it all fit, you officially had too many people crammed into too little space.

I tried to ignore their griping. As much as I despised feeling helpless, how much worse was it for the two of them, who had spent so long at the top of the magical food chain?

Gutenberg slammed through the French doors from the balcony and announced, "The state of literacy in this world is shameful."

"Waiting on your Potter fans?" Ponce de Leon sat in a rocking chair, reading *Harry Potter and the Goblin's Scepter*. He had begun the book last night. Every reader helped build the book's magic, after all.

I, on the other hand, had been forbidden from touching the book until I finished the damn poem, for fear—not entirely unjustified—that I would lose focus on my work.

Gutenberg waved his own copy in the air. "Twenty-three bookstores held surprise midnight release parties last night. The rest put the books out this morning when they opened. Tens of thousands of copies should be in people's hands by now, but what are they doing?"

"Some people work on Tuesdays." I wondered if Jennifer had officially fired me yet, or if she would wait to do it in person.

He ignored me, turning instead to what looked like a

kind of miniature phonograph. An engraved brass disk began to spin, and Gutenberg peered at the marble-sized black jewel at the center of the disk. This was one of the tools he used to monitor his automatons, who were hunting without success for Meridiana and her army. "I assumed the other books would require an additional day or two, but the Rowling?"

"The *fake* Rowling." Ponce de Leon picked up his smart phone from beside the chair. "You've done a marvelous job of blowing up the Internet today, Johannes. The lack of a decent signal makes it difficult to keep up with the fallout, but your readers may simply be too busy yelling at one another online to actually finish the book."

Gutenberg grumbled something unintelligible and turned toward me. "Aren't you done yet? You were supposed to have this worked out yesterday."

"I had to adjust the spokes." Only when I was rewriting my poem had I spotted another layer of meaning in the original work. The letters within the vertical spoke were decorated slightly differently than the rest, with additional horizontal strokes. After staring at it for three hours, I had finally recognized them as meridian lines. Each of the twelve horizontal lines in those letters extended to the left or right of the center spoke. Tracing the endpoints created an elongated figure eight. If the poem were laid out as a sundial, the shadow would fall on those marks at noon on the first day of each month. Which meant recalculating each one of the lines for our current latitude. "It will be done by dinnertime."

"Assuming you haven't missed anything else."

"Give the boy a break, Johannes," said Ponce de Leon. "Do you want it now, or do you want it right? You know he's almost there. You can feel it as well as I can."

I hunched my shoulders and continued working. Whatever magic simmered within the poem, I couldn't feel it, nor would I be able to touch it once I finished.

Gutenberg and Ponce de Leon would be the ones to infuse the text with their own magic and—if nothing went wrong—retrieve Meridiana's prison.

The experience had given me eyestrain, a throbbing headache, and tremendous respect for Gerbert d'Aurillac's mind. He had buried so much meaning within these lines. I wasn't about to admit it to Gutenberg, but I was terrified I had overlooked something vital.

Gutenberg dragged a chair across the floor and sat down beside Ponce de Leon. They reminded me of grumpy cats sharing a sunbeam. Gutenberg glared at the book as if he could intimidate it into producing the scepter.

Ponce de Leon turned a page. "I enjoyed the scene where Harry consults the paintings of former headmasters. The description of the artwork was quite striking, and his interaction with Snape hit just the right balance of snark and grudging respect."

Gutenberg grunted.

"The Quidditch scene dragged on a bit, though. And on page sixty-seven, you've got Neville going out alone to the forbidden forest, but then suddenly he's with Ron and Luna. This is why you need proofreaders, Johannes."

I stared, poetry forgotten. "*You* wrote that book?"

"Shut up," snapped Gutenberg.

"You have a distinctive voice," Ponce de Leon continued. "Even after all these years. You've gotten much better. I thought the ongoing romance between Ron and Hermione was particularly well done."

I had to be one of the only living people who had ever seen Johannes Gutenberg *blush*. "You told me you had hired a fanfic writer, a woman—"

Gutenberg lowered his head, ignoring us and pretending to read. I knew perfectly well that he could see and manipulate a book's magic without ever opening the cover, but he buried himself in the pages, his eyes darting to and fro.

"He did," Ponce de Leon said. "In a manner of speaking. Check online for work by 'Darcy Nacht.' That's the alias you've been using lately, isn't it?"

I jumped out of my chair and headed toward Nicola's computers.

"If you so much as touch that keyboard, I will turn you into a caterpillar and feed you to your own fire-spider," Gutenberg said.

"Don't worry." Ponce de Leon winked at me. "I'll change you back before Smudge eats you."

Gutenberg's expression convinced me I was better off not pressing my luck. I clamped my jaw, pressed my lips together, and returned to my work.

"There's nothing shameful about fanfiction," Ponce de Leon said. "That piece you did about Shakespeare and Elton John—"

"Not now, Juan." Gutenberg had picked up his copy of *Harry Potter*. "It's ready."

Ponce de Leon's face darkened. "Johannes . . ."

"I know," he said without looking. "But Meridiana has been fighting to return to our world for a thousand years. We've always known something was working to claw its way back and destroy us all. This is why I *created* Die Zwelf Portenære. Twelve Doorkeepers to guard the way. We cannot allow her to succeed."

"Meridiana wants to supplant God," Ponce de Leon said. "If you attempt to eliminate magic, to rewrite the world as you see fit, how are you different?"

"False equivalency? You're better than that, Juan. Besides, if it comes to that and I do use this spell, wouldn't that prove it was all part of your God's plan?"

I turned toward Ponce de Leon. "You believe in God?"

"You sound surprised."

I was, a little. "Everything in the Bible can be explained by magic. With all you've done, all you've seen, how can you still believe?"

He smiled at me. A little sadly, I thought. "With all you've done and seen, how can you not?"

"Proselytize later." Gutenberg's fingertips sank into the paper. He grimaced. "Never attempt libriomancy with your own work. It's like repeatedly slamming your brain in a toilet seat, then flushing it away."

"Lovely simile," said Ponce de Leon. "You should use that for your next story."

Gutenberg reached deeper, burying his hand and forearm in the book. He blinked sweat from his eyes. I couldn't tell if his exertion was from the mental dissonance of working with his own book, or the relatively small pool of belief empowering that book.

Gutenberg stiffened as though he had been hit by an electric shock. At the same time, Ponce de Leon jumped from his chair. He turned in a slow circle, searching the room. "We're not alone."

"I feel it," said Gutenberg through gritted teeth. "Isaac, fetch Nicola."

I ran onto the balcony. Nicola was already sprinting toward the farmhouse. She must have sensed it, too.

"She's on her way," I said.

Gutenberg began to drag the Goblin's Scepter from the book. From the description he had shared, the scepter was supposed to be a thing of beauty, made of carved gold inlaid with silver and jewels, and topped with a magical sapphire. The handle Gutenberg struggled to pull free looked like a blackened stick from a burnt-out campfire. Thin metal prongs grasped his wrist like burnt fingers.

Ponce de Leon stood opposite Gutenberg, his hands stretched out like he was holding an invisible glass dome over the book. "Isaac, gather the poem and get out of here."

I nodded and began scooping up my pages and notes.

"How did she find you?" Ponce de Leon sounded calm, but his hands were trembling.

Gutenberg grimaced. "I couldn't say. Either she sensed my attempt to use the book, or more likely, she heard rumors about its release and correctly surmised this was a Porter-sponsored publication."

Nicola burst through the door, breathing heavily. She took one look and began to sing.

I had heard her sing before. I realized now that I had only heard a fraction of her power. Her voice flooded the room, every word pounding through my body, shaking the bones from within.

It was also the first time I had heard Billie Holiday's "Ill Wind" sung in the style of a professional opera singer.

"Thank you, Nicola." Ponce de Leon relaxed whatever it was he had been doing, snatched his cane from the air, and pressed the tip to the scepter.

I wasn't sure how I could hear him over the sound of Nicola's singing. Perhaps it was something deliberate on her part, to make sure we could still communicate.

"It's digging into my flesh," Gutenberg said tightly. "And it appears to be growing. Severing it from the book won't—"

"You'd prefer I remove your arm?" Ponce de Leon put a hand on the side of Gutenberg's head. For a second, I saw the ghost of a long, silver blade extending from his cane. He slashed downward, cutting through the scepter. Gutenberg stumbled back, the broken artifact still clinging to his wrist.

A shadow squeezed up from the book, tearing pages loose from the spine. Blackened paper swirled through its body. It flew past me to slam the door, then paused as if assessing the room. Charred pages continued to rip from the book, flowing after the shadow as it moved toward Nicola.

I pulled my shock-gun and brought the lightning. The gun's magic didn't hurt the ghost, but if nothing else, maybe magic lightning would keep the damn thing pre-occupied while it countered my attack. For a few seconds, at least.

"I had hoped going print-only would allow us to escape Meridiana's notice." Gutenberg grabbed the blackened stump of the scepter and tried to pry it from his arm. "She didn't try to stop me from creating the scepter. She simply redirected its power to try to use it against me. I should have anticipated this."

"She does have twice your experience," said Ponce de Leon. He had set his cane aside and was probing the skin of Gutenberg's wrist, like a doctor examining a wound.

A second shadow started to climb from the book. Nicola walked toward us, her song a palpable force hammering the ghost back.

"Johannes . . ."

"I know." Gutenberg grimaced. "Give me the book. I might be able to reshape the scepter back to its proper form and salvage this mess."

The false Harry Potter book fluttered through the air like a bird, alighting in Ponce de Leon's outstretched hand. I couldn't see what he did, but the second ghost vanished through the pages like it had fallen into a pit.

"She redirected the scepter's power?" I asked. The scepter was designed to lock away the world's magic. Meridiana had turned it against Gutenberg. "What does that mean?"

"It means she's unraveling my spells, one by one," said Gutenberg.

Ponce de Leon stepped around behind Gutenberg. With one hand he held the open book steady. With his other, he guided Gutenberg's hand and the scepter back toward the pages. "Read, dammit."

I heard pounding from the other side of the door. The ghost must have locked or reinforced it. Moments later,

Lena's fist punched through the wall beside the door-frame.

Ponce de Leon helped Gutenberg press the broken scepter against the page. "If you can't separate it, I may need to temporarily remove the forearm."

I waited for the scepter to vanish back into the book, but all that happened was the jagged metal tore a hole in the page.

"I can't. She's locked away too much of my magic." Gutenberg looked toward me and started to laugh, a sound that blended despair and genuine amusement at the irony. "It seems I need another libriomancer to assist me."

Ponce de Leon was powerful, but he had never learned or mastered libriomancy. Nicola was a bard. I didn't know if the Porters had a single libriomancer in all of Wisconsin. Even if they did, by the time someone got here ...

Gutenberg's hand was pale. The scepter had cut off the circulation. He looked up and nodded. "Do it."

Ponce de Leon tossed the book aside. His belt slid loose like a snake and coiled around Gutenberg's arm: a makeshift tourniquet. Ponce de Leon lowered him gently to the ground. He grabbed a ballpoint pen and used it to draw a blue ring around Gutenberg's arm below the elbow.

"Modified fairy ring?" asked Gutenberg.

Ponce de Leon nodded. "Infused with fire, so this *will* hurt. I'm hoping to cauterize the wound as much as possible."

I continued my attack on the remaining ghost. Lightning seared the wallpaper behind it and started a small fire on the wall, but the ghost itself was still strong, diverting or dissolving every shot.

I glanced down, both horrified and fascinated, as

Ponce de Leon prepared his spell. I had read of fairy rings being used as a form of gateway. In this case, the ring would open a gate through Gutenberg's arm, which should instantly and cleanly sever flesh and bone.

Ponce de Leon kissed the back of Gutenberg's head, and then the blue ink flashed orange. Gutenberg cried out. The flames died instantly, but the smoke remained, filling the air with the smell of burnt meat.

Ponce de Leon was already dressing the stump with bandages he seemed to have pulled out of the air. "Hold still, *mi amor*."

Gutenberg's head sagged against Ponce de Leon's chest. His face and lips were pale and covered in sweat. His remaining hand shook uncontrollably.

I had cataloged countless books with the power to regrow an amputated limb, but the physical loss would be secondary. I kept shooting, trying to keep the ghost at a distance. "What about his magic?"

Ponce de Leon looked over as though he had forgotten I was here. "Gone. Locked in a fashion similar to your own."

Gutenberg opened his eyes. "It's a remarkably unpleasant sensation." His voice trembled. "I've not felt this vulnerable for centuries."

"It *can* be reversed?" asked Ponce de Leon.

"Possibly." He looked over at the book. "I can't see the damage. How bad is it?"

"The book is charred beyond use, and continuing to ooze raw magic." Ponce de Leon picked up his cane. "Don't move."

He stood and walked toward the remaining ghost. I stopped firing.

The ghost attacked, but Ponce de Leon was faster. His cane impaled the thing through what might have been its heart. He didn't break stride, pushing it backward until he pinned it against the wall. He twisted the cane, and the shadow writhed in pain. Blue and green flame crackled outward.

Gutenberg looked over at me and tried to sit up. "It looks like we'll need to find you another libriomancer to assist with the poem."

"Be still," said Ponce de Leon. "Don't make me use magic to force you to rest."

Gutenberg grimaced. "It stings. All those words, melting away."

A month ago, I would have called this justice. I was the final entry on a long list of people Gutenberg had robbed of their magic. Wasn't it right that he finally understand what he had done?

But knowing what he was going through made it impossible to feel any kind of satisfaction over his loss. "I'm sorry."

He pressed his lips together, then sighed. "As am I."

Nicola had stopped singing at some point. I hadn't even noticed. She crouched beside Gutenberg to examine the bandaged stump and began a new song. A little of the tightness eased from his body.

"Thank you," he said. "Isaac, would you and Nicola please help me to my feet?"

"You need rest, dammit," said Ponce de Leon.

"Meridiana now knows we're here," he said, reaching for Nicola's hand. "We have little time."

Ponce de Leon shouted something in Spanish, and the last remnants of the ghost disappeared. The fire from my lightning died as well. At the same time, Lena finished ripping through the wall. She stepped inside, swords raised. Smudge crouched on her shoulder. "What happened?"

"Gutenberg tried to create the scepter." I stared at the man who had revolutionized the world of magic. He could barely stand. His pale, damp face and trembling body suggested he was slipping into shock. "Meridiana—"

Ponce de Leon raised a hand. "Don't move."

"I hear it, too," said Nicola.

The room was silent. Ponce de Leon gripped his cane with both hands. I readied my shock-gun, though I didn't know where to aim.

Ponce de Leon spun, his eyes wide. "Johannes, get away from—"

What remained of *Harry Potter and the Goblin's Scepter* opened of its own accord. A broken shaft of blackened gold shot through the air to embed itself in Gutenberg's chest.

The impact knocked him to the floor. His dead eyes stared in surprise and confusion.

UNLIKELY ALLIES

WASHINGTON, D. C.—The National Rifle Association has joined with the American Civil Liberties Union to protest a bill proposed yesterday in the United States Senate.

The proposed bill, which sponsor Susan Brown called the "Magical Security Act," would set restrictions on the use of magic within the United States of America. The law would make all magic illegal for anyone under the age of eighteen. Individuals eighteen years and older would have to apply for a license to practice magic.

A national poll earlier this week suggested that roughly fifty percent of U.S. citizens were somewhat skeptical or very skeptical about recent reports of magic throughout the world. The other half believed *something* supernatural was indeed happening, though theories ranged from magic to aliens to religious miracles.

"I have seen proof of magic with my own eyes," said Brown. "If I'm wrong—if the growing body of evidence turns out to be a hoax—then we lose nothing by passing this law. But if magic is real, and if it presents as serious a threat as recent events suggest, then we must act immediately to protect the safety of the American people."

Dwayne Williams of the NRA disagreed. "This is a clear Second Amendment issue." Williams appeared at a press conference wearing a T-shirt showing a bearded wizard in robes and a pointy hat, along with the words, *"You can take my wand when you pry it from my cold dead hands."*

"Every American has the right to self-defense. I don't believe in witchcraft, but the truth is, we don't know what's out there. If magic is real, this legislation would cripple our ability to protect ourselves. We've been down this road before. They imprisoned Japanese citizens in World War II because people were afraid. They impose burdensome regulations on law-abiding gun owners because people are afraid. Now Susan Brown wants to lock up magic-users, not for any violation of the law, but because they're afraid."

Karla Henson of the ACLU had a slightly different view. "This bill is a blatant attack on religious freedom. Will Wiccans, Pagans, Vodouisants, and others whose belief involves the practice of magic be expected to register with the U.S. Government? Magic, if it exists, isn't a weapon any more than my hand or foot are weapons. A martial artist can kill with a single strike, but we don't require them to be licensed by the government. Magic is a part of who these people are, as much as their blood and bones. This is a critical junction in our history. We have the opportunity to set an example for the world, to show that we value freedom over fear."

Williams encouraged NRA members to rally at both the state and national level. "The choices we make today will shape our country and the world for decades to come. Let's make sure our leaders do the right thing."

Chapter 12

BLOOD SEEPED FROM THE wound in Gutenberg's chest. Nicola crouched beside him and sang a low hymn. "There's no pulse. No mental activity. He's dead."

With all the experiences I'd had since the Porters found me, those two words marked this as the most unreal. It was like she had announced the sun would no longer rise each morning.

"He died almost instantly," she continued. "He would have felt the impact, perhaps a split second of pain, but nothing more. The scepter is no longer magically active. I'm not sure about the book."

Ponce de Leon raised his cane. "Get back."

His words were utterly cold. We scrambled out of the way. He pointed his cane at the book, and death poured forth. White fire disintegrated a three-foot hole through the floor, but the book floated in the air, pinned by magic. Another ghost tried to crawl from the pages. The light seared it to nothingness as it emerged.

The air smelled of salt and ice. Floorboards crumbled like sand. The lamps flickered and died. I backed away and shielded my eyes from the light of Ponce de Leon's assault. It was like looking into the heart of a star.

When the flames finally disappeared, nothing remained of the book. White hoarfrost covered Ponce de Leon's cane, though why frost should be a side effect of such intense heat was beyond me. Perhaps some sort of backlash.

Magic could cheat death, as Gutenberg and Ponce de Leon had done for all these years, but no spell could reverse it. Ponce de Leon turned toward the body, raising his cane as if he was determined to try anyway.

I turned so that my shock-gun was hidden behind my body and adjusted it down to setting four, hoping I wouldn't have to use it. He knew what would happen if you tried to restore function to a corpse, but he wasn't thinking rationally. At best, he would probably just create a host for another of Meridiana's ghosts. At worst . . .

"He's gone," said Nidhi. I hadn't noticed her joining us. Her face was drawn. She watched Ponce de Leon like he was a pacing tiger.

Slowly, he lowered his cane. He limped to Gutenberg, moving more heavily than I had ever seen him do. He gripped the bar in Gutenberg's chest. Metal scraped bone as he pulled it free. He tossed the inert bar aside. It struck the floor with a dull clunk. "I know."

Nobody else moved. He opened Gutenberg's jacket and pulled the fountain pen from the inside pocket. I expected him to give it to Nicola, but instead he handed it to me. "You'll need this, I suspect."

The pen was heavier than I had imagined. From the weight, it had been carved and shaped from real gold. It was as thick as my index finger, polished mirror-smooth. I pulled the cap free and studied the tip. The curved diamond nib was etched with precisely flowing lines, tiny letters engraved into the metal. I would need a magnifying glass to read them. "What for?"

He ignored me, instead retrieving Gutenberg's wallet, phone, keys, and a small leather-bound notebook. He offered all but the last to Nicola.

"We can't stay here," said Nicola. "Meridiana knows where we are, and the police will be coming."

None of us moved. I couldn't stop replaying the last few minutes in my mind, imagining everything I might have done to stop this from happening. If I had finished deciphering d'Aurillac's poem sooner . . . if I had kept Smudge inside where he could have warned us instead of letting him go with Lena . . .

"Nidhi, please get Gutenberg's carpet bag," said Nicola. "Lena, would you carry the body? We can't leave it behind."

Lena nodded and fetched a blanket from the bed, which she used to wrap Gutenberg's body. Nidhi retrieved the carpet bag from atop the dresser.

Ponce de Leon brought both hands to his face and wept.

Lena sat next to me in the Jeep, her hand tight around mine. Nidhi sat on Lena's other side. Nobody had said much since leaving the B&B.

Nicola had gathered or destroyed any magically incriminating evidence, then herded us outside. She stopped long enough to sing excuses to the owners, making sure they wouldn't remember any details about who we were or what had happened.

I kept thinking about the body in the back of the Jeep, the corpse of the man who had invented libriomancy. All that knowledge and experience, gone.

We stopped at a red light, and Nicola twisted around to pass her cell phone to me. "In the contacts list, you'll find an entry for 'Handbasket, Helena.' Call that number and tell whoever answers that it's February of 1468, then hang up."

The month and year Gutenberg was supposed to have died. I dialed the number and delivered the message. The woman on the other end was silent for several seconds before asking, "Are you sure about that date?"

I looked at the spots of blood speckling my shirt. "Yes." I hung up and returned the phone. "What happens now? With Gutenberg gone . . ."

"I don't know," Nicola said flatly. "Gutenberg prepared for this, but many of his preparations were magical in nature. The senior masters will form a temporary council to lead the Porters and assess the situation. The automatons will go into a kind of magical standby mode for now."

"Word will spread quickly," said Ponce de Leon. He sat in the front, still as a statue, save for the slight movement of his jaw. "Johannes' death will embolden the enemies of the Porters. Creatures hidden for centuries will venture into the light."

"What *exactly* happened back there?" Nidhi asked.

"Meridiana twisted Johannes' spell." Ponce de Leon stared out the window. "She turned the scepter against him, stripped him of his protection. She's stronger than we realized."

"We'll need another libriomancer to retrieve Meridiana's prison," said Lena.

Nicola shifted lanes. "The nearest libriomancer is Heather over in Minneapolis. I'll tell her to meet us at—"

"We don't need a libriomancer." I rolled Gutenberg's pen back and forth on my palm.

"You have an alternative?" asked Nicola.

"Maybe." My thoughts were beginning to break free of their shock. "We'll need to stop at a bookstore."

"Who?" asked Lena.

"Bi Wei." Her power over books was as great as Gutenberg's had been, if not stronger. The magic that had helped her to escape Gutenberg's assault on her home and kept her alive for so long was similar in many respects to Gerbert d'Aurillac's spell. Unfortunately, she was also an avowed enemy of the Porters.

I guess it was a good thing I wasn't a Porter anymore.

The first bookstore we found didn't have *A Dance with Dragons* on the shelves. According to the man working behind the counter, it was currently their hottest seller. Nobody could keep the book in stock, thanks to the mysterious message in the front. As if George R. R. Martin needed the additional royalties.

He directed us to the local library, where the librarian explained there was a two-page waiting list. Back in the parking lot, I called two more bookstores and three other libraries, with similar results. "That's everything in a forty-mile radius," I said, disgusted.

Lena cleared her throat. "Does it have to be that particular book?"

"We need something the students of Bi Sheng will be watching." I didn't know for certain that Bi Wei would see a message in *A Dance with Dragons*, but since she had used it to send her own, it made sense that they would have a copy on hand, if only to see whether the Porters were able to dispel or modify her letter.

Lena twisted around and dug into her bag, eventually producing a familiar red book. "What about this?"

I immediately shook my head. "We can't—"

"My book. My decision."

"What is it?" asked Nicola.

I didn't answer. Bi Wei had given this book to Lena. Its magic was identical to the books the students of Bi

Sheng used. This copy held Lena's story, her sense of who she was and who she wanted to be. It was also a secret we had kept from the Porters, one which had come directly from the hands of their enemy.

"It's a book that might help us communicate with Bi Wei," said Lena.

Nicola studied the book. Everything about it announced its origins, from the cloth binding to the rice-paper pages. But instead of arguing, she simply asked, "What makes a student of Bi Sheng a better ally than another Porter?"

"They've known about the Ghost Army for longer than the Porters have existed," I said. "Meridiana is as much a threat to them as she is to us. And I trust Bi Wei." I had shared Wei's memories. I knew her to be both strong and cautious. More importantly, she understood book magic and the nature of these ghosts well enough to combat them, better even than Ponce de Leon.

I waited for Nicola to point out that Bi Wei was also an avowed enemy of the Porters. She said only, "You get started on that while I coordinate with the Porters. I'll find us a hotel for the night."

I paused, repeating her words in my head and comparing it to the script I had expected. "Oh. Okay, right. Thanks."

A half hour later, we were checked into a room with two queen beds. Our accommodations had been going steadily downhill over the past week. The furnishings reeked of cigarette smoke. A faded painting of a triple-masted sailing ship hung over the small desk in the corner. Peeling wallpaper and a brown water damage stain in the corner announced that maintenance and upkeep were low on the priorities list, but all in all, it wasn't much worse than my first apartment.

I turned on the television and found a nature documentary for Smudge. He was warier than usual as he emerged from his cage, but soon he was darting to and fro, trying to catch wild lemurs. I was a little worried he would melt holes in the screen, but he seemed content to play.

I needed to find food for him. A tarantula could survive on a few crickets a week, but Smudge had a much hotter metabolism. I'd have to slip out tonight and hunt for worms and bugs to go with his candy treats.

Ponce de Leon remained with the Jeep, keeping watch over Gutenberg's body. Nidhi had disappeared into the shower. Nicola sat on a folding luggage stand in the closet, arguing on the phone with what sounded like at least three other Regional Masters. I wasn't sure if she had chosen the closet for privacy or for the relative security of the enclosed space. From the bits I overheard, she wasn't happy.

I brought Lena's book to the desk and opened the cover.

Lena sat on the bed, her back against the mounded pillows, her legs folded. "Do you think she'll be able to do it?"

"Bi Wei isn't exactly a libriomancer, but her magic is all about the essence of books. If anyone can make this work ..."

"That's not what I meant." She tapped her forehead. "Your magic. That's the other reason you wanted to bring Bi Wei into this. You're hoping she'll be able to undo whatever Gutenberg did to you."

"Even if she can, there's no guarantee that she will. Stopping Meridiana and the Ghost Army is one thing, but helping an ex-Porter?" I twirled the pen through my fingers. "I'm trying not to think about it. Every time I touch something magical—the shock-gun, the vampire blood, even this pen—it's like ripping open a scab, and it keeps getting harder. Getting more *difficult*," I amended before she could make any lewd comments.

She smirked, but let it pass. "We'll keep trying. Bi Wei, Ponce de Leon, Nicola . . . someone should be able to help you. And if they can't, I want you to remember something."

"What's that?"

She kissed me hard enough to make my skin tingle from my neck to the base of my spine. "I didn't fall in love with you for your magic."

"Thank you." I nodded and turned back to her book.

"How do you know that pen will write something she'll be able to see?"

"I don't," I said. "But Gutenberg used this pen to lock books. That means whatever he did had to carry through to all copies of those books." I turned the page, uncapped Gutenberg's pen, and began to write.

Every surviving student of Bi Sheng had a book like this, and every one of those books included the same block-printed pages in the front. It was those pages I defaced, though the ink left no visible mark. I had to trust Bi Wei would see my message. I angled the desk lamp to help me see the faint indentations in the paper where I had penned her name.

I hesitated. I needed to be circumspect, since I had no idea who else might read this. That meant no mention of Gutenberg's death or what specifically I was asking for.

"Writer's block?" asked Lena.

"Something like that." How could I reassure her this wasn't a Porter trick? Bi Wei knew what the Porters had done to me. I believed she trusted me, to an extent. But I couldn't even prove I was the one writing the message. Anyone could have taken Lena's book and used it to lure Bi Wei into a trap.

Nicola's voice cut through my thoughts as she argued with the other Regional Masters. She was louder than usual, as if anger or frustration or simple grief had adjusted her volume. "Gutenberg said a show of force should be the *last* resort. We need to build goodwill. We can't do that with automatons."

I looked at Lena, who shrugged.

"Suppose your plan worked," Nicola said a moment later. "Say we wiped out a terrorist organization or overthrew a dictator. Imagine we somehow managed to do so without a single civilian casualty. Any such action will still create enemies. Even those who approve of the results will fear our power and the potential threat we pose. We need to tread carefully. In time, we can—" She paused. "Then what about Weronika? She's been visiting hospitals and healing terminal patients. If more Porters could—no, I understand. Miss Palmer has made that quite clear."

"Who's in charge with Gutenberg gone?" Lena asked softly.

"I'm not sure." I had never paid enough attention to politics within the Porters. I had no interest in working my way up the ranks, or being anything except a researcher. Magical bureaucracy was still bureaucracy, and I wanted nothing to do with any of it. I had unconsciously started thinking of Nicola in Gutenberg's place as head of the Porters, but she was one of many Regional Masters. Not necessarily the most senior or the most powerful, either.

Although the whole question could be moot soon. Between the world discovering magic and Meridiana doing her best to destroy . . . well, pretty much everything, there was a real possibility that the Porters wouldn't survive. Gutenberg had been the pin holding the organization together, and even he had struggled to keep things from fragmenting.

"What would you do?" Lena asked.

"What do you mean?"

"If you were in charge. Say Nicola and the rest decide to promote Isaac Vainio to be Gutenberg's replacement. What's the first thing you'd do?"

"Order Nicola and everyone else involved to check in with their therapists, because that would mean they'd lost their damn minds. Then I'd probably resign with extreme prejudice."

She folded her arms.

"Okay, fine. I'd start by offering an olive branch to the students of Bi Sheng." I looked down at Lena's book. "To be honest, I don't know how the Porters fit in a world where magic is out in the open. Are we scholars? A global police force? Saviors or conquerors or both?"

Lena smiled. "I'm surprised you wouldn't immediately set out to colonize Mars."

"I'd save that for the second month, along with getting Fox to put *Firefly* back into production." I glanced over at Nicola, who was still listening to whoever was on the other end of the line. "How do you map the future of the world?"

"You don't," Lena said softly. "Not alone."

Nicola drummed her hand against the wall of the closet. She spoke more slowly, deliberately choosing each word. "I agree, which is why our first priority is to retrieve the armillary sphere. As the senior Porter on site, I intend to—" She straightened. "I don't believe you have the authority to do that."

Lena and I had given up any pretense of not listening in.

"Naturally. I trust you'll inform me once the vote is complete." Nicola hung up a moment later, but remained seated. When she saw us watching, she said, "They believe I'm responsible for Gutenberg's death."

"The hell you are," I said.

"Who believes that?" asked Lena.

"Cameron Howes, and at least two other Regional Masters." She stared straight ahead. "If enough others agree, they can appoint another person to oversee this region."

"Cameron Howes is a pretentious, narcissistic, igno-rant pustule of a man." I was surprised by my own vehe-mence.

"I know," Nicola said, so matter-of-factly that I had to grin. "He sees Gutenberg's death as an opportunity, and he's not alone. He wants me replaced by someone he can control."

I stood up and started toward her, intending to offer comfort, but she flinched when I got close. I stopped moving.

"You need to reach Bi Wei and finish your poem," she said. "I . . . need you to leave me alone. Please." She sounded brittle, as if that flat monotone contained within it a scream of rage and grief. Nicola was at her breaking point. She had lost not only Gutenberg, but four of her animals, creatures she cared about as if they were family.

"Of course," I said softly. "Sorry."

She nodded and left the room.

Lena took my hand. "It's not you."

"I know." I stared at the closed door, listening to the fading sound of Nicola's humming. Eventually, I re-turned to the desk and Lena's book. "If Howes and the others find out we're reaching out to Bi Wei, it will give them one more reason to get rid of Nicola."

"People like Howes don't need reasons," said Lena. "All they want are excuses and justifications. If you hold back to try to protect Nicola, he'll just find them else-where."

I squinted at the page, trying to reread the few lines I had written. There was no need to share our location. Bi Wei should be able to find us through her connection to Lena's book. But how to prove it was us . . .

I thought about the first time I had read Bi Wei's own book, before her return to this world. Bi Wei had written of her first experience with magic, a story whose power and joy resonated with my own discovery. She had hiked into the hills with her great grandaunt, where they read an old star chart and used its magic to study the sky, to see beyond what was visible to the naked eye.

I remembered her joy, preserved all those years by the magic of her readers. I picked up Gutenberg's pen, jotted down three more sentences, and began to sketch the constellations.

I traced the final letters of Gerbert d'Aurillac's poem at about one in the morning, then sat back to try to stretch the cramps from my hand.

Lena had slipped out an hour before to search for a suitable tree for the night, and I hadn't seen Ponce de Leon since we arrived. Nicola had paid for a second room, saying she needed solitude. Nidhi was currently sleeping on one of the beds, leaving the other for me.

I turned off the desk lamp, stripped down to my jeans, and prepared for bed as quietly as I could. Despite my exhaustion, it took forever to fall asleep. The unfamiliar bed only made things worse. Throughout the night, I jerked up at the slightest sounds: a door opening or closing down the hallway, a car door slamming in the parking lot. Even the noise of Nidhi's breathing seemed amplified.

I gave up around six in the morning and made my way, bleary-eyed, to the shower. Nidhi was still snoring when I finished. I picked up my T-shirt, sniffed, and grimaced. Everything smelled of smoke. Gutenberg had provided us with extra clothes that almost fit, but those had blown up with his apartment. I should have just jumped into the shower fully clothed.

Now where had Smudge gotten off to? I hadn't remembered to put him back into his travel cage last night. "Please tell me you stayed in the room," I whispered.

I kept the bathroom light on with the door cracked as I searched the room. Smudge could creep through surprisingly tight cracks and gaps. I didn't think he could have squeezed beneath the door, but I wasn't certain. Maybe he had gone on a midnight raid to see if anyone had left food in the hallway. Worse, he might have found the vending machine and crawled inside to stuff himself with sugar.

I checked the corners of the room, behind the desk and my bed, and the curtains before stopping to think. He would want somewhere warm and dry. He wasn't by the heater. I bit my lip and checked Nidhi to make sure Smudge hadn't curled up with her for warmth.

I finally found him behind the mini-fridge, pulled into a fuzzy ball and enjoying the heat of the compressor. I scooped him into his cage and set him on the windowsill, grabbed my shock-gun, and snuck out of the room.

The hotel offered a complimentary continental breakfast. My first thought upon seeing it was rather less than complimentary. A young man with unkempt hair to the middle of his back was setting out a bowl of questionable-looking apples beside a cafeteria-style cereal dispenser. I grabbed the best of the fruit and a bowl of technicolor sugar puffs and made my way to the table closest to the television on the wall.

A morning news host was interviewing Randall Nickles, a noted skeptic who had spent the past decade debunking the claims of psychics, ghost-hunters, alien abductees, and other stories of the supernatural. He wore a simple navy suit with no tie, and appeared utterly relaxed as he deflected one question after another. To listen to him talk, the various reports of magic were the result of overeager Internet rumor-mongering, human gullibility, and wishful thinking.

I imagined what would happen if word got out that Randy was a high-level field agent for the Porters.

"That doesn't look like food."

The soft, worried voice made me jump. "You got here faster than I expected."

Bi Wei sat down on the opposite side of the table. "Your message implied that this was an urgent matter."

Bi Wei had changed since I last saw her. Now, only a month after her rebirth, her English was flawless. She was dressed in a red-and-white floral dress with matching flip-flops. Black-framed designer sunglasses were pushed up on her brow.

"You could say that." I scooped a spoonful of stale cereal into my mouth. "You look like you're adjusting well to the twenty-first century."

"Your world is amazing and terrifying, but the people are much the same."

"That sounds like something Gutenberg would say."

She tilted her head to one side. "What happened to him?"

I hesitated, but if I wanted her help, I needed to tell her the truth. She was strong enough to pull the details from my thoughts anyway. The fact that she hadn't already done so was another point in her favor.

I told her about the attack, about Meridiana's prison and the Ghost Army, and about Jeneta.

"The sǐ guǐ jūn duì, Meridiana and her army, exist in the river of magic that runs through the Land of Midday Dreams." She smiled at me and added, "I remember your distaste for the poetic, but our poetry helps us to see and understand that river, as if through a glass-bottomed boat. Meridiana has clouded the purity of those waters, but we felt the ripples of Gutenberg's death."

I could hear her fighting to control conflicting emotions. Gutenberg's automatons had killed her peers. Her teachers. Her own brother. What would Nidhi say if she were here? Something gentle and nonjudgmental. "After five hundred years, I imagine that was hard to process. Overwhelming."

"For all of us, yes. We wept. We raged that Gutenberg would never be called to account for his actions. And we grieved. Not for the man, but for . . ." She brought her hands together. "For the waste, perhaps."

She studied me more closely. "Your magic remains buried by Gutenberg's spell. How did you contact us?"

I pulled the gold pen from my pocket.

She took it and turned it in the light. "This pen belonged to Johannes Gutenberg."

"How can you tell?"

"His magic is distinctive."

The hotel doors swung open, and Lena strode into the lobby, yawning. "Good morning, lover. Hello, Wei. Ooh, donuts!" She hurried to the counter, returning with a bowl of cereal and a glazed donut that looked far too plastic for my liking. "There's a lovely maple in the park a block from here," she said. "Eighty years old, give or take. Strong and sweet. Is Nidhi awake yet?"

"She was sleeping when I left," I said.

"She's not a morning person." She tore the donut in half, took a bite, and turned toward Bi Wei, who was watching with a bemused expression. "How's Guan Feng?"

"Very well, thank you. Feng has been staying with us. She's served as a guide to your world."

Guan Feng was a "reader," and had guarded Bi Wei's book for years before her restoration. Not only did she act as Bi Wei's protector, it was her duty to read the book each day. The belief—the faith, really—of such readers was what had helped Bi Wei and others like her to survive for so long. I suspected most readers possessed some form of low-level magic as well.

"Last week, she taught us how to 'Google' things," Bi Wei continued. "It's amazing. A living library, eternally growing, all contained within your computers." She fixed her attention on me. "With Gutenberg gone, who commands the Porters? Will they leave us in peace?"

"I don't know," I said, answering both questions at once. "Between Meridiana, Gutenberg's death, and your letter, the Porters are scrambling to stay on top of things. That letter was like setting off a firecracker in a hornet's nest."

"Familiarity with the field of battle is worth more than a thousand swords," she said. It sounded like a proverb, but I didn't recognize it. "The Porters know this world. It gave them an advantage. Thanks to our letter, the battlefield is changing."

"Confusion and chaos give Meridiana an advantage, too," I pointed out. "If you help us—"

"The Bì Shēng de dú zhě prefer to fight our enemies in our own way." She picked a tiny red ball of fruit-flavored crunch from my bowl and studied it.

"What way is that?" asked Lena.

She hesitated before answering. "Meridiana's pollution spreads through all who drink from the river of magic. We lost four of our number to her poison."

"I'm sorry."

She nodded. "Alone, we would have all fallen in time, but together we can stand against the current."

"Less metaphor, please," I said.

"Our individual stories are now one. I share the senses of my fellow students. When one of us weakens, the rest of us cleanse his or her story."

I shifted in my chair and casually dropped my hand toward my shock-gun. "What does that mean, exactly? Am I talking to Bi Wei, or to all of the students of Bi Sheng?"

"Both." She smiled. "For so long we were alone. Five

hundred years of solitude. I am still Bi Wei. I remember my life, my family, and my ancestors. I have a voice."

"What happens if they overrule your voice?" I had read countless books about group minds. They rarely ended well.

"They wouldn't do that. But they share their thoughts and experiences, and I would be foolish to ignore them." She popped the cereal into her mouth and grimaced. "This is *not* food."

"Don't mock the Sugar Fruit Puffs," I snapped. Her answering grin eased my tension slightly.

"We didn't choose this path lightly, Isaac. Not only does our bond help us to resist Meridiana, but as the magic flows through us, we're able to purify it of Meridiana's influence. Like the wetlands cleansing the river."

"Can you stop her?"

"She will weaken in time, but it will take centuries for us to undo the damage she's caused. And if she escapes her prison, our combined strength may not be enough."

"Then help us," said Lena.

"The Bì Shēng de dú zhě don't trust the Porters." Before I could respond, she added, "But I will help the two of you if I can."

I sat back in my chair, wondering what exactly I had gotten us into. "Thank you."

"It's good to see you again, Isaac Vainio. What is it you need?"

"I've translated the poem Gerbert d'Aurillac used to hide Meridiana's prison. Without magic, there's no way for me to reach into that poem and retrieve it."

Bi Wei set the pen on the table between us. "This isn't the kind of magic Bi Sheng taught."

"It's not libriomancy, either. I'm not completely sure how it works. I hoped that together, we would be able to figure it out. Assuming you're willing to try . . ."

"Of course she'll try." Lena looked at me like I had

asked whether the Earth was round. "She geeks out about this stuff as much as you do. A thousand-year-old word puzzle that reeks of forgotten magic? Do you think for an instant Wei is going to turn her back on that?"

Bi Wei grinned. "When do we begin?"

MesaCon, Arizona's premier fantasy convention, is proud to announce the addition of an exciting new programming track to this year's schedule.

"Magic: Busting the Myths" will feature discussion about the apparent emergence of magic in the world today. We have three popular fantasy authors, a historian, a professor of mythology, and an ordained minister who have all signed on to participate.

Some of the panels we're hoping to present include:

Johannes Gutenberg: Man or Magician? A fifteenth-century court record describes Gutenberg as the master of "a secret art." For generations, we assumed this referred to the printing press, but the Bi Wei Revelation suggests otherwise. Could the father of the printing press have been a sorcerer? Panelists review known facts about Gutenberg's life and discuss who he really was.

The Future of Fantasy. What happens to the fantasy genre when magic becomes real? Does *The Name of the Wind* get moved to "alternate history"? Should *Dracula* go into the biography section? How will readers suspend disbelief when they know an author got the magic wrong? Does true magic mark the death of fantasy?

Magic Is Real. Now What? If magic is real, what does that mean for the world? What new problems are we going to face, and what problems will become a thing of the past, solved with a wave of a wand? Are we headed for a grimdark dystopian future or an era of unimagined peace and prosperity?

Magical Myth Busting. In an age when a single click can forward rumors across the globe, how are we supposed to separate truth from hoax? Our panel discusses popular hoaxes of the past and presents tips on filtering out the junk. From manipulated photos to paranoid conspiracy theories, learn how to check your sources and find the facts.

I, for One, Welcome Our New Wizard Overlords. For every Gandalf, there's a Sauron. For every Harry Potter, a Lord Voldemort. What's to stop these dark forces from seizing power? Assuming they haven't done so already!

If you're interested in being on programming or have suggestions for panels or guests, please e-mail program@mesacon.biz.

Chapter 13

BI WEI GRUDGINGLY ACCEPTED a cup of apple juice, though she refused to try the tea, calling prepackaged teabags "abominations against civilization."

By now, a handful of other people had joined us in the dining room, so we tried to keep the conversation light as Lena and I finished eating.

"The show is called Pī lì," Bi Wei was saying. "The puppetry is amazing. Magical, in its way. Feng also introduced us to the work of Jim Henson."

"Has she shown you *Labyrinth*?" I asked.

"Not yet, but we'll ask her about it. Her favorite is *The Dark Crystal*." She looked more closely at Lena. "You seem different."

Lena held out an arm. Bi Wei touched her index finger to Lena's inner elbow and traced an invisible line. I guessed she was sensing the branches Lena carried within her.

"Interesting." She touched Lena's palm. "How long can they survive inside of you?"

"Almost a month so far. They're stronger when I grow the shoots and let the leaves absorb the sun."

"If the tree grows too strong, it could overpower the flesh," Bi Wei warned. "Are you certain this is safe?"

"They haven't hurt me yet." She tilted her head toward me. "If you want to talk about dangerous, ask Isaac about his trip into space to break into a vampire-owned satellite."

There really wasn't any good response to that. I looked around to see if anyone had overheard, then downed the last of my juice and brought the Styrofoam dishes over to the garbage. When I came back, Lena was talking to Bi Wei about the optimal environment for growing bamboo. "I can make a lot of things grow, but northern Michigan gets nasty in the winter. I don't imagine bamboo would survive."

"You might try máozhú bamboo," Bi Wei said. "If you lent the new shoots your strength to protect them from frost . . ."

They were still discussing Lena's plans for her new garden when we returned to the rooms. We found Nicola waiting in the hallway in front of our door. Her wet hair had dripped dark spots onto the shoulders of her shirt. I had a hard time reading her expression, but she seemed calmer than yesterday. A pair of black earbuds was looped around her neck. She studied the three of us, devoting most of her attention to Bi Wei.

Bi Wei bowed slightly from the head and shoulders.

Nicola pressed the left earbud into place and began to sing. Bi Wei merely waited, her hands clasped in front of her. I got the impression of a silent conversation passing between them, or perhaps it was a test.

Whatever it was, Bi Wei apparently passed. Nicola pursed her lips, stepped to the side, and opened the door to our room. Without a key. Damn, I missed magic.

Inside, Nidhi was awake and dressed, and was brushing her hair in front of the mirror.

"I grabbed you breakfast, love," said Lena, tossing a cinnamon raisin bagel her way.

I dropped a piece of cereal into Smudge's cage and checked the temperature of the air above him. He seemed cool enough. A bit nervous, but certainly not scared of Bi Wei. I caught Lena watching us, and gave her a small, reassuring nod.

"Is this the poem?" Bi Wei whispered, moving toward the desk.

"Gerbert's original is on the left."

"Wā," she breathed.

A month ago, I would have understood the word. My magically powered universal translator might be gone, but I could still recognize her excitement and awe. "It's amazing, isn't it?"

"It is." Her forehead crinkled. "But it's also *wrong*."

"It's outdated." I turned on the lamp, then pointed to the second, larger poem I had finished last night. "This version should be accurate for at least the next two weeks. Maybe longer, depending on how precise the spells are."

"It's beautiful." She sat down and pulled the lamp closer. "I can't read the words, but we can see ideas. The stars within the pages."

I did my best to stifle the envy those words roused, but it wasn't easy. I could appreciate the cleverness of d'Aurillac's work, but I couldn't truly *see* it. Not like Bi Wei could.

She sorted through my notes until she found the translation, complete with the various constellations highlighted in different colors. She grinned up at me. "I'll expect you to provide such gorgeous puzzles every time you call for my help."

"I'll do my best."

She read as fast as I did. Maybe a tiny bit faster. "This was a man who found beauty in structure and order," she said. "Despite his grief and fear, you can feel his love for this work. The satisfaction of fitting each letter into its proper place."

"D'Aurillac saw no boundary between science and religion, math and magic," I said. "He tried to incorporate them all."

"The poetry of the stars." She touched one of the constellations. "The letters of her name are the heart of the poem—this triangle here, and the base of these two spokes. The rest of the poem is structured around her."

"Can she do it?" Ponce de Leon stood in the doorway, looking like he had aged ten years overnight. He had changed into a gray pinstripe suit with a silk tie the color of arterial blood. But he leaned against the door like a man exhausted beyond endurance.

"I think so," said Bi Wei. She looked from me to Lena.

"Bi Wei, this is Juan Ponce de Leon," I said.

She stared. "Who?"

Ponce de Leon almost smiled. "Thank you. That's the most refreshing thing I've heard in years."

"I spoke with Babs Palmer earlier this morning," said Nicola. "She has instructed me to bring the poem to her so she can supervise a team of Porter researchers, who will retrieve the sphere in a safe, controlled environment. She's also ordered me to cease all contact with 'potential enemies' who might attempt to use Meridiana against us."

"Potential enemy?" Ponce de Leon made a face. "It lacks panache. I prefer to be called 'rogue' or 'outlaw.'"

"What gives Babs the right to tell you what to do?" asked Nidhi.

"Nothing, which is why I'm currently ignoring her orders." Nicola's chin rose slightly. "But she's correct about the danger. Meridiana murdered Gutenberg through a magically active book. We don't know what she might be able to do through the poem or the sphere. We can't risk retrieving it here."

We needed somewhere we could hide out and study Gerbert's creation without being disturbed. Somewhere Meridiana and her ghosts would have a harder time reaching. The werewolves would probably take us in, but I didn't want to put Jeff and his pack in that kind of danger. "Oh, crap."

"What is it?" Lena reached for her bokken.

"I never called Jeff. He probably thinks Mahefa Issoufaly tossed my body into a ditch somewhere." I grabbed my phone and sent a quick text: Still alive. Blood worked, thank you! Also, Mahefa is an asshole.

Bi Wei was scanning the poem again. Back and forth her hands moved, touching letters like a musician playing an instrument. I saw the movement, but I couldn't hear the music.

"Babs also wants Gutenberg's body turned over to her," said Nicola.

"Is that so?" Ponce de Leon rested both hands on his cane. "I've tended to Johannes' remains. Please tell the Regional Master that she's welcome to bring any requests or complaints to me personally."

My phone buzzed with Jeff's reply: Glad ur not dead. Try 2 stay that way.

I was sick of running and hiding, and judging from the frustration charging the air like an overloaded power line, I wasn't alone. But we needed that sphere before we could act against Meridiana. Like Dorian Gray's painting, the sphere held her true life, keeping her safe from anything we could do. "What about Fort Michilimackinac?"

"Meridiana knows of the Porter archive beneath the fort," said Bi Wei.

"The whole world knows, thanks to your letter."
Nicola didn't sound angry, but then, she rarely did.

"Michilimackinac has Porter magic protecting it," I
said. "Along with the spells left there by French traders.
It's only a day's drive." Before I could say more, Smudge
scurried to the top of his cage, bits of brightly colored
sugar melted to his mandibles. I lowered a hand to check
his temperature. "Wherever we're going, we should leave
now. The fire-spider just went to yellow alert."

Lena moved to the window and peeked through the
curtains. "Nothing out here."

Nobody spoke as we gathered our things. I tucked my
notes into the briefcase and checked my shock-gun.
Nicola pressed her earbuds into place. Lena sharpened
her wooden blades.

Ponce de Leon's knuckles were white around his cane.
He waited impatiently at the door, as if he couldn't wait
to confront Meridiana. Bi Wei was right behind him,
sorting through books in her leather handbag.

We were checked out of the hotel within five minutes.
I scanned the parking lot, searching for whatever was
worrying Smudge. Waves of red fire rippled over his
back.

"We should switch vehicles," said Nidhi. "Preferably
to something that isn't stolen."

"Nobody will notice us." Ponce de Leon gestured toward the Jeep. "I saw to that in Chicago. The police will
see us, but the memories will slip away like ice melting
through their fingers. I use the same spell on my own
cars. I prefer not to worry about speeding tickets when I
drive."

Bi Wei slowed. "That truck . . ."

A U-Haul truck sat beside our Jeep. Through the window, I made out the silhouette of a man. I checked
Smudge, whose flames jumped higher, confirming my
wariness.

"It wasn't there earlier this morning," said Lena.

The door opened, and the driver climbed out. He wore a dark green trench coat, and a black baseball cap shielded his face, but the skin of his neck sparkled where the sun touched it, marking him as Sanguinarius Meyerii.

Sparklers were tough to beat, even with magic. On any other day, I'd have braced myself for a fight that would almost certainly have ended with me broken and bleeding on the pavement. But I was surrounded by some of the most powerful people I knew, and after bracing myself to face Meridiana, a vampire was such a relief I laughed out loud.

He scowled and pounded the side of the truck. The back slid open. Three more people emerged, all muffled against the sun.

"This won't take long," said the driver. "We just want the blood-thief."

I raised my hand and smiled. "That would be me. How did you find us?"

"We heard about your little adventure in Rome, so we reviewed the videos and photos online. When we spotted Mahefa in the background, we decided to pay him a visit. He told us everything . . . after a little persuasion. He had some of your blood left, which he handed over to us."

I checked the other three vampires, wondering which one had tasted my blood and used it to track me down. It was an unusual gift among vampires, but not unheard of.

They spread out as they approached. Nidhi tapped my shoulder and pointed to the roof of the hotel, where two more vampires waited. When they saw us looking, they flew down behind us. One landed on the roof of a Mini Cooper, denting it inward. The other dropped lightly to the blacktop between us and the hotel door.

"Tell your Porter friends not to try anything." The driver blurred closer. "I can rip out your throat before any of you can crack open one of your magic books. But we've been instructed to make your death ... memorable."

"They're not Porters. Aside from her, I mean." I cocked a thumb at Nicola. "Look, we're in a hurry, and this is a *really* bad idea. Any chance we could reschedule for next week? I promise I'll come down to Detroit to clear things up with your queen. Alice Granach is still running things in the salt mines, right?"

Lena had her bokken. Nicola's hands twitched to a rhythm only she could hear. Ponce de Leon held his cane in one hand, a cold smile on his face. And then there was Bi Wei.

"Take him," said the sparkler. "If he resists, kill his friends."

By my estimate, the fight lasted no more than twenty seconds.

Ponce de Leon burned the sparkler to ash where he stood. One of the flying vampires tackled Lena, only to scream and roll away with a bokken through her leg. A single swipe of the second bokken separated her head from her neck. Nicola's song lulled a third to sleep.

The rest were unfortunate enough to reach Bi Wei.

Wind swirled around us, tossing the screaming vampires into the air. The sky turned gray, and dust choked the air.

Of those twenty seconds, half were spent watching a miniature tornado carry the undead trio out of sight.

Bi Wei removed her sunglasses and wiped the dust from the lenses. "I was reading *The Wonderful Wizard of Oz* yesterday before I received your message. It was inspirational."

The Porters had transferred their Midwest archive to Fort Michilimackinac after the destruction of the MSU

Library in East Lansing. Located at the tip of Michigan's Lower Peninsula, the fort was a moderately popular tourist attraction, as well as the site of an ongoing archaeological dig. The latter presented a challenge at times, as there were certain artifacts and discoveries the Porters preferred remain hidden, but a little judiciously applied magic prevented anyone from digging too deep in the wrong spot.

I spent part of the drive on hold with the Detroit vampire nest. Deb DeGeorge had given me the number for one of Alice Granach's fledglings who apparently doubled as her administrative assistant. After twenty minutes of waiting, the fledgling picked up again and said, "Mistress Granach will be with you shortly. If you would just—"

"Keep waiting while you try to trace the call? That's not going to happen." Not with the amount of magic shielding the Jeep. "Look, we just dusted half the team you sent to kill me and sent the rest off to Oz. I know you're pissed about the blood thing, and you're right. That was rude of me. I don't have time for this right now, and so far, I haven't told the Porters or anyone else the details about your orbiting blood banks. Tell Granach if she wants a war, I'll tell the whole damn world, and we can make bets as to which agency shoots them out of the sky first. *Or*, she can call off the hunt, and we can talk about reparations like civilized beings."

"I . . . will pass your message along to Mistress Granach."

"Threatening the head of the Detroit nest," Lena said once I had hung up. "You're quite the diplomat."

"Granach isn't stupid. They got Mahefa, so by now they know he set me up. Killing me anyway to send a message makes sense, but not if it costs them more than they gain."

"You hope," said Nidhi.

"Yah."

Nicola glanced back. "What is this about other blood banks?"

"Ask me again once I've heard back from Alice Granach. In the meantime, I want to study that poem."

Thankfully, she didn't press the matter, and we spent the rest of the drive in relative quiet.

The fort was smaller than I remembered. I hadn't been here since I was fifteen. My parents had spent that summer trying to show my brother and me as many Michigan historical landmarks as possible. It hadn't been my most thrilling summer vacation.

Nicola had an annual pass, while the rest of us had to purchase tickets in the gift shop. We could have climbed the chain-link fence that surrounded the grounds, but there was no reason to risk attracting attention.

To the right, the Mackinac Bridge stretched across the water, dividing Lake Michigan from Lake Huron. To the left was a refreshment stand and a small playground built like a miniature fort, complete with a tiny toy cannon pointing out at the water. A woman in Ojibwe garb was working around a small campfire up ahead, beside the sidewalk that led to the wooden walls of the fort. A man dressed as a fur trader welcomed us when we reached the northern entrance.

The wooden palisade enclosed a scattering of buildings and open grass. Tourists wandered through reconstructed homes, barracks, and other structures, while park employees in period costumes answered questions, chopped wood, tended the small gardens, and tried not to look bored out of their minds.

Everything we saw was a reconstruction. The fort had been burned to the ground in the late 1700s, when the British relocated to Mackinac Island. But the spells laid by the French traders and soldiers who originally built the fort had survived the flames.

"You've got that look on your face," Lena said fondly.

"What look?"

"You're mentally reading this whole place like it's a history textbook."

I gave an offended harrumph. "Just for that, I won't tell you how the Ojibwe took control of the fort in 1763."

Lena touched each building in turn as we walked. Wasps crawled over many of the wooden shingles, but they left her alone.

"Who's working the archive?" I asked.

"Jackson Chapin transferred up from East Lansing four weeks ago." Nidhi turned toward a small wooden cabin beside a grassy hill, near the southwest corner of the fort.

Chapin had been the archivist at the MSU library before it was destroyed. He had minimal magic, barely strong enough to earn a place among the Porters, but he knew the title of every book on his shelves by memory. He was brilliant, stern, and likely to be of very little help in a magical battle.

A sign on the cabin named it the Chevalier House. Inside, a narrow stairway led down into the old powder magazine. This was one of the few areas to have survived the British torches. It was here that the original magic was strongest, and here that the Porters had quietly moved in.

Glass walls protected the blackened stumps of the original palisade, displayed for tourists. Nicola waited for another family to move along to the next exhibit, then took a silver key from her pocket. She studied the cylindrical steel lock on the glass. The key was the wrong shape, but when she touched the tip to the lock, the cylinder melted aside to reveal a second, older-looking keyhole. She inserted the key and turned it a full three hundred and sixty degrees. To the left of the display case, a section of wall swung open.

Cool, dry air drifted out. The hallway beyond was built of wood, caulked with what looked like white mud or plaster. A pair of flickering fluorescent bulbs hummed overhead. Nicola replaced the lock and led us inside. Ponce de Leon pulled the door shut behind us.

A small video camera was mounted in the corner above a second door at the end of the hall. Patches of green moss covered much of the wooden door. On the ceiling directly in front of us was a steel pipe and what looked like a sprinkler head. "What do they run through the pipes? Lethe water?"

"I think so," said Nicola. "Though I'm not certain which type."

Various authors had written about the memory-wiping properties of the river Lethe, each one giving it his or her own twist, and in the process providing the Porters with a range of forgetfulness potions. Should anyone manage to make it this far without authorization, they would soon find themselves back in the parking lot with no recollection of how they had gotten there.

Nicola pressed her hand to the largest patch of moss, which rippled and molded itself to her fingers. The door opened inward to reveal the business end of an eighteenth-century blunderbuss. The brass barrel lowered a moment later, and Jackson Chapin stepped aside to welcome us in.

Jackson looked like he would be more at home on the rugby field than in a library. Tall and broad, with a rectangular head and a quarter-inch buzz cut, he appeared even more imposing in the cramped confines of the archive. An ID badge hung from a lanyard around his neck. "Master Pallas? What's going on?"

Nicola stepped past him. "We need to use this facility. Isaac and Bi Wei will be working at your desk."

The archive was less than half the size of our former facility in East Lansing, and had an odd blend of modern and colonial furnishings. The gleaming white floor and walls reminded me of a laboratory, but the wooden writing desk in the corner was two hundred years old if it was a day. Fluorescent light fixtures hung from old square timbers overhead.

Sealed crates filled the room, stacked from floor to ceiling. There were no shelves here, but each crate was meticulously labeled. They looked strong enough to safely transport high explosives.

"Is there a problem?" asked Jackson.

"Not yet." Nicola turned on the desk lamp. Every power cord in the room ran to a single silent generator in the corner, roughly the size of a home dehumidifier.

Hanging from the wall above the desk was a six-inch wide image of a white rabbit, created with porcupine quills. I hadn't seen this particular piece, but I recognized Jane Oshogay's work. She was Jackson's predecessor, and had been killed when Meridiana's ghosts attacked the archive earlier this year.

I spread the finished poem on the desk, weighing down the edges with a stapler, a pencil holder shaped like a wooden barrel, and a dog-eared copy of Charlotte Brontë's *Villette*.

"Interesting." Jackson peered over my shoulder. "The Latin reads like gibberish. I take it this is some form of code?"

"Something like that." With a sigh, I surrendered my chair to Bi Wei.

"When you free the sphere, Meridiana will know." Ponce de Leon moved to stand on the opposite side of the chair. "I believe the passive enchantments in this place should prevent her from locating us immediately, but she will devote all of her energy to finding us."

"Whoever she is, she'll have her work cut out for her," said Jackson. "The old underground timbers are like heat sinks. Any escaping magical energy within the fort is absorbed and masked as part of a constant low-level emanation. It's ingenious. From what we can tell, the original runes were carved into the heartwood using some species of powderpost beetle, though nobody knows how the beetles were controlled."

Lena coaxed a branch from one of the rafters, growing it until it was strong enough to hold Smudge's cage.

"Can you do it?" asked Nicola.

Bi Wei chewed her lip. "Meridiana stole the lives of our fellow students. We will do this, not for your Porters, but for them and the rest of the world."

"That works for us," I said before anyone else could answer.

She scanned the pages again. Her eyes followed the outer triangle, then worked inward along each spoke. She whispered to herself, pronouncing the Latin words without hesitating or stumbling. At the beginning of each seemingly nonsensical stanza, she repeated the name "Anna."

"Be careful," I said quietly. I didn't think Meridiana could strike through the poem, not without a copy of her own, but I had been wrong before. Both Nicola and Ponce de Leon stood ready to act. I split my attention between Bi Wei and Smudge, trusting the fire-spider to warn me if everything went to hell.

After about five minutes, Ponce de Leon leaned closer. "Remarkable. The letters are changing."

"Changing how?" I asked.

"They shine in the light," said Jackson. "Like metal or glass." He adjusted his glasses. "Master Pallas, what precisely is this woman attempting to accomplish? If this presents any kind of risk to the books preserved here—"

"Life is risk, Mister Chapin," Ponce de Leon interrupted. "At least, any life worth living."

Bi Wei's fingertips slipped through the page. She

jerked back, and now even I could see gleaming threads clinging to her nails like liquid bronze.

"Be ready." She reached into the poem again.

The sound of ripping paper made me cringe. Threads of smoke rose from the paper where Bi Wei's fingers disappeared. Metal letters climbed her hands, gradually fading into invisibility on her tan skin.

"We can feel the sphere," she said through clenched teeth. "It's hot. Almost too hot to touch."

"If I may?" Ponce de Leon touched her arm. I couldn't tell what he did, but Bi Wei visibly relaxed.

"Thank you."

The paper around her fingers blackened and curled upward. I wondered if Jackson had a fire extinguisher tucked away in here. If we burned down the Porters' new archive, Gutenberg would—

The thought of Gutenberg's name conjured the memory of his final, surprised grunt. The sound in my mind was so real, it was as if I was back in the room watching him fall. I swallowed and focused on Bi Wei's efforts.

The paper continued to burn, though there was no visible flame. I watched my own handwriting melt into Bi Wei's skin, one metal pen stroke at a time. It didn't seem to hurt her, but it was a disconcerting sight after a very disconcerting week.

"It's heavy." Bi Wei flinched. "This is like pulling a wasp nest from a branch, feeling the insects buzzing inside."

"Meridiana can't hurt you from within the sphere," I said.

"You're certain?"

I hesitated. Gerbert d'Aurillac hadn't believed Meridiana would be able to escape at all, but she had learned to reach beyond her prison. "She won't do anything to stop you from retrieving the sphere."

Bits of ash fell away like carbonized confetti. I double-checked Smudge for signs of anxiety or fear. He was preoccupied with grooming the bristles on the top of his head, rubbing his forelegs over his scalp like he was trying to fix a stubborn cowlick.

Like a magician revealing a final trick, Bi Wei lifted her hands. The remnants of the poem dropped onto the desk, leaving her holding the bronze globe I had seen during my conversation with Gerbert d'Aurillac.

She set the sphere on the desk, moving as slowly and carefully as if it were a bomb primed to explode.

I reached out to touch the sphere. Despite the heat Bi Wei had described, the metal was cool to the touch. The rings were polished and utterly clean of dust or corrosion. I might not be able to sense the magic, but I could still appreciate the craftsmanship that had gone into this sphere: the precisely drilled holes, the rings mounted to various axes, the images etched into the metal.

I peered at the model of the Earth, suspended at the center like an oversized olive on a bronze toothpick. "Hello, Meridiana."

The Egyptian government has declared a state of emergency following the apparent assassination of three high-ranking officials, including the vice president.

A group calling themselves the Shadows of Liberation claimed responsibility for the deaths in a video posted shortly after the assassinations. The video was released in English as well as Arabic, and warns that all who would disrupt the dream of a peaceful Egypt through greed and corruption will meet the same end.

"For many years Egypt has suffered the tyranny of evil men, but the instruments of man cannot stop us," proclaimed a hooded man holding a small, colored cap in his hands. "We stand on equal terms with the hidden powers of this world, and we will seize from them the reins of the nation."

The man then placed the cap upon his head and vanished, as if by magic.

The reference to standing on equal terms with hidden powers, as well as several other quotes, appear to have been drawn from the novel *Arabian Nights and Days*, a modern retelling of the tales of Scheherazade, by Nobel-laureate Naguib Mahfouz. One of the tales in Mahfouz's 1979 work describes an invisibility cap that matches the appearance of the cap used in the video.

The Shadows of Liberation have published a list of future targets, whom they describe as traitors to the Egyptian people.

Egypt's president was quick to denounce the Shadows of Liberation as a terrorist organization, and dismissed their apparent magic as simple camera trickery.

Chapter 14

PONCE DE LEON PULLED a silk handkerchief from his pocket and draped it over the sighting tube. "According to Isaac, this tube was how His Holiness trapped Meridiana. Best not to risk anyone accidentally looking through the eyepiece and joining her."

Bi Wei pushed the outermost ring to the right. When she removed her hands, it crawled slowly back to its prior position.

"Do you think Meridiana can feel you messing with her rings?" I asked.

Before anyone could answer, the rest of the metal rings scraped into motion. The sighting tube rose, lifting the handkerchief like a flag. The small spheres of the sun and moon inched along their orbits. When everything came to rest, the sphere was in an entirely different configuration.

I looked up, trying to imagine the position of the sun. Whatever the sphere was showing, it wasn't the current position of the heavens.

Bi Wei poked the rings again, but the sphere didn't react.

"Perhaps it's miscalibrated," Jackson suggested.

I pointed to the azimuth, the flat, vertical ring. "It's adjusted for forty-six degrees latitude, which runs through the northern part of Michigan's Upper Peninsula."

"But we're not in—"

I clapped a hand to Jackson's mouth. "Important safety tip. The sphere has a wannabe goddess inside, and she'd like nothing more than to squash us all, just as soon as she can figure out *where we are*."

He was right, though. We were south of the bridge, putting us several degrees lower than the sphere indicated. I touched the flat band of the ecliptic ring, which was divided into months and days, and marked with the signs of the zodiac. I looked at the sun, projecting where it would intersect the ecliptic at sunrise and sunset.

Lena pulled me back from the sphere. "What's wrong, Isaac?"

I rubbed my arms against a chill that started deep inside my body. I pointed to the position of the sun. "If I'm reading this right, the sphere is set for about ten in the morning on January fourth."

"That date means something?" Bi Wei asked.

"My birthday." But the sphere was moving again, faster than before. Metal hummed as the rings spun and slid into position. I waited for it to stop. "Anyone here born at eleven at night on the twentieth of June, around thirty-five degrees latitude?"

The sphere spun to life.

"I was born in early summer, hours after the sun had set," whispered Bi Wei.

I found it reassuring that the sphere seemed to recognize Bi Wei as an individual.

"It's returned to January fourth." Ponce de Leon touched the metal rings, but nothing happened. "The sphere seems to like the two of you."

"It's listening to us," said Bi Wei.

I thought back to the mythology of Gerbert d'Aurillac, scraps of rumor and legend I had read over the past week. "It's doing more than that." I dropped to one knee, bringing my face level with the sphere. "It reacted every time one of us asked a question."

"I asked you what was wrong," Lena pointed out. "The rings didn't move."

"Every time we asked a yes/no question," I amended. "The stories said d'Aurillac possessed a brazen head, a bronze oracle that would answer any question." I imagined the small orbs of the sun and moon as eyes peering through wild, tangled rings of metal hair. "Did Gerbert d'Aurillac use you as an oracle?"

Nothing. I sat back on my heels, glaring at the sphere. Why would it react to some questions but not this one?

"Did Nidhi eat the last of my Mackinac Island Fudge ice cream last week?" asked Lena.

The sphere moved again, coming to rest in early December. Lena's jaw tightened. "I don't know the exact date of my birth, but I first stepped from my tree in the winter, several weeks before Christmas."

"This is wrong." Bi Wei reached into the sphere to touch the moon. "The moon should be new on this date."

"How can you tell?" asked Nidhi.

She stared through the sphere. "We can see it."

"Maybe it's not equipped to guess the birthday of a dryad," said Jackson.

"That's not it." I grimaced. "It's because I ate Lena's ice cream, not Nidhi. Sorry about that, by the way. I bet the sphere shows the proper configuration for a yes, but introduces a mistake for no." Which would explain why it hadn't moved when I asked if it was an oracle. The answer was yes, but the sphere had already adjusted itself to my birth date. "Can Meridiana hear and remember the questions we ask?"

The rings and planets whirled through time, returning to the positions of my birth. *Yes.*

"Can Jeneta be saved?" I asked. "Restored to who she was, free of Meridiana's influence?"

Nothing happened, but when Bi Wei repeated the question, the sphere moved back to June 20. *Yes.*

"Assuming it's answering honestly," Nidhi pointed out.

"It's impossible to be certain, but we don't believe she has a choice," said Bi Wei.

"Are they ever going to have a woman play the Doctor on *Doctor Who*?" I asked.

Nothing happened. Either the sphere didn't consider my question worth answering, or else it couldn't answer questions about the future, perhaps as a built-in protection against paradox.

It was Lena's turn. "If we chuck you into a smelting furnace, will that destroy Meridiana?"

This time, the moon was in the correct position, but the date was off. *No.*

"If anything, that would release her," said Ponce de Leon. "I believe Johannes had the right approach. He intended to end Meridiana's miniature universe, to bring about the end of days. Would *this* put an end to Meridiana?"

The sphere moved again. We looked to Ponce de Leon for confirmation. For once, he appeared unsettled. "I didn't think that through. I . . . don't know the precise date of my birth," he admitted.

"Ask it a question you know the answer is yes," I said.

"Right, of course." He paused a moment. "Am I wearing shoes?"

We all reflexively looked at his feet, but the sphere didn't move. Meaning the answer to both of his questions was yes.

"Looks like your birthday is March thirteenth," I said. "I'll have to remember to send you a card."

"Does Meridiana know where we are?" asked Nicola.

The sphere spun to August 5, only a few weeks ago. "Happy late birthday," I said.

Nicola looked to Bi Wei, who shook her head. "It should be a first quarter moon."

"How can you know that without knowing the year of my birth," said Nicola.

"The configuration is just wrong. Like a poem with one character out of position."

Assuming Bi Wei's reading was correct, we were safe for the moment. To the sphere, I said, "Gerbert trapped Meridiana—you—in this thing. How did you start to escape?"

It didn't respond, of course. I needed a yes/no question, which meant I had to figure it out myself, then ask for confirmation.

Had Gerbert d'Aurillac made mistakes in his spellcasting? Or perhaps Meridiana was simply too strong to remain contained forever. She could have worked for centuries, a prisoner chipping away at the walls of her cell, until she punched a hole to the outside world. Gutenberg had been aware of her presence more than five hundred years ago, and of the ghosts she had drawn to herself. "Is the Ghost Army trapped in the sphere with you?"

No.

"Has Meridiana altered the magic of her prison?" asked Nicola.

Yes.

"How the hell did she do that?" I asked. Neither Nicola nor the sphere responded. "Can you be disassembled without freeing Meridiana?"

Silence.

The Porters had experimented with oracular magic before, but it was tricky to say the least. Anything connected to libriomancy ran the risk of distorting its answers to align with the originating text rather than the real world. Ask a crystal ball about your future, and likely as not it would show you spoilers from the story it came from. But d'Aurillac's work had no libriomantic component.

I sat down at the desk and held my hand behind my back. "Can you perceive how many fingers I'm holding up on my right hand?"

Yes.

"Cool. What about the individual cells of my body? Can you perceive them?"

Yes.

"Can you distinguish between healthy and sick or dying cells?"

Yes.

I turned to Lena. "You could use this thing as a medical scanner to screen for cancer and disease. I bet it would do instant pregnancy testing, too. If we could—"

Ponce de Leon coughed quietly. "Perhaps we should get on with it before the temptation to play with the oracle distracts us from our true goals."

"Too late," I said. "I'm distracted."

"Jeneta Aboderin." Nidhi rested a hand on my shoulder. "The Ghost Army. Gutenberg. Focus, Isaac."

Jackson straightened. "Wait, what about Gutenberg?"

"The Regional Masters haven't shared that news yet." Nicola paced the length of the room. "They believed it would be 'too disruptive.'"

Ponce de Leon reached toward the sphere, stopping with his hand an inch from the surface. "Meridiana is a thousand-year-old sorceress trapped within that armillary sphere. Yesterday, she murdered Johannes Gutenberg."

"I don't know who you are, sir," said Jackson, "but you must be mistaken. Gutenberg—"

"I apologize for my rudeness. My name is Juan Ponce de Leon."

Jackson stared at Ponce de Leon, then at the sphere. He stepped back from both, as if he wasn't sure which was the greater threat. "I don't understand. You were banished. The Porters . . ." He swallowed, then looked at Bi Wei. "I know Doctor Shah and her bodyguard, and I'm familiar with Isaac. Who are you?"

"My name is Bi Wei. We are the Bì Shēng de dú zhě."

He turned to Nicola, silently pleading for an explanation.

"I'll need you to provide details on all of the fort's enchantments," she said flatly.

"I . . . I should go."

"No, you really shouldn't," said Ponce de Leon without looking up.

"The fort," Nicola repeated.

Jackson chewed the side of his lower lip, then nodded. "I have a copy of Jane Oshogay's instructions in the file cabinet beside the desk. It's basically a user guide for the whole fort."

While they reviewed the defenses, I returned my attention to the armillary sphere. All magic had limits. What were Meridiana's? "If I took you outside in the daytime, would you be able to see the stars?"

Yes.

"But you don't know where you are right now?"

No.

I silently thanked those paranoid French traders. "What about planets? Can you see them?"

Yes.

D'Aurillac had created so much more than a simple prison. This would have been an unimaginably important tool. While it couldn't describe the skies to him, it could confirm or deny his observations and theories. "Can you see planets outside of our solar system?"

No.

So much for using Meridiana to prove the existence of alien civilizations.

Nidhi sat down on the edge of the desk beside me. "Are you all right?"

"What do you mean?"

"You physically pulled away when I mentioned Jeneta's name, before. Your shoulders are tight as rock, and you're talking faster than usual."

"I'm okay. I'm just—"

"You haven't been okay for a while now." She reached out to touch one of the sphere's rings. "You remind me of a story I read a year or so back, about a village in Kenya. A pair of cheetahs had been eating the villagers' goats. Cheetahs are unbeatable sprinters, but they can't run forever. The men waited until the hottest part of the day, then chased the cheetahs on foot. Eventually, both animals collapsed from exhaustion."

"We don't have time for this, Nidhi."

"You never have time," she said firmly. "Ever since Gutenberg took your magic, you've been too busy running. You can't run forever."

My vision blurred. I looked away, but I knew she'd seen me blinking back tears. Guilt and loss and grief battered through walls already weakened by exhaustion. I pressed my palms against my head, as if I could physically force everything back. I was painfully aware of everyone in the room watching me—or in Jackson's case, deliberately *not* watching.

"Gutenberg carved out a piece of your soul," Ponce de Leon said gently. "He believed it was for the best, but such losses leave deep scars. You've nothing to be ashamed of."

I knew they meant well, but his words just made me angry. Like I was a broken animal to be pitied. Wasn't I one of the lucky ones? Unlike too many people who had died without knowing why, I had survived. "I don't need to run forever. Just long enough to bring Meridiana down."

"All right. But when this is over, I want you to talk to someone." Nidhi raised a hand before I could object. "It doesn't have to be a therapist. Take a walk with Lena. Go out drinking with Jeff if you want to."

I turned back to the sphere. "What I don't understand is why d'Aurillac hid this away in a poem. This sphere could have done so much for his work and research. Sending it away would be like . . . like permanently cutting off your Internet connection."

"The horror," Lena said, giving a mock-shudder.

"Maybe he felt guilty," Nidhi suggested. "Gutenberg enslaved others to power his automatons, but he was forever conflicted about them. Gerbert d'Aurillac might have felt the same about using his former student."

"Let's ask her." To the sphere, I said, "Did Gerbert d'Aurillac enchant this intentionally to allow you to indicate yes or no, but with no other voice?"

Yes.

"A true voice might have allowed her to use magic," Nidhi suggested. "Or to persuade someone to free her."

As a precaution, it made sense to limit Meridiana's ability to communicate with the outside world, but I couldn't see Gerbert d'Aurillac forcing her to serve as his own personal oracle. The man whose memories I had touched had never been cruel. Imprison a murderess, certainly, but this? He would have been revolted by such enslavement. There had to be another reason, something we were missing.

I unhooked Smudge's cage from the ceiling as I thought. He had been squeezed in that flattened rectangle for too long. I opened the door and let him scurry up my arm. He crouched on my shoulder to watch the sphere, as if it was a metal monster ready to pounce.

"Rotting *hell!*" Lena staggered backward into the wall, both hands clutching her ribs.

Nidhi and I were at her side a moment later, each of us grabbing one of her elbows to support her.

"What's wrong?" asked Nicola.

Lena jerked free of my grip and slammed a fist against the wall behind us. The blow left a foot-long crack. Through gritted teeth, she said, "That *really* hurts."

She appeared uninjured. "Your tree?" I guessed.

Lena nodded.

Whatever was happening, it had to be in response to us retrieving Meridiana's prison. "There should be Porters near the house. Nicola can contact them—"

"Meridiana has a message for us." Sweat beaded Lena's brow, and her eyes brimmed with unshed tears.

"You can hear her?" Ponce de Leon asked sharply.

"She's carving the words into my oak." Lena took several quick, tight breaths. "She wants to meet to discuss a truce."

"The question isn't whether or not it's a trap," said Ponce de Leon. "It's whether or not we can turn the trap to our advantage."

"I can't allow it." Nicola was insisting the only safe choice was to ignore Meridiana's offer and proceed as planned. "The moment any of us approach Meridiana, she'll rip the location of the sphere from our memories and send her forces to take it and kill the rest of us."

"There are ways of shielding those memories," said Bi Wei.

Nidhi and I sat with Lena. Sweat drenched her skin. Dark lines twitched and bulged on her arms as the grafts inside of her responded to the ongoing assault on her tree. Her lips parted. Through clenched teeth, she said,

"Meridiana is threatening to release the Ghost Army if we refuse to talk."

"Can she do that?" asked Jackson.

Behind him, the armillary sphere reconfigured itself in response to his question. A brief exchange between Jackson and Bi Wei over the date of Jackson's birth confirmed the answer: *Yes*.

"She's desperate," said Ponce de Leon. "We know Lena can survive the death of her oak. If we strike quickly enough—"

"Are you that confident you can destroy the sphere before she looses her army?" I asked. "And what about Jeneta?" I spun to face the desk. "If we destroy the sphere, will Jeneta Aboderin be harmed?"

Yes.

"Will she die?" I pressed.

The sphere didn't respond.

"Jeneta is one child." Ponce de Leon raised his cane like a baseball bat, and for a second I thought he meant to physically smash the sphere. Instead, he rested it on his shoulder and sighed. "We might yet find another way to rescue her, but if we can't, she's too dangerous a weapon to leave in Meridiana's hands."

"She's not a weapon," I shot back. Nobody answered. They didn't have to. With the exception of Jackson, we all knew what Meridiana had accomplished with Jeneta's magic.

"Is Meridiana's offer of a truce genuine?" Nidhi spoke so quietly I almost missed it, but the sphere heard.

Yes.

"If Meridiana releases the Ghost Army now, will she be able to control them?" I didn't know which possibility was more frightening.

No.

Ponce de Leon swore under his breath.

"We're at a stalemate," I said. "We've got Meridiana's

life in our hands, and she has the Ghost Army." As well as Jeneta and Lena's oak. To the sphere, I asked, "Can you hear us if we move into the hallway and shut the door?" The archive was both physically and magically soundproofed, but we didn't know the sphere's full abilities.

No.

I kissed Lena on the forehead and stood up, leaving her with Nidhi. I tapped Ponce de Leon and Nicola, who followed me out of the room.

"You have an idea?" asked Ponce de Leon once the door was closed behind us.

"Maybe." I turned to Nicola. "Who took over tech support for the Porters after Victor died?"

"Kirsten LaMontagne."

I didn't know the name. "Meridiana is using Jeneta's magic. Together, they're working libriomancy beyond anything I've seen, but it's still done through e-books and other electronics. Her monsters? Transformed using books from her e-reader. The devourers she sent through the television in Chicago? She probably uploaded them somehow."

"Where are you going with this?" asked Ponce de Leon.

I smiled. "Ask Kirsten how close I'd have to get to hack Jeneta's e-reader."

If I hadn't known how much trouble was waiting at my house, Smudge would have warned me. The closer Lena and I got, the more he flattened himself against the floor of his cage, red flames rippling over his back like the northern lights.

"What the hell?" Parked cars lined my street, most of them clustered directly in front of my place. A few had pulled onto the grass, and a white news van blocked the driveway. I had to drive to the end of the block to park the Jeep. "This doesn't look good."

"Meridiana is in my grove." Lena had stopped sweating, but her face remained pale. "There's a crowd. I can feel their feet on my roots."

"The Ghost Army?" I checked my shock-gun out of habit, reached for Smudge's cage, then changed my mind. Bringing Smudge along wouldn't warn us of anything we didn't already know. It would simply put him in danger, too.

"I can't tell."

As we walked back to the house, I searched the street for the Porters who were supposed to be watching the place. I didn't find them.

Lena readied a single bokken, leaving the second thrust through her belt. I switched my gun to a lower setting, one that would stun but not kill. None of our weapons were likely to do much against Meridiana herself, but hopefully it wouldn't come to that.

A familiar, shrouded figure approached us on the street. I fought the urge to look away. So long as the burqa hid the gorgon's gaze, we were safe. Lena and I spread apart as we walked, wordlessly preparing to hit the gorgon from both sides should things go wrong.

"Hello, Deanna," I said.

"Deanna?" Lena repeated.

"That was her name, back when she was a Porter. Before Meridiana killed her. Deanna tried to warn me about Meridiana's angel, back in Rome."

The gorgon turned to me. "Meridiana asked me to give you this." Her slender, jaundiced hand offered an old e-reader.

I checked the monochrome display, but didn't touch it. "Douglas Adams?"

"This is for your protection." Her words were like

honey and tea, sweet and seductive, with a thick Texan drawl. You barely noticed the shifting and hissing of her hair. "I'm told the effect is called a 'somebody else's problem' field. Stay close to the reader, and nobody else should pay any attention to your presence." She stood motionless for several seconds, like she was listening. "Your phone. Please turn it off."

"No way. I've got an open connection to Nicola Pallas. If that call goes dead, so does Meridiana."

"All right." She motioned for me to take the e-reader.

I hesitated, but if Meridiana wanted to kill us, she didn't need to trick me into taking an e-book to do it. My fingers brushed Deanna's. Her skin was hot and dry. I wondered if she was warm or cold-blooded. Between the sun and the burqa, she couldn't have been comfortable.

"Do you remember who you were?" asked Lena.

She stopped in midstep and studied Lena closely. "Do you?"

Deanna led us around the house. A little over a month ago, Jeneta Aboderin and I had sat on the deck discussing dreams and magic and poetry. Now Meridiana waited before a crowd in front of the oaks. Her angel perched twenty feet up, white wings outstretched among the branches.

Meridiana looked much as she had the last time I saw her. She wore a pink-and-white leather jacket with fake jewels decorating the sleeves. I assumed they were fake, at least. Colorful plastic beads clicked at the end of her braids. She stood upon a tangle of roots, giving her an extra foot of height over the crowd. Her own e-reader was clutched in her left hand.

"There are forty or so people here," I muttered for Nicola's benefit. "Including a news crew near the front." Their camera was rolling. Jeneta's parents would see this. What was I supposed to tell them when they called?

Lena and I each held one end of the older e-reader,

but that didn't stop Jeneta—Meridiana—from spotting us. She gave a brief nod of acknowledgment, then addressed the crowd. "If you had a plentiful supply of water and came across a man dying of thirst, would you refuse to offer him a drink? Would you stand by and watch him expire?"

The angry muttering made me suspect Meridiana had been working them for a while, stoking their emotions. I couldn't tell if she was using magic to strengthen her influence.

Deanna wove through the crowd and slipped between the trees of the grove, disappearing into the shadows.

"Magic is not a thing to be feared," Meridiana continued. "The world is sick, starving for hope. How many people have died in conflicts that could have been solved with magic? How many loved ones have you lost to disease and death? There is a vacuum, an emptiness in the world where magic was always meant to exist. Thanks to those who hoard their secret power, that void has come to be filled by suffering and despair."

The worst part was that I couldn't entirely disagree. Obviously, things weren't as simple as she made it sound. Magic brought new dangers of its own. And yet the Porters had the ability to help so many people . . .

I glanced down at my phone and activated the app Kirsten had e-mailed me. It immediately began pinging for other devices. It picked up a number of other smartphones as well as the neighbors' wireless modem, but I didn't see Jeneta's e-reader on the list yet.

Meridiana raised her hands to quiet the crowd's anger. "The men and women who kept this secret are human, just as you and me. We are all flawed beings under God. But their flaws have brought the world to the edge of damnation. You know of the Porters, I assume?"

Shouts of affirmation and accusation. By now, everyone had seen or heard about Bi Wei's letter.

"The Porters have unearthed an artifact from a thousand years ago, a prison for unimaginably powerful souls, ghosts who would devour this world."

She looked at me when she said "devour." My nails dug into my skin. Jeneta was the one who had coined the term "devourers" for the Ghost Army, during a conversation here in my backyard.

"I can protect this town. I can prevent another massacre like the one you suffered before." Meridiana pointed to the angel. "This is Binion, a friend who found the courage to leave the Porters to help me do what's right. He, Deanna, and a handful of other courageous souls will do everything in their power to stop an even greater threat."

What I wanted was to send a bolt of lightning into Meridiana's lying mouth. But their magic was strong enough to deflect or dissolve anything I could throw their way, and in the unlikely chance something did get through, it would hurt Jeneta more than Meridiana. Binion hadn't *chosen* to leave the Porters. Meridiana would have battled him to exhaustion, transformed his body, and ripped out his mind, replacing him with one of her ghosts. Whoever he had once been was gone, either dead or sent to join Meridiana's ghosts, to be tormented in his afterlife until nothing remained but power and madness.

"The Porters hope to use this prison on me, to bind me with the mindless souls of the dead. And then they would destroy it." She raised her voice, and her next words sounded like she was standing right beside me. "I brought you here to warn you. If the Porters destroy the sphere, they will release an army of ghosts upon the world with no one to control them. Whatever your fears, nothing would be worse than such unchecked chaos and death. They will destroy everything and everyone they touched."

"Do you think she's right?" Lena whispered. "Would destroying the sphere free the Ghost Army?"

"I don't know." Meridiana knew her prison better than anyone. She might be bluffing, but she had to know we'd use the sphere to confirm anything she said. Which suggested she was telling the truth. I raised my phone. "Nicola, could you relay that question to the sphere?"

"What *is* that angel thing?" asked a man near the front of the crowd. "Is it safe?"

"He is exactly what he appears to be." Meridiana extended a hand.

Binion's wings stirred powerful gusts of air as he dropped to the ground beside Meridiana. He towered over the girl like a god. People near the back shoved to try to get a better view.

"Magic is real." Meridiana tilted her e-reader and tapped the screen. "If Binion's presence doesn't convince you, perhaps this will."

She began to read. I couldn't understand the language—Italian, maybe?—nor could I sense the magic itself. But I felt its effects. Her spell stirred a sense of longing, reminiscent of the siren's song, though thankfully not as potent. Her intonation changed, and now laughter spread through us all. I found myself grinning as well.

Without magic of my own, there wasn't a damned thing I could do to fight it. Plugging my ears didn't stop her spells from penetrating my body and manipulating my emotions. Bi Wei and Ponce de Leon had shielded my memories of their location, nothing more.

The next spell evoked rage. Meridiana cut it off after only a few seconds, but it was enough to bring several people to blows. I realized I had turned my shock-gun to maximum and brought it to bear on Meridiana.

"That was no sleight of hand," said Meridiana. To the camera, she added, "Those of you watching on your televisions will have felt only an echo of my power."

An echo which hadn't entirely faded, or maybe the

angry thudding of my pulse was the aftermath of adrenaline. I slowed my breathing, trying to calm myself enough to think clearly. I needed to get close enough for my phone to connect to Meridiana's primary e-reader.

Meridiana bowed her head. "Isaac Vainio was given the gift of libriomancy, the magic of books. He could have used that magic to help you all. Instead, he brought the Porters' war to Copper River. How many of you lost friends and family to the monsters that fought in your streets?"

Too damned many. I handed the e-reader to Lena and pressed into the crowd. "Why don't you tell them where those monsters came from?"

Meridiana folded her arms. The creak of her leather jacket was the only sound. I could see confusion on people's faces—friends and neighbors squinting at me as I stepped out of range of the old e-reader's magic.

"You spent a thousand years gathering the broken shells of the dead," I said. "Building your army. *You* sent them to attack Copper River. I did everything I could to stop them." My voice cracked. "I was the one who found Loretta Trembath after one of your creatures killed her."

I remembered every detail: the web of cracks in the smashed windshield, the flattened metal, the wide, frozen eyes of a woman I had known and joked with for years. I hadn't told anyone about finding her body, or how she and others haunted my nightmares.

"You blame me for that attack?" asked Meridiana. "I thought your war was against the students of Bi Sheng. Another innocent group the Porters tried to destroy. Or was it a battle against one of your own, a father who turned against the Porters after the death of his son? You have so many enemies, so many secrets, it's difficult for me to keep track."

I snuck another peek at my phone. Bingo. We had the signal.

"I asked for a truce," Meridiana continued. "And you brought a weapon to kill me."

In my anger, I had forgotten about the damned shockgun holstered at my hip. "Tell them whose body you've taken. How you violated Jeneta Aboderin's mind and infected her thoughts."

Meridiana looked to the camera. "Jeneta Aboderin was a brilliant, gifted, trusting child. The Porters lied to her family and lured her here under false pretenses so they could study her magic. They failed to protect her from the darker side of magic, the things that live and wait in the shadows. Isaac and his brethren used her, until her mind was damaged beyond repair. I saved her, and she welcomed me."

"That's a lie." Only it wasn't, not entirely. I *had* failed to protect Jeneta, and Meridiana knew it.

The crowd moved with restless energy, and I heard my name muttered over and over, growing louder and angrier with each repetition. I had no proof of Meridiana's actions, and they saw me as a liar who had betrayed their trust.

I had lived most of my life in Copper River, but suddenly I was no longer one of them. I was an outsider. I picked Lizzie Pascoe out of the crowd. If I couldn't get the crowd to listen to me, maybe I could reach them as individuals. "Lizzie, you would have died in that attack on Copper River if I hadn't gotten you inside. I pulled you off the street . . ."

She stared at me like I was a stranger. Dammit, the Porters had erased her memories to try to cover their tracks. She didn't remember how close she had come to dying. The Porters had effectively eliminated anything I could use to defend myself.

"You know me," I said. "You knew my parents. I've never done anything to hurt any of you, or to endanger this town."

"How many werewolves live in Tamarack?" Meridiana's words were soft, but her power carried them to every ear within a hundred feet. "Or should we discuss the vampire you befriended in Marquette? The one who was so fond of the blood of young Boy Scouts. What other threats have you concealed from your friends and neighbors?"

Shit. The longer she kept me on the defensive, the more I looked like a criminal and a liar. I spread my hands. "You told me you wanted a truce."

"I do. Bring me the sphere, and I promise to protect you from the Ghost Army. I will make sure Copper River is safe. Or do you care so little for your home that you would sacrifice it to protect your own power?"

"What the hell are you, Isaac Vainio?" shouted Jaylee Parker.

Walt Derocher shoved me from behind. "We buried my cousin after that attack. The cops tried to tell us it was a bear what did that to her."

My bowels and gut clenched as I realized what was about to happen. I shoved the phone into my pocket and tried to back away, but I was too late. A stone glanced off of my temple, making me stagger. I reached for my shock-gun, but before I could draw it, they closed around me, grabbing and punching and kicking.

I fell to the ground and rolled to the side. A boot smashed into my upper arm. Someone else stomped on my hand. I kicked a heel into the stomper's groin and tucked my other arm over my head for protection.

Everyone had grieved for the loss of friends and family. They had watched, afraid, as stories of magic and monsters spread. And Meridiana had brought me here to be a target for their anger and their fear.

I saw my boss, Jennifer Latona, standing a short way back. She wasn't attacking, but neither did she do anything to try to stop the others. Our eyes met, and she turned away.

Pain jolted my lower back. Hands seized my shirt and hair, hauling me brutally to my feet.

I heard the crack of wood against bone, and thought for a second someone else had struck me. Instead, Jaylee Parker cried out in pain and staggered back. Lena's bokken hummed through the air and another man fell, clutching a broken knee. She grabbed me with one hand, sweeping her bokken through the air with the other as she dragged me toward the street.

Jaylee held her arm and wept, but nobody followed us. Already the old e-reader's magic was working, causing them to forget about me, just as I had forgotten Lena's presence until she stepped in. They looked around in confusion, seeking another outlet for their anger.

Meridiana said nothing. She simply watched as the mob turned toward my house. They didn't know I was here, but they remembered me. They remembered Meridiana's accusations, and the deaths of their loved ones.

I tried to get up, but Lena's grip was unbreakable. "They'll *kill* you."

The fire started on the deck. I had to believe it was more of Meridiana's magic. No matter how hurt and afraid they were, I couldn't accept that the people I had lived with my entire life would deliberately set my house ablaze. But as the flames began to spread, they did nothing to stop it, either.

Black smoke rose from the deck. Siding warped and cracked. A window shattered. The fire crept inside, consuming the faded blue curtains my father had hung in that room when I was eight years old.

The mob fell back. Some looked frightened. Others shocked, as if they were beginning to realize what they had been a part of. Nobody looked at one another. Nobody spoke. The news van backed out of the driveway and sped away.

I raised my weapon. I couldn't stop this, but Meridiana could.

She smirked and tapped the screen of her tablet. When she pulled her finger away, a tiny orange flame perched on the tip. She gave a meaningful glance toward the trees of the grove.

I holstered the gun and shouted, "This is your truce?"

Her smile grew, and she curled her fingers into a fist, extinguishing the threat. "This is a warning. A preview of things to come should you release the Ghost Army."

"You're assuming nobody else can command them," I said.

"If the children of Johannes Gutenberg and Bi Sheng could control my army, don't you think they would have done so by now?" She walked toward us, flanked by Deanna and Binion. "I've stood with one foot in the land of the dead since my birth. Thanks to my teacher's betrayal, I spent most of my life in the liminal state between reality and nonexistence. The dead are more real to me than you are, Isaac Vainio. What makes you believe you or anyone else could take them away from me?"

"My boundless hope and optimism," I said flatly.

She smirked. "Life is an ephemeral, fragile thing. Even to those such as Johannes Gutenberg. You're children, terrified of what waits in the shadows. You saw how quickly fear turned your friends and neighbors against you. This is what the rule of the living has brought about: a world fragmented by petty, shortsighted men who rule over mindless sheep.

"I mean to make this world whole. To unite the living and the dead. You can accept that and live, or you can try to fight. Destroy me, and you damn this world to the mercy of the dead."

"Free Jeneta, and I'll talk to the others about your sphere."

"I offered to spare Copper River, and you demand more?" She cocked her head to the side so the plastic beads in her hair clicked together. "Bring me Gerbert d'Aurillac's armillary sphere, and I will give you back Jeneta Aboderin. I will restore your magic. And I will find a place for you in my empire. It's a generous offer, Isaac Vainio. But if you continue to fight, Jeneta will be the first to die upon my rebirth. Her body will burn, and her soul will serve me forever."

Meridiana's ghosts were little more than animals, beaten and tormented into madness, until nothing remained but hatred and power. One way or another, I couldn't let her do that to Jeneta.

"It's no longer a question of winning," said Meridiana. "Letting the Ghost Army ravage your world unchecked will be far worse than anything you fear I might do."

The wind shifted, slamming a wall of smoke and heat into my body. I retreated until I could breathe again, if uncontrolled coughing qualified as breathing. Meridiana and the others backed away and disappeared in the darkness.

The flames spread through my house like hatred. Smoke detectors wailed pitifully, their voices smothered by the cracking sound of my home being consumed. I tried not to think about the books I could have used to stop this. Books to slow time. Books to extinguish even magical flames.

Sirens screamed in the distance. Lena dragged me to the road, then ran to her grove. She sank her hands into the closest of the oaks. Overhead, branches shied away from the house, pulling their leaves out of reach. I lost sight of her when she moved to the next.

The first to arrive was a pair of police officers. Within minutes, they had been joined by a fire department SUV, fire truck, and ambulance.

By then, there was no saving the house. The fire chief

interrogated me as his team fought to drown the flames and keep the fire from spreading. His questions felt unreal, like a voice from a dream.

Are you the homeowner? Was anyone else inside? Is there anything dangerous or explosive in the home? Were you here when the fire broke out?

I kept my responses short and as truthful as I could, but I could tell he wasn't buying it.

He crouched in front of me and checked my eyes with a flashlight. "You're saying you just came home and your house was on fire? There were no candles, no forgotten cigarettes, no dying appliances you forgot to shut off before you left?"

I shook my head.

"How'd you get that black eye?" he asked. "Your hand looks pretty busted up, too. What happened?"

"Got into a fight at work."

"Any chance the other fellow did this?" He pointed to the fire.

"No, he—he doesn't know where I live." Dammit. I could see him getting more and more suspicious.

"Have you been drinking?"

"Not yet." I looked toward the house as gouts of water assaulted the flames. "I'll probably start soon enough, though."

"I've been doing this job twenty-three years, Isaac. I've seen a lot of houses burn. There's always a reason."

My phone buzzed, making me jump. The text message said *Let me speak to him.* I had forgotten Nicola was still listening on the other end. I gave the chief an apologetic look, exchanged a few quick words with Nicola, then handed him the phone. "This woman says she saw something."

I heard the faint, metallic echo of Nicola Pallas' song from the speaker, and then he was returning my phone. He stared at me for a moment longer, brows furrowed like he was struggling to remember, then shrugged. "Thanks, Mister Vainio. The EMTs will be around to check you over. I'm sorry about your home."

I returned the phone to my pocket and watched as my roof caved in, sending geysers of sparks into the sky. As water gradually turned the earth to swamp. As smoke and ash smothered everything in gray.

Five hours I waited, while Lena hid within her trees. The closest oaks had been singed, but they had survived. The fire crew inspected the wreckage, soaking every potential hot spot.

It was a long time to think. Meridiana's offer might have been genuine, but she knew the Porters couldn't go along with it. There had to be another reason for her so-called truce. To warn us about the Ghost Army going free if we destroyed the sphere? She could have carved that warning into Lena's tree.

A second fire truck had arrived at some point during the night, this one out of Tamarack. I hadn't even noticed. One of the EMTs had me sign a form officially refusing a ride to the hospital. I signed left-handed, keeping my right arm as still as I could. They had splinted two of the fingers and bandaged a cut on my leg.

The chief returned a while later to go through a well-rehearsed but sympathetic checklist of things to do and not to do. Call my insurance company. Don't go into the wreckage. Call if I remembered anything about how the fire might have started.

I nodded and thanked him and spoke whatever words would send them away the soonest. Once the last truck finally left, Lena emerged from the oaks to join me. She looked unreal, untouched by the gray and black that had leached the color from the rest of the world.

"I'm sorry," she said.

I dug out my phone. The battery was almost dead, but

we were still connected to Nicola. I put her on speaker and asked, "Did we get Meridiana's e-reader?"

"We have a snapshot of its contents, and we'll be able to see any time she downloads something new."

"Good. We'll be back soon." I hung up. Lena had to help me to my feet. My limbs had stiffened, and I could feel each punch and kick my neighbors had landed. "I need one thing before we go."

Most of the house was a sinkhole, the wreckage having collapsed into the basement. But the garage was built on solid ground, having been added on when I was in elementary school. Lena was strong enough to pry the worst of the debris aside, using blackened timbers as enormous levers.

Beneath it all sat the car I had stolen from Ponce de Leon years ago, a black Triumph convertible, four decades old and laced with magical enchantments that had protected it from the flames. The exterior was filthy, but the damage hadn't touched the inside. I opened the door, shifted it into neutral, and released the parking brake. Together, we rolled the car down the driveway and into the street.

I fetched Smudge from the Jeep and brought him back to the Triumph. I sat down in the driver's seat and gasped. At a minimum, a couple of my ribs were out of place, if not broken. Half of my face felt heavy and swollen. My lower lip was cut, and blood oozed every time I spoke.

I closed my eyes. "On second thought, maybe you should drive."

Dear Isaac,

I saw the newscast out of Copper River. You're really one of them, aren't you? One of those book-wizards, the Porters.

I remember the weirdness before you went away to college. I thought I was imagining things. Where would my brother get a stack of real gold coins? And that pet spider of yours, the one you kept insisting was some kind of mutant tarantula?

You lied to me.

I can't blame you for that. I know we didn't exactly get along in those days. And you needed to keep your secrets, I get it. The Porters probably had rules and oaths and all that.

But we grew up. You graduated and got your job at the library. I married Angie and had kids. You and I stopped fighting over stupid stuff.

And then the accident happened. Lexi was five years old. Do you know what it's like trying to explain to your five-year-old daughter that if we don't let the doctors cut off her leg, the infection will kill her? Or to know that even the amputation might not save her?

She's had four surgeries to try to repair the damage from the crash. To pin her pelvis back together. To ease the pressure on her brain. Depending on the results of her next MRI, we may have to go back for number five before the end of the summer.

I never said how much it meant to us that you flew out here after the accident. That you watched Lexi's brother and brought us badly cooked meals and did everything you could to help.

Only you didn't, did you? You didn't do <u>everything</u>.

Maybe you had good reasons. Maybe your precious secret was more important than your niece. Well, the secret's out now, and Lexi deserves better. She deserves the chance to be a kid, and she shouldn't have to go through life like this because some drunk blew through a stop sign.

People tell Angie and me how strong we are to take care of Lexi. How she's such a special girl, and we're amazing parents. How God never gives anyone more than they can handle.

This has nothing to do with God. This is about a fifty-two-year-old woman who was too wasted to drive, and a brother who chose not to use his magic to help his niece.

I haven't said anything about this to Angie or the kids, but I can't hide it from them forever. Sooner or later, they're going to see the story. They're going to know what you are.

I don't imagine you can go back in time and stop the accident, but there's got to be something you can do. Lexi is in pain every day. Her hips, her back, her knee . . . some days it takes hours for her to fall asleep, even with her meds.

Isaac, if you don't help that little girl, I swear to Christ I'll never forgive you.

Your brother,
Toby

Chapter 15

I HAD GROWN UP in that house. It could be rebuilt, but so much of what it held was gone forever. Old novels, many of which had been autographed and personalized by authors now dead. The crooked tile floor my parents had installed in the bathroom more than ten years ago. Memories of helping to haul ruined carpet and old boxes out of the basement one spring after the sump pump failed, and later launching paper boats into the three inches of standing water from the bottom step.

The loss hurt, but not as much as the way the crowd had turned on me. It was like something from *Lord of the Flies*, primitive savagery summoned to the fore by fear. I had known many of them for most of my life. Played with them as kids.

I glanced in the rearview mirror and wished I hadn't. Dirt and blood crusted the side of my swollen, bruised face. A bloody gash crossed my forehead. I hadn't even felt that one.

"You know she's probably following us," Lena said. "Hoping we'll lead her to the sphere."

I hadn't even thought of that. I was more tired than I thought. I rested my head against the window and watched the grassy dunes and the lake beyond. Clouds obscured the moon and stars, and the waves were all but invisible in the blackness.

My phone buzzed. I glanced at the text message. "Nidhi says they're ready to destroy the sphere, but they won't do it until we have a way to contain the Ghost Army. She also said the Porters saw the footage of us and Meridiana. They're preparing a press release of their own."

Meridiana wanted to build an empire of the dead, and the Porters were worried about public relations.

"We should take the scenic route," I said. Paradoxically, we were probably safer right now than we had been in weeks. If Meridiana was hoping we'd lead her to the sphere, she couldn't exactly kill us. She could damn well wait as long as it took for us . . .

I sat up, barely noticing the pain in my side.

"What is it?"

"Meridiana didn't have to meet with us in person. What did she gain by dragging us out to Copper River and burning down my house?"

"Beyond stopping the Porters from killing her, trying to tail us back to the sphere, and beating you half to death?"

"She was stalling." Meridiana was jerking us around like puppets. I checked the time. The sun would be coming up soon. "Several hours to drive here. Longer to wait with the fire department."

"Why? What is she waiting for?"

"Hell if I know." As long as we held the sphere, we had the better hand. The moment we figured out how to neutralize the Ghost Army, Meridiana was done. Logically, she should be putting all of her energy into getting the sphere back, not wasting time manipulating the people of Copper River or tormenting an individual librarian. Unless she had another way of nullifying our advantage.

Lena pursed her lips. "When Master Sarna taught me stick fighting, he said that nine times out of ten, the one who wins the fight will be the one who acts instead of reacts."

"Did he have any advice on what action to take when you were outnumbered and outgunned?"

"Run away. Failing that, figure out who presents the biggest threat and focus your attack on her. Take that one down, and the rest might decide to leave you alone."

"I like it." More importantly, I was pretty sure I knew where to start.

We were halfway back to the fort when Lena adjusted the door mirror and said, "There seems to be an angel following us."

The Triumph was enchanted to prevent magical spying, but it wouldn't help against a flying minion. We had kept the top up, so I had to roll down the window to spot him. He didn't appear to have any trouble keeping up, despite the fact that we were averaging ninety-five on the highway.

"Who do you think he used to be?" Lena asked.

"Meridiana called him Binion." I sat back and grimaced. Twisting like that had aggravated the throbbing in my side. "There was a libriomancer by that name who lived out west. I didn't know him personally. From what I've read, he was a bit of an asshole. Way too full of himself and his own power. But that doesn't mean he deserved this."

She switched gears and pushed the needle past a hundred. I opened the glove box. From the back, behind a box of Band Aids and an old tire gauge that doubled as a wand for jumping dead batteries, I pulled out a miniature disco ball the size of a golf ball.

"Should I ask?"

"Nope. Merge with that line of cars up ahead." I hung the disco ball on the rearview mirror. It began to rotate back and forth. "You might want to shield your eyes."

The tiny square mirrors brightened. Beams of light stabbed out in all directions. The light passed through us with no effect, but every vehicle it touched changed appearance, taking on the compact, glossy black body of a 1973 TR-6 convertible. Which was, I suspected, particularly distressing for the parents in the minivan, whose three screaming children now appeared to be riding in the open trunk.

A second burst of light rendered the kids invisible. Duplicates of Lena and me appeared in our vehicular doppelgangers.

Cars screeched and swerved. Horns blared. Several convertibles pulled over to the side of the road. Others continued on. I heard one driver—he sounded like a teenager, though it was hard to tell, since he looked exactly like Lena—screaming excitedly about his new sports car.

"Ponce de Leon used this trick years ago when the Porters were after him," I said. "The write-up was funny as hell. One of the vehicles he hit with his illusion was hauling cattle. The field agent wasted five minutes trying to interrogate a cow."

Our pursuer circled overhead, clearly uncertain. Even if Binion had been tracking us by our magic, spells now clung to every one of the dozen or so vehicles on this stretch of the road. He swooped lower, arms outstretched. One of the cars reverted to its proper appearance as he stripped the illusion away. We followed two more Triumphs off the next exit ramp, driving slowly and casually, like we had no idea what had just happened.

A half mile down the road, I peered out the window and searched for Binion. He was staying with the cars on the highway, probably assuming we had chosen that route for a reason, and would therefore keep going after tossing out our magical distraction. One by one he tore their magic away, but he couldn't catch them all. I held out my fist toward Lena, who grinned and bumped it with her own.

Damn, I missed being able to do this stuff on my own.

I texted Nidhi to let her know we were in the clear, then tried to find a position that would let me rest. I closed my eyes, but every time I began to drift off, pain jolted me from half-formed dreams of Gerbert d'Aurillac's armillary sphere and the smell of smoke.

"*Paeniteo*," I whispered.

"What's that?"

"One of the words from the poem d'Aurillac used to hide Meridiana away. It means repent." I thought about the connection I had shared with Gerbert, and his guilt for not recognizing Meridiana's evil sooner.

He felt responsible for the damage she had caused, the pain she had inflicted through her lies. He had known how dangerous she was. But he also pitied her. She was without mercy, but Gerbert d'Aurillac wasn't. He could be flawed and vengeful and petty, but he strove to do better. He had also been close to Anna's family. He even loved her, in his way.

I couldn't be certain, but my gut—or else the lingering memories from Gerbert's mind—told me I was on the right track. "*That's* why he gave Meridiana the ability to speak from her prison. He wanted her to be able to repent. He could ask her if she atoned for her sins, and she was forced to answer honestly. I'd bet that if she were ever able to answer yes, it would free her."

How long had he waited and prayed before realizing Meridiana would never feel guilt for her actions? What he had intended as a chance for redemption had only added to her never-ending torment. Meridiana could have freed herself at any time, if only she had been able to lie, something she had done so effortlessly in life.

I shifted in my seat, and fresh pains pierced my body. "What is it?"

"Maybe I should have gone to the hospital after all." I breathed through clenched teeth. I couldn't fully inhale. On the right side, my lung felt like someone was jabbing it with a jagged stick. I pulled up my shirt to see that much of the skin over my ribs had turned purple.

Lena swore and pushed the gas pedal to the floor. I dug my fingers into the seat as we zipped through traffic. I hoped Ponce de Leon's magic would protect us from the police, and Lena's reflexes would keep us from smashing into cars and trucks that might as well have been parked.

By the time we reached Fort Michilimackinac, I could no longer focus on anything but the pain. I needed help just getting out of the car.

Nicola was waiting for us in the parking lot. The moment her song reached my ears, the pain eased somewhat, enough for me to walk without gasping.

She didn't bother buying tickets this time. Her song turned every eye away as we passed through the gift shop. My ribs ground together with each step.

Ponce de Leon and Bi Wei met us on the other side of the gate. I sagged to the ground and closed my eyes as they used their magic to begin repairing damage. A man dressed like a British soldier approached, asking if I was all right.

"Low blood sugar," said Ponce de Leon. "He'll be fine." He waited for the man to leave, then added, "We all heard your confrontation with Meridiana. That was an interesting strategy, Isaac. Walking *toward* the angry mob. I take it American schools don't teach self-preservation?"

"I was out sick that day." I worked my jaw back and forth, then touched my forehead. The swelling was gone, and there was only a dull ache as I rubbed away the dried blood, all that remained of the scabbed cut.

"I'm sorry about your home," said Nicola.

"Thanks." I gasped as my ribs moved beneath my skin. When I could speak again, I asked, "Any progress on the sphere?"

"Gutenberg's plan will work," said Bi Wei. She and Lena helped me to my feet. "He locked most religious texts, but we've torn through his locks before. We can apply them to Meridiana and bring her to an end."

The students of Bi Sheng could open any text in the archive, but they couldn't restore my magic. At least not *directly* . . .

I set that idea aside for the moment. "If we kill Meridiana, we unleash the Ghost Army. We have to find another way to contain or destroy them first, and we don't have much time. I think she's been stalling. With her prison restored to the world, she might have found another way out."

"Right now, Meridiana's power is limited," said Ponce de Leon. "And still she was able to use Jeneta to kill a five-hundred-year-old libriomancer. If she escapes and regains her full strength, she could be unstoppable. If she's stalling, that's all the more reason to act now."

"Not yet." I wondered if anyone else noticed the hitch in his voice when he spoke of Gutenberg's death, or the way he avoided his name? "You fought her ghosts one at a time, with help. If we destroy the sphere, how much destruction will they cause while we hunt them down? And once it comes out that the Porters were responsible for releasing the Ghost Army, we'll turn the whole world against us."

"Does that matter, Isaac?" Ponce de Leon's words were flat, as if to relax his hold on his emotions would unleash them all in a single catastrophic eruption. "Those forced to make impossible choices are rarely loved. If it's approval and reputation you care about, then you have no place here."

I thought back to the blows crashing into my body, to my friends doing their best to break me. "This isn't about reputation. It's about turning every one of us into a target for angry, frightened people."

"People like us have always been targets," he said. "You've lived in an era of unprecedented safety and security. Locked away in your magical tower with your books and your research."

"When I wasn't out fighting madmen or trying to stop a magical war, you mean?" I shot back.

Nidhi cleared her throat. "Yelling at one another probably isn't the best way to deal with your grief and exhaustion. Isaac, if you don't like the plan, focus on finding a better one."

She had the habit of being right at the most annoying times. "I've *got* a better one," I said. "But I need to ask the sphere a couple of questions first."

"And then what?" asked Ponce de Leon.

"Research, just like you said." I stood up and tested my limbs. My body was bruised and sore, but I could move without screaming. It was enough. I started toward the fort. "I'll peer into that sighting tube, climb into Gerbert d'Aurillac's contraption, and figure out how Meridiana's been controlling her ghosts."

The armillary sphere seemed heavier than before, as if it had somehow doubled in mass since I left. I tapped one of the rings. The cold metal hummed like a tuning fork.

Folklore described d'Aurillac's creation as a brazen head. Standing here, I could feel Meridiana watching me from within her prison.

I fixed my attention on the central sphere. "If I look through the sighting tube, will I be drawn in and trapped with Meridiana?"

The sphere shifted slowly into the configuration of my birth. *Yes.*

"Isaac, I can't pull you back from this," said Bi Wei. "If we can't get you out, you'll be destroyed along with Meridiana."

I yanked Ponce de Leon's handkerchief off the end of the sighting tube. "All you have to do is ask me if I repent. That's the magical escape pod d'Aurillac worked into his prison. Isn't that right?"

Yes.

Oh, good. I would have been embarrassed as hell if I'd been wrong about that. "Will my entering or leaving the sphere help Meridiana to free herself?"

No.

"That's it?" asked Lena. "Just ask if you repent? Or does it have to be specific to work?"

The sphere moved back and forth, unable to answer three simultaneous and contradictory questions at once. I was reminded of old episodes of *Star Trek*, where Captain Kirk logic-bombed various evil supercomputers into destroying themselves. Somehow I doubted that would work here. "Will repenting for a specific sin, like stealing my brother's Easter candy when I was nine, work?"

No.

I had to repent for everything. To acknowledge and ask forgiveness for all my sins. Dammit, I hadn't set foot inside a church for two years, and now I'd have to go to confession.

"What if you're unable to truly repent?" asked Bi Wei.

"Then I'll have a lot more time to look around inside this thing and figure out how it works."

"This isn't your fault," Nidhi said gently.

I blinked. "What isn't?"

"What happened to Jeneta. To your home and the people of Copper River. None of this is your fault."

I took another slow breath. "Don't play therapist with me, Nidhi. Not now."

"Looking into that thing could kill you," she pressed. "It's a stupid risk."

"Stupid risks are what I do," I countered. "I'm good at them. As long as you're here to pull me back—"

"You're assuming there will be anything left for us to rescue," Ponce de Leon pointed out. "You will be entering a universe where Meridiana is a literal god. She might destroy you."

"Will you kill me if I join you in there?"

Nothing. Another question the sphere couldn't answer.

"What about the block on your memories?" asked Nicola. "If she can bypass that spell, she'll know where we are."

Ponce de Leon picked up his cane. "Erasure is probably the safer path."

"Wait." I turned back to the sphere. "If I look into this tube, will Meridiana have access to my thoughts and memories?"

Yes.

Damn. "All right, but I want Bi Wei to do it, not you."

He stepped back with an amused smile and waved his arm in a "Be my guest" motion to Bi Wei.

I did my best to relax as Bi Wei approached. She circled me twice, then stopped. Her fingers stretched out like a conductor preparing to direct a full orchestra.

"I'm ready," I said.

Her mouth quirked. "It's done."

I looked around, trying to reconstruct the past few minutes. I couldn't recall what it was she had done to my memory, only that it was important Meridiana not find out. "I do *not* like this. How long was I out?"

"She spent fifteen minutes pulling thoughts from your head," said Ponce de Leon. "Delicate work, but she did well, considering her lack of experience. You should know within the next day or two whether there were any unfortunate side effects. Hopefully you won't need to be toilet trained all over again."

I scratched my cheek with my middle finger, and he smirked.

"Will Isaac survive?" asked Lena.

The sphere didn't move. "Too many variables," I said. "We've got to find out the old-fashioned way."

I looked to the ceiling, imagining the sky beyond. I needed to align the sighting tube with the pole star. It would be easier if I knew where we were, but that shouldn't matter. "Which way is north?"

Bi Wei rotated the sphere about thirty degrees to the right. "It's ready."

Lena cupped my face and kissed me. When she finally broke away, I held her close. Home and magic came in many forms. Our noses brushed together, and I rested my forehead on hers. "I'm sorry for being such an asshole lately."

"Don't worry." Her lips tickled mine when she spoke. "Once this is over, I expect you to make it up to me. With interest."

"We'll check in with you every five minutes," said Nicola. "Simple yes/no questions. Meridiana may try to answer as well. With Lena and Nidhi's help, we'll try to select questions only you could answer."

"Give me half an hour, then ask if I repent." That should give me enough time to explore Meridiana's prison, and if I needed more time, I always had the option of looking into the tube again.

I moved to the other side of the desk and folded my arms tight, as if I could physically contain the anxiety expanding within my chest. There was excitement as well, eagerness to see the inside of d'Aurillac's master-piece, but excitement wasn't even in the same weight class as the fear. "Allons-y."

I saw Lena grin as she recognized the *Doctor Who* reference. Before I could change my mind, I leaned forward, and peered down into the sighting tube.

The interior of the tube was polished to a mirror finish, perfect despite its age. Light reflected from the sides, elongated like I was racing through space in an old SF film. Colors stretched toward me. As I fell, I found myself thinking *this* was the effect Kubrick had tried to achieve in *2001: A Space Odyssey*.

I saw the Earth first, a bronze sphere so dark it appeared black. Violent clouds swirled beyond the globe, their edges lit with metallic flame. They spun like a hurricane, with the Earth floating above the eye.

Without a physical form, I had no sense of scale. My awareness plummeted toward the metal world that could have been as small as a single molecule or as large as the Virgo Cluster. But the magic flowing through it—

I could feel magic.

Laughter echoed through space. My laughter. Gutenberg had carved his spell into my flesh, and I had left that flesh behind. I was complete again.

Other spheres entered into my awareness. A bronze moon orbited the Earth. Silhouetted metal flames ringed an enormous sun. All the celestial landmarks of d'Aurillac's time were here, separated by the vastness of space yet so close you could stand on the surface of the Earth and press your palm to the rust-red metal of Mars.

Beyond it all, an enormous wall of bronze circled the sky, setting the boundaries of existence. A second wall intercepted the first, constellations chasing one another along a never-ending metal trail. The stars were abstractions, artistic renderings that formed bulls and lions and hunters, with points of metal fire scattered over the outlines.

Magic held each world in its proper place. Magic was light and gravity and momentum and perspective. I felt myself drawn into the pattern of Gerbert d'Aurillac's spell, like I was a being of liquid iron and this place a nexus of finely balanced magnetic fields.

I explored the emptiness between the metal bands. I saw nothing to represent the sighting tube which had pulled me in. Nor did I find Meridiana herself, which was troubling.

How had this thing endured for so long? I couldn't get a damn toaster to last more than a few years, but d'Aurillac's work had outlasted nations. Books lost their magic over time, as did most libriomantic spells. What kept this place going?

"I do."

I searched for the source of the voice that filled all of existence. I found it at the intersection of the two enormous metal bands. Seated with her back against a bronze wall as high as a city block was the woman who had invaded my thoughts to taunt me when Gutenberg took my magic, the woman I had glimpsed from the bottom of Euphemia Smith's pond. Meridiana sat upon a throne built into the wall behind her, the back melting into the metal, leaving her seated over the emptiness of space. The horizontal wall rippled outward like a riverbed. Light green corrosion spread like mold where the back of the throne joined the wall.

Meridiana's arms and legs were fused to the chair, as if she had fallen partway into the molten bronze, only to have it harden around her. Even her skin was bronze, cold and perfect.

Her eyes were empty pits to the stars, though these

stars didn't twinkle like those in the real world, nor were they the stylized etchings of the constellations. These were the stars as seen from space, with no atmosphere to block your vision. Pinpoints of slowly shifting light, like an entire galaxy whirled within her.

She must have been aware of me, but she gave no physical sign. I crept closer, feeling the power pouring from her to the rest of the universe.

Most of the brazen heads I had seen in museums were cast as solid works of bronze, but Meridiana's features had been welded together from more pieces than I could count. She looked like d'Aurillac's memories of Anna, with a rounded face and a strong, cleft chin. Her nose had been broken, and appeared flattened and bent to the left. Lashes like scimitars shone in the orange light that bathed this world. Rippling layers of metal hair cascaded past her shoulders like a waterfall, each lock sharp enough to cut flesh.

Why would she have a metal body while I was form- less? Was this part of d'Aurillac's magic, or something she had constructed for herself over the centuries?

Looking into her eyes, I saw her memories as if they were my own. Meridiana was the heart of this universe. Her magic powered this prison, keeping the lifeless worlds and stars in motion.

I could sense it drawing strength from me as well, us- ing my magic and will to maintain a delicate, never- ending balance. It was nothing, a single mosquito drinking my blood, but that drain would never end.

Meridiana was strong enough to survive such a drain for years. Decades, perhaps. Not centuries. Not a thou- sand years. Not alone. But then, Meridiana had never been alone.

In her memories, I saw her begin to lose herself. I shared her desperation as she joined with her prison, adopting the bronze skin as her own and praying it would help her to hold on. I watched her reach out to the dead . . .

I pulled back from her thoughts before they could drown me. How long had it been since I looked into the tube? I had no sense of time here, but surely five minutes had passed by now.

I tried to focus on the problem at hand. I turned back to study the storm raging beyond Earth. Everything else I had seen related in some way to the armillary sphere d'Aurillac had constructed, but that was different, distinct from his plan. I flew toward it, but like a reflection in a window, it remained beyond my reach.

"Isaac, do you remember the first time you touched the life in my oak?"

The words reverberated between brass worlds. Trust Lena to come up with a question only I could answer.

Beyond the bronze sky, I saw Lena looking down at us. I saw not her physical body, but the entirety of her existence. I saw her oak and her flesh and the branches growing within her all at once. I saw Nidhi and myself, our desires twined through Lena's core.

I also saw the effects of the book Bi Wei had given her. Its magic had grown like a lattice of spun glass, a skeletal tree within Lena's skin. Its power was fragile, but it was real, stabilizing her identity and personality.

I could have wept with relief, if I had possessed a body with which to do so. *The book had worked.* If I died, that book would help her to remain herself.

I saw Lena's birth, those hours before she emerged from her tree, when her mind first stirred. And I remembered our hands intertwined, pressing against rough bark, feeling the water flowing through the trunk and into the branches, the roots sunk into the earth, the leaves rustling in the wind. Instinctively, I reached out to bring this world into balance with the moment of her awakening. Stars crawled through the sky. Planets whirled past one another, until I had given Lena her answer. *Yes.*

Meridiana was watching me now, though her head hadn't turned. Her eyes had faded, a patina of brass dimming the distant stars. The hinged jaw opened. "Welcome to Purgatory."

CLOWNING AROUND FOR BOOKS

When: This Sunday at 1:00 p.m.

Where: The corner of 21st and Yale St., across from the West Branch Baptist Church.

What: A clown-themed counterprotest to celebrate books and piss off closed-minded idiots.

Our local bigots are at it again, this time adding book-burning to their list of "wholesome Christian" activities for the family.

You probably know them for their lawsuit-trolling ways, including picketing funerals and other public events, but it didn't take the Neanderthals at the WBBC long to jump on the anti-magic bandwagon with a "Bonfire of Books" this coming Sunday.

They've announced a long list of titles to be burned for promoting "sins" like homosexuality, premarital sex, false religions, profanity, promiscuity, adultry [sic], birth control, transgenderism, polyamory, interracial marriage, abortion, alcoholism, feminism, socialism, welfare, and magic.

We all know Pastor Tom Briggs is a walking skidmark in a bad suit, and his congregation is a stain on Christians everywhere. The police are looking into whether or not the church has filed for the proper permits for this event, but given the number of lawyers in Briggs' flock, there's unlikely to be any legal reason to stop them.

And that's as it *should* be. Freedom of speech is easy when it's speech we approve of. The true test of freedom is what we do when people like Briggs and his ilk mount their soapboxes and show their asses to the world.

Fortunately, freedom of speech doesn't mean freedom from mockery and other consequences. So grab your wigs and your oversized shoes, your makeup and your juggling clubs, and join us this Sunday for a circus-themed counterprotest. We'll have readings all day from the most outrageously "offensive" books we can find, including a special event at 3:00 with Leslie Bliss, a local author of popular lesbian erotica. The library will be selling refreshments, with all profits going to the purchase of banned books for their shelves.

Don't have clown garb? No problem! Show up early for free face painting.

George Bernard Shaw once said, "I learned long ago, never to wrestle with a pig. You get dirty, and besides, the pig likes it." Well, we're not going to fight these illiterate pustules of humanity. We're going to ridicule them into total and utter irrelevance.

Chapter 16

"NICE UNIVERSE YOU'VE GOT HERE."
I wasn't certain how I spoke without a physical body, but I seemed to be able to vocalize as long as I didn't think about it too hard. "Any leaks I should know about?"

Meridiana didn't answer, but I could feel her attention vibrating through my core, like speakers with the bass maxed out. I silently thanked Bi Wei for erasing the pertinent pages of my memory.

I could sense the planets, the flow of Meridiana's magic, the enormous metal bands that bordered our universe, everything *except* the glowing hurricane below. Was it illusory? But even an illusion required magical energy. I studied the individual clouds, each one distinct in shape and color, distended like toffee. There were hundreds. Thousands. "That's the Ghost Army, isn't it?"

I couldn't feel them because they weren't really here within the armillary sphere. They existed in the real world, trapped in Meridiana's orbit.

She'd been telling the truth. Destroying this place

wouldn't destroy the Army of Ghosts. It would set them free. "How did you find them all, let alone control them?"

Her cold stare gave no answers. I returned to her throne. I could feel her magic, but I couldn't interpret it, any more than I could read ancient Sanskrit. I studied the hammered bronze, wishing I could peel it back to expose the spells within. I could almost see the words etched into the metal.

With that thought, the words grew clearer. Each one carried memories. Stories.

I had forgotten none of this was real. We weren't truly floating within the armillary sphere. The planets, the rings, these were simply manifestations of Gerbert d'Aurillac's spell. I was like a character from a computer game seeing the world's code for the first time.

If I could see it, could I manipulate it as well? I envisioned the word *sleep* joining the text beneath Meridiana's skin, but nothing happened. That was probably for the best. If I could control her, she could certainly do the same to me, and she had spent a lot more time learning how to function in this place.

But I could still read. I looked past the rippled sheen of metal to the text beneath. It was something I had managed a few times before, seeing the spells that lived in Gutenberg's skin, or the magic of Lena's tree, but those examples had all involved libriomancy.

At its heart, libriomancy was no different than any other magic. Nicola used music to wield and shape her spells. Ponce de Leon was powerful enough to use little more than will alone, aided by that cane he carried. Libriomancers tapped into the same power; we just used books to understand and control it.

I had said before that all stories were magic. It had never occurred to me that all magic was stories.

Words flew past too quickly to read, but I absorbed them anyway. I read Meridiana's rage at Gerbert d'Aurillac's betrayal, and beneath her fury, her grudging respect for how well he had prepared his final trap.

I looked beyond Meridiana to where bands of celestial text told the story of the stars as d'Aurillac had understood them. I saw the names of the constellations, written in Arabic but melting into English as I read. Beneath the constellations lay the writing that had informed his work, including the very text from al-Sufi I had referred to when trying to decipher his poem.

I read of his interactions with Meridiana—Anna—as well. He had tutored Anna and her brother both, but Otto had never been a magical or intellectual match for his sister. And so Gerbert d'Aurillac had favored Anna. I read of his pride in her abilities, and his horror when he realized he had helped to empower a monster. And I read his hope.

Gerbert d'Aurillac's faith flowed through every line of this prison. Faith in God's plan for Meridiana and the world, and faith in Meridiana herself, that she would one day turn from the darkness and seek redemption.

"Isaac, does anything of Jeneta Aboderin survive?"

Ponce de Leon's question hurled me downward. I dove through the bronze Earth, seeing both the molded wrinkles of land and water and the story of the world's creation, translated through d'Aurillac's theology and education. I could have stayed there for hours, but the question compelled me to seek out the answer.

My vision split apart. I saw Jeneta walking through the woods, flanked by mythological creatures. At the same time, I looked beyond the armillary sphere to the Army of Ghosts, to a single wisp in the storm, battered about like a handkerchief in a dryer. Within that swath of thinned life and memories, I glimpsed a swirl of text.

I know why the caged bird beats his wing
Till its blood is red on the cruel bars;
For he must fly back to his perch and cling
When he fain would be on the bough a-swing;

Joy and relief flowered from my core, pulling the
worlds into alignment in response to Ponce de Leon's
question. I recognized the snippet of "Sympathy" from my
time working with Jeneta. It was from *The Collected Poetry of Paul Laurence Dunbar*. I searched my memory,
then called out what I could remember of the final stanza.

It's not a carol of joy or glee,
But a prayer he sends from his heart's deep core,
But a plea, that upward to Heaven he flings.
I know why the caged bird sings!

I thought I sensed a change within the storm, a tiny
flicker of recognition. I silently thanked Ponce de Leon
for choosing that question, for helping and forcing me to
find Jeneta.

She slipped away, lost in the clouds despite my attempts to hold on. But she *had* heard me. Given centuries, I might have learned to communicate with the rest
of the ghosts, and to control them as Meridiana had
done.

Reluctantly, I turned away from Jeneta and the other
trapped souls to face Meridiana. As I did, the metal wall
behind her rippled like air over the blacktop in midsum-
mer. I moved closer. What had caused the corrosion
around her throne and wrinkled the wall?

Though the metal face never moved, I felt Meridiana's smile. Words flowed beneath her mask, a palimp-
sest of text, layer upon layer superimposed over the
figure before me. I peered deeper.

That was a mistake. Those words—her magic— entangled my thoughts like seaweed and dragged me deeper. The armillary sphere faded to blackness, and I began to drown.

"Isaac, do you repent?"

Nidhi's question saved my life.

The magical foundations of Meridiana's prison seized us both, forced us to respond. Trapped within this universe, unable to lie to myself, I realized how difficult a question it truly was. A few days earlier, I would have answered no. I would have justified and rationalized everything, from running off to outer space to bargaining Lena's blood to risking my life and those of my loved ones.

After all, that first trip into space and the deal that went with it had given us the key to finding Meridiana's prison. If I had been short with the people around me, it was because I was so intent on saving Jeneta's life. How was that a bad thing?

Only that wasn't what I had been doing. I had been running away, both figuratively and literally. From my own failure to protect my friends and neighbors. From the fear of a life without magic. From guilt and helplessness. And from the people who wanted to help . . . people who needed my help.

Yes.

The planets moved without conscious thought, and then I was tearing free, even as Meridiana shouted her own answer. *No.*

Lena caught my arms and kept me from hitting the floor. I was rigid as steel and acutely aware of every physical sensation. The pressure of Lena's hands on my muscles. The smell of my own sweat. The way my clothes rubbed my skin as my body seized.

"What's wrong?" asked Lena.

Nidhi shoved something soft under my head. Nicola was singing, and Ponce de Leon was doing something with his cane. Darkness clouded my eyes. I felt like a dinosaur had stepped on my chest.

"He's not breathing," said Nidhi.

Bi Wei pressed a hand over my chest. My heart spasmed, sending blood through my stiffened limbs. I lurched onto my side and vomited. Silty water spewed from my stomach and lungs, and then I screamed.

I felt like I was being flayed from within as the life slowly spread through my body, but the next breath was slightly easier. Sweat covered my body. I tried to move, but my limbs were like softened clay.

Everyone was watching me. Ponce de Leon held his cane ready. Nicola's head bobbed to unheard melodies. How much magic had they prepared in case something else escaped with—or within—me?

"What happened?" asked Lena.

My teeth were chattering too hard to answer.

"It's Isaac," said Bi Wei. "*Just* Isaac." The others relaxed.

"Meridiana did something to you," guessed Ponce de Leon.

I managed a nod. My mouth was a desert, and my sinuses felt like water balloons squeezed to the bursting point. "Thirsty."

Jackson fetched me a Vernors. The carbonation burned my throat, and I coughed up the first swallow, which triggered another bout of vomiting. Water spilled out of my mouth and nose.

When the upheavals subsided, I reached for the desk. Lena helped me stand. I touched the sphere first, then one of the books stacked beside it. I felt nothing. Magic was once again lost to me. "Somebody box that thing up," I croaked. "I don't want her listening, or jumping in to answer our questions."

Nicola emptied a crate of books and lifted the sphere into it. She sang a spell as she sealed the crate. I didn't recognize the song, but hopefully it would give us some semblance of privacy.

I took another drink of Vernors, then collapsed into the chair. "Gerbert d'Aurillac's sphere was designed to hold a single human soul. But the dead were a part of her from birth. When she was locked away, they remained free. They sustained her, and over the centuries, she learned to control them." I took a deep breath. "I need to know exactly what's on Jeneta's e-reader."

Jackson tapped the keyboard of his laptop to pull up the program they had used to remote view the e-reader. "Can you sort them by date?"

"What are you looking for?" asked Nidhi.

I scanned the list. "In the beginning, it was all Meridiana could do to survive. She had to consume the power of the dead to maintain her universe. Over time, she learned to send her ghosts out to gather others, particularly those with magical abilities. She used them not just for sustenance, but for their knowledge. And for the past five hundred years, the majority of her victims have been libriomancers."

"Are you suggesting she can do libriomancy?" asked Jackson.

"Through Jeneta, yes. And Meridiana knows more about libriomancy than anyone alive today." I grabbed a pencil and began jotting down titles. "That's how she created the monsters that follow her around. Imagine libriomantic possession turned inside out. Instead of a character from a book worming his way into your mind and taking control, Meridiana takes that character's story and uses it to reshape a living being, to turn them into extensions of her own mind and will."

"What about Jeneta?" asked Nidhi. "If Meridiana's ghosts and the people they possess are a part of her—"

"Meridiana silences the voices of those she consumes,

but she can't destroy Jeneta without losing her libriomancy. And Jeneta is her way out." I stabbed my pen at the list of books. "Look at what she's been checking out. *The Magician's Nephew. The Looking-Glass Wars. Princess Nevermore.*"

Nobody reacted.

"All portal fantasies, about gateways between one world and another. And in each one, the magic portal was a body of water." I gestured to the puddles on the floor. "That's how she means to escape. The metal around her throne was corroded. The bronze rippled like waves on a pool. She intends to use these books to create a portal to herself."

"How close is she to completing this portal?" asked Nicola.

"I didn't have much time to study her plan before she tried to drown me, but I think she'll need to bring the sphere to whatever portal she's preparing in our world." I sat back and grinned. "Now ask me how we're going to stop her."

Lena sighed. "How?"

"The same way we free Jeneta. By separating their stories." I could see they didn't understand. I wasn't sure I did. I turned to Ponce de Leon. "How do you experience magic? What do you see and feel when you command those energies?"

"Wind." His expression changed, losing a little of the tension he had carried since Gutenberg's death. "It's like being at sea. You learn to sense the air, to anticipate every change and adjust your sails to capture the breeze. I've always been able to feel it."

I turned to Nicola. "I'm guessing you don't see magic at all. You hear it."

"Not exactly," she said. "It's . . . there's a *pressure* inside me. I don't hear the magic as much as I feel it pounding through my body. The music is how I get it out."

That left Bi Wei. Of all of us here, her magic was closest to my own. She had spent centuries clinging to existence through her book. She carried the imprint of that book within her, helping her to resist Meridiana's call. "Look at Lena and tell me what you see."

"A being of magic," she said slowly. "The strength of her tree within her body, flowing through her weapons. The ties linking her to you, and to Doctor Shah. The power of the books of Bi Sheng growing inside of her. And the threads of the book that bore her, woven through it all."

"Good. Now, can you read it?" I pressed. "Can you read her?"

Her eyes and mouth compressed. "We can make out the words of her book."

"Not the book, *her*." I jumped up and pointed toward Smudge. "You're not looking the right way. Try to read Smudge. Stop thinking of him and his book as separate things."

She blinked. "I don't understand what you're saying."

"Slow down." Nidhi had slipped into clinical mode, calm and soothing. Her hand circled my wrist, her fingers pressing to check my pulse. "You're manic. What else happened in there?"

I set the list on the desk. She was right about the mania. I was exhausted and my throat felt like I had swallowed a cheese grater, but I didn't care. "When I was inside the sphere, I saw Meridiana. I *read* her. Her history, her power . . . I saw magic in a way I've never experienced before. I can't explain it, but I know how to fight her."

"How?" asked Lena.

"Bi Wei, what did you do to unlock *Nymphs of Neptune*?"

"I forced the lock." She shook her head. "I've already told you we can't do the same for you. It was unpleasant and inelegant, and would likely destroy your mind."

"I know, I know. I don't need you to unlock my mind. I just need—" I looked around. "What I *really* need is to get to the archive at Fort Michilimackinac. The books there would let me . . . why are you staring at me like I just turned back into a newt?"

"Our apologies. We forgot." Bi Wei tapped my forehead, sharing her own memories with mine.

I shivered as I realized where we were. I had been seeing this place all along without recognizing it. "Wow. That's just creepy."

I grabbed one of the crates and brought it to the desk. This room held the books taken from the Porter archive at Michigan State University. The books that had survived its destruction, at any rate. That made it *my* archive, the place where the books I had reviewed and recommended for locking would have ended up, back when I was working as a cataloger for the Porters.

"What are you searching for?" asked Nidhi.

"Robert Jordan." Packets of desiccant were positioned in each one to absorb moisture. Thin, sturdy plastic sheets separated layers of books. I pawed through all three layers, then shoved the box aside. "The *Wheel of Time* series. Where is it?"

Jackson pointed to a crate near the bottom of the center pile.

Lena lifted the three boxes on top and set them aside without straining. Jackson opened the crate. I pressed close as he pulled out stacks of books.

"There," I said. "*Towers of Midnight.*" There were at least ten different editions, paperback and hardcovers in various languages. I snatched the English mass market paperback.

Ponce de Leon wrinkled his nose. "Modern fantasy is little more than juvenile escapism and anachronistic longing for a time that never existed. I've never understand the appeal."

"That's because you suck." I sat down at the desk, skimming for the reason the Porters had locked these books in the first place. I jabbed a finger at the pages. "Balefire."

"What does it do?" asked Nidhi.

"Burns things out of existence. When it's strong enough, the effect extends backward through time. It makes it so that something never existed at all."

"If you unmake the sphere, you'll just set Meridiana free," said Bi Wei. "And the ghosts are capable of diffusing and deflecting every spell we throw at them. We have no reason to believe this balefire would be an effective weapon."

"Let me worry about Meridiana." I pulled out Gutenberg's gold pen and slammed it onto the desk. "Use the balefire on this."

Nobody moved. Ponce de Leon was the first to speak. "Isaac, think this through."

"I have."

"You'd have your magic back." Nidhi's face and her tone were equally unreadable.

"That's right," I said. "And we'll have the resources of every book Gutenberg locked with that pen."

"These books are dangerous." Jackson stepped sideways, moving closer to the door and the blunderbuss he had set in the corner.

"More dangerous than Meridiana?" I countered.

"If you alter the past, don't you risk erasing us all from existence?" Nidhi was a fan of comics, meaning she had a decent understanding of how messed up things could get when you started trying to unravel and rebraid different timelines.

I shook my head. "It won't really change the past. Every experiment the Porters have tried suggests you *can't* alter history. It takes too much power to even try."

"Then why bother with the pen?" asked Ponce de Leon.

Bi Wei picked up the pen, holding it between us. She appeared to be looking through the pen into my eyes. "To change the present."

"Exactly," I said triumphantly. "Every spell that thing created should dissolve."

"Even if this works," said Nicola, "think of what you could unleash." Her hands were twitching again. "Plagues, superweapons, predators who could be worse than Meridiana. All available to any fool of a libriomancer who decided it was worth the risk."

"Fools like me, yes," I said impatiently.

"Like anyone who has left or been thrown out of the Porters," she continued. "There are others whose magic and memories were taken from them, Isaac. People whose true loyalties lay elsewhere. Will you be responsible for opening the way to all-out magical war?"

"Every lock can be broken," I said. "The Students of Bi Sheng exposed the Porters, but they haven't tried to use these books against us. If . . . *when* Meridiana escapes, she will."

"You're risking an awful lot on theories," said Nicola.

"They're *good* theories. Better than anything else we've got." Into the silence that followed, I added, "If it's any consolation, I think I should be able to lock the books again once we're done."

It was probably wrong to enjoy the way they stared.

"You know how to lock books?" asked Ponce de Leon. "Even without the pen I made for Johannes?"

"Gutenberg was locking books before you gave him that pen, right? All I need is one locked book. I should be able to read that lock, to peel back its magic and duplicate it. It's the same concept I'm talking about with Meridiana's ghosts, just a slightly different application."

"This is the worst excess of conjecture and wishful thinking," snapped Jackson. "We don't know if Isaac is capable of any of this."

"He believes he is," said Bi Wei.

"I once met a woman who believed she was abducted by aliens who looked like the Teletubbies," Jackson shot back. "That doesn't make it true."

"Enough." Nicola raised a hand, and Jackson fell silent. "Doctor Shah, what is your assessment of Isaac's current mental state?"

"I'm not his doctor," said Nidhi. "I can't—"

"It's all right," I said quietly. "Tell them the truth."

She looked at me, then nodded. "Isaac has been depressed since he lost his magic. He blames himself for the deaths of his friends and neighbors in Copper River, and for the loss of Jeneta Aboderin. He has isolated himself from others. The combination of guilt and depression has made him significantly more reckless than usual.

"His judgment is questionable. Last night, he was physically assaulted, and his home was destroyed. He is physically, mentally, and emotionally exhausted. If he were a Porter agent, I would order him pulled from the field immediately."

Lena took my hand and squeezed.

"Isaac has pinned his guilt, desperation, and powerlessness on one thing: regaining his magic." Nidhi turned toward Nicola. "And you should help him."

"He's unstable," Jackson protested. "You just said so!"

"Yes, I did." Nidhi's voice hardened ever so slightly. "And even in the depths of that instability, he successfully discovered Meridiana's identity, learned of her origin from Pope Sylvester II, and figured out how to retrieve her prison. Isaac's focus and performance in other areas of his life have been erratic, but when it comes to Meridiana, he's been more effective than anyone within the Porter organization. If he says he can stop Meridiana and her ghosts, then it's my professional opinion that you should trust him."

I felt simultaneously exposed, humbled, and grateful. "Thank you."

Nicola picked up *Towers of Midnight*. "Thank her by making sure Meridiana doesn't conquer the world and kill us all."

From: Whitney Spotts
To: Nicola Pallas
Subject: FWD: Real-Life Superhero Busts Drug Dealers

Ms. Pallas,

This story has been making the rounds online today:

A man calling himself "The Wizard" is claiming responsibility for the capture of four alleged drug dealers on the streets of New York City. Dressed in a black trench coat and carrying a staff that could have come straight out of Middle Earth, The Wizard describes himself as a modern-day superhero who uses magic to make his city safer for everyone.

A fedora and black mask cover his head and eyes, and a long gray beard obscures his face, making identification difficult. However, authorities do have a recording from a 911 call in which The Wizard let the city know where they could "pick up their trash." Assuming his voice hasn't been altered, the accent suggests he's a local from the Brooklyn area.

While real-life superheroes aren't a new phenomenon, The Wizard appears to be the real thing. Witnesses describe him using a spellbook to conjure a maelstrom of garbage, a "trashnado," that attacked the suspects, subduing them with only moderate injuries.

Many people applaud The Wizard's efforts, but the police have announced a zero-tolerance policy for vigilantism. More importantly, if magical superheroes are now patrolling our streets, can supervillains be far behind?

Between the accent and the "trashnado," this sounds like Jerry Howze. I thought he was restricted to cataloging. Jerry's got to be what, a hundred years old by now?

Will someone please yank him off the street before he gets his ass killed?

Thanks,
Whit

Chapter 17

I SORTED THROUGH ONE book after another, setting most aside. Some were simply too destructive. Others might be able to stop Meridiana, but would probably take out the rest of Copper River along with her.

I hesitated over Pearl North's *The Boy from Ilysies*. A magical pen capable of literally rewriting the world had potential, but a single careless word could unintentionally kill us all, and Nicola had just asked me not to do that. Not to mention the amount of power it would take to use such an artifact. I could char myself into ash with the first spell. On the other hand, the conclusion to the series, *The Book of the Night*, contained a library of pretty much every book on Earth. *That* would be handy.

Bi Wei pored through Jordan's brick of a novel, unraveling Gutenberg's lock. Jackson and Ponce de Leon watched over her shoulders. I longed to do the same, but for the moment, I remained blind to the manipulation of magic.

I wiped my hands on my shirt and tried to swallow. If this didn't work . . . It *should* work, according to everything I knew about magical theory, but what we didn't know far outweighed what we did. And it wasn't like anyone had ever tried this before.

"We're ready," said Bi Wei a short time later. Too short. I had picked out only three books that might help. "You'll want to back away."

Jackson had already cleared the desk of everything save Gutenberg's pen. We pressed together on the far side of the room as Bi Wei reached into the pages of *Towers of Midnight*. She tilted it toward the desk, and what looked like droplets of blinding light spilled from the edge.

This was magic Gutenberg himself had deemed too dangerous to use. I looked toward Nidhi, who shrugged as if to say, *It was your idea.*

I felt like I was back on my very first roller coaster with my mother and brother. I could almost hear the clacking of the wheels as we climbed higher and higher toward the top of what she described as "Shit Peak." I had no idea what awaited us on the other side. All I knew was that there was no going back, and to fail at this point was to fall off the tracks and die. And that whatever happened, it was better than turning back.

Light sprayed forth to envelop the pen. Its afterimage burned purple on my retinas.

The room spun around me. I dropped to one knee and pressed my hands to the floor. I could feel Gutenberg's pen burning its invisible tattoo into my skull all over again, only this time my skin felt inflamed, blistered by fire and smoke that tried to burst free, as if Bi Wei had poured the balefire directly into my flesh.

Maybe this hadn't been the best plan after all.

I closed my eyes and clutched my head, physically trying to keep my skull from exploding.

I heard the angry words Gutenberg had spoken that day in Lena's grove a month before, as Meridiana dug her way into my mind like a mining drill crushing through stone. I remembered his pen carving a single word into my being.

Sileo.

For the past month, I'd been unable to accept the silence, the emptiness where there had once been magic. I'd spent every waking moment trying to flee from it.

I looked to where Bi Wei continued to send balefire onto the pen. Beyond them, Smudge was burning like a highway flare. Ponce de Leon was working to keep Smudge from setting the room on fire. The archive had protections from normal fire, but it was best not to take chances with the magical variety.

Jackson was shouting. Nicola was singing. Lena was saying my name. Their voices battered my senses. I pressed my hands to my ears, but it didn't help. I couldn't shut them out.

I sank to the floor. I felt like I was back in Wisconsin, drowning in Euphemia's pool.

"Stop fighting it." Ponce de Leon's voice, cutting through the noise.

My breath huffed through my nostrils. My heartbeat battered my chest. I closed my eyes and thought about a night on a lake months before, the paddles tucked inside the canoe as Lena and I drifted lazily through the water, looking up at stars and the cloud-misted moon.

Sileo.

I relaxed my hands and turned inward, seeking stillness. Seeking silence. Not an empty void, but acceptance. This would work or else it wouldn't. There was nothing I could do to change that.

For the first time since Gutenberg's pen touched my scalp, I heard the magic. A humming, like the buzz of insects, crept into the silence to rouse my nerves.

"Isaac?" Lena sat beside me, her arms circling my waist.

"I'm all right." I opened my eyes and touched a hand to my face. My cheeks were wet.

I pushed myself up and hobbled toward the desk. The balefire had burned a hole a foot wide through the antique wood. It had taken out the floor as well, leaving a deep crater in the dirt below.

Bi Wei was pale, but otherwise appeared okay. The Jordan novel, on the other hand, was black with magical char. The balefire must have channeled enough magic to burn out the book in a single use.

"How are you feeling, Isaac?" asked Nidhi.

I touched the three books I had set aside. Only one was unlocked: a large, thin hardcover, its power warm to the touch. Decades of untapped belief begged for release. The others must have been locked with some other magic than the pen Bi Wei had erased from existence.

I turned to the end of the book, where the magical items' descriptions were laid out. Skimming these pages conjured memories of the clatter of plastic dice on the dining room table from years ago, the last time I had read an earlier edition of this particular role-playing manual. I scanned a paragraph, and my fingertips slid into the pages.

"Whole," I whispered. "I feel whole."

"All the books in the Porter archive, and you created a headband?" asked Lena.

"That's right." I carefully tied the silk band around my forehead. "It gives me plus six to intelligence, which should boost my IQ about twenty to thirty percent, not to mention helping with spellcasting." The magic headband couldn't impart new knowledge, but it would help me to process the information I had.

To Ponce de Leon, I asked, "Could I borrow your cane?"

He pursed his lips, then shrugged and tossed it to me. It was heavier than I expected. I held the cane horizontally in both hands and thought back to what I had learned in Gerbert d'Aurillac's prison, how I had looked past Meridiana's appearance to the magic underneath. Words woven together at a subatomic level.

"What are you doing?" asked Nicola.

"Making sure I know what I'm doing."

"Better late than never," Lena murmured.

The cane was beautiful, but nothing about its appearance shouted *magic*. There were no carved runes, no magical jewels tucked into the wood. The tip was hard black rubber, textured for traction. I tried twisting the handle, but it didn't budge. No sword or wand hidden away, either.

I slowed my breathing, searching for the calm silence I had touched only minutes earlier. I had done this before. I remembered touching the roots of Lena's oak and reading the words of her book. I had reached into those words to seize control of her grove's magic. But Lena was a creation of libriomancy, and *Nymphs of Neptune* was a book I had read and remembered. This cane was neither.

But it was magic, and like everything else, it had a story of its own. A story that began with the death of a tree and the shaping of the wood. The cane was older than I realized. Ponce de Leon's magic kept it looking new and perfect.

Words flitted past my vision. I let them go. Trying to chase them would break my focus. I waited in silence as each brushstroke of text outlined the cane's history.

"Gutenberg gave this cane to you." It had been the early part of the twentieth century. They were in Petra, Jordan.

"That's right," he said quietly.

But it was Ponce de Leon who had enchanted it. I

watched him wrapping spells around the wood and metal, but I didn't truly understand how the power fit together, any more than I understood how a sculptor transformed a lump of marble into a masterpiece. I saw him strip the polish and rub a thick, dark oil into the wood. He hardened the metal in flames so hot they couldn't be seen. And then he raised the cane to the sky and captured the wind.

The cane showed me another story, one that threatened to pull me back down into despair. Ponce de Leon's blood dripped down the wood, absorbed into the cane before it reached the end. The power of the Fountain of Youth healed his body, just as it always had before. I read his hopelessness, the emotions and passion he rarely let the world see.

"You tried to kill yourself." I spoke without thinking.

"Yes," he answered in the same neutral tone. "It was after my banishment. After my final split from—from the Porters." When he spoke again, it was with morbid humor. "I didn't try particularly hard, and as you know, I'm rather difficult to kill."

"I'm sorry." I hadn't intended to violate his privacy, only to confirm that I could read magic.

"It would seem you've mastered a new aspect of your art," he said mildly.

Not mastered. Not yet. Reading wasn't enough. I had to be able to control that magic.

"How does that work?" asked Lena. "He spends a few minutes in a metal ball and comes out with new magic?"

"Not new," I said. "A better understanding of what I can do. It's like spending your whole life looking up at the night sky from the city, then finally seeing the stars from space, without lights or atmosphere to distort your view. There's so much more . . ."

"It's not unheard of," said Ponce de Leon. "My master

called it baptism. The apprentice would meditate for days, fasting until his body weakened enough for him to leave it behind. The goal was to become one with magic itself. When he returned to himself—*if* he returned—he often brought new insight and abilities back with him."

"Like the students of Bi Sheng," I said, thinking of everything I had seen Bi Wei and her fellow refugees do. They had existed in that magical limbo for five hundred years, and it had changed them. They were far stronger now than when Gutenberg attacked their temple.

"The Land of Midday Dreams," said Bi Wei. "Great grandaunt told me about a river made of the dreams and fears of every man, woman, and child. Where even the strongest soul could lose herself and wander forever, or be consumed by the demons that swam within the dreams. The Ghost Army."

"The practice of baptism was mostly abandoned when I began my study." Ponce de Leon crouched in front of me, peering into my eyes like a doctor. "We thought it a myth."

Not a myth, but a technique made far more danger-ous once Meridiana had been trapped within the river, waiting to drown whoever passed by.

I wanted more than anything to sit down with Ponce de Leon and Bi Wei and mine every magical rumor and legend from their memories. If they were correct, Merid-iana's existence had fundamentally altered the study and practice of magic. What else had we lost or forgotten over the centuries?

I looked at the cane. This was the knowledge I needed right now. Reading the cane's story was one thing. Ma-nipulating it was another. The magic in that cane was unlike any I had performed.

But what was libriomancy, truly? Jeneta had proven it wasn't the ink and paper that held the magic. Laser-etch a story into ten-thousand hockey pucks and hand them out to fans, and I could theoretically use those pucks as easily as a midlist mass-market paperback.

This cane was unique, but its story was stronger than any book. It had been "written" by Juan Ponce de Leon, after all. I reached for the words and let them flow past in silence. I found myself again in that moment of despair and loneliness. Ponce de Leon had believed nothing could truly split the bond between him and Gutenberg. They might have fought over the years, but each relied on the other for support and comfort. The betrayal tore at my chest. They were strangers from another time, the only two people on Earth who understood where the other had come from, and what they had left behind.

"Isaac . . ." Lena pointed to the cane.

Blood seeped from the wood like sap.

I drew my fingers through illusory words that clung to my hand like cobwebs. I could do it. I could pull them apart, separate the layers and undo at least some of what Ponce de Leon had done to this cane over the years.

Instead, I carefully stroked the text back into place, laying it down like stain on wood. The blood followed, until nothing remained but the unbroken ebony surface.

I sat back, shaken by the magic I had done and the power of Ponce de Leon's despair.

"Nothing is eternal," Ponce de Leon said at last. "That doesn't stop us from longing for permanence and security." He took the cane and kissed the metal handle. "You've given us quite the demonstration, Isaac. Can you do the same when faced with Meridiana and her creations?"

"I hope so." My stomach grumbled. It had to be getting close to lunchtime, and I hadn't eaten since yesterday. "But first, do you have any snacks around here?"

Meridiana had protected herself from magical spying. Not even Ponce de Leon could snoop on her that way. But she hadn't thought to block more mundane approaches, like hacking into her e-reader to monitor her Wi-Fi usage. We had tracked her to a one-mile area near Copper River. Given that her planned escape involved a water-based portal, she had to be along the river.

Nicola, Jackson, and Bi Wei would remain at the fort to guard the armillary sphere and monitor her e-reader. That left me, Lena, Nidhi, and Ponce de Leon to spearhead the attack.

"We'll need a second vehicle," I said as we made our way out of the fort, passing a family posing for photos with a man in the red uniform of a British soldier. "I kind of left the Jeep in Copper River, and the Triumph only seats two. Sorry, I didn't think that through."

I wasn't happy about stealing another car, but short of creating a flying carpet or taking our chances with teleportation—

The smell of burning fire-spider rose from my hip, and I stopped walking. Bright lights, like a trio of flashbulbs, heralded the arrival of three wood-and-metal goliaths in the parking lot ahead. Each one carried a man or woman in its arms. The size difference made their passengers look like children.

"We might also need a new plan," I said quietly.

The automatons stood like statues, eight-foot-tall golems with metal skin and glassy eyes, polished to capture the light. Their armor was made up of metal keys, possibly the same blocks Gutenberg had used in his early experiments with printing. Those blocks imprinted libriomantic spells into the wooden flesh of the automatons, drawing on the magic of the Latin Vulgate Bible, just as Gutenberg himself had done.

I could read those spells from here, a tightly woven mesh of Biblical verse protecting them from assault and diverting the attention of people walking past. Any camera pointed in that direction would show only a blurred shadow.

The people they were carrying—two women and a man—moved to inspect my car. I recognized Babs Palmer and Cameron Howes. The other woman looked like Sarieha Ward, a researcher from the East Coast. She clutched a stack of books in her arms. Babs spotted us and pointed.

I could see Babs' silent command to the automatons. The closest of the golems tore through a section of fence, opening the way for Babs and the others.

Cameron, a stocky man with a bush of dark curls and an eye-searing magical green cloak, looked me up and down. "Nice cape."

"Thanks." In addition to my magic headband, I had created a small wand, a ring, and a red-and-yellow cape, which I had safety-pinned to one side of my shirt to keep it away from Smudge's flames. "I like your cloak. We should talk cosplay some time."

"We're not here to fight you, Isaac." Babs was a muscular woman, and her accent made me imagine her roping cattle from horseback like a caricature from a bad Western, despite the fact that she was a practicing lawyer with a known distaste for animals. Some kind of personal shield protected her body, humming like an old refrigerator and giving her skin a glassy shine in the sunlight.

"Jackson called you?" I guessed.

"It wasn't him," said Cameron. "But when he failed to return home, his wife grew worried. Her phone calls were eventually forwarded to us." He gestured to Ward, who began walking toward the fort. One of the automatons followed like an overeager half-ton puppy.

Ponce de Leon had vanished. If he was smart, he'd gotten out of here the instant the automatons popped into view. Right now, the Porters were probably trigger-happy enough to attack him on sight if they realized who he was.

"Automatons won't help against Meridiana," I said. "You have to know that, which means you brought them to use on us."

"Not unless you force us." Babs stopped a short distance away. "What the hell have you done? Every archive on the planet is reporting books suddenly unlocking themselves."

"Spells all over the world go haywire, and you automatically assume I was involved? I don't know whether to be flattered or insulted." I saw no visible weapons, but when I squinted, I could read the faint text of the magic worked into her skin. "Do you have enchanted tattoos? That's so cool. What do they do?"

She folded her arms. "Where is the armillary sphere, Isaac?"

I played out one scenario after another in my head. Lena and I had fought automatons before, but even if we managed to stop these three, we were also facing two Regional Masters, both of whom would have prepared themselves before coming here. I didn't recognize Cameron's cloak, but I suspected it would protect him from most attacks, and I would need time to read and understand Babs' tattoos.

"It's in the archive," I said cheerfully. "Which you already knew, right? You're just starting with the easy stuff to see how cooperative I'll be?"

She tilted her head in acknowledgment.

"I've been inside the sphere," I continued. "I got a nice, good look at Meridiana and the Ghost Army. I know how to stop them. I can free Jeneta and the others, then lure the ghosts into the sphere with her before we destroy it."

"We've put together a different plan." Cameron was smiling. It made me nervous.

Babs touched a jeweled cuff on her left ear and cocked her head, like she was listening to voices we couldn't hear. "We have Nicola," she said to Cameron a moment later. "Jackson is with her."

Nothing about Bi Wei. I kept my face neutral as Cameron stepped forward. "Please hand over any weapons or magical items you're carrying. Including the spider."

I thought back to the books Sarieha Ward had been carrying. "Sarieha had a copy of Damon Knight's *A for Anything*."

"So she did." Babs touched her forearm, and I saw the power within those tattoos building. One passage looked like it would create a web of magical energy. Another had something to do with diverting attacks back on her enemies.

Babs had claimed the automatons weren't here to fight us. I thought she was just trying to play nice, but she meant it. They weren't here to fight at all. Their purpose was much worse. "You can't do this."

"What is it?" asked Lena.

"*A for Anything* was written back in the late fifties." I didn't take my attention from Babs. "It opens with the introduction of a 'gismo,' a small, simple device capable of duplicating anything it touches. Money, machines, human beings."

"Or automatons," said Nidhi.

I scoured my memory. It had been so long since I read the book. "It was a simple wooden cross with a pair of glass and metal cubes, kind of like three-dimensional circuits. Hook one up to whatever you want to duplicate, flip the switch, and then there are two. Gutenberg locked that book the day it came out. I must have unlocked it when I destroyed his pen."

Only a handful of Gutenberg's original automatons still survived. He was said to have hated the things and what it cost to create them: a broken human mind, trapped within wood and metal, acting as the magical battery to give each automaton life.

"They're going to erase one of the automatons," I said, watching Babs' expression. "Like wiping a hard drive. Then they'll use Knight's gismo to build an army, a thousand empty soldiers. Each one nigh invulnerable. Each one lacking only a mind to animate it."

"Why destroy the Ghost Army," Nidhi asked, "when you can enslave them instead?"

"Enslave them how?" asked Lena.

She and I had come across the broken remains of an automaton months before. I remembered piecing together broken metal disks from the automaton's "brain." Engraved on the disks had been the name *Johann Fust*, a competitor of Gutenberg's from the 1400s. I assumed the name was part of the spell binding Fust's spirit to the automaton, but from what I had seen of the Ghost Army, most of them were so far gone they didn't remember their own names.

Babs shrugged. "As I recall, Isaac was able to hitch a ride in one of these things and control it without engraving his autograph on its brain. And there are plenty of books about trapping and controlling ghosts."

Instead of an army of ghosts led by a thousand-year-old parasite and wannabe goddess, we would have an army of unstoppable warriors under the control of a splintering magical organization, one with a history of aggression and paranoia, not to mention a power vacuum at the very top.

Tourists and mock historical figures were streaming out of the fort. A spell trailed from Babs' hands, leading them away like sheep.

"This is a really, *really* bad idea," I said. "The students of Bi Sheng think of the Porters as conquerors and destroyers. They've already outed us to the world. Now you want to escalate things by unveiling your own magical army?"

"Your President Roosevelt was fond of saying, 'Speak softly and carry a big stick; you will go far,'" said Cameron.

"The problem with carrying a big stick is the temptation to use it," I said. "Like Gutenberg did, when he tried to wipe out the students of Bi Sheng. The instant they find out about your automatons, it will be all-out war." And Bi Wei was likely still hiding within the fort. She'd see what they were up to the minute they began.

"To those who survived, that attack happened only a month ago," Nidhi said, adding her urgency to my own. "They watched their friends and family die. The memories are open wounds. Do this, and you'll destroy any chance of peace."

"Automatons are more than capable of hiding until they're needed," Cameron said dismissively.

He might have been right, if not for Bi Wei. She had lost her brother when the automatons destroyed her temple. That she had been able to trust me at all was a miracle, as was the fact that the arrival of Babs and Cameron with automatons in tow hadn't triggered an instant and violent response.

I tried to calculate my odds against Babs, Cameron, and automatons. They weren't good.

Babs must have seen my intentions on my face. "Don't do anything hasty, Isaac. Take off the cape and whatever other magic you're carrying, and we'll talk."

I considered warning them about Bi Wei, but I couldn't see that helping. Babs and Cameron were pushing for control of the Porters. They couldn't back down. Even if they managed to subdue her, all of her fellow students were tapped into her mind and senses. They would see what happened, and they would know the Porters remained an active threat to them all.

Slowly, I removed the cape and tossed it onto the ground between us. Testing my abilities on Ponce de Leon's cane in the safety of the archive had been one thing. Now it was time for the field test.

I stared at the cape, reading the magic and belief woven through the garishly colored fabric. I saw both the rules from the book and the belief of countless gamers who had used this particular artifact. Not to mention the arguments between rules-lawyers who wanted to push the cape's capabilities to the very edge. And beyond, if the game-master let them get away with it.

"Do the other Regional Masters know about this?" Lena asked.

Cameron snorted. "They'd spend a month arguing and forming committees to study the problem, and we'd be dead of old age before they made a decision. Why do you think Gutenberg bypassed them so often?"

"Look how that worked out for him," Nidhi said quietly.

Screams from within the fort gave me the distraction I needed. I tore the cape's magic free and wrapped it around myself. I stretched the web of words to embrace Lena as well, then reached for Nidhi . . .

The magic buckled. Three people were too much. The rules could only be pushed so far. Hoping Nidhi would understand, I refocused the cape's power.

Lena and I disappeared.

FEDERAL BUREAU OF INVESTIGATION

FILE NO: 16824-17

☑ New File

☐ Update to Existing File

NAME: Isaac Samuel Vainio

ALIASES: None

PHYSICAL DESCRIPTION

SEX: M
RACE: Caucasian
HEIGHT: 5'9"
WEIGHT: 155 lbs
HAIR COLOR: Blond
HAIR LENGTH: Short
EYE COLOR: Brown
SCARS/MARKS/TATTOOS: None

FAMILY: Unmarried, no children. Cohabitates with Lena Greenwood. One brother: Toby. Parents: Erik and Heidi Vainio.

CRIMINAL HISTORY: Member of the magical organization known as the Porters. Suspected involvement with the disappearance of Ted Boyer (Marquette, MI). Suspected involvement with the murder of Ray Walker (East Lansing, MI). Suspected involvement with multiple, unexplained deaths in Copper River, Michigan (see case file C89626.)

KNOWN ASSOCIATES: Nicola Pallas (File 16821-23). Nidhi Shah.

Property of the U.S. Government. For internal use only.

Chapter 18

LENA AND I rematerialized within the Chevalier House's basement, just outside of the archive. The inner door was open. Nicola and Jackson were slumped unconscious against the wall. Nicola had been gagged and bound as well, presumably to keep her from using magic if she recovered. Ward and her automaton must have caught them by surprise.

I could see the spells laid over them like blankets, keeping them asleep. Given time, I could probably reverse them, but we didn't have time. "Where did they go?"

Lena jogged to the end of the hallway and opened the outer door. "No sign of her here. What the hell did you do, by the way?"

"That cape is what's called a Wondrous Item. Once per day, it allows your character to open a dimensional doorway. I used to play a dwarf rogue who caused all sorts of mischief with one of those capes."

I found the armillary sphere in the crate where we had left it. Nothing else had been touched, as far as I could tell. I checked Nicola and Jackson more closely.

Both were breathing normally, and had no obvious injuries.

Shouts from aboveground gave me a good idea where Ward had gone. Lena snatched the armillary sphere, and seconds later we were running up the stairs and out of the house.

We found Sarieha Ward facedown on the ground in front of Damon Knight's magical gismo. Her automaton lay beside her, its head separated from the torso. Sarieha had removed several metal disks from the head, presumably "wiping" it of its current occupant in preparation for the magical cloning process.

It wasn't the automaton that made Smudge burst into anxious flames. It was Bi Wei. Power swirled around her, raw and unformed and terrifying. I couldn't tell whether or not Sarieha was still alive, but if she was, Bi Wei intended to change that. "Wei, stop!"

The eyes that turned toward me were wide with rage and terror. Bi Wei stood in the eye of a magical maelstrom. I could see Meridiana's tendrils stretching toward her, seeking her heart and mind. Meridiana fed on those who channeled too much magical power. But Bi Wei didn't stand alone. Shadows surrounded her: the other students of Bi Sheng, lending her strength.

"The Porters are *not* going to do this!" I gestured to the automaton. "I won't let it happen."

Cameron and his automaton materialized atop the north wall.

"Oh, shit." The automaton reached toward me, and I saw a line of familiar Latin flare to life. *Pluit ignem et sulphur de caelo et omnes perdidit.* "Incoming!"

Sulfurous flames poured forth. Cameron wasn't playing around anymore. Neither was Bi Wei, who diverted the attack and spun, carrying the fire like a dancer twirling her partner, then launching it back at Cameron.

Lena tossed the sphere to me and sprinted toward the

wall. I dropped to one knee and checked Sarieha. Her legs were broken, but she was alive. I turned my attention to the automaton's head. With its inner workings exposed and its defenses down, I could have destroyed it, but Babs and Cameron had two others they could use to build their army. And since Sarieha had gone to the trouble of opening this one up for me ...

I twisted the ring on my hand, another of the items I had pulled from the gaming manual. I hadn't planned on using the ring's three wishes until I faced Meridiana. Then again, when had any of my plans worked out the way I wanted? I crafted my first wish in my mind, examining every word for loopholes before speaking it aloud.

While I worked on the automaton's head, Lena plunged her hands deep into the northern wall. Branches sprouted from the palisade, twining around Cameron's arms and legs. Lena directed other branches to attack his automaton, while Bi Wei countered the automaton's magic.

I finished my work on the automaton's head and turned my attention to the armillary sphere. Magic poured forth from the ring, and the second of the three jewels disappeared. The sphere vanished from the grass.

Babs and her automaton appeared on the eastern wall. I yanked out my shock-gun, adjusted it to the highest level, and fired at the platform beneath her. It collapsed under their weight.

Another branch trapped Cameron's arm. Bi Wei raised her hands. Dozens of shadows moved with her, preparing to finish him off.

I switched to a nonfatal setting and shot her in the back. Electricity fragmented over her body, and she fell.

"Come on!" I shouted.

Lena left Cameron fighting to free himself. Babs and her automaton were already getting back to their feet. Lena scooped Bi Wei into her arms, and we ran toward the southern gate. Smudge's cage banged against my hip with every stride.

Fire washed through the gate behind us, but they didn't chase us. Why bother? Their first priority would be to find the sphere, and they could see neither of us had it.

Ponce de Leon waited for us in the parking lot, leaning against the Triumph with his arms folded. I was a little surprised. With Gutenberg gone and the Porters crumbling, I had half-expected him to do the pragmatic thing and get the hell out of here. Instead, he got in and started the engine, leaving the door open.

"Do you have Nidhi?" Lena shouted.

"They put her into an enchanted sleep. She's resting comfortably in the passenger's seat."

"We could have used a hand back there," I said.

"I've squared off with automatons before. I'd prefer not to do so again."

I didn't have time to argue. "We have to get to Copper River. The Triumph isn't big enough to—"

Ponce de Leon didn't move. "How long has it been since you stole my car, Isaac?"

"Technically, I didn't steal it from you. It was in storage. Confiscated after you snuck into France back in seventy-nine. All I did was fudge some paperwork."

"You were clever enough to forge Porter requisitions, but you've yet to uncover everything this car can do." He tucked his cane behind the seats. "You'll want to stand back."

He pulled the choke out as far as it would go, sealed the air vents, then turned on the hazard lights. With a satisfied smile, he turned on the radio and pressed the fourth station button.

The transformation was too swift for me to follow, though scraps of magical text taunted me as they flew past. The car's body spread outward. Paint melted into the metal, leaving the appearance of hammered steel. The door slammed shut, locking Nidhi and Ponce de Leon inside.

Lena and I fell back. The car was now three times as wide as before and almost twice as long. Portholes the size of dinner plates spread equidistantly around the upper portion. A ramp hissed down to the pavement, and Ponce de Leon beckoned us inside.

I didn't move. "Are you telling me I've had my own *flying saucer* all this time?"

"It's a shame you didn't steal the manual. It will be cramped, but we should all fit, and this form makes much better time. We may need to stop for gas, though." He sat in a padded metal-backed swivel chair at the exact center of the ship. A curved control panel arced in front of his lap, studded with toggle switches and bright lights in primary colors. "What do you think? One of your libriomancers helped me with the layout."

The ramp lifted, leaving only the low illumination from the lights hidden in the base of the walls. A chrome control stick, two-handed and reminiscent of something you'd find in the cockpit of a jumbo jet, rose from the instrument panel. Lena set Bi Wei on the floor, then moved to sit with Nidhi.

"You turned your car into a UFO," I said.

He looked over his shoulder at me. "How do you know I didn't turn my UFO into a car?"

There were no chairs or seatbelts, only metal plating for the floor and a circular bench that ringed most of the ship, with a gap for the ramp. The walls curved up around us, suggesting that the engines and electronics were all locked away in the lower half.

The floor buzzed as we rose into the air. The wall in front of Ponce de Leon turned transparent, a viewscreen showing the Mackinac Bridge stretched out before us.

"This is awesome," I whispered.

He glanced over his shoulder. "You should see my DeLorean."

And then we were off, streaking through the sky toward Copper River. I couldn't tell if the ship somehow knew where it was going, or if Ponce de Leon had a hidden GPS on that console. Most of the lights and switches were unlabeled and incomprehensible, though they looked extremely cool.

"I feel like we should stop to burn a crop circle," I said. Instead, I turned to study the spell keeping Nidhi asleep. After a few minutes, I was able to peel the magic away. I did my best to preserve the spell, transferring it like a sheet of gold leaf and laying it over Bi Wei. Her legs twitched, and her breathing deepened.

I dug out my phone to begin putting the rest of my plan into effect. "Can you fly lower? I can't get a signal up here."

Ponce de Leon dropped the ship through the clouds, taking us lower and lower until we were skimming over the treetops. I stared at the phone, but I couldn't bring myself to use it.

"What's wrong?" Lena asked. She sat with one arm around Nidhi's shoulders.

I closed my eyes, but when I did, I saw the graves from a month before. "Meridiana knows we're coming. We need help. But anyone I drag into this fight might not walk away."

"Don't drag them," said Nidhi. "Tell them the truth. Let them choose for themselves."

My heart was pounding as hard as it had during the fighting at Fort Michilimackinac. In some ways, I was more scared of this phone call than I had been to enter Gerbert d'Aurillac's sphere. At least with the sphere, I had only been risking my own life and sanity.

I started with Jerry Beauchamp, who answered after the fourth ring. I hadn't seen Jerry or his family among the mob at my house, but given the speed of gossip in this town, he would have heard about it by now. And about me.

"This is Isaac Vainio. I—yah, I know you're at work." I hadn't, but I should have realized.

"What do you want?" Jerry asked warily.

"It's not what I want. It's what I need." I wiped my other hand on my jeans. "I need to tell you the truth. And I need your help."

Ponce de Leon hadn't lied about the ship's speed. We reached the northern coast of the U.P. in a half hour, and the Copper River Public Library five minutes later.

We landed on the side of the road across from the library. The ship blocked both the sidewalk and one lane of traffic. I crept down the ramp, shock-gun in one hand. I neither saw nor felt magic aside from our own, and Smudge was relatively unworried.

A man stopped on the far side of the road with an overweight toy poodle on a leash. My jaw tightened. Andy Rosten had been part of the mob that attacked me and stood by while my home burned.

He didn't move. The sight of me emerging from a flying saucer with what looked like a revolver in my right hand might have had something to do with that.

I strode purposefully toward the library's back door, stopping only to nod in his direction. "Good afternoon."

I could see him trying to say my name, but no sound emerged.

There were only a few people inside, and they stayed out of my way as I stocked up on books. Alex was working the main desk. "Isaac, what are you doing? You know you need to check those out first."

I turned around.

He raised his hands. "Or you could do it later."

When I emerged, more people had gathered to stare at the UFO. Andy hadn't moved at all, though his dog was pulling impatiently at the leash. He flinched when I glanced his way.

"How are the twins?" I asked.

"Good." His voice squeaked a little. "They're . . . they're good."

"Did they ever pick up those *Justice League* books they reserved?"

He nodded.

"Glad to hear it. Tell Cindy I said hi."

Just down the street was a small flower garden surrounding a set of copper statues commemorating the original miners of our town. I pulled out a wand, and seconds later the miners and their full cart of ore were shrinking to the size of children's toys. I tucked the wand away, scooped the three statues and cart into my hand, and turned to go.

Andy was practically a statue himself. I gave him a quick salute with the wand, and he flinched.

Once inside the saucer, I sat down beside Lena, who had been watching through one of the portholes.

"I think he might have soiled himself," she commented, putting a hand on my thigh. "You look like you enjoyed that."

"Damn right." I tossed one of the statues in my hand.

"And you needed miniature statues why?"

I grinned. "It's a surprise."

Lena and Nidhi exchanged a look of exasperation.

"Where are we going?" asked Ponce de Leon as we lifted off.

"She's at the river. Fly north."

He turned in his seat and raised a single dark eyebrow.

I winced inside. "Please."

We landed in a picnic area about a half mile from the river. Nidhi stayed with the ship. Or the car. Whatever you wanted to call it. If it transformed into a flying saucer, what other modes might it have? Assuming we all survived, I needed to see if I could read the different layers of magic worked into the body.

Flames rippled over Smudge's back as we climbed out. Ponce de Leon had been kind enough to conjure me a passable imitation of the old leather duster I used to wear as a field agent. The extra pockets allowed me to better stock up on books. It also gave Smudge a leather-insulated shoulder to cling to instead of being confined to his cage.

We had gone only a few steps when a shadow flew toward us. Meridiana's warrior angel, Binion, cut through the sky like an overgrown owl. He crashed into Lena with an impact that would have shattered the bones of an ordinary human. They rolled through the grass together. I concentrated, intending to strip his angelic story away, but before I could act, he cinched an arm around Lena's neck. The other pinned her arms to her sides, preventing her from drawing her weapons.

I raised my gun. Bodies conducted electricity well enough for me to stun them both. But when I pulled the trigger, the lightning dissipated before reaching them.

"Buzzing the town in a UFO isn't subtle." Binion pressed Lena's head sideways, straining to crack her neck.

"I wasn't going for subtle," I said. "Let her go."

Ponce de Leon readied his cane. I forced myself to relax, to read the currents of Binion's strength and power.

Lena wedged her chin down, trying to force it into Binion's elbow to create a gap so she could breathe. She bent her knees and sank lower, then rammed her elbows backward.

It shouldn't have worked. Binion was as strong as Lena. Probably stronger. But he gasped and released his grip. His hands went to his sides, where blood darkened his robe.

Lena spun to face him. Six-inch wooden spikes had grown from her elbows. Binion drew his sword and swung at her head. She blocked the blow with a forearm now covered in thick bark. The thunk of steel hitting oak echoed over the grass.

Lena continued to transform as she fought. Plates of bark grew over her exposed flesh. Wooden spikes jutted from her knees. Sharp wooden spurs slid from the backs of her hands, reminding me of Wolverine's claws from the *X-men* and making me suspect Lena had been reading Nidhi's comics again.

Binion tried to take flight, but she caught his leg. He reached down to grab her hair. She rammed the spurs on her left fist through his forearm and slammed him to the ground.

He bellowed a most unangelic curse as he bounced to his feet. His right fist snapped out to strike Lena's face, rocking her head back. But even as blood dripped from her nose, she lunged again, slicing and stabbing.

I could see Binion trying to drain her magic, but there was too much, and Lena was striking too quickly.

The crack of a hunting rifle made me jump. Binion staggered, his left arm hanging uselessly.

Lizzie Pascoe stepped out from the woods, rifle raised to her shoulder. Binion moved sideways, trying to keep Lena between himself and Lizzie. He thrust his sword. Lena knocked it aside and punched him in the sternum, driving wooden spurs into his chest. She ripped them free and dodged to one side, allowing Lizzie to put a bullet into his chest.

The sword slipped from his bloody fingers, and he fell face-first to the ground.

Lena hadn't even needed to use her bokken. This was an aspect of her magic I had never imagined. If she could stretch her power like this, what else could she do?

Lizzie turned her weapon toward Lena.

"Wait!" I waved my arms and ran to stand between them. I could understand Lizzie's fear. Aside from the brown rings of her eyes, nothing human remained of my lover. She was a being of wood, with overlapping plates of bark for armor. Even her teeth had grown thicker, encased in fine-grained cellulose. The blood dripping from her nose was thick as syrup. "That's Lena."

The rifle didn't move, and I realized that putting myself in the line of fire of a woman who had recently helped burn down my house and beat the shit out of me was, perhaps, a poor tactical choice.

"Yah, I . . . I know," Lizzie said at last. She lowered her rifle. "I saw her fighting before . . . before all *that*." She looked from Lena to me to Ponce de Leon, and then to the flying saucer behind us. "Is there anything more you want to tell us?"

"Sure. That's not a real UFO, the gentleman there is five hundred years old, and there's a woman trying to break out of a prison built by a pope a thousand years ago. And thank you."

She shook her head and glanced at the grass by her feet. "Isaac, I don't know what the hell's going on, or what you and your girlfriend really are. But about what happened before . . ."

Another monster bounded out of the woods before she could finish. Grotesque and scarred, with yellowed skin. I remembered seeing him in Gutenberg's apartment building, right before it exploded. Up close, the misshapen features helped me to finally place why he looked so familiar.

"You're Frankenstein's monster!" I fished one of the shrunken statues from my pocket. "Awesome!"

Like the rest of Meridiana's puppets, he had both the physical strength of his distorted body and the magical powers of her ghosts. I could see that magic reaching toward me, seeking to disarm whatever spells or weapons I might have prepared.

With a grin, I hurled the tiny statue straight at him.

Under normal circumstances, the wand I had used should have kept the statue miniaturized for up to eighteen hours, depending on the roll of the die. But with his magic stripping my spell away like a swarm of hungry piranha, the statue returned to its normal size—and mass—in midair.

Its velocity, on the other hand, was unchanged. I saw the monster's rheumy eyes turn round, and then the full-sized metal mining cart knocked him flat onto his back. He lay staring up at the clouds, simultaneously moaning and gasping for breath.

I wanted to stop to study how his body worked, how the muscle and bone from different corpses grafted together so powerfully. Not to mention what an EEG of his brain activity might show. How did magic compensate for the body's automatic rejection of foreign blood and organs? Or was the immune system dead as well, its functioning replaced by Meridiana's magic?

Instead, I turned to Lizzie. "Stay behind us."

She stared at me, then at the monster on the ground, then back at me. "Damn right I'm staying behind you!"

In my peripheral vision, I saw Smudge slip from my shoulder. I caught him instinctively. My fingers closed not around the body of a hot, bristling spider trying to pretend he meant to do that, but a small stone statue, perfect in every detail. His petrified forelegs were raised as if in protest.

I felt sick. Smudge had been my companion since high

school. I cupped his body in my hands, too stunned to speak.

"What happened?" Lizzie raised her rifle and searched the woods.

"Don't look!" I jumped in front of her. Which way had Smudge been facing when he fell? I grabbed a copy of *Heart of Stone* from my pocket. I had catalogued this book myself, and had taken it from the library on the chance that we'd face Meridiana's gorgon again.

I carefully slipped Smudge into an inner pocket, then opened the book and pulled out a pair of mirrored sunglasses. The glasses were enchanted to show magic and to protect the wearer from visual-based attacks.

Deanna Fuentes-McDowell—the gorgon—strode toward us, her burqa thrown back. I glimpsed skin like sandalwood, black serpentine hair, and brown eyes full of unimaginable sorrow. I dropped the book and reached for my shock-gun.

Through the darkened lenses, I saw the ghost controlling her. It stretched toward me, devouring the magical discharge from my weapon, then stripping the protection from my glasses.

The transformation began with my own eyes. My vision clouded as lens, cornea, and ocular fluid solidified. My lids blinked once over gritty stone, and I had just long enough to swear silently at my own stupidity.

Author Margaret Stone died at 3:15 this afternoon at Providence Portland Medical Center, two hours after being shot by a gunman who broke into her home.

Stone is best known as the author of the *Red Death* series, set in a post-apocalyptic plague world inhabited by humans and vampires. The third book, *Red Night*, was a *New York Times* and *USA Today* bestseller, and Stone recently announced that the books had been optioned by a major film studio.

Eric Crocker, the alleged killer, was arrested at the scene and is being held for psychiatric evaluation. Crocker's online presence paints a picture of a long-time genre fan, a man whose love of science fiction and fantasy border on the obsessive. His recent posts describe his growing alarm over the revelation of the supernatural, particularly the magic known as libriomancy.

"It's real," Crocker shouted as he was forced into a waiting police car. "I've always known it was real. Witches and ghosts and aliens. She was one of them, spreading poison through her words. We have to fight back. We have to stop them before it's too late!"

Margaret Stone's first book was *Time Wyrm*, a critically acclaimed but commercially unsuccessful adventure published in 1991. She went on to write twenty-six more novels, two of which were finalists for the Nebula Award, one of science fiction's highest honors.

Stone was also an outspoken advocate against animal cruelty. Her work often featured the rescue of abused animals, and for the past five years, she ran an annual fundraising auction for the American Society for the Prevention of Cruelty to Animals.

Stone is survived by her husband Christopher Hooks and their three children. In lieu of flowers, the family asks that donations be made in Stone's memory to the ASPCA at http://www.aspca.org/donate.

Chapter 19

IN A WAY, the loss of sight saved my life. Blindness helped eliminate the distractions of the real world, letting me concentrate on the magic racing through my body, petrifying every cell. My thoughts translated that magic into Greek text, excerpts from stories and myths thousands of years old.

My lungs felt like they were filling with sand. Silence closed around me as my inner ears hardened. I tried to peel back the words, to chip them away and free my heart to beat, my lungs to expand once more.

I was used to touching a book to manipulate its magic. In this case, the gorgon had sent her stories through me. I captured the words, the belief and terror that had grown up around the myth of Medusa and her sisters. Athena's curse transforming the gorgon's beauty to this monstrous form. The battle between Perseus and Medusa. The blood that was both deadly poison and healing elixir. And of course, the gaze that turned her victims to statues.

Much of the text was irrelevant. The venom of her hair, the tale of her birth. All that mattered were the passages fighting to fossilize my body.

One word at a time, I chiseled them back.

Stone rasped through my throat. I blinked, and the darkness changed to a grainy mess of clouds and shadows. Cold, numb fingers curled. My palm felt like dried plaster. Skin flaked away, the pain jolting my nerves. I stopped trying to move for fear I'd accidentally snap off a limb.

The gorgon was running toward me, little more than a slash of gray through the static of my vision. Other figures moved awkwardly to intercept her, their heads turned away to protect them from her curse. I focused not on the gorgon's body, but on the magic flowing through her, the words that stretched out like tendrils of stone to my body. I seized those words in my mind and hurled them back.

She stumbled, her feet turned heavy and unresponsive. My blood pounded so hard that my still-healing veins threatened to split from the pressure. Like a mirror to a laser, I turned her own curse against her.

She stopped moving. The last of my petrified body melted back to flesh as the gorgon's power rebounded through her. Much of her body was already stone. The serpents of her hair moved sluggishly, like snakes in a torpor from cold. Two ghosts swirled around her, seeking to dissolve my counterspell as it spun muscle and bone into rock.

I reached for the stories Meridiana had used to re-make Deanna's body. As I unraveled them, her hair fell limp. Scales dropped away, leaving thick-curled black locks. The curse died along with the gorgon's form, and Deanna slumped to the ground.

For a moment, I thought I had saved her, but her body was still. You couldn't restore life to the dead, and I had spoken to Deanna's ghost in Rome.

Sweat stung my eyes. I dropped to one knee and took Smudge from my pocket. As quickly and carefully as I could, I peeled away the spells that had come from Deanna.

"Meridiana knows we're here," said Ponce de Leon. "We need to—"

"Shut up." How long since Smudge had been petrified? Sixty seconds? Maybe more. I flung my useless sunglasses aside and squinted at the tangle of magic that defined the little fire-spider. I hadn't read his book in ages, but I could see the individual passages crumbling. "Come on, dammit!"

I had restored his body, but he wasn't moving. I snatched one of the dying fragments of magical text, a passage in which Smudge accidentally set fire to his owner's oil-slick fingers. I knew these books. I remembered the scene. I clung to that memory, used it to restore the broken text, and wrapped it around Smudge's body.

Sweat stung my eyes. Line by line, I raced to repair my friend. I felt someone crouch beside me—Lena, from the sound of creaking wood.

My eyes were dry from my time as an almost-statue. My vision hadn't completely returned either. Black clouds fogged the edges of my sight. I restored another scene, this one a fight between Smudge and a zombie.

One of Smudge's legs twitched. Slowly, he began to stir.

I wanted to jump to my feet and shout, *Holy shit, did you see that?* This was Gutenberg-level libriomancy, and I had done it! I had stopped a gorgon and saved Smudge—and myself as well.

"This sort of thing is normal for you, eh?" asked Lizzie, gesturing toward Frankenstein's monster and the ex-gorgon.

"No, that was new." My clothes still felt gritty, but I didn't care. I was alive, as was Smudge. Though he had curled into a tight, glowing ball, like a lone ember in the smoldering grass. I pulled a jellybean from my pocket and offered it to him.

"Are you all right?" asked Lena.

I rubbed my eyes. It didn't help my vision. "Good enough."

"Then we should be going," said Ponce de Leon.

I nodded. Once Smudge cooled enough for me to return him to my shoulder, we walked down the trail toward the river.

Meridiana stood knee-deep in the water on the far side, gathering magic from her e-reader. Behind her was a naga, an enormous seven-headed serpent that had twined three of those heads around a fat birch tree. An ogre of some sort stood beside Meridiana, with fists like moldy sacks of meat hanging in the water. A winged monkey straight out of Oz perched in the branches overhead, along with what could have been a harpy, or maybe a fury. And standing in the darkness beyond was Death personified, a tall black-robed figure with a scythe.

"I know you took the sphere from the fort, Isaac." Meridiana's attention remained fixed on the water. Ghosts swirled around her, ready to intercept any magical assault. "You should have left it in Gerbert's poem."

The water in front of her was a circle of perfect blackness. I tried to decipher the magic in the portal, but where the water itself was smooth as glass, the spells Meridiana had poured from her e-reader were like swirls of ink, diffusing through one another and rendering the whole thing unreadable. I pulled out my phone and tapped the screen. The wireless signal here was faint, but I didn't need much. "And you shouldn't have saved all of your books on one device."

Her ghosts moved to counter my assault, but this had nothing to do with magic. This was all about Kirsten LaMontagne's skills as a hacker. The dead had no way of blocking the wireless command that reset Meridiana's e-reader to factory default settings.

She screamed. Had any of her books remained in its

memory, I had no doubt she would have killed me on the spot. But it would take time to restore her electronic library.

Unfortunately, the loss of her e-reader didn't undo the spells she had already cast. The portal remained, as did her ghosts and her monsters.

"Bring him to me," she shouted.

The flying monkey and the harpy—definitely a harpy, now that I could see her better—launched themselves from the trees. When they were halfway across the river, a series of gunshots rang out like firecrackers. The monkey splashed down into the water, while the harpy managed to wing her way to a pine tree, where she clung to the branches and nursed her bleeding shoulder.

The smell of gunpowder drifted through the air. I had counted five shots, and they had come from both sides of the river. Tee Jandron stepped into view holding a pump-action shotgun. Walt Derocher was with him, dressed in camo and holding the rifle he used for hunting bear. I spotted Jaylee Parker a little way down, one arm in a sling, the other extending a black revolver toward the naga.

Meridiana flung her e-reader away and yanked out her cell phone. Magic shimmered into existence from whatever books she had stored on her phone, shielding her and her creatures from the bullets.

More shots rang out, and the world turned to chaos. The ogre waded toward us. The bullets only seemed to annoy him. Behind me, Ponce de Leon leaned forward to jab his cane into the edge of the river. The water froze around the ogre's legs, trapping him in place.

The kitsune had drawn a pair of chrome-plated pistols and was returning fire against my reinforcements. Death and the naga were both coming toward me.

Lena scaled an old maple tree like she was Spider-Man, her fingers sinking into the wood. Twenty feet up, she plunged both hands into the maple. The entire tree shuddered. Thick roots punched free of the dirt and reached for the naga.

Meridiana's ghosts were everywhere. They freed the ogre from Ponce de Leon's magic, weakened Lena's hold on her tree, and turned my shock-gun into a useless paperweight. I concentrated on Death, trying to rip the myth and magic from its mortal frame, but something struck me from behind.

I hit the ground hard enough to knock the wind out of me. When I looked up, the cloaked skeleton stood at my feet. I knew he was a construct of myth and magic, but it was *profoundly* disturbing to look up and see Death himself looming over you. Fingers of yellowed bone tightened around the old, curved wood of his scythe.

Branches from Lena's tree reached for his neck. He caught the closest with one hand. Lena screamed as the branch dried and crumbled.

I scooted back. "You know, in some stories, Death lets his victims challenge him for their lives. I don't suppose I can interest you in a game of Monopoly?"

He raised his scythe.

A lopsided grin crept over my face. "Before you kill me, you might want to check your cloak. It seems to be on fire."

The skull tilted in what I assumed was confusion. He twisted around to see flames creeping up his back. Smudge raced higher, leaving a trail of fire behind. Death tried to strip off his cloak, but he couldn't do that while holding the scythe. By the time he tossed the flaming cloak away, leaving a naked and somewhat less imposing skeleton standing in shin-deep water, Smudge had managed to hop onto his shoulder.

Death reached for the fire-spider. Smudge was quicker, darting up the jawbone and then disappearing into the left eye socket.

Death's skull lit up like a jack-o'-lantern.

I wasn't sure the skeleton could feel pain, but he was certainly upset. He dropped his scythe and stumbled back. Thin, yellowed fingers dug into his eyes, but judging by the flickering red flames, Smudge had squeezed through the back of the eye into the larger brain cavity.

I studied the skeleton for a moment, but my vision wouldn't focus. Black smoke obscured the words of his enchantment. He was doubled over now, gripping his own head like a bowling ball.

I crawled to retrieve the discarded scythe.

Lena would have reminded me that this was a victim, just like Jeneta. And she would be right. But whoever he had been before, that person was already dead.

I swept the scythe's blade through the neck. It was an awkward strike, but it worked. Death collapsed in a clattering pile of bone. I snatched the skull before it could roll into the water.

Smudge crawled out of the skull onto my arm, turned to survey his work, and began cleaning his forelegs.

"Show-off," I said.

The staccato cracking of gunfire had mostly died down. Ponce de Leon was struggling against a swarm of ghosts, and it looked like he was losing. Lena had knocked the kitsune's guns away, and they were battling hand-to-hand. Lizzie Pascoe was slumped against the base of a tree. She wasn't moving.

I concentrated on Meridiana, searching for the stories I had seen within the celestial sphere. Meridiana's stories, binding her to Jeneta Aboderin.

The harpy tackled me from behind. The naga struck my legs. I saw Smudge fall, but I couldn't catch him this time. Talons gripped my head, grinding my face into the pebbled riverbed. I tried to get my mouth above the water, but the harpy was too strong. I clawed at her wrists as they dragged me toward Meridiana. I tried to fight, but I couldn't think, couldn't concentrate on anything but the need for air.

I felt Meridiana's magic crawling through my thoughts, searching for the location of the sphere. I heard her cry of triumph as she uprooted the memory she needed. The water's distortion made it sound far away.

The harpy wrenched my head up. I gasped for breath and searched for Smudge. I had no idea whether or not the fire-spider could swim.

Ponce de Leon hurled a spell, but Meridiana deflected it into a nearby tree, which shrank to little more than a sapling. Some sort of reverse aging magic. Nice.

"You thought you could hide the sphere from me?" she asked.

I coughed and spat river water. "I won't fetch it back."

"I didn't ask you to." She stepped to the edge of the portal.

"How did you overcome the problem of textual misalignment?" This kind of libriomancy risked sending things into the world of the book, which essentially destroyed whatever you were trying to teleport. Maybe blending the magic of multiple books somehow canceled out the effect? For an instant, I could almost see how she had layered the different stories into the water, and then the harpy's fist thudded against my temple.

Meridiana ignored me. I saw her guiding the portal's magic toward the memory she had stolen from me. Ripples spread from the center, rebounding from the edge as if trapped by an invisible barrier. She looked at me, either making sure I had no final tricks, or else wanting to be sure I saw her triumph. Grinning wildly, she plunged her hands into the river.

Triumph turned to shouts of rage and pain. Bubbles and steam roiled from the portal. A cracking sound like the snapping of giant bones filled the air as the water tried to freeze and boil at the same time.

Meridiana screamed, her hands and forearms trapped in the ice. Unearthly cold spread outward, and fog obscured normal vision.

I twisted around, reaching for the stories within the naga and the kitsune. I didn't have time to destroy them, but I tugged at their magic long enough to make them let go. They staggered away from me. I crawled through the water, following Meridiana's cries until I reached her side. Once there, I pressed a hand to her side, searching for what remained of Jeneta Aboderin. For the girl who had rolled her eyes at my obtuseness and fed raisins to Smudge and taught minnows to dance to the magic of her words.

"'For he must fly back to his perch and cling,'" I muttered, quoting the fragmented Dunbar poem I had shared with her from within Meridiana's prison. "'When he fain would be on the bough a-swing.'"

What Meridiana had done to her monsters was crude and clumsy compared to the magic smothering Jeneta's mind. The gorgon had been a human body wearing a mask of story; with Jeneta, the transformation was internal. Meridiana's thoughts were welded to her own.

"Jeneta would have known better than to reach into that portal." I tugged harder.

"Stop," Meridiana snarled. "I'll kill her." I saw her power turn inward. Deep within the tangle of text and magic, Jeneta cried out in pain.

"No, you won't." A shadow moved through the fog, coalescing into the shape of Nidhi Shah. She gripped an oddly shaped pistol with both hands.

"What took you so long?" I sagged back in the water. "I told you that as soon as she reached into the portal, I'd need you to get out here and save my ass!"

"There was a harpy in the way," said Nidhi. "I had to wait for Lena to take care of it."

"You're going to shoot us?" Meridiana sneered. "Go ahead. Murder the poor girl."

"You don't know what that is, do you?" I grinned. "You knew about *Harry Potter and the Goblin's Scepter*. But you missed the other books the Porters put together. That's a JG-367 from *The Foretelling*. I made it for Nidhi on the way over. It's locked in exorcism mode. She's not going to shoot Jeneta. Just you."

Nidhi pulled the trigger, and a line of crackling amethyst light speared Meridiana's chest. I saw her summon her ghosts to disrupt the JG-367's magic. With her attention distracted, I reached for the ambition, the hatred, the stories Meridiana had donned over the centuries, the legends she had built and fed upon. Her dreams and her hunger. One story at a time, I added my efforts to the JG-367 to pull her out of Jeneta's body.

Nidhi's gun crumbled away, but it had given me enough. I felt Jeneta fighting back from within. Her assault was desperate and instinctive, but between the two of us, we finished what the JG-367 had begun. She collapsed onto the ice, her forearms still frozen in place.

I crouched beside her. "Can you hear me?"

Jeneta nodded, a movement which transformed into shudders. I tried to undo the portal's magic, but I had overexerted myself. My eyes refused to focus.

Ponce de Leon strode across the river. His cane rapped the ice, and Jeneta's hands pulled free. I felt the portal's magic start to dissolve.

Jeneta's fingers were frozen claws. She was crying and shaking, and it was all I could do to hold her as Ponce de Leon worked a second spell. Slowly, warmth flowed through her flesh.

I tried to rise, but she clung to my arm. Together, Nidhi and I half-dragged, half-carried her to shore while Ponce de Leon continued to dispel the portal. Soon, all that remained was a frigid berg of ice in the middle of the river.

I saw the naga pinned beneath a tangle of roots. There was no sign of the kitsune or the harpy.

The three of us collapsed on the dirt. "Has anyone seen Smudge?"

Jeneta pointed a shaking finger behind me.

"Huh." I cocked my head to the side. "That's new."

Smudge stood *atop* the water, burning as hot as I'd ever seen him and floating on a cushion of steam like a tiny, pissed-off hovercraft. He was trying to crawl to shore, but his legs simply passed through the steam. Ponce de Leon dipped his cane beneath Smudge and carefully lifted him free.

"Isaac?" Jeneta whispered.

I looked at Nidhi. She was the therapist. If anyone was supposed to know what to say to a teenager who had just regained control of her body and mind from a psychotic millennium-old sorceress . . . But she simply nodded at me and walked away, leaving the two of us alone.

"I'm . . . I'm sorry about your hands," I said. "And your e-reader. And, you know, everything."

Jeneta didn't answer. She was shuddering so hard she could barely speak.

"Come on." I took off my jacket and wrapped it around her shoulders. Her skin was cold. Sweat beaded her brow. Her teeth chattered.

Smudge scrambled up my leg, steam rising from his back. I scooped him into Jeneta's lap. She brought her hands over his body for warmth.

"Is she gone?" Jeneta balled her fingers into a fist.

"Sort of. She's still trapped in the sphere, and—"

Before I could say more, Jeneta punched me in the face.

"You told me I was safe at camp!" Her tears spattered my shirt as she continued hitting me. The blows were wild, but strong enough to bruise. "I *told* you about the nightmares and the devourers, how they hated me. You said I'd be safe. You *lied* to me!"

"I didn't know—" I caught myself. I might not be a

therapist, but I knew this wasn't the time to argue. "I'm sorry. I thought you'd be safe. I'm so sorry. I've been searching for you every day since you were taken."

She landed one last punch to the center of my chest, then collapsed against me.

"I'm sorry," I whispered again, holding her as she sobbed.

I'm pretty sure I was crying as well.

SPECULATIVE FICTION WRITERS GUILD SUPPORTS AUTHORIAL FREEDOM

The Speculative Fiction Writers Guild (SFWG) was founded in 1974 for two purposes:

1. To support, educate, and promote our authors.
2. To promote speculative literature in all its forms.

Our membership has struggled with the revelation that magic exists—particularly the school of magic known as libriomancy. The idea that products of our imagination could be made real and brought forth into the world has shaken our entire community. Some of our members have cosigned a letter pledging never again to write stories that could be used to create new tools of destruction. Others have begun working on books with which they hope to improve the world. (Although like any community, we don't always agree on the best way to do that.)

As writers of speculative fiction, our job is to imagine the possibilities. We see the potential risks of libriomancy as well as the potential hope, and we understand the backlash against our genre. We understand the fear of the unknown.

It's important to remember that speculative storytelling has been with us for millennia. The *Epic of Gilgamesh* is more than four thousand years old. Lucian's *True History* introduced aliens and space travel in the second century AD. Stories of powerful sorcerers and futuristic technology have entertained, inspired, and enlightened. What these stories have *not* done is cause the fall of civilization, despite the existence of magic.

The official position of SFWG has always been that authors should be free to write without fear of censorship. But as authors, we also recognize that words have power. The role of the storyteller is an important one, and carries great responsibility.

Some publishers and editors are working to revise their submission guidelines, asking that stories not include new and potentially deadly elements. SFWG is collaborating with several other writers' organizations to develop "Best Practice" guidelines that would ease fears for publishers while allowing authors the freedom that is essential to creativity and art.

However, SFWG *strongly* protests the legislation proposed today in the Canadian House of Commons that would allow the government to ban and destroy books based on arbitrary criteria and uninformed fears. The false sense of security such measures might bring about are not worth the price we would pay in freedom of expression and thought.

In short, *Fahrenheit 451* was never meant to be an instruction manual.

Connie Allen
President, SFWG

Chapter 20

"IT LOOKS LIKE MOST of Meridiana's minions bolted when you pulled her out of Jeneta," said Lena. She and Ponce de Leon had been searching the immediate surroundings.

"Thanks." None of us were up for a prolonged hunt, but if I told Jeff what had happened, he could probably find some werewolves who would be eager to track the remnants of Meridiana's forces.

"How's your vision?" asked Ponce de Leon. He was sweating hard, and blood soaked his left sleeve. "Black spots floating around the edges?"

His question chilled me more than the icy water soaking my clothes. "How did you know?"

"I've seen it before. You think magical charring only happens to books?" He tapped the side of his head. "I saw how you were working your magic. Almost entirely visual, which suggests where the damage would begin."

I had charred books before, pouring too much power through the pages and reducing them to supernaturally blackened ash. Imagining the same thing happening to my eyes and optic nerves made me shudder.

"Why do you think sorcerers use wands and staves?" He raised his cane. "Better to char a piece of wood than your own body. It's not a perfect solution, of course. The sorcerer still channels and controls the magic, but it helps."

Lena kicked a chunk of floating ice. "Would you like to explain what the hell just happened? How did you freeze her portal?"

"I couldn't destroy the sphere, and no matter where I sent it, I figured there was a good chance she'd rip the location out of my head and retrieve it. So I sent it somewhere that would bite back. According to the rules, the three wishes I pulled out of the gaming manual can duplicate the effects of any spell. But the teleportation spell I used requires the caster to be familiar with the destination." I grinned. "Fortunately, I've been to the moon."

Ponce de Leon chuckled. "The question is, can you get the sphere back?"

"Not at the moment, unfortunately. I used up all three wishes." I rubbed my hand. "That may be a moot point by now, though."

"Did you say you've been to the moon?" asked Walt Derocher.

I hadn't heard him approach. I tensed as others from Copper River closed around me. One hand moved toward my gun before I caught myself. Last time, the mob had tried to kill me, but there was no anger on their faces now. Only shock and exhaustion and pain. "Yah, that's right. It was just the one time, and I didn't get to do much sightseeing."

I searched the crowd. Where was Lizzie? I didn't see Tee Marana, either. My gut knotted tighter. "How many . . . ?"

Walt knew what I couldn't bring myself to ask. "Two dead, and we've got three people in dire need of a hospital. Tee's in the worst shape, and nobody's been able to find Rusty Isham. Is there anything your . . . your magic can do to help?"

Dammit. That was fewer casualties than I had feared, but it was still too many. "I think so. I can—"

"Allow me," said Ponce de Leon. "Isaac has seriously overexerted himself, and his work is only beginning."

"These people helped us because I asked them," I said. "Don't tell me I can't help them. I owe them at least that much."

"You helped to save their town and their world." He turned to accompany Walt. My gut told me once he finished whatever healing spells he had planned, he wasn't coming back.

"Nidhi, could you stay with Jeneta?"

She folded her arms, and I got the sense she was more than willing to tie me to a tree to prevent me from further burning myself out, magically.

"No magic. I promise." I looked after Ponce de Leon. "There's something I need to do."

The rest of my things were scattered outside the UFO where I had left them. I dug through my bag and pulled out a metal canister. I found Ponce de Leon sitting beside Tee Marana. Tee was alive, and the bullet wounds in his chest and gut slowly healed as I watched. Ponce de Leon was doing something to a compass and a cigarette butt. He handed the compass to Walt. "This will take you to Rusty Isham."

I waited for them to go. "I have something for you."

He blinked in surprise. "As we discovered earlier, it's not even my birthday."

"This is what's left of the vampire blood I stole." I offered it to him. "I thought you could use it to talk to Gutenberg. To say good-bye."

He stared at the canister. His lips parted, but he didn't speak. He reached out to take the canister, holding it as carefully as if it were porcelain instead of heavily insulated steel. Tears dripped down the sides of his nose, but he didn't bother to wipe them away. "Thank you, Isaac."

"You're welcome." I looked over my shoulder toward the river. "And thank *you*."

He stood and raised his cane in salute. "Good luck."

Babs Palmer arrived two hours later, accompanied by about twenty automatons. Their arrival created a strobe light effect powerful enough to trigger seizures. In my case, it simply added to the throbbing pain in my skull.

"Took you long enough," I said. Lena and I were resting at the base of a pine tree. Everyone else had cleared out as soon as they found Rusty, who had lost an arm to Death's scythe. He would have died if he hadn't been able to get his belt tightened around his shoulder as a makeshift tourniquet. Ponce de Leon had healed the stump, and I'd promised to restore his arm as soon as I got a good night's sleep.

I pointed to the clearing. "Would you believe that asshole Ponce de Leon stole my car?"

"You stole it from him first," Lena said. Her appearance was human once more, soft and warm and beautiful.

"The Porters will be reviewing your history and actions," Babs said after a long pause. "I know you were able to save Jeneta."

I yawned and rested my head on Lena's shoulder. Her arm snaked around my waist, her thumb hooking through the belt loop of my jeans. I waved a hand at the automatons. "I take it you found the sphere and built your army of toy soldiers."

"We sensed the magic of Meridiana's portal when it activated, and were able to trace its power to the moon.

You're fortunate we were able to retrieve it before she did."

"Well, Meridiana was suffering from brain freeze." I clamped back laughter at my own bad joke. If I started giggling, exhaustion and giddiness would make it impossible to stop. "I knew you'd be searching for it. I figured you'd have an automaton hop up for a quick moonwalk within minutes of Meridiana trying to grab it."

"And if you'd been wrong?" Babs asked. "If she'd gotten her mitts on the sphere first?"

"This wasn't exactly how I'd intended things to go," I admitted. "I had to improvise a bit when you and your friends showed up at the fort."

Babs straightened, visibly trying to get back on script. "Based on your results, we *might* be able to overlook your other actions and restore your position in research. We'll also be assigning Jeneta to a Porter psychiatrist. I know you've been concerned about her. However, you need to tell us everything you know about Ponce de Leon and Bi Wei, and where they might have gone."

"They left." Bi Wei had slipped away during the battle. I had no idea where Ponce de Leon had gone. All I knew was that I would be unlikely to find him unless and until he wanted me to.

"How many of those things did you make?" Lena asked, waving lazily at the automatons.

"We weren't able to capture all of the Ghost Army," Babs admitted. "Some escaped. But we have five hundred new automatons."

It was the first thing she'd said that truly bothered me. "You had the sphere. How could they just escape?"

"We miscalculated the amount of magic it would take to duplicate a thousand automatons."

At least half of the Ghost Army was still out there. Damn their ambition. "I guess that makes you king of a pretty big magical hill, eh? What about the sphere itself?"

"Destroyed, along with Meridiana."

"You hope." It saddened me to know Gerbert d'Aurillac's masterpiece was no more.

"The ghosts aren't the only threat," Babs continued. "The Porters are splintering. The students of Bi Sheng are out there, waiting for us to drop our guard. And there are other rogues to worry about, like your Spanish friend. Christ only knows what the rest of the world's going to want to do to us as the truth spreads."

"Where's Nicola Pallas?" I asked.

Babs must have heard some unspoken threat in my tone. She frowned, and the two closest automatons stepped forward. "She'll be given a fair hearing. Most likely, she'll be dismissed from the Porters with strict rules limiting her use of magic."

"Yeah." I dragged the word out. "I don't think that's going to work for me. How about instead you give Cameron a ring. Tell him to let Nicola go. I don't know if she'll want to stay with the Porters or not, but I think we should let her make that choice."

Automaton magic surged to life, preparing to counter any spells I might attempt. As if I had the energy for that.

"Oh, please. I'm too damn tired to fight you." I raised my hands in surrender. "I'll tell you what, though. I can understand why Gutenberg locked some of those gaming manuals I found at the fort." I waved my fingers, admiring my ring with its three now-empty settings. "The craziest campaign I ever ran, my brother's dwarf wizard got hold of a ring of three wishes. There are limits to what you can use wishes for, of course. Let's say, in theory, you wanted to wish all the automatons out of existence. A direct assault like that is just too much. You probably couldn't use it to destroy Meridiana or prevent her from ever being born, or anything like that, either. It would take too much power."

I slid the ring from my finger and tossed it to Babs.

"On the other hand, you could use a wish to transport an object to another location, like the moon. Or to create a moderately powerful, single-use magical item. Something like a silver tack enchanted with a pair of spells. Maybe a maximized dispel magic and a force orb. Automatons have defenses against that sort of thing, so the trick would be to plant it *inside* the head. Difficult, unless you already have a partially disassembled automaton to work with. Then you could get within its protective spells. If all went well, the first spell would dispel and destroy the ghost, and the second would blow the automaton apart from the inside out."

I tilted my head. "But even then, you've only managed to sabotage a single automaton. Unless someone was using a magical gismo to duplicate that automaton . . . and everything inside of it."

Babs was three shades paler by the time I finished my monologue. Power shot from a beaded bracelet around her left wrist. My body went rigid. I couldn't move or speak. She forced her way into my thoughts, searching to find whether or not I was telling the truth.

I was. I let her see the memory of how I had rammed the enchanted tack into the inside of their decapitated automaton, hiding it in the shadow behind the metal neck joint. And then I let her find my third and final wish. The one I had used to create a magical remote that would trigger those spells. I had shaped it into a silver ring in the shape of an oak leaf.

"Where is the remote?" she demanded.

"Oh, that? I figured you'd try to stop me, so I gave it to Lena."

Beside me, Lena twisted the ring on her middle finger. Twenty automaton heads exploded in unison. The concussive force toppled me onto my back. As I waited for my ears to stop ringing, I studied the magic Babs had used to trap my body and peeled it back, one story at a time.

Babs groaned. Wood and metal shrapnel had pelted her body. She was alive, but in no condition to fight. I had gotten a few cuts and bruises myself, but my jacket had protected me from the worst of it.

I walked over to remove the bracelet from her wrist. I also took a magic wristwatch, a sidearm, her cell phone, and three books tucked away in her purse. Once she was magically defenseless, I checked her pulse and made sure none of her injuries were life-threatening.

Decapitated automatons fell all around us, their magical armor clinking to the ground in pieces. I saw no sign of active magic, or of the ghosts Babs had imprisoned within them.

"I was really hoping that would finish off all of the Ghost Army." I sat down in front of Babs and crossed my legs. "Congratulations. In your rush to set yourself up as the next Gutenberg, you let half those things loose in our world. I wonder what the other Regional Masters are going to say about that."

"You destroyed our only means of fighting them," she replied.

"The only means? A libriomancer should have more imagination than that." I slid her phone through the dirt. "Now how about you make that phone call to Cameron and tell him to turn Nicola loose? I suspect he'll also want to know why the rest of your mechanical army just exploded."

Twenty-four hours later, I was sitting in the Detroit Metro Airport with Lena, Nidhi, and Jeneta, watching the flow of arriving and departing passengers.

Jeneta glanced up from her book—a paperback collection of late twentieth-century poetry—and frowned. "Those things make you look like a nerd."

I pushed the black-framed glasses higher up on my nose. The earpieces weren't adjusted quite right, and the lenses weren't perfect, being designed to help correct damage from cataracts, but they were better than nothing.

The charring of my vision continued to give me trouble, especially when reading or trying to drive at night. Not that driving was much of an issue, since my truck had burned up with my house and Ponce de Leon had taken the Triumph. Sure, it was technically his car, but I really, really liked it.

"They're not nerdy," said Lena. "They're 'geek-chic.'"

Jeneta's feet tapped anxiously against the floor. She scanned the crowd again. To distract her, I set Smudge's cage atop her duffel bag and offered her a packet I had been saving for the right occasion.

Before, she would have lit up. Now, it was as if everything about her had been dimmed. But her crooked smile as she accepted the gift was progress. "For Smudge?"

"He's never tried Pop Rocks before. Don't give him more than three to start with until we see how he does."

She tore open the packet and poured a pile of irregular pink crystals into her hand. She took her time selecting three, then offered them to Smudge.

Smudge carefully plucked the crystals from her fingertip and gobbled them down. Jeneta tossed the rest of the handful into her own mouth.

Spiders had far less saliva than human beings, and if it wasn't enough to dissolve the candy and release the pressurized bubbles of CO_2, this could be rather anticlimactic. If the candy didn't break down until it was in his stomach, I'd just have a belching fire-spider. Which could also be entertaining.

Thirty seconds passed. A minute.

There was a faint crackling sound, and Smudge

jumped back as if he was trying to escape from his own mouth. A puff of red fire passed over his back, vanishing as quickly as it had appeared. He turned to glare accusingly at Jeneta. A second puff of flame followed the first.

Jeneta giggled. "I think they gave him hiccups."

Smudge flamed one more time, groomed his face, and trotted back to the side of the cage to beg for more.

"I think he likes it," said Lena.

Jeneta nodded, but kept her attention on Smudge. I wondered again whether bringing her here had been a good idea. The last time she was in this airport, Meridiana had been in control of her body. We could have arranged to meet her parents anywhere. But she had insisted, and Nidhi said it was important to let Jeneta make her own choices, to help her start to regain a sense of control.

"Do you think Meridiana is really gone?" Jeneta asked quietly.

Much as I wanted to lie, I owed her more than that. "I'm not sure. Nicola confirmed that the sphere was destroyed, and the pieces are magically inert. We know the remnants of the Ghost Army are still out there. I've heard of two attacks since last night, but they weren't planned or coordinated the way they were when Meridiana was around."

I was pretty sure Nicola hadn't slept at all since leaving Fort Michilimackinac. In addition to helping organize a response to the ghosts, she was also reviewing Gutenberg's notes to try to catalog everything I had undone when I destroyed his pen. They would be months or years cleaning up that mess.

"I've also spoken with Bi Wei," I continued. "She's agreed to meet with Nicola. I'm hoping the Porters and the students of Bi Sheng will be able to work together to hunt down the surviving ghosts."

"Meridiana let me see what was happening sometimes," Jeneta said. "What she—what we were doing. Like when those people tried to kill you and burned down your house. We manipulated their emotions, pushed them into turning on you, but they were already scared. They're going to be scared of me, too."

"Some of those same people helped us save you," Nidhi said gently. "Despite their fear."

Lena pointed to the gates. "There they are."

Mmadukaaku and Paige Aboderin raced through the crowd toward their daughter. The sight of them shattered every wall Jeneta had built up. By the time they reached each other, Jeneta was sobbing. The three of them sat down right there on the floor, heads together, arms around one another, like a rock in a river of people.

Nidhi, Lena, and I all stood, but none of us wanted to interrupt this reunion. Lena positioned herself "upstream," forcing others to veer around. Nidhi and I followed suit, trying to give Jeneta and her parents a modicum of space.

Jeneta had spoken to them on the phone, but I got the feeling they hadn't truly believed until this moment, when they could see and touch and hear their daughter in person.

When they finally rose, Jeneta's parents stood close together, keeping her between them. They turned toward us, and I suppressed the urge to wipe my palms on my jeans. No words could undo the pain I had caused them.

Mmadukaaku was a large man in a rumpled brown suit. Sweat darkened the collar of his green shirt. He stood like a statue, appearing to neither blink nor breathe as his brown eyes berated me.

Paige was almost as tall as her husband. She stood with her chin raised. One arm clasped her daughter. The other pressed tightly to her own chest.

The silence bored deeper into my guts, like a spindle

knotting my intestines. I was the one who had met them back at the beginning of summer to explain how their daughter would be spending one day a week at a "library internship." I was the one who had repeatedly lied to them after Jeneta disappeared. Who had stopped answering their calls.

I tightened my jaw and clenched my teeth, bracing for whatever came next.

Still they did nothing. Said nothing. I was tempted to punch *myself* in the face, just to break the tension. They were going to make me speak first. So be it. "I'm—"

My throat turned to stone, and my eyes blurred. I shook my head furiously, fighting for control. I heard Lena and Nidhi moving closer, not speaking, but offering their strength.

"Your daughter," I said, trying a different approach, "is amazing."

"Yes, she is," said Paige.

"She saved my friend's life." I nodded toward Lena. "Earlier this year."

"With magic." The anger in Paige's words made it clear this wasn't a question, but a challenge. She knew the truth. They both did. They wanted me to acknowledge that truth.

"Yes."

I wouldn't have thought Mmadukaaku's body could tighten any more. If he had been stone before, now he was wrought iron, hard and immovable and glowing with fury.

"You took her from us to teach her magic," Mmadukaaku said quietly.

"That's right. Jeneta is a libriomancer. She can manipulate the magic of stories, though she prefers poetry."

A muted smile flashed over Paige's features.

"You're one of those Porters," Mmadukaaku continued. "We saw you on the news."

"Not anymore. The Porters aren't happy with me right now, either."

"Papa." Jeneta's whisper silenced us as effectively as magic. She pulled her parents toward the bench and picked up the small cage. "This is Smudge. I e-mailed you about him, before."

"I remember. He's beautiful." Mmadukaaku actually smiled. Right up until Jeneta offered another Pop Rock to Smudge, causing him to backfire again. Mmadukaaku stepped back. "God have mercy."

"He's not dangerous," Jeneta said. Which wasn't entirely true, but I held my tongue. "The first time Isaac showed him to me, I thought of the Anansi stories you used to tell. Smudge is a trickster at heart. Yesterday he fought a skeleton to help Isaac and Lena rescue me."

Her parents turned to me, their skepticism and confusion palpable.

I shrugged. "Smudge is . . . he's spunky. Very loyal, too. And he likes Jeneta a lot. Mostly because she spoils him with junk food."

"I wonder where she learned that," Lena commented.

"What happens next, Mister Vainio?" Paige asked.

It was Nidhi who stepped forward to respond. "Now you take your daughter home. Let her adjust to her old life. Try not to pressure her. Don't expect her to do everything she used to do right away. Give her time. She'll let you know what she's up for. Have a close friend visit her at home before she tries going out. When she's ready, have her go out with one or two people before she starts going to any parties."

"Jeneta doesn't go to parties," Mmadukaaku said.

I don't think he noticed Jeneta's reaction. I did my best to keep a straight face so as not to give her away.

"She'll probably have nightmares," Nidhi continued. "Certain sounds, smells, and sights might trigger panic. This isn't something you can fix. All you can do is to be there for her." She handed a business card to Mmadu-kaaku. "Any of you can call me at any time."

"You're a doctor?" asked Paige.

"A psychiatrist. I've worked with people who've had bad experiences with magic, though I have no magical abilities myself."

Mmadukaaku was visibly relieved at that last part.

To Jeneta, Nidhi said, "The fact that you're standing here proves how strong you are. But that doesn't mean you have to do this alone. You're *not* alone, and I meant what I said. Call me any time, day or night. If I'm with a client, I'll get back to you within an hour."

"Thanks," Jeneta mumbled.

"Will she be safe?" asked Paige. "We saw the video of those people attacking Isaac and his house. What's to stop others from doing the same to our daughter? She was on television, too. The whole world saw her. The news people have already discovered who she is. Someone posted our home address on the Internet. We're talking about moving, but what happens when they find her?"

"Getting an unlisted address and number is a good start," I said. "There are things I can do to help you stay off the public's radar, if you'll let me. The Porters have done witness protection-type work before."

"You said you weren't part of the Porters," Mmadu-kaaku said sharply.

"I'm not. But one of the Regional Masters owes me a pretty big favor." I moved toward the pile of luggage and other belongings. "In the meantime, I have a gift that might help."

Jeneta looked almost as wary as her parents. Lena winked at her as I uncovered a small traveling cage, identical to the one Smudge used.

Jeneta's mouth and eyes turned to near-perfect circles when she saw the small red-spotted spider inside the cage. She brought both hands to her mouth and looked at Smudge, as if to make sure I hadn't pulled some sleight-of-hand. "Is that . . . ?"

I held out the cage. "The second book in Smudge's series included an encounter at a fire-spider nest. This was one of the spiders written into the background. She wasn't given a name or much of a personality, which I think eased her transition to our world. I was up all morning helping her to adjust. But being a fire-spider, she should have the same basic potential as Smudge."

Jeneta extended trembling hands to take the cage. The fire-spider backed into a corner, the bristles on her back glowing like tiny matchsticks.

I passed Jeneta a plastic bag full of chocolate-covered ants. "Feed her these, and you'll be her best friend forever." To her parents, I said, "Fire-spiders can sense danger. Smudge has saved my life more than once. You'll need to keep her somewhere that isn't flammable, but if you install a smoke detector over her cage, she'll be able to alert you to any threat. I hope she never has to, but if she does, get out of there and call me."

"Thank you," said Mmadukaaku, though I wasn't sure he meant it.

"She'll need crushed stone to line her cage. You can buy crickets to feed her from any pet store." I frowned at Jeneta. "Don't let her just eat sweets all the time."

"I won't," she promised.

"If you have other pets, keep them away from her for their own safety, at least until she gets used to them." I pulled a small carry-on sized cooler from below the bench. A printed label on the top read, *Contains Live, Harmless Invertebrate for Scientific Research.* "I've taken care of the paperwork. You'll need to leave her in the cooler for the flight, but you can take her on the plane with you."

The inside of the cooler was lined with obsidian gravel

and contained a pair of small hand-warmers for heat. "Crack the lid before you board and after you land. She'll have plenty of air for the flight."

"Does this mean my fire-spider and Smudge could—"

"There will be *no* breeding of the fire-spiders," I said firmly.

Jeneta pouted, but it couldn't smother the excitement in her eyes. That left only one other matter. I faced Jeneta's parents. "Many of the stories you've heard are true. There are vampires, werewolves, and more. The woman who took Jeneta did so using what she called the Ghost Army. Some of those ghosts are still out there. It would help us find and stop them if we could work with Jeneta and ask her about the things she experienced. But if you or she say no, we'll find another way."

They didn't answer immediately, which was encouraging. Mmadukaaku and Paige looked at one another, carrying on a silent conversation. Finally, Paige put her hand on Jeneta's shoulder.

Jeneta stared at her fire-spider. "They'll be coming for me. For all of us who do magic. I want to help."

Mmadukaaku looked at Nidhi.

"It would help her regain a sense of control over her own life," Nidhi said quietly.

He pressed his lips together like he wanted to stop the words from escaping. "All right."

"Thank you." I smiled as Jeneta offered an ant to her spider. "What are you going to call her?"

"Nkiruka." She raised her head. "It means a good and hopeful future."

My name is Isaac. I've been a libriomancer for most of my adult life. Until recently, I was a member of the organization known as the Porters.

I've seen these people sacrifice their lives to protect you from monsters that would haunt you for the rest of your days. I've also seen them commit the pettiest acts of greed and selfishness.

Both of these extremes remind me that they're human. The Porters aren't gods. None of us are. We're simply people who have learned new ways of poking the universe and making it react.

I recently got some advice from a . . . I guess you'd call him a friend. (Though if he was a *real* friend, he'd return my car!) Anyway, he's lived through this kind of world-altering change before, and he says it's going to be a bumpy ride. He also reassures me that we'll get through it. Empires rise and fall. Human beings live and die, but humanity survives. It's what we're best at.

None of which is all that comforting when you discover a nest of vampires living a half mile below your local supermarket, eh? Or see winged monsters terrorizing ancient churches.

You're going to hear that magic is a dangerous threat that needs to be eradicated, and that it's the salvation of mankind. There's truth to both sides. Magic is powerful, dangerous, and potentially deadly.

So was the printing press. So was language for that matter, and nuclear power and gunpowder and the Internet and so much more.

Magic is amazing. I've walked on the moon. I've spoken with men who died centuries before I was born. I've seen treasures that were thought lost to history, and I've met beings who taught me that there's no limit to the variety and imagination of our universe.

According to myth, Prometheus stole fire from the

gods, and was sentenced to eternal torment for his crime. Well, the Porters aren't gods. Nor should humanity have to steal the magic you've helped to create.

Magic is a gift. Like fire, it can burn. And like fire, it's going to change everything.

You're gonna love it.

Bibliography

Titles marked with an asterisk (*) were made up for this book.

Al-Sufi, Abd al-Rahman. *The Book of Constellations of the Fixed Stars*.

American Psychiatric Association. *Diagnostic and Statistical Manual of Mental Disorders, Fifth Edition (DSM-V)*.

Bradbury, Ray. *Fahrenheit 451*.

D'Aurillac, Gerbert. *Selected Writings on the Mind of God*.*

Baum, L. Frank. *The Wonderful Wizard of Oz*.

Beddor, Frank. *The Looking-Glass Wars*.

Britain, Kristen. *Green Rider*.

Brontë, Charlotte. *Villette*.

Collins, Suzanne. *The Hunger Games*.

Conrad, H. Allen. *Time Kings*.*

Dahl, Roald. *Charlie and the Chocolate Factory*.

Dunbar, Paul Laurence. *The Collected Poetry of Paul Laurence Dunbar*.

Glenday, Craig. *Guinness Book of Records*.

Golding, William. *Lord of the Flies*.
Gray, Henry. *Gray's Anatomy*.
Herbert, Frank. *Dune*.
Ikeji, Lisa. *Heart of Stone.**
Jordan, Robert. *Towers of Midnight*.
Knight, Damon. *A for Anything*.
Kress, Nancy. *Beggars in Spain*.
L'Engle, Madeleine. *A Wrinkle in Time*.
Lewis, C. S. *The Lion, The Witch, and The Wardrobe*.
———, *The Magician's Nephew*.
Lucian of Samosata. *True History*.
Mahfouz, Naguib. *Arabian Nights and Days*.
Martin, George R. R. *A Dance with Dragons*.
McCaffrey, Anne. *Dragonflight*.
North, Pearl. *The Boy from Ilysies*.
———, *The Book of the Night*.
Pan, Stuart. *The Foretelling.**
Regan, Dian Curtis. *Princess Nevermore*.
Rothfuss, Patrick. *The Name of the Wind*.
Rowling, J. K. *Harry Potter and the Goblin's Scepter.**
Travers, P. L. *Mary Poppins*.
Shelley, Mary. *Frankenstein*.
Stoker, Bram. *Dracula*.
Stone, Margaret. *Red Night.**
———, *Time Wyrm.**
Wright, James. *Nymphs of Neptune.**

Coming soon from DAW,
the fourth novel of *Magic ex Libris*
by Jim C. Hines:

REVISIONARY

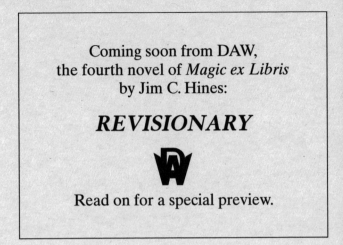

Read on for a special preview.

"I thought you'd made plans for all of this."

"There have always been contingency plans for the revelation of magic, as well as for my own death."

"What happened? Did you forget to share those plans with anyone else?"

"To paraphrase Von Moltke, no plan survives beyond the first encounter with the enemy. The more rigid the plan, the more thoroughly it shatters. I left the Porters with certain goals and strategies. Proper disposal of my body, for one. Delegation of power to a small group, no more than six. The importance of international neutrality. The safety and security of our own people. Most importantly, a focus on the long term that could help us all survive the short-term chaos and upheaval."

"Define 'short-term.'"

"Historically speaking? Years. Decades, most likely."

"And how many people are going to lose their lives as a result of that chaos?"

"As you've said, magic can't predict the future."

"But it can damn well guess."

"By my estimate? Millions . . ."

THE SERVICE THE PORTERS were using for transportation and security in D.C. wasn't scheduled to pick us up for at least another hour. I took a copy of Neil Gaiman's *Neverwhere* from my jacket while Lena hailed a cab.

"Where to?" asked the driver, an older woman in a yellow headscarf with the gruff voice of a long-time smoker.

I scooted into the back and handed her a ten. "Just keep it parked here for a minute, eh?"

"You waiting for someone?"

"Not exactly."

Lena sat down beside me. "Shortcut?"

"I hope so." *Neverwhere* was one of the books I'd been rereading lately as part of my own research. I might not be able to create a stable portal from Vegas to the U.P. yet, but I'd learned a few tricks in the process.

I'd also accidentally sent a pair of lab rats off to either Alpha Centauri or possibly a wardrobe in London. I doubted Vince would ever forgive me for that one.

I turned to a page marked with a blue post-it note. I could recite the scene from memory, but it was simpler to touch the book directly. Every page had its own texture, as unique as a fingerprint. I could feel the individual letters, the ink pressed into the paper, like a blind man reading embossed print in the days before Braille.

Gaiman had created a character named Door. I'd experimented with her magic back at the lab, but this would be my first time using it in the field.

My fingertips sank through the paper, touching the world so many of Gaiman's readers had visualized and dreamed about. While that world was fictional, the belief and imagination of his readers was quite real. That was where the story's true magic came from, with the physical book serving as a magnet and anchor for that cumulative belief.

The driver twisted around. "What are you doing back there?"

"We'll be on our way in a moment," said Nidhi.

Libriomancy in its most common form allowed us to grasp an object from a story and pull it into our world, transforming belief and potential magical energy into physical reality. Assuming said object would fit through the pages.

If that was 101-level libriomancy, what I'd been working on for the past year was graduate work.

My vision blurred, like I'd been reading too long in poor light. My mother used to tell me I'd ruin my eyes that way. As it turned out, she hadn't been entirely wrong.

I yanked off my glasses and slipped them into my shirt pocket. The spots of shadow floating around the edges of my vision grew worse, but the book's text sharpened. The damage to my eyes was a result of magical charring, and behaved similarly to early cataracts. Glasses helped me to compensate, but paradoxically made it harder for me to truly see magic.

I reached deeper into the book. My hand touched Door's back. Rather, the composite imagination of Door's back. I wasn't actually touching the outline of her shoulder blades, or feeling the faint beating of her heart. I was touching readers' belief. Belief in the character, and belief in her particular ability.

"Our driver is getting twitchy," Lena commented.

"I'm almost done." From here, I could have plucked an object from Door's hand and created it in my own. But instead of pulling anything physical from the page, I grasped Door's ability and drew it into myself. Lines of text crept up my skin. In essence, I was making myself an extension of the book.

This kind of libriomancy carried two major risks. For one thing, the magic came from a fictional universe. Any portal I created would want to connect back to that non-existent universe. If I screwed up, we'd be lucky to find ourselves lost in the sewers of London. If we were unlucky, the magic would try to send us into Gaiman's fictionalized London.

Since that world didn't exist, it would just kill us instead.

Then there was the danger of letting a book get into your head. As the story flowed through my blood, I could hear the characters calling me. When I looked around, it was as though the fictional world had been overlaid with this one. I saw our driver staring at my truncated arm, watched her mouth move, but I heard the murmurs of the London crowd, saw tunnels and subway lines passing through the cab, smelled the damp fog . . .

"Isaac?" Lena touched my neck, helping ground me in the real world.

I placed my other hand on the inside of the cab's door and pushed the story through my body, into the metal and plastic of the car. The words were like a windstorm trying to escape, trying to return to their book.

Slowly, I forced them to a place I knew well enough to overwrite the fragments of *Neverwhere* clawing at my thoughts. "It's like herding cats across a stream."

I opened the door and climbed out to find myself emerging from the back of a pizza delivery car parked on the side of a road.

Had Gutenberg been alive, I'm sure he would have cast this spell without a second thought, putting us down on the front steps of the Capitol building. Given another five hundred years of practice, I liked to think I'd have done the same. But Gutenberg was gone, and I was still learning how to target this stuff.

"What the hell are you doing?" The shout came from

a young woman on the sidewalk across the road, carrying an empty red delivery bag. "Get out of my car!"

"Sorry!" I stumbled away from the car, shoved *Neverwhere* back into my jacket pocket, and checked on Smudge. He didn't look happy, but he wasn't about to set anything on fire either, which meant the driver probably wasn't going to pull a gun and shoot me just yet. I glanced around. I'd put us down in East Lansing, on the campus of Michigan State University. "Technically, we weren't in your car. We just—"

"What do you mean 'we'?" She hurried across the road and pushed past me to check the back seat, which was empty. She tossed the delivery bag into the back, aimed her cellphone at my face, and snapped a picture before dialing what I assumed was the police. "What did you take, asshole?"

"Nothing," said Lena as she emerged from the car.

The poor woman jumped so hard she dropped her phone. Lena caught it before it hit the pavement.

I checked the magnetic sign on the top of the car. "Georgio's, eh? I used to eat there all the time when I was an undergrad." I pulled out my wallet and handed her a twenty. "I'm sorry we scared you. Consider this part of your tip for the night?"

She stared at me, then at the car, where Nidhi now appeared to be climbing out of nothingness. "That's . . . that's magic."

"Pretty cool, isn't it? If I had more time, I'd tell you how it worked."

"He would," Lena said. "Even if you asked him to stop."

I glanced at the three-story brick building across the street. "That's Mason-Abbot Hall, which puts us on the northeast corner of campus, about ten miles from Lansing." I turned back to the delivery driver. "How'd you like to make a bigger tip?"

*   *   *

"If traffic doesn't pick up soon, I'm going to fly the rest of the way," I muttered.

"You can do that?" Our impromptu driver's name was Callie, a second-year communications major who had agreed to drive us into Lansing only after getting a selfie with Lena, and another with Smudge.

"I can. The FAA gets cranky about it, though."

Callie swerved into another lane, then slammed the brakes. "Looks like they've closed 496 and Saginaw both. I'll get you as close as I can. Is it true this was a terrorist attack?"

"We don't know yet," said Nidhi.

Lena was studying her hands. "I should get rid of these," she said, touching the buds on her knuckles. "It's probably safer for everyone if I pass for human."

I wanted to argue, to tell her to be herself. I looked at Nidhi and saw the same conflict in her eyes. Neither of us spoke as the green buds slowly absorbed back into Lena's skin.

Callie broke the silence. "There was a campus march for Marcus Visser last week. A real werewolf came to speak. It was pretty intense. The cops showed up at the end. Six people got pepper sprayed." She turned north and snuck a block closer before hitting another line of stalled traffic. "I think this is as close as I can get you."

"It's close enough." I handed her another forty bucks and climbed out of the car. I could see the capitol dome a short distance away, past bumper-to-bumper traffic. "Thanks."

She rolled down her window. "Hey, that libriomancy stuff. Is that something anyone can learn? I was thinking of changing majors."

"Sorry. It doesn't work that way."

The noise hit hard: horns blaring uselessly in the streets, sirens wailing, shouts and chants in the distance. I heard dogs barking as well, but I couldn't tell if they were pets howling at the noise or police dogs trying to track the perpetrators.

Then there were the people making their way toward the capitol. Many of them had similar expressions of shock, confusion, and grief. Others had skipped past grief to rage. Even if I hadn't known where I was going, the flow would have carried us to the site of the attack.

A uniformed police officer was diverting traffic up ahead. Another officer on horseback trotted up the opposite side of the road. Two helicopters circled overhead. From what I could see, one was a news chopper, while its louder big brother looked military.

Lena took the lead, being the best equipped to deal with any physical confrontations. Nidhi and I followed close behind, letting Lena serve as our icebreaker. I split my attention between Smudge and the crowd, watching for potential magical threats.

Yellow barricades blocked the streets at the intersection of Ottawa and Capitol. Beyond those barriers, ambulances and police cars lined the roads. The news vans had parked farther off. It looked like every camera crew in the state was pressed up against the yellow tape surrounding the capitol building, along with reporters from some of the national outlets.

The tension after the hearing in D.C. had been bad, but at least that had been in daylight, with a short, clear path to our escape.

The emotion here was colder. Harder, and more unstable. Officers in riot gear were doing their best to keep things under control. I found myself holding my breath, like I was afraid of setting off an explosion. Sweat trickled and tickled down my back.

All reporters were being kept back with the rest of the crowd. Several were calling out to the officers and detectives for statements, while others interviewed random bystanders. I eavesdropped long enough to overhear one reporter say something about werewolves and an unknown number of casualties. I turned up the collar of my duster and approached the nearest uniformed officer, keeping my hands in full view.

"Sir, you need to stay back." This was a man clearly practiced in using his voice as a tool to keep people in line, and his tone suggested he was equally prepared to use other tools if his words failed to do the trick.

I glanced back to make sure none of the reporters were paying attention. The last thing I wanted was to get mobbed by news crews looking for a sound bite. "My name is Isaac Vainio. I'm a libriomancer, one of the directors for New Millennium and a member of the Porters. We can help."

He looked the three of us over. "Nobody gets across that line. Especially magic-using types."

I understood his paranoia, even as frustration tightened already-tense muscles in my neck and jaw. For all he knew, we were here to finish the job the werewolves had begun.

I looked past him to the two ambulances parked on the sidewalk. Their crews were checking over a small group of people with blood on their clothes. A short distance beyond was a white FBI truck, possibly a command vehicle. I also counted three other police and FBI trucks, and six state and Lansing police cars.

I glanced at his badge. "I know your people and the EMTs are doing everything they can, Officer Blackwell. But if it's true werewolves did this, then anyone could have been infected, and we have a very limited window to help them. I'm the only person within a hundred miles who can guarantee those people remain human."

He jerked his chin at Nidhi and Lena. "They're libriomancers too?"

"I'm Doctor Shah," said Nidhi. "I've been with the

Porters for more than fifteen years." She touched Lena's arm. "Ms. Greenwood is my assistant."

"Depending on what species of werewolf did this, the survivors could be a danger to your officers," I pressed. "I've consulted with the State Police in the past. They can vouch for me."

He stepped back and spoke to someone on his shoulder-mounted radio, never taking his attention off of us. I couldn't make out the response, but a moment later he raised the police tape and beckoned for us to step through. He patted each of us down, a process that took much longer with me, given the number of books tucked into my duster pockets. By the time he finished, two more people had joined us.

"Identification." The speaker was a middle-aged woman in a state police uniform and vest, with the kind of laser focus and determination that made me think she could work this case for thirty-six hours straight on nothing but coffee and attitude.

Her companion was an older man with the face of a balding bulldog and an FBI badge clipped to his belt. Between the street lamps and various floodlights that had been set up, I was able to make out that his name was Steinkamp, and he was a Special Agent from the Magical Crimes Unit in the Detroit Field Office.

Nidhi and I produced our licenses. The police officer inspected them both, handed them back, and looked expectantly at Lena.

"I don't have one." Lena held out one hand and produced a single green bud from the palm of her hand. "Michigan's DMV still refuses to grant a driver's license to nonhumans."

"She stays here," said Steinkamp. "We've had too many people contaminating the scene as it is."

"It's all right," Lena said, before Nidhi or I could argue.

"Sign here." The officer, whose badge read ROWLAND, passed me a clipboard. I jotted down my name, title, organization, and the date and time, then handed it to Nidhi to do the same. "You touch *nothing* unless absolutely necessary. Blackwell's going to be your police escort. You obey his instructions at all times. Understood?"

I nodded, trying not to let my impatience show. "How did the werewolves get inside?"

Rowland didn't answer. Steinkamp scowled. "There was a fucking student group scheduled for a five o'clock tour. The werewolves waltzed right in with them."

"Are the students all right?" asked Nidhi.

"Define all right," said Rowland. "Terrified enough they'll be pissing their beds for a month, but physically they're fine."

"Four people have been taken to Sparrow hospital," said Steinkamp. "The rest of the wounded are being checked over by the EMTs. We've got agents interviewing witnesses across the street, several of whom have already been treated for minor cuts and scrapes."

"I can call Nicola and ask her to send a Porter to the hospital," said Nidhi.

"The Evidence Response Team is inside with the coroner," Steinkamp continued in a softer voice. "They haven't taken the bodies away. Is there anything you can do . . ."

"Raising the dead has been tried before. It wasn't pretty."

Rowland clucked her tongue. "I guess there are limits to magic after all."

"You have no idea."

Agent Steinkamp was staring at me, like I was a book he couldn't quite read. "Mister Vainio, have you ever heard of an organization called Vanguard?"

I shook my head and glanced at Nidhi, who did the same.

"Get moving," said Rowland. "Blackwell, make sure they sign out with me before they leave."

Blackwell walked us toward the ambulances. The vehicles provided some degree of privacy, but plenty of gawkers strained to see what was happening. One of the EMTs moved to intercept us.

"They're here to help," said Blackwell. "He's one of those book wizards."

"Libriomancer," I corrected as I moved toward a woman with a blanket around her shoulders. Her knee and thigh were bandaged, and blood matted her scalp, but none of her injuries looked severe. I tugged a small crystal vial from a heavily padded pocket inside my jacket. "My name's Isaac. Have you ever read *The Lion, The Witch, and The Wardrobe*?"

She nodded. "My niece loves those movies."

"This is from the book. It's the healing cordial Lucy was given by Father Christmas. A single drop will heal you inside and out."

"You can't use magic on her," said the EMT.

"Except in life-or-death situations," I snapped. "This woman was mauled by a werewolf. Do you have anything in your ambulance that will stave off lycanthropy?"

The woman's face went pale, and she swayed on her feet. Nidhi shot me a *look*, then took the woman's hand and began talking in a low, calm voice. "You're going to be fine. What's your name?"

"Margaret. Margaret Edwards."

I peered over the top of my glasses, searching the woman for any magical residue in her bloodstream. She was clean. No trace of lycanthropy or other magical infection, but I saw no need to mention that until after I'd healed her injuries. I'd be damned if I was going to let anyone else suffer today if I could help it. "Do me a favor, Margaret, and stick out your tongue?"

She did so, and I used a dropper to transfer a tiny

bead of Lucy's potion onto her tongue. She swallowed, pain or shock preventing her from asking questions. Within seconds, her body started to relax. She poked cautiously at her knee. "That's it? I'm . . . better?"

"One hundred percent human," I said. "Not a trace of werewolf in you."

She tentatively tested her bandaged leg. "Thank you."

The EMT looked from me to Margaret and back. "All right, I'm convinced. Bring that bottle and come with me."